Joseph Florimond Loubat

A Yachtsman's Scrap Book

The Ups and Downs of Yacht Racing

Joseph Florimond Loubat:

A Yachtsman's Scrap Book
The Ups and Downs of Yacht Racing

ISBN/EAN: 9783337396343

Printed in Europe, USA, Canada, Australia, Japan

Cover: Foto ©Andreas Hilbeck / pixelio.de

More available books at **www.hansebooks.com**

A

·YACHTSMAN'S SCRAP BOOK,

OR THE

Ups and Downs of Yacht Racing.

EDITED BY

J. F. LOUBAT.

NEW YORK:

BRENTANO BROTHERS.

1887.

This Scrap Book of my cruises and races in the Enchantress, I dedicate to the memory of her designer and sailing master, the late Captain Robert Fish.

New York, April, 1887.

J. F. LOUBAT.

CONTENTS.

CHAPTER V.

THE CAPE MAY CHALLENGE CUP RACE.

CHAPTER VI.

Mr. J. F. Loubat's Gift to the Pilots.

CHAPTER VII.

The Enchantress Goes to Cowes.

CHAPTER VIII.

An International Yacht Race.

SOCIETE DES REGATES DU HAVRE.

CHAPTER IX.

The International Channel Match.

YACHT CLUB DE FRANCE.

CHAPTER X.

THE PRINCE OF WALES'S CHALLENGE CUP RACE.

CHAPTER XI.

MR. LOUBAT'S FIRST EUROPEAN CHALLENGE.

CHAPTER XII.

THE ENCHANTRESS IN ENGLAND.

CHAPTER XIII.

The Enchantress in Russia and in Sweden.

CHAPTER XIV.

Mr. Loubat's Cup to the Royal Albert Yacht Club.

CHAPTER XV.

The Yacht Racing Association.

CHAPTER XVI.

The Rule of the Road at Sea.

CHAPTER XVII.

Mr. Loubat's Second European Challenge.

CHAPTER XVIII.

The Loubat Cape May Cup Race.

CHAPTER XIX.

Miscellaneous.

CHAPTER XX.

The New York Pilot Boat Joseph F. Loubat, No. 16.

CHAPTER XXI.

The Death of Captain Robert Fish.

LIST OF PLATES.

A YACHTSMAN'S SCRAP BOOK.

CHAPTER I.

THE NEW YORK YACHT CLUB.

The Evening Post, New York, July 1, 1874.

THE NEW YORK YACHT CLUB.

THE ORIGINAL MEETING.

On the afternoon of the 30th of July, 1844, a number of gentlemen, in pursuance of a previous notice, assembled on board the yacht Gimcrack, then lying off the Battery, for the purpose of organizing a yacht club. There were present John C. Stevens, Hamilton Wilkes, John C. Jay, George L. Schuyler, Louis A. Depau, George B. Rollins, James M. Waterbury and James Rogers. At that meeting it was resolved that the title of the club be the New York Yacht Club; that the gentlemen present be the original members of the club; that John C. Stevens be commodore thereof; and that a committee of five be appointed by the commodore to report rules and regulations for the government of the club. The following gentlemen were appointed, namely: John C. Stevens, George L. Schuyler, John C. Jay, Hamilton Wilkes, Captain Rogers. It was further resolved that the club should make a cruise to Newport, Rhode Island, under command of the commodore, and Friday, August 2, at 9 o'clock A. M., was the time appointed for starting. At this meeting the following yachts were represented:

```
Gimcrack.....................John C. Stevens
Spray........................ Hamilton Fish
Cygnet.......  ...............William Edgar
La Coquille.....................John C. Jay
Dream....................George L. Schuyler
Mist........................Louis A. Depau
Minna..................James M. Waterbury
Petrel.....................George B. Rollins
Ida...........................Captain Rogers
```

THE FIRST CRUISE.

On the 2d of August the foregoing yachts, with the exception of the Ida, sailed on the first cruise of the New York Yacht Club. The fleet stopped at Huntington, on Long Island, New Haven, Gardiner's Bay and Oyster Pond Point, arriving at Newport on Monday afternoon, August 5, and leaving again for New York on the 11th. From these modest beginnings thirty years ago, has grown the present magnificent fleet composing the New York Yacht Squadron, numbering thirty-eight schooners, twenty-two sloops and nine steamers.

THE FIRST DINNER AND THE FLAG.

The next meeting of the club was held at Windust's, in this city on the 17th of March, 1845. Some routine business was transacted ; new members were elected, and the secretary was requested to have a flag ready for exhibition at the next meeting. The first Yacht Club dinner took place at the Astor House on the 9th of April, 1845. At a meeting at Delmonico's on June 3, 1845, a flag was adopted.

THE FIRST RACE.

The first trial of speed between the yachts took place on the 17th of July, 1845, from off the Elysian Fields, under the direction of the Committee of the Regatta, the following yachts entering for the race: Cygnet, 45 tons; Sibyl, 42 tons; Spray, 37 tons; La Coquille, 27 tons; Minna, 30 tons; Gimcrack, 25 tons; Newburgh, 33 tons; Addy, 17 tons; The Lancet, 20 tons.

THE OLD CLUB HOUSE AT HOBOKEN.

At that time the Yacht Club House was at the Elysian Fields, Hoboken. Old members will remember its charming location and the pleasant dinners which were had there in early spring, and during the yachting season. On the 18th of February, 1846, a first appropriation of $500 was made to furnish this cottage Club House. On the 24th of June following, a further sum of $250 was appropriated for the same purpose. In those early days economy was more necessary, and more widely practised than in the present age of greenbacks and "inflation." William Edgar, treasurer, in February, 1846, read his report of the receipts and expenses of the club since its formation, showing a balance in his hands of $881.13.

THE MARIA.

Commodore Stevens's yacht, the Maria, modelled by himself, embodied at that time all the latest improvements in naval architecture. She was built entirely for speed, and was for many years the crack boat of the squadron. But she was not destined to carry the flag of the New York Yacht Club abroad to achieve the great triumph over our English cousins at the Royal Yacht Squadron regatta at Cowes, in 1851.

THE AMERICA.

The America, whose name has since become famous among nautical men the world over, was built and modelled by George Steers for John C. Stevens, Hamilton Wilkes, George L. Schuyler, James Hamilton, J. Beekman Finlay and Edwin A. Stevens, who were jointly interested as her owners. She was launched in 1851 in this city from the yard of W. H. Brown. She was 94 feet on deck from stem to stern, and measured 170 tons, custom house old tonnage. She was built with a stipulation that she should beat any vessel in the country, and any one of her size in England. In this event the builder was to receive $30,000 for her. But before she crossed the ocean she had four or five trials with the Maria—by the wind, with the wind free, and before the wind—and the Maria proved the faster craft in every trial. The America was accordingly purchased for $20,000, and sent over to test her speed with the English yachts in compliance with an invitation from the members of the Royal Yacht Club at Cowes.

THE VOYAGE TO EUROPE.

She sailed from New York on the 21st of June, 1851, with a crew of thirteen, all told; and arrived at Havre on the 12th of July, after an excellent passage of twenty-one days, during which she was under the reduced canvas of a temporary suit of sails. At Havre she was painted and refitted before sailing for Cowes, where she arrived on the 31st of July. She excited considerable interest among the members of the Royal Yacht Squadron and other yacht clubs at Cowes, and was visited by a great number of persons interested in nautical affairs.

THE CHALLENGE.

On arriving at Cowes, Commodore Stevens issued the following challenge: "The New York Yacht Club, in order to test the relative merits of the different models of the schooners of the Old and New Worlds, propose through Commodore Stevens to the Royal Yacht Squadron to run the America against any number of schooners belonging to any of the yacht squadrons of the kingdom, to be selected by the commodore of the Royal Yacht Squadron. The course to be in some part of the English Channel outside of the Isle of Wight, with at least a six-knot breeze. This trial of speed to be made at an early day, to be selected by the commodore of the Royal Yacht Squadron. The fact whether there be such a breeze on the appointed day to be decided by the commodore of the Royal Yacht Squadron. And if on that day there shall not be at least a six-knot breeze, then on the first day thereafter that such a breeze shall blow." Here was a gage thrown down to the whole kingdom, the only stipulation being that the America should be matched with schooners, and that she should at least have a six-knot breeze. This was bold language for a stranger in a strange land. But the Englishmen were shy, very shy, in taking up the gauntlet. Finally Mr. Stevenson, of the Titania accepted the challenge.

THE ROYAL YACHT SQUADRON REGATTA.

Meanwhile the America was entered for the Royal Yacht Squadron regatta, which came off on the 22d of August, 1851, at Cowes. The race was for the Royal Yacht Squadron Cup of £100. There were eighteen entries. It is needless to repeat here the thrice-told tale of the victory of the America. Suffice to say that, starting at 10 o'clock A. M., she went around the Isle of Wight and passed the flagship as winner at 8 h., 34 m.; the Aurora was announced at 8 h., 58 m.; the Bacchante at 9 h. 30 m.; the Eclipse at 9 h. 45 min.; the Brilliant at 1 h. 20 min.; no account of the rest. The cup was awarded to the owners of the America. At a dinner given at the Astor House on October 1, 1851, by the New York Yacht Club to Commodore John C. Stevens, Edwin A. Stevens, and Colonel J. A. Hamilton, on their return home from their triumphal cruise in the America, the Commodore spoke of the race as the race for the "Queen's Cup"; and the cup won by the America has been misnamed the "Queen's Cup." It was, as before stated, the Royal Yacht Squadron Cup.

THE RACE FOR THE QUEEN'S CUP.

The America entered for the Queen's Cup with nine other yachts; but as there was but a six-knot breeze she did not start with the squadron. She went out, however, as far as the Nab Light, and it is said she made one reach with the most extraordinary movement from the Nab to Stokes Bay, and by another tack rounded the Brilliant in gallant style. To accomplish the same feat the Alarm took ten tacks and the Volante made about twenty. The America did not leave the starting point for an hour and five minutes after the yachts had started to compete for the prize, but she accomplished the distance, upwards of seventy-two miles, within ten minutes of the Wildfire, and gained in rounding forty-five minutes. If, therefore, the "Yankee," as she was called, had proceeded with the match, she would have won a second prize.

THE RACE WITH THE TITANIA.

The match between the America and Titania came off on the 28th of August, 1851. The course appointed for the trial was that they should proceed outside the island to a distance of twenty miles southeast of the Nab Light, where a station vessel was to be placed, and the yachts, having rounded the same, were to make their way back to the Nab Light. The America was an easy winner. She received no more challenges.

SUBSEQUENT HISTORY OF THE AMERICA.

It may not be uninteresting to follow the fortunes of this remarkable vessel. Before leaving England, Commodore Stevens sold her for £5,000 to John de Blaquire, captain in the Indian army, who sold her to Lord Templeton, from whom she was bought by Mr. Pritchard, a shipbuilder at Northfleet, England, and rebuilt by him in 1859 and sold to H. E. Decie, who made a cruise in her to the Mediterranean. After that time nothing was heard of her until, during the late Rebellion, she was found by the United States frigate Wabash, scuttled in the St. John's River, in Florida. She was raised, brought north, repaired, rigged, and used as a practice-ship for the cadets at the United States Naval Academy at Newport, in Rhode Island, and afterwards at Annapolis, in Maryland. On August 8, 1870, she was entered for the regatta against the British yacht Cambria, and came in fourth, making the race over the New York Yacht Club course in 4 h., 23 m., 51 s. Mr. Decie, during his ownership, changed her name to Camilla, under which name he

made the cruise to the Mediterranean, and arrived thence at
Savannah, in Georgia, by way of Porto Grande, Cape de Verd,
in April, 1861, where he, no doubt, sold her, which accounts for
her being on the American coast at the time of the Rebellion.

THE WANDERER.

The members of the New York Yacht Club have ever been
prompt to preserve untarnished the fame and honor of the organization. We find many instances of this in looking over the
annals of their proceedings, and cite a notable instance of their
action in such matters, had at a general meeting held February
3, 1859. In a communication to the Senate from the President
of the United States, January 12, 1859, the fact having been
officially stated that a cargo of more than three hundred negros
from the coast of Africa had been landed in Georgia, from the
schooner Wanderer, and the vessel thus designated being on the
list of yachts forming the New York Yacht Squadron, it was
unanimously " resolved, that the name of the yacht Wanderer
be erased from the list, and that William C. Corrie, proprietor
of said yacht and a member of this club, primarily for his
deliberate violation of the laws of the United States, but more
especially for being engaged in a traffic repugnant to humanity
and to the moral sense of the members of this association, be
and he hereby is expelled from the New York Yacht Club."

PATRIOTISM OF MESSRS. BENNETT AND IVES.

During the first year of the Rebellion, Messrs. Bennett and
Ives offered their yachts—the Henrietta and the Hope—to the
United States government. They were duly accepted and commissioned as revenue cutters, in which capacity they did efficient
coast service from the port of New York down to Florida.

THE HENRIETTA, FLEETWING AND VESTA.

We next hear of the Henrietta in September, 1865, as beaten
by the Fleetwing in a race around Cape May lightship. In
October of the same year she was beaten by the Vesta over the

same course.   Nothing daunted, the Henrietta in 1866 entered
the lists against her victors for the great Ocean Yacht Race and
a purse of $90,000, each competitor putting up $30,000.   This
contest was at the time a subject of the deepest interest, both
here and abroad.

THEIR OCEAN RACE.

On the 11th of December, 1866, these three schooners, of
little more than two hundred tons each, assembled at Sandy
Hook to start across the Atlantic Ocean, having chosen that in-
clement season, as most likely to afford a quick passage.   The
Vesta, built by David Caril, and launched in 1866, was supposed
to embody the most recent improvements in the way of speed.
The Fleetwing, built by J. B. Van Dusen, and launched in 1865,
was one year older.   The Henrietta, modelled by William
Tooker, and built by Henry Steers, was launched in June, 1861,
and was therefore at the time of the race five years old.   There
had been wonderful improvements in naval architecture since
August 2, 1492, when Columbus set sail from the little port of ˙
Palos with three frail vessels to cross the same ocean in search of
the Spice Islands, the mythical kingdom of Cathay and the
Great Kahn.   Could we but see a model of the Nina or the
Santa Maria alongside that of the Sappho, how interesting
would be the study !   Columbus was seventy-one days at sea before landing at St. Salvador at sunrise on the morning of Octo-
ber 12, 1492.   The three schooners of the New York Yacht
Club from Sandy Hook were not so long in reaching Cowes.

> The Henrietta arrived in 13 days, 21 hours, 55 minutes.
> The Fleetwing "   " 14 "   6 "   10   "
> The Vesta   "   " 14 "   6 "   50   "

SUBSEQUENT HISTORY OF THE HENRIETTA.

In preparing for the Ocean Race, the Henrietta had her
spars considerably reduced, and her bowsprit shortened.   After
returning home, she was laid up, and subsequently sold to R. H.

Harrington, for the fruit trade, made several successful voyages, and was lost on the coast of Honduras, December 16, 1872, on a voyage to New York.

THE SAPPHO AND THE DAUNTLESS.

In 1869 the Sappho, W. P. Douglas, owner, made the shortest trip across the Atlantic, which has yet been accomplished by a yacht, sailing from New York to Queenstown in 12 d., 9 h., 36 m. The Dauntless, J. G. Bennett, owner, made the same trip the same year in 12 d., 17 h., 6 m.

INCORPORATION OF THE CLUB.

In 1865, an act incorporating the New York Yacht Club was passed by the New York Legislature. By it " Edwin A. Stevens, Ambrose C. Kingsland, Alexander Major, Robert S. Hone, William H. McVickar, Anson Livingston, Hamilton Morton and such other persons as are now associated as a yacht club in the city of New York and may hereafter become associated with them," were constituted a body corporate by the name of the New York Yacht Club, to be located in the city of New York, for the purpose of encouraging yacht building and naval architecture, and the cultivation of naval science, with authority to purchase and hold any real or personal estate to an extent not exceeding one hundred thousand dollars. The motto of the club on its corporate seal is, *Nos Agimur Tumidis Velis.*

THE CLUB HOUSE ON STATEN ISLAND.

In the spring of 1868 the club purchased from Mrs. N. H. Wolfe, for a Club House, a property on Staten Island, near the lower landing, for the sum of $24,000, paying $9,000 cash and the balance remaining on mortgage. It contained two acres of land, sloping down to a road which separated it from the shore, about one mile this side of the narrows. Sitting on the wide piazza of the Club House—a large roomy cottage in the English style—one sees every vessel coming into the port of New York. With a good glass we can distinguish the features of those on deck.   Until 1868 the site and Club House at the Elysian Fields, Hoboken, had been gratuitously furnished for the use of the club by John C. Stevens, Robert Stevens, and Edwin A. Stevens. On the occasion of moving to their new abode, the club, in an engrossed letter to Mr. Edwin A. Stevens, expressed their high appreciation of such courtesy and liberality.   The Staten Island property was subsequently sold.

THE PRESENT CLUB HOUSE IN THE CITY.

In November, 1872, the club took possession of its present commodious rooms, over the American Jockey Club, in the handsome building on the southwest corner of Madison Avenue and Twenty-seventh Street.   This house was originally built for club purposes, and is admirably adapted to its present uses.   The Yacht Club occupy the whole of the second story, consisting of three rooms, comfortably and luxuriously furnished.   The walls are covered with models of yachts.   There are at least a hundred and twenty different models.   The front room, looking upon Madison Avenue, contains magazines, newspapers and other periodicals.   The walls are covered with nautical engravings. Over the mantelpiece, and above a beautiful model of the Sappho, which stands thereon, hangs a portrait of Commodore Stevens.   The middle room contains large and comfortable sofas and writing tables.   The bar-room occupies a portion of the third room.   There are four hundred and sixty-three members.   The entrance fee is fifty dollars.   The yearly dues are twenty-five dollars.

THE MODELS OF THE YACHTS.

The model of every yacht entered for a regatta is the property of the club, and is retained in its possession ; and no person other than a United States naval constructor shall be permitted to copy it, unless he shall have obtained written authority from the owner or builder of the yacht.

THE ENCHANTRESS.

The New York Yacht Club will not be formally represented

in English waters this season; but Mr. J. F. Loubat, an American gentleman, who makes his home abroad, while on a visit to this country last year bought from George S. Lorillard the yacht Enchantress. During the past winter he has had her lengthened and altered in England, under the direction of her original modeller, Robert Fish, at an expense of some fifteen or twenty thousand dollars. Mr. Fish went abroad not only to superintend the lengthening of the Enchantress, but likewise to act as sailing master for Mr. Loubat. We wish Mr. Loubat success, and we have no doubt that when the Enchantress is next heard from she will give a good account of herself.

THE PRESENT OFFICERS OF THE CLUB.

The officers of the club for the year 1874 are as follows:

Commodore—James Gordon Bennett.
Vice-Commodore—William P. Douglas.
Rear-Commodore—George L. Kingsland.
Secretary—Charles A. Minton.
Treasurer—Sheppard Homans.
Measurer—A. Cary Smith.
Fleet Surgeon—L. De Forest Woodruff, M.D.
Regatta Committee—William Krebs, Edward E. Chase, William B. Bend.
House Committee—Fletcher Westray, George W. Kidd, John G. Beresford, Thomas T. Lawrence, N. D. White—the secretary, *ex-officio*.

CHAPTER II.

THE AMERICA.

The Illustrated London News, London, Saturday, May 15, 1851.

NEW AMERICAN YACHT.

A yacht is now building at New York, to complete with the English yachts, next summer at Cowes.

The builder, Mr. W. H. Brown, is to receive about one-third more than her value (say £24 a ton) if she succeeds in outsailing any competitors of the same tonnage in England. Her construction is on a novel principle; drawing 10 feet, aft, she tapers away forward to about half that draught, and is totally without any gripe. Aft, her keel is about 30 inches deep, diminishing in depth forward, and gradually ascending in a graceful curve into cutwater and stem. Her tonnage, 175 tons; length, 94 ft.; extreme breadth, 23 ft., 6 in.; depth of hold, 9 ft. Her timbers are a foot apart, filled in on both sides with eighteen pigs or bars of iron, which weigh 12 cwt. each, and have small projections or shoulders, which let into the timbers, and prevent any contact with outside planking. In addition, eighteen square pigs, each $1\frac{1}{4}$ cwt., are placed on the main keel, fitting exactly between the timbers. She has, therefore, upwards of 21 tons of ballast, built and tightly wedged into her sides. As she only requires about as much more ballast, it is calculated that she will be able to stow it with great ease, and have room to spare.

She is cross-braced inside with long iron bands, well secured to the timbers. The intelligent foreman, Mr. Steers, as well as the American gentlemen who are to own her, if she succeeds, are very sanguine of success.

This is an original and spirited undertaking, and will, if successful, completely alter the present system of yacht architecture. We do not, however, think she can compete with the sharp and deep English yachts. Whatever the result may be, it cannot fail of being extremely interesting and valuable to both countries. As a model, she is artistic, although rather a violation of the old established ideas of naval architecture.

The Illustrated London News, London, Saturday, August 9, 1851.

ARRIVAL OF THE AMERICAN CLIPPER YACHT AMERICA, OF THE NEW YORK YACHT CLUB.

Accustomed as we have been to witness the symmetrical models of our own yacht clubs, we confess our opinion falters when a model of an entirely different construction, so contrary in every respect, both in build and rig, is presented to us. In our former remarks we termed the America to be "rather a violation of the old established ideas of naval architecture," which all must candidly confess to be the case. In lieu of "straight lines," we have curved and hollow lines; instead of spars loaded with rigging, top hamper, and numberless small sails, we have stately masts with scarcely a rope to support them; the propelling power being in substance, and not in sum. In fact, instead of the "phantom ship," we have before us a " rakish piratical-looking craft," whose appearance in by-gone days in the Southern Atlantic would have struck terror into the soul of many a " homeward-bounder." But this yacht has traversed the Atlantic on a different mission; and opportunely in the year 1851, the citizen of the States brings her for fraternal competition with the aristocracy of our own island.

Since her arrival she has been visited by nearly every member of the Squadron, and by several scientific and naval gentlemen, and all appear to be gratified with the inspection. As some discrepancy has already appeared in the accounts of the America we have taken some pains to verify the following.

She was solely designed and constructed by Mr. George Steers, of the firm of Messrs. George and James R. Steers, of New York, who are now on a visit to this country in the yacht. To the talents of the builder, the New York Yacht Club is indebted for several of the specimens which grace their list; among which we may name the sloop Syren, of 85 tons; the schooner Cornelia 90 tons; Sybil, 58 tons; Cygnet, 52; Coquille, 37; several of the celebrated New York pilot boats; the W. G. Wagstaff, 104 tons, supposed to be the fastest vessel of her time; and subsequently the well-known Mary Taylor, of 75 tons, the smartest vessel in the States. As it has been whispered that the yacht, after all, has been designed and constructed by one of our own countrymen, we have authority for stating that Mr. George Steers was born in New York, and is the son of the late Mr. Henry Steers, a native of Dartmouth, England, and once connected with our naval establishment, at Plymouth, but emigrated to the United States, and established himself in that country.

The America belongs to the New York Yacht Club, and is, according to American register, 171 tons; she is owned by J. C. Stevens, Esq., the commodore of the N. Y. Y. C., and by Messrs. C. A. Stevens, H. Wilkes, and J. B. Finlay. Her dimensions are:

	Feet.	In.
Length over all	94	0
Length of keel	82	0
Extreme breadth	22	6
Breadth moulded	22	0

The dimensions of spars—Foremast, 79 ft. 6 in.; mainmast, 81 ft., with $2\frac{7}{8}$ in. to a foot rake to both masts; bowsprit (hollow),

32 ft., 17 of which only is outboard ; fore gaff, 24 ft. ; main gaff, 28 ft.; main boom, 56 feet.

She carries three standing sails, viz.: jib, foresail, and mainsail; the foot of the latter as well as of the jib laces to the boom; she also sets a main gaff-topsail. Her forestay is very heavy, and is the principal supporter of the foremast. The internal arrangements of the America are in chaste style, with a due regard to comfort. The fore-cabin is 21 ft. by 8 ft., with 14 berths (seven on either side) for the crew, besides state-cabins for the master and mate. The galley, or cook's department, is apart, between the fore and after cabins, a great desideratum in warm climates, which comfort, as regards the men, has been overlooked in our yachts. The fore-cabin is ventilated by a circular sky-light, 3 ft. in diameter. Between the galley and main cabin there are two large state-rooms; there are also two other state-rooms, a pantry and wash-room.

The cock-pit, as it is termed, is a circular opening abaft, of 30 ft. circumference, from which is the entrance to the main cabin. On the starboard side is the bath-room, and on the opposite is a clothes and wine-room ; and under the cock-pit is the sail-room. The main cabin, or saloon, is fitted with sofas, of mahogany and velvet, corresponding furniture, with a splendid carpet. Lockers extend the whole length of the cabin, with plate-glass panels. The internal decorations are Chinese, white and gold, with mahogany reliefs. On deck, by the mainmast, there is a break, which gives the appearance of a raised quarter-deck; the bulwarks are only fourteen inches. She has a plain raking stern-post, and a large gilt eagle, etc., on the stern, which is elliptical. The workmanship of the whole is perfection. She is all smooth outside, and would be taken for an iron vessel by a keen eye. The shrouds under the line, about two-thirds down, are covered with white canvas, which gives her a light appearance.

Her crew consists of seven hands before the mast, two mates, cook, steward, boy and master—in all, thirteen hands.

Whatever may be the result in her trials with some of our fast yachts, we trust that the introduction of this novel specimen will be the means of cultivating that good feeling which ought to prevail among all who contend for the palm in a fair spirit of rivalry. The owners are far beyond any mercenary ideas or speculative purposes, and, we understand, are ready to allow her sailing qualities to be tested with any yacht that may be selected for the purpose; and, as the gain of "a cup," or a pecuniary prize, is not their object, we have no doubt, ere long, we shall be able to record something definite on the subject.

The Illustrated London News, London, Saturday, August 30, 1851.

THE CHALLENGE MATCH BETWEEN THE AMERICA AND THE TITANIA.

This exciting contest, in which all the yachting world has evinced such deep interest, took place on Thursday off the Isle of Wight. The America was undocked at Portsmouth dock-yard at half-past nine on Wednesday night, and went out of harbor at half-past five on Thursday morning, and at 10 A. M. she started from Cowes, and ran down to the Nab, which she left at eleven, in competition with the Titania iron schooner, 100 tons, the property of Mr. R. Stephenson, M. P., for a race of twenty miles out and twenty miles in. They started, steering S. E., with a strong wind from the W. N. W. At five o'clock the America returned in sight from Portsmouth, when about ten miles outside the Nab, but nothing could be seen of the Titania at that time. Ultimately the America completed her course and became the winner by 52 minutes.

ROYAL YACHT SQUADRON REGATTA.

VICTORY OF THE AMERICA.

The race at Cowes, on Friday se'night, for the Royal Yacht Squadron Cup of £100, furnished our yachtsmen with an opportunity of "realising," as our trans-atlantic brethren would say,

From The Illustrated London News, August 30, 1851.

what those same dwellers beyond the ocean can do afloat in competition with ourselves. None doubted that the America was a very fast sailer, but her powers had not been measured by the test of an actual contest. Therefore, when it became known that she was entered amongst the yachts to run for the cup on Friday, the most intense interest was manifested by all classes, from the highest to the humblest, who have thronged in such masses this season to the Isle of Wight; and even her Majesty and the Court felt the influence of the universal curiosity which was excited to see how the stranger, of whom such great things were said, should acquit herself on this occasion. The race was, in fact, regarded as a sort of trial heat, from which some anticipation might be formed of the result of the great international contest, to which the owners of the America have challenged the yachtsmen of England, and which Mr. R. Stephenson, the eminent engineer has accepted, by backing his own schooner, the Titania, against the America.

Among the visitors on Friday were many strangers—Frenchmen *en route* for Havre, Germans in quiet wonderment at the excitement around them, and Americans already triumphing in the anticipated success of their countrymen. The cards containing the names and colours of the yachts described the course merely as being "round the Isle of Wight;" the printed programme stated that it was to be "round the Isle of Wight, inside Noman's Buoy and Sandhead Buoy, and outside the Nab." The distinction gave rise, at the close of the race, to questioning the America's right to the Cup, as she did not sail outside the Nab Light; but this objection was not persisted in, and the Messrs. Stevens were presented with the Cup. The following yachts were entered. They were moored in a double line. No time allowed for tonnage :—

	Tons.		Owners.
Beatrice, schooner	.. 161	..	Sir W. P. Carew.
Volante, cutter	.. 48	..	Mr. J. L. Craigle.
Arrow, cutter	.. 84	..	Mr. T. Chamberlayne.
Wyvern, schooner	.. 205	..	The Duke of Marlborough.
Ione, schooner	.. 75	..	Mr. A. Hill.

	Tons.		Owners.
Constance, schooner	218	..	The Marquis of Conyngham.
Titania, schooner	100	..	Mr. R. Stephenson.
Gipsy Queen, schooner	160	..	Sir H. B. Hoghton.
Alarm, cutter	193	..	Mr. J. Weld.
Mona, cutter	82	..	Lord A. Paget.
America, schooner	170	..	Mr. J. B. Stevens, &c.
Brilliant, 3-mast schooner	392	..	Mr. G. H. Ackers.
Bacchante, cutter	80	..	Mr. B. H. Jones.
Freak, cutter	60	..	Mr. W. Curling.
Stella, cutter	65	..	Mr. R. Frankland.
Eclipse, cutter	50	..	Mr. H. S. Fearon.
Fernande, schooner	127	..	Major Martyn.
Aurora, cutter	84	..	Mr. T. Le Merchant.

At 9.55 the preparatory gun was fired from the club house battery, and the yachts were soon sheeted from deck to topmast with clouds of canvas, huge gaff-topsails and balloon-jibs being greatly in vogue, and the America evincing her disposition to take advantage of her new jib by hoisting it with all alacrity. The whole flotilla not in the race were already in motion, many of them stretching down towards Osborne and Ryde to get good start of the clippers. Of the list above given the Titania and the Stella did not start, and the Fernande did not take her station (the latter was twice winner in 1850, and once this year; the Stella won once last year). Thus, only fifteen started of which seven were schooners, including the Brilliant (three masted schooner), and eight were cutters. At 10 o'clock the signal gun for sailing was fired, and before the smoke had well cleared away the whole of the beautiful fleet was under weigh, moving steadily to the east with the tide and a gentle breeze. The start was effected splendidly, the yachts breaking away like a field of race horses; the only laggard was the America, which did not move for a second or so after the others. Steamers, shore-boats, and yachts of all sizes buzzed along on each side of the course, and spread away for miles over the rippling sea—a sight such as the Adriatic never beheld in all the pride of Venice; such, beaten though we are, as no other country in the world could exhibit; while it is confessed that anything like it

was never seen, even here, in the annals of yachting. Soon after they started a steamer went off from the roads, with the members of the sailing committee, Sir B. Graham, Bart., Commodore Royal Yacht Squaldron, and the following gentlemen :—Lord Exmouth, Capt. Lyon, Mr. A. Fontaine, Captain Ponsonby, Capt. Corry, Messrs. Harvey, Leslie, Greg, and Reynolds. The American Minister, Mr. Abbott Lawrence, and his son, Col. Lawrence, *attache* to the American legation, arrived too late for the sailing of the America, but were accommodated on board the steamer, and went round the island in her ; and several steamers, chartered by private gentlemen or for excursion trips, also accompanied the match.

The Gipsy Queen, with all her canvas set, and in the strength of the tide, took the lead after starting, with the Beatrice next, and then, with little difference in order, the Volante, Constance, Arrow, and a flock of others. The America went easily for some time under mainsail (with a small gaff-topsail of a triangular shape, braced up to the truck of the short and slender stick which serves as her maintopmast), foresail, fore-staysail and jib; while her opponents had every cloth set that the Club regulations allow. She soon began to creep upon them, passing some of the cutters to windward. In a quarter of an hour she had left them all behind, except the Constance, Beatrice, and Gipsy Queen, which were well together, and went along smartly with the light breeze. The yachts were timed off Noman's Land buoy, and the character of the race at this moment may be guessed from the result:

	H.	M.	S.		H.	M.	S.
Volante	11	7	0	Beatrice	11	9	15
Freak	11	8	20	Alarm	11	9	20
Aurora	11	8	30	Arrow	11	10	0
Gipsy Queen	11	8	45	Bacchante	11	10	15
America	11	9	0				

The other six were staggering about in the rear, and the Wyvern soon afterwards hauled her wind and went back towards Cowes.

The America speedily advanced to the the front and got clear away from the rest. Off Sandown Bay, the wind freshening, she carried away her jibboom; but as she was well handled, the mishap produced no ill effect, and during a lull which came on in the breeze for some time subsequently, her competitors gained a trifling advantage, but did not approach her. Off Ventnor the America was more than a mile ahead of the Aurora, then the nearest of the racing squadron; and hereabouts the number of her competitors were lessened by three cutters, the Volante having sprung her bowsprit, the Arrow having gone ashore, and the Alarm having staid by the Arrow to assist in getting her off But from the moment the America had rounded St. Catherine's point, with a moderate breeze at S. S. W., the chances of coming up with her again were over. The Wildfire, which, though not in the match, kept up with the Stranger for some time, was soon shaken off, and of the vessels in the match, the Aurora was the last that kept her in sight, until, the weather thickening, even that small comfort was lost to her. As the America approached the Needles, the wind fell, and a haze came on, not thick enough however, to be very dangerous; and here she met and passed (saluting with her flag) the Victoria and Albert Royal yacht, with her Majesty on board. Her Majesty waited for the Aurora and then returned to Osborne, passing the America again in the Solent. About six o'clock, the Aurora, being some five or six miles astern, and the result of the race inevitable, the steamers that had accompanied the yachts bore away for Cowes, where they landed their passengers. The evening fell darkly, heavy clouds being piled along the northern shore of the strait; and the thousands who had for hours lined the southern shore, from West Cowes long past the Castle, awaiting anxiously the appearance of the winner, and eagerly drinking in every rumor as to the progress of the match, were beginning to disperse, when the peculiar rig of the clipper was discerned through the gloom, and at 8 h. 34 m. o'clock (railway time, 8 h. 37 m., according to the Secretary of the Royal Yacht Squadron) a gun from the flag-ship announced her arrival as the winner of the cup. The Aurora was announced at 8 h. 58 m.; the Bacchnnte at 9 h. 30 m.; the Eclipse at 9 h. 45 m.; the Brilliant at 1 h. 20 m. (Saturday morning). No account of the rest.

On the evening after the race there was a very brilliant and effective display of fireworks by land and water along the Club House Esplanade, at which 6000 or 7000 persons were present. A reunion took place at the club house; and the occasion was taken of Mr. Abbott Lawrence's presence to compliment him on the success of his countrymen. His Excellency acknowledged the kindness in suitable terms, and said that, though he could not but be proud of the triumph of his fellow-citizens, he still felt it was but the children giving a lesson to the father.

On Saturday evening the America sailed from Cowes to Osborne, in consequence of the intimation that the Queen wished to inspect her. The Victoria and Albert also dropped down to Osborne. At a quarter to six, the Queen embarked in the State barge, accompanied by his Royal Highness Prince Albert and suite, and on nearing the America, the national colors of that vessel were dipped, out of respect to her Majesty, and raised again when her Majesty had proceeded on board. Her Majesty made a close inspection of the America, attended by Commodore Stevens, Colonel Hamilton, and the officers of the yacht. The Queen remained on board half an hour, and expressed great admiration of the general arrangements and character of this famous schooner. On her Majesty leaving, the American colors were again dipped, and her Majesty proceeded in the barge to Osborne, where she arrived at half-past six o'clock.

HER MAJESTY'S CUP.

On Monday the contest was for the splendid cup presented by her Majesty, and took place at Ryde. Up to the hour of starting it had been fully expected that the American clipper would give another proof of her extraordinary powers, and great was the disappointment when the announcement was made that she would not start. The following were the entries for the Queen's Cup, the course being round the Isle of Wight:—

YACHTS.	TONS.	OWNERS.	FLAGS.
Volante	48	J. L. Craigie, Esq	White.
Fernande	127	Major Martyn	Purple and orange.
Surprise	15	W. H. Woodhouse, Esq.	White, black Maltese.
America	170	Commodore Stevens	Blue, with stars.
Alarm	193	J. Weld, Esq	Red and white.
Wildfire	42	F. Thynne, Esq	Blue and white chequered
Fanny	92	H. Young, Esq	————
Bacchante	80	B. H. Jones, Esq	Blue and white cross.
Constance	218	Marquis of Conyngham	Blue, with red hand.
Destiny	107	C. P. Leslie, Esq	————

At ten o'clock the yachts took their station off Ryde pier, when, in consequence of there not being the desideratum for the America—viz.: a six-knot breeze, she declined starting with the squadron, and the Fernande and the Constance were also withdrawn.

At five minutes after ten o'clock the starting gun was fired from the commodore's yacht, the Brilliant, when the Wildfire, belonging to the Cork Regatta Club (which, though not in the race on Friday, headed the American clipper for a considerable distance on that occasion), was the first to get under weigh towards the westward with a light breeze from the W. S. W., with a strong ebb tide, followed by the Bacchante, and close in her lee by the Volante and Alarm.

The Needles were rounded as follows:

	H.	M.	S.
Wildfire	1	15	0
Bacchante	1	18	0
Volante	1	23	0
Alarm	1	23	0

In making up to the starting point off Ryde, the Volante, who appeared to have been rather badly handled, made a series of short tacks, and the Alarm taking advantage of this, made a long tack, and succeeded in first arriving off the Brilliant schooner, when the signal gun proclaimed her victorious. The following is the time of arrival:

	H.	M.	S.
Alarm	5	26	0
Bacchante	5	30	0
Volante	5	30	0
Wildfire	5	31	0

Just before the vessels above-named had got in, the raking America was seen making her way round the Nab Light, and, with a most extraordinary movement, made one reach from the light to Stroke Bay, and by another tack rounded the Brilliant in gallant style. To accomplish the same feat that the America had performed, the Alarm took ten tacks, and the Volante made at least twenty for the same distance. Although not in the match, and not leaving the starting point, as has been stated, for sixty-five minutes after the rest, the " Yankee " clipper, now become the wonder of the south, rounded the Brilliant at 5:41, thereby accomplishing the distance within ten minutes of the Wildfire, and gaining in round numbers, forty-five minutes. Had the America, therefore, proceeded into the match at the appointed hour, there can be no doubt that the same fortunate result would here have greeted the " flying stranger," as she succeeded in obtaining last week at Cowes against the entire Royal Yacht Squadron.

At about six o'clock, the visitors on the pier were much satisfied on observing the Fairy steam-yacht approaching from the direction of Osborne, with the Royal standard flying from the main; and it was soon made known that Her Majesty, Prince Albert, and the Royal children were on board, who had come down to witness the yachts which had contended for the prize, which it is Her Majesty's intention to confer annually upon the club. After coming opposite the pier, and receiving the hearty plaudits of the spectators, the Fairy proceeded on her return to Osborne.

The day being the birthday of His Royal Highness Prince Albert, a Royal salute was fired from the club-house in honor of that day and a similar demonstration was made by the Vengeance, 90, lying at Spithead, which was gaily dressed with colors of all nations from stem to stern. There were also several sailing and rowing matches among the small craft of that place, the funds for which were provided by Her Majesty.

The America was fully described in our journal for August 9. As many of our readers may not be conversant with the technicalities of ship-building terms, we have endeavored in the accompanying diagram, to give the relative position of the beam (or extreme breadth), as it occurs in the old style of yacht, and in the America.

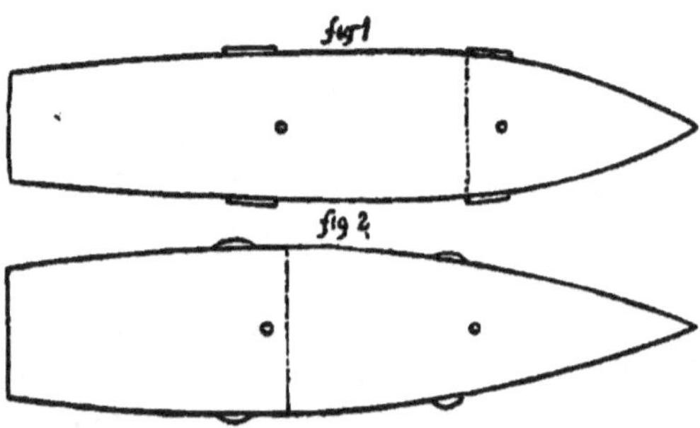

Fig. 1. respresents the shape of vessels on the old plan—the dotted line being the position of the beam.

Fig. 2. Plan of the America.

CHAPTER III.

THE ENCHANTRESS.

Land and Water, London, July 1, 1871.

THE AMERICAN SCHOONER YACHT ENCHANTRESS.

THIS is a new vessel, built by Mr. Fish, owned by Mr. Lorillard, and sailed by Captain Reuben King; and all four—the vessel, her builder, owner, and sailing master—are perfect types of their several species as produced on the other side of the Atlantic. This, perhaps, conveys no impression to those people who are not acquainted with the Americans and their yachts, and we may therefore be permitted to say that, taken in the order already named, the four are respectfully beautiful, talented, accomplished, and bold. The Enchantress, lying where she now does among a cluster of English yachts in Cowes harbor, looks lovely; so graceful and so rakish; so taut and yet so well balanced; so racer-like, and yet so stiff and safe. A little to the south of Bannister Quay, where she is lying, there are a good many schooners; one, the very last launched from the yard of a celebrated builder, and truly they are hideous by comparison with the stranger. They seem all of one pattern, wall-sided, straight-sheared, sharp-ended boxes, while she looks like a swan sitting on the water. Mr. Fish, her constructor, is renowned as a most successful designer of yachts, and many hundreds of vessels of all sizes, perhaps the most celebrated of which are the Truant, the Challenge, and the Meteor, owe their being to him. It is not our present business, however, to discuss men, but ships, and having introduced the Enchantress with these remarks on her general appearance and the characteristics of her people, we will describe the vessel in detail.

The Enchantress is a large vessel of some 300 tons or more. She is broad in the beam, and shows a rather low freeboard, with a great deal of shear, and she has raking masts and bowsprit with a steave, so that thus far we look upon comparatively familiar forms; but below water she is after a new pattern, which is as yet strange both in America and England. Although this shape may claim to come originally from America, yet the most conspicuous example of it, so far as we know, is now sailing her trial matches, having been launched under the name of the Livonia only a few weeks back at Cowes. We see the shape therefore produced both in England and America, and certainly in America first; but it is better to call it "new" than to give it any nationality, because it is so totally unlike any of the models which we are accustomed to regard as peculiar to either one country or the other.

This strange form of the immersed body of the vessel has its origin in the peculiar shape of the midship section. The direct resistance, or, in other words, the area of this section, is reduced until it is the smallest possible, or, at any rate, the smallest we ever saw. One of the ideal "racing machines" is here realized; not the simple plank on edge, with its lower extremity weighted; but the two planks—one on edge affording the lateral resistance and one (lying flat) nailed on top of it, affording the stability. She is a vessel with a deck and keel, and little else; the only modification of this exaggerated form being that the junction of the two is not pronounced in a sharp angle, but is affected by the interposition of curves in the transverse sections. Here is a sketch of her midship section; not drawn to scale from a model or correct draught, but merely by eye and from memory:

To look at this section and realize to oneself that at no other place is this vessel even so bulky as this, must impress one with the fact that there is very little of her anywhere. She is, fact, the leanest ship we ever saw. The Livonia has the same sort of "hollow" bottom, as it may be called; but her bilge is much

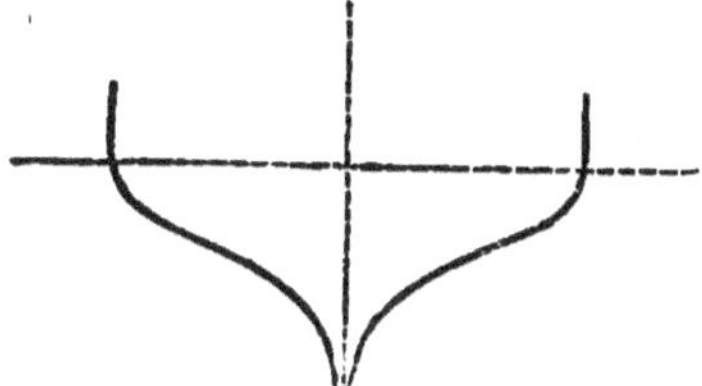

fuller, and extends further down into the water, than that of the Enchantress, and, as a consequence, we find the Livonia started with 70 tons of ballast (how much more she has now we can't exactly say), while the Enchantress, which is a much larger vessel, has but 60. Both these vessels depend chiefly for their stability (at least, so we think) on their form ; and if this be so, a very curious and interesting question arises as to why the Livonia proved tender—too tender to race, and the Enchantress stiff enough to brave the Atlantic, and prove herself a safe and good sailor in all weathers. In the first place, we must be understood to agree with our correspondent "C. E. S.," who wrote a letter about the Livonia the other day, when he seems to doubt the accuracy of calculations which go to show the Livonia's centre of gravity to be below her centre of buoyancy. We cannot imagine such to be the case ; and, supposing we are right, the answer to the question as to why the Livonia was more tender than the Enchantress would seem to be that her bilge is unnecessarily full—that is to say, this bulky part of the hull is too *deeply* immersed, and in piling in the ballast to sink the vessel to her proper water-line, the centre of gravity was raised faster than the centre of buoyancy. This has been pointed out before, but then the Enchantress was not here to bring forward, as an instance of a larger vessel with nearly the same proportion of depth to breadth, with a less powerful bilge, and carrying less ballast, and yet being stiffer altogether. The moral of all this is that to strive after a combination of stability by form and stability by ballast is vain. If you go in for a stiff shape, it seems better to make no concessions to the requirements of the opposition sort of stability, and give up all hope of getting the centre of gravity below the centre of buoyancy.

In addition to having a lean middle piece, the Enchantress has fine ends. Her bows are, perhaps, not finer than the Livonia's, but her after end certainly is, and especially at her load-water-line, where instead of a full curve nearly all the way from the greatest breadth to the stern post, we have here a Scott Russell wave line. Below this again, the water-lines at both ends are extremely sharp; and four or five feet beneath the surface of the water there is scarcely any body to the vessel at all.

The stern is of the usual American graceful form, and joins the keel at a round-up forefoot. The keel, however, contrary to the modern custom, is nearly straight; and it has considerable drag, so that the draught aft is some feet more than it is forward. The stern-post rakes about three or four feet, and the counter is rather long and slight.

With this much description, and with the help of the sketch of her mid-ship section, those who take an interest in the subject and have not an opportunity of seeing the vessel for themselves, may be able to form an idea of the shape of the Enchantress's hull. Beyond this, however, it would be quite impossible to give a fair idea of her general appearance to any one who does not know the sort of thing to expect, and even those who saw the Sappho, Dauntless, and Meteor last year would not be quite prepared for the Enchantress. She is handsomer and more rakish; and a visit to the island only for a look at her, would be well repaid. We have read legends of slavers, and pirates, and buccaneers, and corsairs, and the like, with long, low, black hulls, and towering spars; and, behold, in this vessel we have the realization of all the most facinating pictures of such that Marryatt ever drew, or youthful imagination ever invented. Although her spars are to our English eyes quite gigantic, yet she is in cruising trim; in proof of which it may be asserted that though a larger vessel, yet she has the poor old Meteor's mainsail now bent; and the Meteor's hemp shrouds too are over her mast heads. Still, her people say that, rigged as she is now, she can fly; and—although we are persuaded that her hull below water is not the shape that salt water likes—yet we can readily believe the report, and if asked why, should say because she is so " fine " and so " fair."

A good sea-boat she has proved herself to be. She has been seen running before a heavy gale of wind in the Atlantic, with both gaff-topsails aloft, when the sea was so high that the large vessels near her have been hove-to and their decks swept.

Now why cannot a match be made between this vessel and the Livonia? Although the Enchantress's racing sails are in New York, we hardly think this would prove an obstacle; for Americans are too fond of sport to let anything stand in the way of a good match; and if the proposal was made, there can be very little doubt that it would be accepted; and the match would be far more interesting than any of those which the Cambria sailed against the Americans last season and the season before.

The Daily Telegraph, St. Johns, New Brunswick, July 25, 1873.

THE ENCHANTRESS.

This beautiful yacht made her appearance in the harbor yesterday afternoon, and signalled her advent · by firing a salute, which was returned by one of the ships loading on the Carleton side. In a short time one of our staff boarded her, and was very courteously received by the owner, J. F. Loubat, Esq., of New York, who showed him over the vessel. Outwardly, the Enchantress is a very rakish looking craft, with a very sharp bow, fine lines forward, and a very long overhanging counter. She has a moderately flat floor, and is not too much cut away on the bilge, so that, although very fast, she is weatherly and a very dry boat for a yacht. She measures 136 feet over all, and is 115 feet long on the water line, 112 feet 6 inches on the keel. She is 24 feet beam, 11 feet hold, and her draft of water is 13 feet 6 inches. She is a keel yacht. Her official measurement is 118 tons, but she would probably approach 200 tons carpenters' measurement. This vessel was built two years ago by Mr. Lorillard, of New York, as a cruising yacht, and as comfort was considered of more account than speed, she was arranged with a view to furnish the largest amount of accommodation for her inmates. How far this design has been successful can be seen at once by the most casual glance at her cabins, which are of the amplest character. The main cabin is amidships and is very large, and the state rooms are on an equally ample scale. The after part of the vessel is occupied by a saloon after the English model, a capital lounging place in the day time, and at night furnishing comfortable sleeping quarters to those who are too indolent or feel disinclined to go to bed. Forward are the ice-houses, the pantry, the galley, and the quarters of the steward and crew, the latter being amply provided for and supplied with all necessary conveniences for their safety as well as their comfort. The fittings of the cabins are of the most substantial and elegant description. The Enchantress belongs to the New York Yacht Club, and was purchased from Mr. Lorillard some time ago by her present owner, Mr. Loubat. He is accompanied in his present cruise by two friends, Dr. F. G. Snelling and Mr. Gardiner Sherman, Jr. Mr. Robert Fish, the celebrated yacht designer, is also on board this, the finest of his productions. The sailing master of the Enchantress is Reuben King, the first mate, William Dand, and the Sandy Hook pilot, Peter H. Roff. The crew numbers 18 men all told.

When Mr. Loubat left New York, in his fine yacht, he intended to go to New London, but concluded to come further east, and arrived some days ago at Mount Desert, which he left on Wednesday at 6 P. M., arriving here early yesterday afternoon. It is his intention to spend some days here, perhaps to go up river and to cross the bay. It is quite likely that the yacht will go to Halifax, calling at one or two of the ports on the Atlantic Coast on the way. After that the Enchantress will go to Europe, probably to the Mediterranean, where she has already cruised two seasons. At present the vessel is in cruising trim, but still she is able to hold her own with all comers. When she was being built it was predicted that she would be fast, and she has amply fulfilled the expectations of those interested in her. She is probably faster than any other yacht belonging to the New York Yacht Club, except the Sappho. She is kept in admirable order, and is provided with a steam launch, which is also a life boat, a most admirable and useful appendage.

CHAPTER IV.

THE OCEAN RACES.

The New York Herald, New York, September 25, 1878.

Meeting of the New York Yacht Club Last Night—Appropriation of $1,000 for the October Races.

The New York Yacht Club held a meeting last night, rear commodore Kingsland in the chair.

Mr. Colgate moved that the regatta committee be authorized to carry out the instructions of the commodore's letter in regard to the October races.   Carried.

On motion of Mr. Chase the secretary was added to the committee.

It was moved to appropriate $1,000 to defray the expenses for the October races.   Carried.

The following are the prizes to be sailed for at the October races:—

Cup, presented by the commodore, one for schooners and one for sloops, to be sailed for on the first Thursday in October over New York Yacht Club course; value $500.

Cup, presented by the commodore, to be sailed for on the second Thursday of October, by schooners of any organized yacht club, from the anchorage off Owl's Head to and round lightship off Cape May, and return to Sandy Hook Lightship; value $1,000.

Purses, presented by the Commodore, to be sailed for on the second Thursday of October (under direction of the N. Y. Y. C.) by pilot boats, working schooners and smacks (schooners), sailing from any port in the United States. The first vessel arriving to take a purse of $1,000; the first boat arriving of each of the other two classes to take a purse of $250. No class, however, to win more than one prize.

Newspapers in the various seaport towns are requested to call the attention of owners of vessels to the conditions under which these two last mentioned cups are offered. Further instructions in regard to the races will be issued by the Regatta Committee from time to time. Any persons desiring to enter their boats or wishing any information can address Mr. Charles A. Minton, Secretary, No. 26 Broad Street.

The Autumn Regatta of the New York Yacht Club and the Ocean Races under its Auspices—The Conditions and Prizes of the Aquatic Events set down for October 2 and 3.

The autumn regatta of the New York Yacht Club and the ocean races under its auspices are awaited with pleasure, and promise to create a great amount of interest, not only because of the excitement likely to be attached to them, but because of the confidence which many owners place in their gallant craft. The first named of these aquatic events will be sailed on Thursday, October 2, over the usual regulation course, subject to the time allowances and under the sailing regulations of the club. The prizes to be sailed for are two cups, presented by Commodore Bennett—one for schooners and one for sloops, each of the value of $500. The Regatta Committe, comprising Messrs. Fletcher Westray, William Krebs, Edward E. Chase, and Charles A. Minton, have issued the official notice calling attention to the regatta and inviting entries, which will be received by the Secretary of the Club, at his office, No. 26 Broad Street, until Tuesday morning, September 10, at ten o'clock precisely.

In this contest no entrance money will be required. All yachts must carry their private signals at the main peak. The start will be a flying one, and the time of each yacht will be taken as she crosses a line between a stakeboat, which will be anchored in the Narrows, near Fort Wadsworth, Staten Island, and the judges' steamer. The signals for starting will be given from the judges' boat, as follows:—For a preparatory signal, one gun and lowering the yacht club flag on the steamboat, and ten minutes later, for the start, one gun, and the flag will again be lowered. No yacht's time will be taken later than fifteen minutes after the second gun, unless instructions to the contrary are given by the judges on the morning of the regatta. The expiration of the time will be marked by a third gun and lowering of flag. If practicable, a short blast of the steam whistle of the judges' boat will be given when the time of each yacht is taken as she crosses the line in starting and returning.

The course will be from the starting point, as above, to and around a stakeboat, at buoy $8\frac{1}{2}$, on the Southwest Spit, keeping it on the port hand in turning, thence to and around the Sandy Hook Lightship, keeping it on the starboard hand in rounding, and return over the same course, keeping the Southwest Spit buoy on the starboard hand. Yachts must keep to the eastward of buoys Nos. 9, 11 and 13 on the West Bank, going and returning, and will pass between the judges' boat and the stakeboat on arriving home.

THE OCEAN RACES.

The "outside" or ocean contests under the direction of the New York Yacht Club will be sailed one week after the autumn regatta, Thursday, October 9, and there is but little doubt these will be the events of the year and of a character to be remembered by all the participants. The races will embrace, first, a cup of the value of $1,000, presented by Commodore Bennett, to be sailed for by schooner yachts belonging to any organized yacht club, from an anchorage off Owl's Head, New York Harbor, to and around the Lightship on Five Fathom, off Cape May, N. J., and return to Sandy Hook Lightship. Second, three purses of the value of \$1,000, \$250 and \$250, respectively, also presented by the Commodore, to be sailed for over the same course upon the same day, and open to the following class of vessels, hailing from any port in the United States:—

First—Pilot boats.

Second—Working schooners of not less than 25 nor over 300 tons, old measurement.

Third—Schooner smacks.

In this race the first vessel arriving at the winning post will take the purse of \$1,000, the first vessel arriving of each of the other two classes to take a purse of \$250, no class, however, to win more than one prize. These races will be sailed in accordance with the sailing regulations of the New York Yacht Club, which limits the amount of canvas to be carried to the following:— Mainsail, foresail, forestaysail, jib, flying jib, jib-topsail, fore and main gaff-topsail and main topmast-staysail.

The Regatta Committee, comprising the same gentlemen as given above, will issue specific instructions as to the course to be sailed and the rules governing the race, copies of which will be furnished upon application to the Secretary, Mr. Charles A. Minton, at his office, on and after the 25th inst. All entries must be made before twelve o'clock м., October 7, to the Secretary, to whom inquiries relative to the race should be addressed.

These events, occurring in the season of the year when fresh breezes are wont to abound in the bay of New York and along the coast, have given rise to a great deal of interest and speculation in yachting circles and among the friends and owners of the vessels that are invited to enter for the purses named. The latter contest, first of its character in this country, should call out the speedy pilot boats and working schooners which abound in not only these and adjacent waters, but in all our seaport towns, and thus test their sailing qualities in company with the crack yachts of the New York and other club fleets. In doing this mayhap they will accomplish more than winning a purse; they may beat some more pretentious craft over the course, and thus add additional laurels to victory. To aid a full entry in these races it is desired that as much publicity as practicable may be given these conditions by all journals on the seaboard. "The more the merrier" on the 2nd and 9th prox.

The New York Herald, New York, October 8, 1873.

THE OCEAN RACES.

Special Instructions by the Regatta Committee of the New York Yacht Club—How the Competing Vessels will be Distinguished at night.

There can be no question regarding the success of the ocean yacht races to be sailed to-morrow (Thursday), under the direction of the New York Yacht Club. The entries, as given herewith, embrace six schooner yachts of such construction they must make good reports of themselves, notwithstanding the character of the weather; and if it should happen to blow great guns, as it did on Monday during the Meta and Vision match, the respective owners will glory in the occasion and hail the opportunity as most fortunate to test their several models. The names of these pleasure craft that will contest for the $1,000 cup are the Enchantress, Alarm, Clio, Eva, Atalanta and Dreadnaught, a very fine fleet, indeed, and among yachtsmen who are acquainted with the sailing qualities of each, the event will produce much excitement. The performances of the Enchantress and Dreadnaught will be particularly watched, as Mr. Loubat, owner of the former, has challenged Mr. Stockwell of the Dreadnaught, to defend his right and title to the Cape May Challenge Cup on the 14th inst., and, without doubt, the part the latter yacht will play in the ocean race will shape the character of the cup contest. Then there are formidable competitors in the Eva and Clio, both of which did magnificently in the regatta of the 2nd inst., the latter winning the schooner prize. And still more, the new boat of Mr. Astor, the Atalanta, which displayed such qualities of speed when there was but a handful of wind during the late regatta, will "show her hand" around the "outside" course ; and again, the Alarm, which demonstrated what she could do in a gale and heavy seaway at Newport, last Summer will, it is predicted, be at the front around the Lightship on Five Fathom Bank. All in all, the competing yachts are heavy weather craft, and must give an excellent account of themselves from the moment they are started until the finish of the grand race at the Lightship off Sandy Hook.

If there will be interest manifested in the competing yachts and speculation as to the probable winner, there certainly must be genuine excitement among the owners and their friends of the pilot boats that have entered for the purses presented by Commodore Bennett, to be sailed at the same time and over the same course. Seven of these staunch sea craft are on the list, and the several crews are exerting themselves to the utmost for the event. The friendly rivalry among the pilots in this matter is deep and earnest, and yet while each captain will strive to make his vessel reach the winning post in advance of all the others, they hope that no accidents will occur and that the "best boat may win."

Still another class of those that "go down to the sea" are intensely interested in the races—that of those owning working schooners. Four of this class of vessels are entered for the purses, and, if report be true, among them are the crack craft of the waters in and about New York. Much determination will mark the race between these boats, as each crew will "go in to win," and their sailing masters, as well as those of the pilot boats, are among the best in the country. Then there is a class for schooner smacks, but until late last evening but one entry had been received under this head.

The Regatta Committee, comprising Messrs. Fletcher Westray, William Krebs, Edward E. Chase and Charles A. Minton, having the races in charge, issued a few days since the annexed specific instructions and rules to govern the events, which should be carefully perused by all that are concerned.

NEW YORK YACHT CLUB.—OCEAN RACES OCTOBER 9, 1873.

The following cup and purses, presented by Commodore Bennett, will be sailed for on Thursday, October 9, 1873:—

I. Cup of the value of $1,000, to be sailed for by schooner yachts belonging to any organized yacht club, from an anchorage off Owl's Head, New York Harbor, to and around the Lightship on Five Fathom Bank, off Cape May, N. J., and return to Sandy Hook Lightship.

II. Three purses, of the value of $1,000, $250 and $250, respectively, to be sailed for over the same course, upon the same day, and open to the following classes of vessels hailing from any port in the United States:—

First—Pilot boats.

Second—Working schooners of not less than 25 nor over 300 tons, old measurement.

Third—Schooner smacks.

In this race the first vessel arriving at the winning post to take a purse of $1,000; the first vessel arriving of each of the other two classes to take a purse of $250. No class, however, to win more than one purse.

Entries to be made to C. A. Minton, Secretary, New York Yacht Club, No. 26 Broad Street, New York, to whom all inquiries relative to the races should be addressed. No entrance fee required.

These races will be sailed in accordance with the sailing regulations of the New York Yacht Club, and the following

SPECIFIC INSTRUCTIONS.

Two flagboats will be stationed off Owl's Head, about one mile from the shore, and competing vessels will anchor on the morning of the race as follows :—

I. Yachts, fifty yards apart on a line drawn due east from the stakeboat stationed nearest the Narrows.

II. Pilot boats, working schooners and smacks, fifty yards apart on a line drawn due east from the stakeboat stationed to the northward of the first line.

In taking position in line each vessel may select its own, in the order of its arrival at the anchorage. Mainsails, foresails and gaff-topsails may be set before starting, unless otherwise ordered by the Regatta Committee.

Yachts will be required to carry their private signals at the main peaks, and working schooners and smacks will carry designating numbers in the middle of their mainsails, just above the reef points.

THE START.

The competing vessels will be started at three o'clock, P. M. precisely, and the signals, which will be given from the judges' steamer the steam yacht "Herald," will be as follows:—

For a preparatory signal—One whistle and the New York Yacht Club signal on the steamer will be lowered; and, ten minutes after, for the start, the same signals will be repeated, whereupon all competing vessels will weigh anchors and get under way.

THE COURSE.

The course will be from the anchorage, keeping to the eastward of buoys Nos. 9, 11 and 13 on the West Bank, to and around buoy No. 8½ on the Southwest Spit, leaving it on the port hand in turning, thence to and around the Cape May Lightship on Five Fathom Bank, leaving in on the starboard hand in turning, and back to the Sandy Hook Lightship, passing to the westward of the same, and within 200 yards. Each vessel shall, immediately upon passing the Sandy Hook Lightship, round to and report to the judge stationed on board.

APPROACHING LIGHTSHIPS AT NIGHT.

Any vessel approaching either lightship at night shall, when about half a mile distant, fire two rockets, to apprise the judge stationed on board that she is a competing vessel; and any vessel other than a yacht rounding the Cape May Lightship at night shall, when nearest to it, flash a light upon the number in her mainsail, so that it may be distinquished.

Rockets, lights and numbers for mainsails will be furnished upon application to the Secretary.

The races will be governed by the following extracts from the sailing regulations of the club:—

Rule 7.

Sails.—Yachts contending for prizes may carry sails as follows:—Schooners, mainsail, foresail, fore staysail, jib, flying jib, jib-topsail, fore and main gaff-topsails and main topmast-staysail.

Rule 10.

Objections.—If any objection be made with regard to the classification or sailing of any yacht in a race, such objection must be made in writing to the Regatta Committee before three o'clock, P. M. on the next day after the regatta.

Rule 13.

Sounding.—Nothing but a hand lead and line to be used in sounding during a regatta.

Rule 14.

Tonching Buoys, &c.—A yacht touching any mark, boat or buoy used to mark out the course shall forfeit all claim to the prize, unless as in case specified in rule No. 19.

Rule 16.

Floors and Bulkheads.—All yachts, during a regatta, to keep the floors down and bulkheads standing. No starting or taking in water or ballast permitted within twenty-four hours of the time named for starting, nor any trimming by dead weight allowed.

Rule 18.

Courses.—Any yacht bearing away or altering her course to leeward, and thereby compelling another yacht to bear away to avoid a collision, shall forfeit all claim to the prize and pay all damages that may ensue, unless when two yachts are approaching the windward shore, a buoy or stakeboat together, with a free wind, and so close to each other that the weathermost cannot bear away clear of the leewardmost, and by standing further on would be in danger of running on shore or touching a buoy or stakeboat, then such leewardmost yacht, on being requested to bear away, is immediately to comply, and will forfeit all claim to the prize for not doing so. The weathermost yacht must, however, bear away as soon as the one she hails, if she can do so without coming into contact.

Rule 19.

Rounding Buoys.—When rounding a mark, boat or buoy the yacht nearest thereto is to be considered the headmost yacht; and should any other yacht in the race compel the yacht which is nearest to any mark, boat or buoy to touch said mark boat or buoy, the yacht so compelling her shall forfeit all claim to the prize, her owner shall pay for all damages that may occur, and the yacht so compelled to touch a mark, boat or buoy shall not suffer any penalty for such contact.

Rule 20.

Courses.—Yachts going free must invariably give way for those by the wind on either tack.

Rule 21.

Courses.—When two yachts (by the wind) are approaching the shore, a buoy, or stakeboat together, and so close to each other that the leewardmost cannot tack clear of the weathermost, and by standing further on would be in danger of running on shore, or touching a buoy or stake boat, such weathermost yacht on being requested to put about, is immediately to comply, and will forfeit all claim to a prize for not doing so. The leewardmost yacht must, however, tack at the same time as the one she hails, if she can do so without coming into contact.

Rule 23.

Ruling of Regatta Committee.—The Regatta Committee shall have full power to decide all questions that may arise in the sailing of the regatta, and also to exclude all yachts, which, by their decision, have violated any rule of the Club. There shall be no appeal from the decision of this Committee.

THE ENTRIES.

The entries of the several classes, up to a late hour last night, were as follows:

YACHTS.

Name.	*Owner.*	*Tonnage.*
Enchantress	J. F. Loubat	276.16
Alarm	A. C. Kingsland	225.77
Clio	{ T. B. Asten. / T. C. P. Bradhurst. }	59.18
Eva	E. Burd Grubb	77.50
Atalanta	Wm. Astor	145.41
Dreadnaught	A. B. Stockwell	240.

PILOT BOATS.

Widgeon, No. 10	N. Y. Pilots	105.09
Hope, No. 1	N. Y. Pilots	132.04
Edmund Blunt, No. 21	N. Y. Pilots	——
C. H. Marshall, No. 3	N. Y. Pilots	85.00
James W. Elwell, No. 7	N. J. Pilots	165.00
Thos. S. Negus, No. 1	N. J. Pilots	——
Mary E. Fish, No. 4	N. Y. Pilots	——

WORKING SCHOONERS.

Designating Letter.

Wm. H. Van Name	A	Wm. H. Van Name	180
Reindeer	B	Capt. Howard	140
Sharpshooter	C	F. M. Crossman	120
Racer	D	Eugene Howard	—

SCHOONER SMACKS.

Wallace Blackford	E. H. C. Rogers & Co.	80

LIGHTS, DESIGNATING NUMBERS AND LETTERS.

In addition to the two rockets required to be fired by each vessel approaching either lightships on Five Fathom Bank or

Sandy Hook, the Regatta Committee will instruct the yachts as they round either of these beacons to show the following lights, that they may be easily distinguished.

Enchantress, blue light; Alarm, red light; Clio, blue and red, one after the other; Eva, red and blue, one after the other; Atalanta, two blue lights, one after the other; Dreadnaught, two red lights, one after the other.

The pilot boats will carry their own numbers, but as there are duplicates on the list of entries, the Hope will be distinguished by a large black ball directly under her number.

The letters by which the working schooners and smacks are to be distinguished are given above.

The New York Times, New York, October 9, 1873.

THE OCEAN RACE.

Just now the seekers after amusement must be especially difficult to please if, in the multiplicity of attractions offered them, they cannot find the wherewithal to satisfy their cravings. There was a time when it was considered extremely doubtful if New York could support a single Italian opera, and when a single prima donna or tenor, either graceful or robust, was considered sufficient to meet all our musical requirements. Now we have two opera houses, in which large and fashionable audiences congregate nightly to hear not one, but half a dozen, of the foremost singers in the world. The theatres are open and running briskly, with native and exotic talent, and they who cannot find something to suit them, from Salvani, all the way down to Sothern, from the "Midsummer Night's Dream," to the "Black Crook," must be indeed exacting.

For those to whom the opera is forbidden ground, and the theatre an abomination, there are the harmless pleasures of the lecture-room, and the miracles of the prestidigitateur. They may inspect the wonders of machinery at the American Institute Fair, or view the marvels of art at the Metropolitan Museum. They

may ponder over the exhumed pottery of Crete, or combine re-
ligion with relaxation by going to the pious pantomime and
panorama of "The Pilgrim," where for a most considerate ex-
penditure one may taste all the various delights, as the published
programme informs us, of "painting, song, music, lecture, and
grand transformation finale." And lastly, those who are fond
of sports may choose between the races at Fordham, the rifle-
shooting at Creedmoor, and the regatta of the New York Yacht
Club.

As the latter contest is this time to be an ocean race, it will
probably be, if the wind holds, an exceptionally fine one, and it
may be, as the race between the Meta and Vision on Tuesday
showed, that our amateur mariners may have ample chance to re-
deem themselves from the reproach of overcaution, not to say
timidity, which has been left upon them by some episodes of the
Summer cruise. A yacht that cannot face an ocean breeze, or
even an ocean gale, is little better than a toy, and its racing
hardly deserves a place among the list of manly sports. The
main use and recommendation of yachting, next to its service in
the improvement of marine architecture—to which we have before adverted—the one thing that saves it from the stigma of an
expensive idleness, is the hardihood, vigor, and contempt of
danger that it naturally breeds.

For this reason we would be glad to see owners oftener sail
their own craft, instead of confiding them to professional sailors.
It is difficult to see on what principle a yacht race so conducted
can fairly be called an amateur contest at all. Rather would we
see them emulate the example of Mr. Brassey, the well-known
railway contractor and member of Parliament, who, the other
day, passed his examination and received his full certificate as a
qualified sailing master in all the branches of navigation—the
first instance, it is said, of the kind on record. We wish it
might not be the last. With a few such yachtsmen, this noble
sport would soon acquire a new dignity and importance. And,
we suggest, as one means towards bringing about this desirable
result, that in future regattas a separate and distinct prize shall

be offered for yachts which are so sailed by their owners, or at least by amateurs.

A novel feature of to-day's contest will be an additional race open to pilot boats, working schooners, and schooner smacks, for which two prizes, of $1,000 and $250, are offered by the Yacht Club, and which has attracted a dozen entries. For the yacht race proper a number of our best yachts are entered, including the Enchantress, Alarm, Clio, Eva, Atlanta, and Dreadnaught and, with favoring winds, the contest should be an exceedingly fine one. Few, of course, can hope to see much more of it than the start, though at least two steamers, as will be seen by our advertising columns, will accompany the race to Sandy Hook, and if the weather permits, as far as the Light-ship. All who enjoy this exhilarating and graceful sport, and who do not fear the "white caps," will, we are sure, find their recompense in attending.

The New York Herald, New York, October 10, 1873.

THE OCEAN REGATTA.

From Owl's Head to Cape May for Cup and Purse and Glory—The Clio Leading at Sandy Hook—The Pilot Boats and the Toilers of the Sea Struggling Broadside to Broadside—Brilliant Scene at Bay Ridge—The Fishing Schooner Blackford and Her Walk Over the Course—"Crowding" at the Narrows and "Bunching" at the Southwest Spit.

The great ocean yacht race, from Owl's Head Point around the Southwest spit to Cape May Lightship in New Jersey, and back to the Sandy Hook Lightship, a distance of about 140 miles as the bird flies, and probably 250 miles when the boats are going free and with tacks for wind, began yesterday afternoon, at thirteen minutes after three o'clock. No more beautiful day than Thursday, October 9, 1873, has ever been vouchsafed to the yachtsmen of this or any neighboring city in the United States. The air at an early hour of the morning was as delightful as the dream of a young girl; the sky was clear and of a piercing blue, and the sun, which in the beginning denied an

appearance to its worshippers, came later to gladden all hearts,
and to gild the white canvas of the boats as they lay on the blue
expanse of water between the villa-crowned eminences of Staten
Island, and the autumnal leaves of the crest of Bay Ridge. The
upper bay was swarming with the sails of numerous craft gad-
ding about, toying and tossing and flirting with sun and air, their
crews shouting with enthusiasm and their breasts filled with the
ozone that made the faintest sound or the lightest laugh distinct
as the booming of a bell over the waters of the bay. At about
eleven o'clock the "Herald" steam yacht bearing the Regatta Committee, consisting of Messrs. Fletcher Westray, William Krebs,
Edward E. Chase and Charles A. Minton, together with the representatives of the press, left the Battery and passed down the
bay, with the red cross, white star and blue ground on her bunt-
ing, and was hailed on her track by many welcome salutations
from the shipping, and by deafening screams from the whistles
of steamboats which tore by with the rapidity of demons.

OFF OWL'S HEAD.

At this point the sight was a charming one. Given the
same number of boats, with their snowy canvas and their tall,
unpainted masts and fairy-like rigging, it is doubtful whether
the Bay of Naples or the Golden Horn, nor yet the Golden
Gate of San Francisco, could furnish a surrounding of frame-
work so deliciously still, so calm, so full of nobleness and grandeur. October had brought to the perspective all her purple and rus-
set and fading emerald glories to fill out the season's picture, the
centre of which was a breathing flame of gold from the sun, a
million of miles above in the great dome of the sky. As is
usual where a number of yachts are to contest a race, they
came slowly, some lying in at the verge of the shore of Staten
Island, others looming down fitfully upon the middle point of
concentration, and surging through the foam, rising from their
bows in the blue water like so many sea birds. The "Herald"
under the judicious management of Captain Robinson, was
obedient to every command of the Regatta Committee, and was

busily engaged in delivering instructions to the different yachts, pilot boats and working schooners which had been entered for the race. Rockets and blue lights to be burned around the bleak circle of Cape May Light and at the scarlet iron sides of the Sandy Hook fogship, were distributed to each contesting boat by young Mr. Minton as the "Herald" yacht forged alongside. The steamers Chamberlain, William Fletcher, Arrowsmith and other marine caravansaries came down from the city wharves loaded with people and endeavoring to secure good vantage ground for the spectacle of a sea fight.

THE CONTESTANTS.

The Bennett Cup, valued at $1,000, was offered to schooner yachts of any organized yacht club in the United States, and three purses, amounting respectively to the sums of $1,000, $250 and $250, were offered also by Commodore Bennett to pilot boats, working schooners of not less than 25 or over 300 tons, old measurement, and to fishing schooner smacks. And now to tell of the entries to this ocean regatta, which was probably better favored by wind and weather than any previous regatta ever before contested on the Atlantic coast.

Of schooner yachts there were entered the Enchantress, J. F. Loubat, 276 tons; Alarm, A. C. Kingsland, 225 tons; Clio, T. B. Asten and T. C. P. Bradhurst, 59 tons; Eva, Gen. E. B. Grubb, 77 tons, and the Dreadnaught, A. B. Stockwell, 240 tons.

Of pilot boats there were entered the Widgeon, No. 10, 106 tons; Edmund Blunt, No. 2, 111 tons; James W. Elwell, No. 7, 137 tons; Thomas S. Negus, No. 1, 130 tons, and Mary E. Fish, No. 4, 106 tons.

The working schooners, instead of being designated by numerals, had large letters of the alphabet, nearly ten feet high placed on their mainsails.

The working schooner W. H. Van Name had the letter A on her mainsail, rated at 140 tons, and hails from Staten Island. This is a magnificent boat, painted black, and her crew boasted before starting that there was not a pilot boat in the race equal to her in model and solidity of timber. She is owned by Mr. W. H. Van Name, and any person who saw her sweep by the point of Sandy Hook yesterday must acknowledge that she is fit to compete with any vessel that sails out of New York harbor.

Next on the list of working schooners was the Reindeer, painted white, with the letter B on her mainsail, of 154 tons, W. N. Howard, master, from Cold Spring, New York. The Reindeer is a brick sloop, and is staunch enough and with breadth of beam enough to dismantle a stone fort.

Last, but not least, of all in the schooner smack class, came the little Wallace Blackford, of eighty tons, owned by H. C. Rogers & Co. This boat had enough hamper on her deck to satisfy the mind of a captain of the Black Ball Line. She bore the letter E on her mainsail, and the Blackford was considered the pride of Fulton Market fishmongers.

Captain Baillie sailed the Widgeon, Bob Fish and Captain Pete Roff were on board the Enchantress, Captain Dick Brown sailed the Mary Fish, Captain Sam Greenwood (who sailed the Sappho in her races with the Livonia) stood on the quarter deck of the Van Name, Captain Schofield sailed the fishing smack Blackford, Captain Warner the Elwell, Captain Lewis the Negus and Captain Johnson the Edmund Blunt.

The Regatta Committee distributed the judges of the race on board the different boats in the following order :—Mr. Walter Kane and the Messrs. Jones on the Enchantress, Mr. Stockwell and Mr. Henry Steers on the Dreadnaught, Mr. Asten on the Clio, Rear Commodore Kingsland and Mr. Parsons on the Alarm, and Mr. F. A. Smith on the Negus. To make the race more interesting a private match for a cup valued at $250 was made between the yachts Clio and Eva. Late in the afternoon the Prospero, Mr. Aspinwall's beautiful steam yacht Day Dream the police boat Seneca, the steamboats Charles Chamberlain and Seth Low, and a dramatic looking and ferocious little steam yacht, with a big smokestack and no deck, called the Oliver Doud Byron, came on the ground and added to the brilliant spectacle.

OUTWARD BOUND FOR THE START.

It was now three o'clock, and the hour was approaching when the boats were to be started by the Regatta Committee. Two stakeboats, with the American colors flying from their masts, were stationed off Owl's Head Point, a mile distant from the shore. Near the stakeboats, and with fifty yards distance between them, the yachts Enchantress, Alarm, Clio, and Dreadnaught were lying at anchor. The Atalanta had not yet been seen. The pilot boats, with their big figures standing out vividly on their mainsails, the hardy-looking working-schooners, having their alphabetical designation, and the solitary fishing smack from Fulton Market, were all in line, waiting for the first whistle to prepare for action. The whistle was blown for preparation on board the "Herald" steam yacht, where the Committee were engaged closely watching the movements of the different craft. The red-cross signal fell at this moment and then there was immediate bustle on the deck of every one of the thirteen boats about to take part in the great ocean regatta. Ten minutes elapsed and the last whistle, the signal for starting, was blown with a shriek so loud and long continued that it might have woke the sleepers in Greenwood. At thirteen minutes past three P. M. the vessels all weighed anchor as quickly as possible. The Clio was the first to show to the front with her sails all sheeted well home as the pretty clipper leaped forward, before the breeze. The Eva was close in her wake and the fishing smack not many yards astern. As they drew off to fill, the boats headed towards Fort Hamilton, but soon drew out again into the middle of the entrance to the Narrows. The Elwell was a good fourth, and the other wave-skimmers were all well up. The Vindex—not in the race—had been backing and filling under Fort Richmond, and the schooner Ariel, her peaks gaudy with flags, came out to greet the competing vessels. The wind, which was from the eastward, had dropped considerably, and the lurid sun shone down upon the sea, tinting the tiny wavelets and glinting upon the snowy sails of the noble fleet then moving onward in stately phalanx to victory and defeat.

"DOWN TO THE SPIT."

While the spectators on the regatta boat and on the surrounding steamers were heaping praises in an exciting manner on the plucky little schooners which led the van, there came down among them the great, big Enchantress wing-and-wing, her deck crowded with men, and looking thoroughly as though she was about to enter into a marine contest in earnest. The Enchantress ran down towards Coney Island, and close upon her starboard beam was the majestic Alarm. The Enchantress then jibed her foresail; while passing Gravesend Bay was the pilotboat Edmund Blunt, working splendidly and standing up to her canvass stiff as a tree. Just at this moment the Clio, which was leading the fleet splendidly toward the main channel, caught a gust of wind and had a large hole, about six yards in length, blown into her maintopmast staysail. This retarded her somewhat, and the Enchantress was overhauling her rapidly, when a dirty old tub of a coasting schooner crossed the latter's bow, and she came very near colliding with the pretty Clio. The Dreadnaught picked up a little on account of this; but the coaster, with an unexpected spirit of fairness, got in her way also, causing her to bear up and lose what she had gained. It was as if a lumbering charcoal wagon had crossed two rival four-in-hand teams in Central Park. The Ariel and other outsiders kept away well to the eastward, so as to leave the course clear. At this point the scene was an exceedingly beautiful one, for the wind freshened considerably, and the hindmost boats, catching the breeze first, ran up to their leaders and the whole fleet were bunched, though clear and going well, as the Southwest Spit was reached. Here the "Herald" awaited the swan like craft, and the scene, as witnessed from her deck, was truly magnificent; for the sun flashed and sparkled upon the foam under the sharp prows of the swift-gliding vessels. It was now past four o'clock, and the regatta steamer was soon surrounded by the other "funnel boats" at buoy No. $8\frac{1}{2}$. The fleet passed in the following order, amid the most unbounded enthusiasm and excitement :—

	H.	M.	S.			H.	M.	S.
Olio	4	23	50	Widgeon		4	35	02
Enchantress	4	26	55	Reindeer		4	35	26
Alarm	3	28	45	Thomas S. Negus	4	36	14
Dreadnaught	4	29	09	WallaceBlackford	4	37	05
Van Name	4	29	32	James W. Elwell	4	39	06
Eva	4	29	44	Edmund Blunt		4	39	26
Mary E. Fish	4	34	32					

The "Herald" regatta steamer then started after the clippers. The Elwell was doing very well and was flying foresail, main sail, gaff topsail, forestaysail, jib and jib-topsail, and the Edmund Blunt, who was evidently trying conclusions with her partner, had fore and mainsails, main gaff-topsail, main-staysail, topmast staysail, forestaysail and jib set. The Fulton Market people on the Blackford seemed very excited and were running about wildly, and off the point of Sandy Hook the Mary Fish put her nose under and shipped considerable water. An emigrant packet from Europe came down at this moment, and those aboard of her raised a cheer that rang out a welcome to their American brethren in the tinier vessels.

About this time we all began to feel that this was going to be a big race, and particularly it was noticeable that the larger schooners were buckling down to the work which was cut out for them. We were in the shadow of the Highlands of Navesink, a heavy sea was running, and afar off we could see that the Enchantress was doing her "level best" for the first place, though the Olio was still leading and the Alarm pushing them both to their utmost speed. The regatta steamer then turned her bow homewards, and two of the excursion boats crept out a little further, in a timid way, but soon followed in our wake. The sun sank slowly down towards the western horizon, and as he touched the line dividing sea and sky, he resembled, in his crimson majesty, a giant's golden shield. To the southward we saw a huge flock of white sea gulls circling on strong pinions and dipping their beaks in the brine in search of prey, while over them hovered a great black fish hawk, his sable wings spread like a fashionable fan. A German steamer, deeply laden with freight and passengers, outward bound, passed us and returned us a responsive whistle. In the distance, the serrated tops of the Highlands, resembling a waving woof of indigo, were standing boldly up, and, almost hull down, we saw the Mary Fish fast overhauling the Van Name. A bulky iron ship, built on the Clyde, was being towed past us, and, on being hailed, her Captain stated that she was from Glasgow, eighteen days out. The Edmund Blunt passed us at this moment, and, on being hailed, her sailing master cried out, "You will hear from us to-morrow morning." Following the Blunt comes the Elwell, and as they sweep by through the gloom that is covering Sandy Hook all hands rise to wave their hats and cheer us, as might be expected from the sternmost boat in the race. A few moments elapse, and as the turbulent waves toss and the brisk sea breeze blows in our faces we lose sight of all the fleet, who are stretching away, with bending spars and bellying canvas, for Cape May Lightship.

The World, New York, October 10, 1873.

OCEAN YACHT RACES.

The Start and Position of the Racers at Sandy Hook—Magnificent appearance of the Yachts sailing down the Bay.

A splendid start was made yesterday afternoon on the Ocean Yacht Race to Cape May and return for the prizes offered by Commodore Bennett, and the indications are that the race will be one of the finest and fastest that has ever been made over so long a course. The novelty of the conditions of this race and the varied character of the contestants has attracted more than usual attention to it and interested many classes of persons outside of purely yachting circles. It was, in effect, open to any and all schooners that chose to enter, including the schooner yachts of all organized clubs, schooner-rigged pilot boats, working schooners and schooner smacks. There was no entrance fee for any of the vessels, and there were liberal prizes for all classes. The prize for yachts was a cup of the value of $1,000, and for the other schooners there were three purses, one of $1,000 and two of $250 each. The rule governing the award of these purses was that the first vessel arriving at the winning post should have the purse of $1,000, and that the first vessel arriving of each of the other two classes should have a purse of $250, with the proviso that no class should receive more than one prize. The course was from an anchorage off Owl's Head, around the Southwest Spit, thence to and around the Cape May Lightship on Five Fathom Bank, and back to the Sandy Hook Lightship, passing within 200 yards of the latter.

The competing vessels were as follows :

YACHTS.

Name.	Owner.	Tonnage.
Enchantress	J. F. Loubat	276.16
Alarm	A. C. Kingsland	225.17
Clio	{ T. B. Asten { T. C. B. Bradhurst	59.86
Eva	E. Burd Grubb	77.50
Dreadnaught	A. B. Stockwell	240.00

PILOT BOATS.

Widgeon, No. 10	New York pilots	105.69
Edmund Blunt, No. 21	New York pilots	111.00
Jas. W. Elwell, No. 7	New Jersey pilots	132.00
Thos. S. Negus, No. 1	New Jersey pilots	130.00
Mary E. Fish, No. 4	New Jersey pilots	106.75

WORKING SCHOONERS.

W. H. Van Name (A)	W. H. Van Name	140.00
Reindeer (P)	Captain Howard	154.00

SCHOONER SMACKS.

Wallace Blackford (E)	E. H. C. Rogers & Co.	80.00

There were five other vessels entered for the race, but which failed to appear. They were the yacht Atalanta, the pilot boats Hope, No. 1, and C. H. Marshall, No. 3, and the schooners Sharpshooter and Racer. The letters which are placed opposite to the schooners in the above list were used to designate them when at sea, and were painted on large sheets of muslin, which were sewed on the mainsails of the respective vessels. It will be seen that there was only one schooner smack in the race, so that if she sails over the whole course, she is sure of the purse offered for her class, and she has also a chance of winning the capital prize for schooners. In other words she may win $1,000, and she must win $250.

The day broke bright and beautiful yesterday morning, and it was evident that the racers were to have the most favorable wind and weather that could be desired. There was not a cloud in the sky, the temperature was just cool enough to make the genial sunshine welcome, and there was a brisk breeze from the northeast which dotted the surface of the bay and harbor with long white caps, and which seemed expressly provided for speeding the racers down the Jersey coast. From an early hour of the morning the harbor presented a busy scene with the white-winged schooners working down toward the anchorage, or sailing about in long tacks and displaying their points to the numerous spectators, and with the large number of excursion steamers and smaller craft that were busily plying about the harbor picking up passengers and attending the vessels that were to participate in the race. Toward evening a great many spectators began to assemble upon the points which commanded the best views of the rendezvous, and by the time the start was made the banks of Staten Island and South Brooklyn were well lined with carriages and pedestrians, all eagerly watching the race. The Committee having charge of the race consisted of Mr. Fletcher Westray, Chairman; and Messrs. William Krebs, Edward E. Chase, and Charles A. Minton,; and Mr. Freeman S. Smith was appointed the Judge of the pilot boats. These gentlemen embarked on board of the "Herald" steam yacht at the barge office, and a little after eleven o'clock the judges' boat steamed down the harbor to deliver the signals and instructions to the contestants and to align the vessels. The signals consisted of rockets, two of which were ordered to be fired by every vessel approaching either of the terminal lightships at night—blue and red combination lights—by which the yachts were to be distinguished, and ship lights for the other schooners, which were to be used so as to display the designating letters and numbers upon their mainsails. The first of the contesting vessels encountered by the judges' boat was the Reindeer, which was proceeding to the anchorage under very easy sail, and next the Dreadnaught and Enchantress passed the steamer on their way down. At the anchorage off Owl's Head most of the pilot boats and working schooners had already got into position and dropped their anchors. There were two stakeboats, one exactly opposite Owl's Head and the other 300 yards further down the Narrows. The second of these marked the position of the yachts and the first the position of all the other vessels. Of the yachts the Enchantress and the Eva were the only ones in line. The Dreadnaught was lying under the Jersey shore, and the others were gracefully disporting about the harbor under easy sail, but all showing fine speed. At the last moment a private match for a $250 cup was arranged between the Eva and the Clio, to be determined during the present race. The judges' boat completed the distribution of the signals and instructions, and after awaiting the arrival of all the contesting vessels took up a position to the leeward and between the lines of schooners.

The signals agreed upon for the start consisted of one whistle, and the lowering of the Yacht Club flag as a signal of preparation, and ten minutes after another whistle and another dipping of the flag for getting under way. The start was announced to be made at three o'clock, and at exactly two minutes after that hour the first whistle was sounded, the last orders were given on all the vessels, the men sprung to their posts, and all was life and bustle. At twelve minutes after three the final signal was given, the anchors were raised and the jibs hoisted as if by magic

and the thirteen contestants swung swiftly about with the northeast breeze and dashed through the waves like greyhounds re-
leased from the leash.   The start was one of the most even ever
made, but of the yachts the Clio made the best, and speedily
put herself 200 yards ahead of all her rivals, the Eva following
next, the Dreadnaught and Enchantress coming next and close
together, and the Alarm a slight distance in their rear.   Of the
other vessels the "Pride of the Market," as the Blackford is
called in Fulton Street, got away first, and was followed by the
Edmund Blunt, next by the Elwell and the Negus, and then by
all the others in a bunch.   The wind was a little lighter than it
had been in the morning, but it was dead astern and the fleet swept
wing-and-wing down the Narrows with every stitch of canvas
set, and presented one of the most splendid sights that ever
charmed the eyes of a yachtsman.   The Clio kept her lead, but
the Eva came creeping up in a determined way that showed that
Captain Grubb had no intention of letting that $250 cup get
away from him without a struggle; the Enchantress veered a
few points to leeward and soon passed the Eva; the Dreadnaught
was but little astern of either, and the Alarm was coming rapidly up in the rear.   At this moment an ugly hole appeared in
the staysail of the Clio, caused by a foul with the gaff, and in
a few seconds the wind, which was bellying the sail in fine shape
ripped it from top to bottom, and it was hauled down to be repaired.   The Clio, however, still gallantly maintained her advantage, and swinging around to windward shot swiftly past the bow
of the Dauntless and took her position on the extreme left of
the fleet, which was by this time extended into an irregular cres-
cent, with the Clio and the Enchantress marking the two advanced corners.

This position was maintained without material change down
to buoy No. 8½, on Southwest Spit.   The Clio and Enchantress
were ahead, with the Clio away over to windward, and therefore
nearer the Spit, the Dreadnaught and Alarm were between and
a little behind them and on an exact line with each other, while
the Eva was just astern of the Dreadnaught.   The other vessels

had made some changes in their relative positions, and the Van
Name was away ahead and rapidly picking up the Eva. Close
upon her heels was the Mary E. Fish, and then came the Widgeon and the Reindeer, apparently together, and with the heavier
pilot boats—"Big 7" and the Blunt—bringing up the rear.
The time of rounding the Spit was as follows:

	H.	M.	S.
Yacht Clio	4	23	50
Yacht Enchantress	4	26	55
Yacht Alarm	4	28	45
Yacht Dreadnaught	4	29	09
Schooner Van Name	4	29	32
Yacht Eva	4	29	44
Pilot boat Mary E. Fish, No. 4	4	34	32
Pilot boat Widgeon, No. 10	4	35	02
Schooner Reindeer	4	35	26
Pilot boat Thomas S. Negus, No. 1	4	36	14
Smack Wallace Blackford	4	37	05
Pilot boat James W. Elwell, No. 7	4	39	06
Pilot boat Edmund Blunt, No. 2	4	39	36

From the time of the start to the arrival at the spit, the
breeze had noticeably decreased and had changed towards the
east, so that the "white caps" were no longer visible, and the vessels, when they strung out after rounding the buoy, were compelled to beat down with long tacks to get to sea. As each of
the beautiful craft shot past the Spit, she was greeted with three
shrill salutes from the whistles of the judges' boat and the other
steamers that had assembled there, and which included the
Fletcher, Arrowsmith, Chamberlain and Day Dream. The Clio
made a splendid tack, which slightly increased her lead, and the
Enchantress, which followed her, and was bounding along at the
speed of a race-horse, had to beware of her greater draught of
water, and describe a much wider circle. The Clio, therefore,
managed to retain her lead until out of sight, and there were no
important changes in the relative position of the other vessels.
The judges' boat, under the command of Captain Robinson, gallantly escorted the fleet to Sandy Hook, and was followed by a
dozen other craft, including the steamers already named, and the

yachts Vindex, Columbia, Emilie, Camelia, and Ariel. The racing yachts, as they receded in the distance, and in the mellow sunset, formed one of the finest sea pictures that the Bay of New York has ever seen. The wind was still in their favor and they stood almost erect, with their tall masts and their crowds of canvas giving them the appearance of great white columns reflected against the deepening blue of the horizon. On the judges' boat, a number of rockets and other pyrotechnic pieces which had not been needed in the distribution to the yachts were discharged as a final salute to the fast-fading fleet, and as the sun sank, blood-red, behind the hills of Staten Island, the boat reversed its course and brought the party back to the city.

The favorable start which the yachts have had encourages the belief which was expressed by all the yachting men who observed the start, that the race will be an unusually fast one. The course has been sailed in twenty-five hours, and the yachtsmen yesterday, as they passed the steam yacht on their way to sea, promised they would do it in twenty-four. It is quite possible that the first of the returning fleet may be seen at Sandy Hook early this afternoon, and it seems almost certain that they will return this afternoon or evening. The Regatta Committee are to proceed to Sandy Hook this afternoon to await the finish of the race, and will remain upon the lightship until all of the fleet return.

The New York Herald, October 11, 1878.

THE GREAT OCEAN YACHT REGATTA.

On Thursday afternoon thirteen vessels of schooner rig and of four distinct classes, which have never before met in racing competition, sailed forth under a clear blue sky on a grand ocean race. The fact that five vessels of our trim pilot fleet, whose fame in their line of hardy seafaring is world-wide, were sailing beside five saucy schooners of our racing fleet is a circumstance in itself worthy of note. That two working schooners, one from Staten Island and another from Cold Spring Harbor, brought

their ruddy crews into competition with the pilot boats, and that
a gallant little schooner smack came forward to claim her share
of the race, give us a picture well worthy of the genius of some
such American painter of marine subjects as Moran. That the
race meant downright sailing under conditions which divested
it of the toylike quality of races inshore was evident from the
beginning. It was a test of qualities that are not brought out
in races with land calms threatening to spoil all sport; in races
with subtle knowledge of tides and currents telling more than
the great quality of fast sailing; in races where the exact reach
of every tack under given directions of wind can be calculated
to a nicety. The vessel, in such a race as that started on Thursday, is tested as much as the sailing master, and the result will
prove much more of the true grit in both than the ornamental
regattas, which, in their place, are so very admirable. About
this race there is another feature which Americans can point to
with pride—it marks the entrance of a republican spirit into
contests hitherto laid claim to by a class alone. As that class
is, of necessity, a rich one, it will be gratifying to think that
the men of bronzed face, stout arms and manly heart, by whose
lives coasting commerce is made a nursery of hardy seamen—
men whose grandfathers manned the privateers of 1812, whose
fathers in turn manned the gallant ships that in the war of the
revolution so brilliantly contested with England for the su-
premacy of the seas—are taking their places in the race with
their fortune-favored fellow citizens. It matters not to whom
the prizes fall if the race proves where the best contests are to
be decided and if it marks an innovation in yachting experience
worthy of the aquatic holidays of a republic. The course,
covering from two hundred and fifty to three hundred miles
of actual sailing, is a splendid one, and one of the results of the
race will doubtless be to make it the scene of the future contests
of importance battled in by yachts in the vicinity of New York.
Throughout yesterday the arrival of the winning vessels was
anxiously expected, and the explanation that three hundred
miles cannot be sailed in the time of an ordinary race from

the Narrows to Sandy Hook Lightship and back was made hundreds of times by those learned in the matter to others not so fortunate, but up to the present time the return of none of the yachts has been reported.

The Evening Telegram, New York, October 11, 1873.

THE OCEAN RACE.

The Enchantress the Winning Yacht—Ninety miles in ten hours—An Unprecedented Run from Sandy Hook to Cape May—A Terrible Time at Sea—A Head Wind All the Way Home—The Winning Pilot Boat.

SANDY HOOK, Saturday, Oct, 11—A. M.

The yacht Enchantress passed the lightship here at twelve minutes past six o'clock this morning, and won the race.

The second boat is not yet in sight, but from the report made by the Enchantress it is supposed that the first pilot boat is pilot boat No. 1, Thomas S. Negus, of New Jersey, and that the second yacht is probably the Alarm.

The Enchantress made the run from Owls' Head, L. I., in New York Harbor, the starting point, to Cape May lightship in ten hours, forty-five minutes and thirty seconds, an unprecedented run.

The start was made at twelve minutes past three o'clock on Thursday afternoon, and the Enchantress rounded the lightship at Cape May at one o'clock, fifty-seven minutes and thirty seconds on Friday morning.

There was a fair wind all the way down.

The race was a dead beat all the way back, a heavy head sea running. In the afternoon of yesterday there were light airs for a considerable time, the sea being very lumpy.

After rounding the Cape May Lightship the Enchantress about four o'clock yesterday morning fell into a very heavy sea and split her jib.

There was no time for repairs at the time, but when the morning advanced and an opportunity presented itself it was repaired.

At eleven o'clock she shipped a tremendous heavy sea which carried away the under bobstay, which endangered the jibboom. Things were particularly lively at this time on board the yacht. A tackle was got out and the jibboom secured.

Just at this time the split jib was ripped to its head all through, a heavy sea running. From that time only half the sail was used, it being impossible to bend another, the sea was so high.

Captain Robert Fish sailed the Enchantress and Peter W. Roff was the pilot.

The general interest felt in the result of the great ocean yacht race has in no way abated. On the contrary, the inquiries after the yachts were more numerous this morning than yesterday.

The delay in the arrival of the vessels was, of course, caused as stated in the Telegram yesterday, by the strong northeast breeze which was blowing yesterday morning. Though this has delayed the arrival of the vessels, it was far from spoiling the race or lessening the interest felt on all sides in the result of the contest. The fact is that this wind showed to greater advantage the sea-going and weatherly qualities of the competing vessels.

Along shore the most intense interest is felt in the result of the race on account of the pilot boats and the working schooners.

THE LATEST.

FASTEST SAILING ON RECORD.

The Enchantress passed Fort Hamilton at 9:15 this morning, under full sail.

The yacht was followed by the pilot boat Thomas S. Negus, No. 1, and the third boat in was the New Jersey pilot boat James W. Elwell, No. 7.

If the run to Cape May has been made in the time mentioned it is the quickest run on record by any sailing vessel.

CAPE MAY, N. J., Oct. 11, 1873.

The yachts passed Five Fathom Light at 3:20 A. M. as follows:

Enchantress, first.
Dreadnaught, second.
Alarm, third.
The positions of the other yachts were not obtained.

PHILADELPHIA, PA., Oct. 11, 1873.

A second dispatch from Cape May, N. J., says that the yachts passed at 3:20 yesterday morning, the wind being at the time dead ahead.

The New York Herald, October 12, 1873.

THE OCEAN RACES.

From Owl's Head to the Five-Fathom Bank Lightship off Cape May — Thirteen Vessels Striving for Victory — Working Schooners and Pleasure Craft in the Fleet—Plenty of Wind and Heavy Head Seas—Accidents and Incidents—Beating to Windward One Hundred and Twenty-five Miles—The Enchantress the Winner of the $1,000 Cup and the Pilot Boat Negus the $1,000 Purse—Three of the Racers Home.

ON BOARD YACHT ENCHANTRESS, OFF SANDY HOOK LIGHTSHIP.

Saturday, October 11—6.12 A. M.

Thursday afternoon when the competing vessels in the great ocean races were off the point of Sandy Hook and the Regatta committee of the New York Yacht Club and others on board the steam yacht " Herald " were preparing to bid them adieu and wish them all " good luck," the scene was one that could not fail to delight the most enthusiastic yachtsman. It had been a day particularly charming to commence a contest of the character in which the vessels were engaged, and upon each and every deck of the racing boats were picked crews, veteran pilots, delighted sailing masters, and hopeful owners. It was the fortune of one of the " Herald " reporters to find himself, early that afternoon, on board the Enchantress, where, on deck, were Mr. J. F. Loubat, the owner ; Vice-Commodore Douglas, Mr. Walter L. Kane, Judge for the Committee ; his brother, Mr. Delancey Kane, and Mr. Edward R. Jones, ready to accompany the yacht to victory or defeat. Busy giving orders to the bronzed crew was seen Captain Bob Fish, who modelled the boat, and near him, eager to take the wheel, was Pilot Peter W. Roff, of Staten Island. In like respects it was understood that all the craft whose crews were eager to win the prizes presented by Commodore Bennett were well provided. So, when the point of Sandy Hook was passed, the great ocean race to the lightship on Five Fathom Bank had commenced and was fast becoming exciting. At the time of starting the wind was to the northward, but at this point it had veered to the east-north-east and was breezing freshly. The pretty Clio, with all sail set, was working well to windward ; the Enchantress, with a cloud of canvas, was second ; the Alarm third, Dreadnaught fourth, working schooner Van Name fifth, Eva sixth, and the pilot boat Mary E. Fish, working schooner Reindeer, pilot boat Thomas S. Negus, schooner smack Wallace Blackford, and pilot boats James W. Elwell and Edmund E. Blunt in the positions as named. Passing out by the land, the Enchantress went about on the port tack at 4 h. 26 m., the Clio did likewise at 4 h. 27 m., the Alarm followed suit at 4 h. 28 m., the Dreadnaught soon the same, and now each bent to their business.

Away to leeward, and not to interfere with the manœuvring of the vessels, the excursionists' steamers accompanied us, and gliding swiftly along among these, looking particularly handsome, was the steam yacht Day Dream, upon the deck of which General Aspinwall was observed, in the New York Yacht Club uniform. Though each and every captain of this fleet of clippers knew there was much work and chances of ill-luck before them, they commenced their task with faces lighted up with pleasurable excitement, and the last whistle of the judge's boat left them all in the best of humor, and with the highest hopes of success. On board the Clio, which had crept up to windward in the Narrows, there was an evident determination to keep in advance. She had set foresail, mainsail, foretopsail, jib, flying-jib, and two topsails, and the canvas drew very well. At 4 h. 35 m. the Enchantress, under club foresail, mainsail, jib, flying-jib, maintopmast staysail, and working topsails was gradually lessening the distance. The Clio was in advance. The noble looking Alarm was a short away to leeward, while the Dreadnaught, with all kites set, her big maintopmast staysail being the more conspicuous, was challenging Rear Commodore Kingsland for third place. The saucy Eva followed, and then the Widgeon and Mary E. Fish, of the pilot boats, were earnestly contesting with each other for the post of honor in their class, with the advantage in favor of the latter, and to leeward of these was the trusty-looking Van Name, and among the brush the Wallace Blackford, the schooner smack that entered for the prize and glory attached to the event. The yachts were now flying through the water and the Enchantress on the starboard tack at 4 h. 44 m. went by the Clio, which looked a beautiful picture, and assumed the lead of the fleet that now was out on the ocean heading to the goal far away. The day was fast passing to a pleasant twilight, and the sun glinted its adieu on the snow white canvass of the racers with blinding brightness. Now the fun began in earnest. Five miles distant, at 5 h. 9 m., the Highland lights bearing west southwest, the Enchantress was heading south with the wind fair and leading all her competitors fully one mile.

The Clio, standing on the same tack, was second, one mile astern; the Alarm a like distance to the leeward of her the Dreadnaught half a mile further off, while the Eva, Van Name and others were hull down. The wind was now hauling a little more down the coast, and it was the unanimous opinion of all on the Enchantress that there would be lively work before the night was over. At 5 h. 31 m., we were off Long Branch and on our weather quarter, with sails set, we sighted the Richmond steamer Old Dominion, outward bound, and two miles further away was one of Alexandre's steamships ploughing the deep in the same direction. The western horizon still looked bright with the glories of departing day, and, using a glass, the positions of the competing vessels nearest us were noted to be the same as before given, though we were dropping them fast. There was a rolling sea off this point, and the steamers, as with us, felt its influence. We were now doing very finely, and at 6 h. 4 m., the Alarm, two miles astern, had eaten up to windward of the Clio and was passing her, but it was some time before the saucy craft could be shaken off. One mile to the leeward of the Clio was the Dreadnaught, and far in the fast approaching gloom was the Eva struggling with the Van Name. Darkness settled down upon us at 6 h. 56 m., and heading south by west, the Enchantress was slipping away upon her mission. Here we passed the steamer Old Dominion, her officers acknowledging the " go-by," blew their whistle, which we responded to by a rocket, and the steamer in turn " blazed away " in similar manner from her bow. At 7 h. 10 m., Barnegat light was made, bearing south southwest distant about fifteen miles. The night was clear and beautiful, and as the great golden moon came out of the sea the scene was exquisite.

The wind was now hauling to the eastward and increasing, which sent us skipping along very fast. At 7 h. 55 m., the yacht was kept off half a point, heading south by west-half-west, and at 8 h. 17 m. Barnegat light bore west. We were doing some very nice work now, as at 8 h. 24 m., Alexandre's steamship was abeam, and nothing could be made out astern but the lights of the Old Dominion. The sea was very lumpy on this part of the coast, but the Enchantress carried her sail well, and while owner, officers and guests were congratulating themselves on their good luck a sea broke over her weather rail, and dousing some of the non-workers on deck they went below to change their clothing and repair damages. Little Egg Harbor bore west at 9 h. 45 m., the run down from Barnegat, a distance of eighteen or nineteen miles, having been made in 1h. 28 m. At 10 h. we took in our maintopmaststay sail and jibtopsail and boomed out the foresail, the wind getting lighter. Still we were doing nicely, and at 10 h. 37 m. Absecom blazed in the westward. The wind now backed to the northeast, and at 11 h. we headed southwest by south. It was freshening every instant, and at 11 h. 20 m. Captain Fish ordered the flying jibs to be shifted. The big one was taken in and a smaller one set at 11 h. 35 m.

We were now doing our best, bowling along in the glorious. brightness of the night fully thirteen or fourteen knots, though the sea was becoming more lumpy. At 11 h. 48 m. the balloon topsail was ordered to be taken in and at 1 h. 54 m. it was on deck unbent and clewed up, a neat job. At midnight, Alexandre's steamship disappeared on our weather bow, and then we were left traveling alone in solitary grandeur. At 12 h. 01 m. Friday morning we lowered away the peak and put a single reef in the mainsail, and began preparation to wear around the Five Fathom Lightship. A man was sent up the foremast head at 12 h. 25 m. to look out for the lights of this beacon off Cape May, and at 12 h. 48 m. he sighted them two points on the port bow. At 1 h. 20 m. the foresail was lowered, the topmasts housed and everything made snug for rounding the goal, the sea was very lumpy, but we flew along exceedingly fast, and at 1 h. 10 m. sent up two rockets, in accordance with the instructions from the Regatta Committee. Every man was at his station, and, with showers of drift breaking over the weather bow, we wore around the Lightship at 1 h. 57 m., under jib, small flying jib and reefed mainsail, having made the distance from Owl's Head, about 122 miles, in 10 h. 45 m. We burned a blue light, left the beacon on the starboard hand, and, trimming down on the wind, made a stretch inshore, with our starboard tack aboard. As we passed under the stern of the Lightship Mr. Loubat sang out " Enchantress," which elicited some response, but in the confusion it was not understood. The work now began in earnesst, the wind to the nor'ard and increasing, with a head sea, becoming very nasty. We looked anxiously astern with a view of observing what other rockets were sent up, but nothing was seen until 2 h. 30 m., when two signals were observed in the air, and we knew another vessel was approaching the Lightship, and would soon be bursting on the wind with us—(afterward ascertained to be the Dreadnaught.) At 2 h. 57 m. we set the foresail, and half an hour afterward stood off on the port tack. All the while the water was becoming more turbulent, and at four o'clock the Enchantress was near coming to grief, as she fell into a heavy sea, and, bursting over her bow with tremendous violence, it split the jib one cloth above the leech, making a rent four feet in length. Nothing could be done with it at the time, and, with hopes that it would not become worse, our officers trusted to luck. At five o'clock we stayed and stood toward the beach, and at 6 h. 10 m. just after daylight, sighted the pilot boat Negus, No 1, on the same tack to leeward of us, heading northwest on her lee bow with the Widgeon, No. 10 while about two miles astern of them was another sail, that we could not make out. The Enchantress was heading northwest-half-west and at 6 h. 35 m., "land on the lee bow" was announced.

Shortly after this the Dreadnaught was sighted to leeward of the Widgeon, on the starboard tack, under double reef mainsail, single reef foresail and jib. The Negus was under two lower sails and jib and flying jib ; the Widgeon the same. The sea was quieter at this time, and the Negus and Widgeon had a lively brush together, ending in the Widgeon getting the best of it. But her victory was for a short time, for at 6 h. 48 m. the Negus began to overhaul her, and when they tacked off shore a few minutes afterwards she passed up to windward. At

6 h. 57 m. the Enchantress stood off on the port tack, and one minute after the Dreadnaught went in stays. The latter had just before set her flying jib. The Enchantress now was heading northeast-by-east, and was outpointing all the others and going to windward fast. The reef in our mainsail was shaken out at eight o'clock, and it was very evident that in the lumpy water we hadn't headsail enough. We wanted to shake out the reef in the foresail, but dared not. All the while the Negus was doing admirably, beating the Widgeon and the Dreadnaught, as well as the Alarm, which was now sighted to the leeward of Mr. Stockwell's yacht. Abseccom lighthouse, looking dreary indeed in the morning light, at 8h. 20m., bore northwest by north, and at 10 h. 05 m. the tall, chimney-looking affair, surrounded by dismal hotels and cottages, could be seen with the naked eye. Our friends astern—Negus, Alarm and Dreadnaught—were standing on the same tack, the Widgeon having dropped out of sight. At this time the Dreadnaught looked in trouble, as, settling away her jibs and mainsail, she soon dropped astern. The head seas were getting to be very bad, and, the wind still hanging from the northeast, it was evident, unless it shifted, we would have not only the day but another night to pass on the ocean, and we were not disappointed.

The Alarm stood in shore at 11 h. 56 m., and the Negus went in stays two minutes later. At 10 h. 05 m., Captain Fish expressed a doubt as to our damaged jib holding out much longer, as it continued splitting and was now half way up the sail. Effort was made to "stop" the rent, and it was partially successful. We went about on the port tack to clear Brigantine Shoals at 11 h. 25 m., and but little headway was made against the lumpy water. At 11 h. 45 m. the Enchantress fell into a heavy sea, and, as it tumbled its tons of water over the bow, its terrific force carried away the outer bobstay of the running bowsprit, and for a moment it looked as if the stick would be wrenched clean out of its fastenings. At the same moment, and just when such an event was especially annoying, the ripped jib was split clear to the head. With this disaster on hand all eyes were anxiously cast to leeward to note "just for amusement" how far astern the Negus was, and the distance was adjudged to be five miles, while the Alarm was three or four miles further away. At 12 h. 15 m. we took a reef in the mainsail, laying the yacht "dead to," and got out a tackle, hooking it on a strap at the end of the boom, thus securing it and saving us from an ignominious defeat, after going to the windward of all competitors for hours. Little Egg Harbor was sighted at 12 h. 30 m., and we shook out the reef in our mainsail at 1 h. 15 m., the wind hauling to the north northeast. The Enchantress was heading north northwest, but the delay had materially lessened the distance between the Negus and the Enchantress. The breeze at 1 h. 30 m. freshened, but was still dead ahead. We set our foretopmast at this time, and nine minutes afterwards stood off shore. Again we tacked at 2 h. 10 m., and the fact that we had been racing for hours with one-third of our jib carried away wasn't a pleasant reflection. Yet we held our own with the Negus, who was still six miles to leeward, but going away from the Alarm all the while. No other vessels were in sight at 3 h. 14 m., as Barnegat light was sighted, bearing north by west. All the afternoon these relative positions were maintained by the Enchantress, Negus and Alarm. At 5 h. 10 m. our foretopmast was sent up, the wind getting lighter and hopes of a change at nightfall entertained by all. As the sun was sinking the Enchantress stood in shore with her starboard tacks aboard, heading north northwest and the Negus, on the port tack, was seven or eight miles away, with the Alarm, as before trying to hang to her formidable adversary.

At 6 h. our gaff topsails had been set, and soon after the smaller flying jib was taken in, and the big one ordered to be substituted, but there was much difficulty in doing this work, as the sea was running high and many of the men were worn out. During this trouble, we went astern, and it became a matter of serious conjecture whether it would not cause our defeat. Still, every effort was made by constant watchfulness and good judgment to make up the loss, and at 10 h., 50 m. a nice breeze from the northeast enabled us to fetch up the beach within one point of our course. The sea was still lumpy, but there was more foot to it. We stowed the foretopsail at 10 h. 45 m. as it did not draw. We were now along upper Squam Beach, half way to Sandy Hook, and despite the discouragements of wind and sea, some of the guests of the Enchantress felt hopeful that they might keep their Saturday's engagements in the city. At 12 h. 15 m. yesterday morning the wind shifted to the northward and became lighter, heading us off. Barnegat light was now sunk, and after three tacks at 2 h. 15 m. the welcome blaze of the Highlands loomed up, bearing north-half-west, while we stood off shore on the port tack. Though the ocean was narrowly scanned, nothing could be sighted, and the hope was expressed that we still led the fleet. From this time we stood off and on until 4 h. 9 m. when the Enchantress went in stays, and headed in shore, which, at 4 h. 40 m. brought the lights of the beacon off Sandy Hook in view, bearing north. At 5 h. 10 m. we tacked, and stood off shore until 6 h. 10 m. when we went about and bore away for Sandy Hook Lightship, which we passed to the westward at 6 h. 12m., and all on board gave three hearty cheers when they heard the welcome news that no other competing vessel had been seen.

The judges appointed by the Regatta Committee and the members of the press, stationed on the beacon, returned the cheers as the yacht prepared to beat in for Staten Island. The following table of distances made by the Enchantress during the race down to the Five Fathom Bank Lightship shows a pretty fast run:

	Distance.	Time.
Point to Point.	Miles.	H. M.
Owl's Head to point of Sandy Hook..	15	1 23
Point of Hook to Barnegat..........	45	3 42
Barnegat to Little Egg Harbor...... ..	19	1 28
Little Egg Harbor to Absecom.......	11	0 52
Absecom to Five Fathom Lightship..	31½	3 20
Total distance running down.....	121½	10 45

The beat back required 28 h. and 15 m., making the total run, about 247 miles, in exactly 39 hours.

RUN OF THE PILOT BOAT THOMAS S. NEGUS, NO. 1.

We rounded the Lightship stake boat on Five Fathom Bank, off Cape May, at twenty-four minutes past three o'clock A. M., on Friday   Shortly before reaching the Lightboat, put a reef in the mainsail and took bonnet off the jib. On hailing the Lightboat, reported our name and asked how many of the boats had rounded.   Learned we were the fifth, the Enchantress, Dreadnaught, Alarm and Widgeon being ahead of us.   Then stood on the starboard tack, shook reef out of mainsail and jib.   In half an hour made the Enchantress, Dreadnaught and Widgeon ahead to the leeward.   At daybreak had dropped the Dreadnaught and Widgeon astern to leeward, the Enchantress still leading us, wind blowing quite fresh from north, and a dead beat to windward.   At 4:30 P. M., Enchantress crossed our bow, most of the competing vessels, both yachts and pilot boats, astern in sight to the leeward.

Arrived at the Lightship off Sandy Hook at 8 h. 49 m. 30 s. A.M. Hailed Judges on board, who informed us we were the second boat in, the Enchantress only being ahead of us.

THOMAS S. NEGUS.

WAITING AT THE LIGHTSHIP.

For thirty-six hours, the *Herald* representative, together with half a dozen others, were waiting on board of the Lightship at some seven miles outside of Sandy Hook, to witness the arrival of the contesting boats at the home stake.   Captain Cosgrove, who has had command of Lightship, No. 16 for the long spell of twenty-one years, made all his guests feel at home, and did everything in his power to cheer the weary hours that passed before the winning yacht came in sight.   It was a pleasant sight, for Captain Cosgrove to look upon so many new faces, as he is isolated and shut off from all human kind, as effectually, as if

he were located on a deserted island, during the winter months of the year. Nothing is to be heard but the vibration of the lazy swell of the pathless sea in fine weather, and the rolling and pounding of the iron ship, combined with the terrific screaming of the wind through the rigging and chain cables, in stormy weather. Life in a lightship or shore beacon may do very well for a day or two, because of its novelty, but, unless specially trained for it, the monotony becomes something dreadful to a stranger. During Friday afternoon and night, there were no traces of the yachts discernable, and nothing was heard at the Lightship of any of the contesting pilot boats. At a little after four o'clock on Saturday morning, and a short time before daylight, a vessel was reported rounding the Lightship, and the watch called up all hands to see it. We discerned a schooner with a large mainsail, and having a huge figure "7" painted on the sail. This was supposed to be the James Elwell, No. 7, of the New Jersey pilot boats, in the regatta, and there were exclamations that she had won ; but in a few minutes the mistake was discovered, for the people on board of the stranger, cried out, that it was " pilot boat, No. 7, of New York," and that they were "not in the race," and had heard nothing of the contestants. At twelve minutes past six o'clock yesterday morning, a cry was raised that a yacht was rounding to, and, looking forward, we saw the dirty purple sides of the Enchantress rising under the lofty bow of the Lightship. There was a wild cheer from her decks, as the Lightship spoke the winning yacht, and instantly acclamations resounded through the still morning.

There was an interval of two hours before any of the other boats came in sight to fill up the long gap, but gradually the sails of a trim looking schooner rose on the horizon, and soon it was manifest that, although she had her topsails clubbed, like a yacht, yet she must be a pilot boat. Shortly after this the Thomas S. Negus, No. 1, a brand new pilot boat, rounded to at precisely forty-nine minutes and thirty seconds after eight o'clock. There was a tremendous cheer from about a dozen persons who stood on the deck of the Negus, when they were informed that no pilot boat had preceded them, and their enthusiasm became so great at the intelligence, that the captain of the Negus immediately hoisted a great big burgee and a long whip pennant as a sign that she was the victor. In a few minutes after she was dancing around the Lightship, as if she would like to have a nautical chip knocked off her shoulder. Captain Cosgrove, acting under the inspiration of the moment, fired several shots from a huge navy revolver at the Negus, and ordered his lighthouse colors and the American flag to be loosened, which was immediately done, to every one's satisfaction. Some hours now elapsed, and the next vessel that appeared was the pilot boat Widgeon, No. 10, which passed within hailing distance, but did not round to at the Lightship. It is supposed that all the other vessels have been becalmed, as the three boats reported above, were the only ones heard from up to a late hour last night.

The World, New York, October 12, 1873.

THE OCEAN YACHT RACE.

The Enchantress the Winning Yacht—Stormy Weather—Head Winds and Heavy Tide—Arrival of Pilot Boats Last Night.

The Enchantress, after an unprecedented run from Sandy Hook to Cape May, and a beat back in a seaway that thoroughly tested her seagoing qualities, passed the Sandy Hook Lightship at twelve minutes past six yesterday morning the winner of the yacht prize for the ocean race. The start was made at twelve minutes after three Thursday afternoon. A light northeast breeze was then blowing, and as the yachts strung out after rounding the buoy the Clio led, followed closely by the Enchantress, with the Dreadnaught in close company. Just off the Highlands the Enchantress passed the Clio, and the Southwest Spit was turned in the following order: Enchantress, Clio, Dreadnaught, Alarm, Mary E. Fish and James W. Elwell. The other boats were lost sight of by those on board the Enchantress. An exciting race took place as far as Long Branch, which was passed at half-past six Thursday evening. At this point the Enchantress still led, with the James W. Elwell a point or two astern. Then came the Dreadnaught, followed closely by the Alarm, with the Mary E. Fish last of the first bunch. Everything was made snug for the night, but with the exception of the occasional flash of a colored light nothing was seen of the racers by the Enchantress people until daybreak Friday morning. During the night the yachts kept in the same relative positions as when last seen Thursday night. The pilot boat Thomas S. Negus, however, had crept up, and now led the boats of her class. The Widgeon had also taken a first place, together with two other pilot boats, whose numbers could not be distinguished. At fifty-seven minutes past one Friday morning the Enchantress rounded Five Fathom Light, off Cape May, and ran for home. Just after turning, it came on to blow, and the Enchantress carried away her jib-bobstays head gear and had to lay to to repair damages. The sea was running high at the time, and when the sails were finally set the other yachts had gone their course and were beating back. Under a single reefed mainsail, reefed jib and small jib the Enchantress began to beat back, and it was not until six o'clock when the weather moderated sufficiently to allow a small foresail with the bonnets out to be set. Shortly afterwards the jib was blown away, but the Enchantress continued to run for home, and arrived off the Sandy Hook Lightship shortly after six o'clock yesterday morning. The Judges on the Lightship were astir, and having recorded her time she ran up to Fort Hamilton, where she dropped anchor at a quarter past nine. During the run home the wind varied considerably, veering from north northeast to north northwest. There was a heavy tide running and the Enchantress encountered a head sea all the way back. When the Enchantress had reset her sails after her mishap and began to beat back the other yachts were seen about fifteen miles astern. She was commanded by Captain Bob Fish and Peter Roff was pilot. Captain C. Fairchild was acting captain.

The following yachts had arrived up till two o'clock this

morning :—Enchantress, Thomas S. Negus, Widgeon, James W. Elwell, Mary E. Fish.

THE RACE AS SEEN FROM THE M. E. FISH.

A visit to the pilot-boat Mary E. Fish, of New Jersey, at pier 23 East River, last night at half-past one, just as she arrived from sea, elicited the following information : Leaving with the rest at three o'clock Thursday, with a light northeast wind, the Fish kept in the midst of the fleet until the Hook was passed. At the Southwest Spit was near Enchantress, schooner A, and another yacht. At five o'clock the wind was northeast. The Fish was the first pilot-boat around the Spit. With two tacks she went around the Hook. The fleet kept pretty close together as far as could be seen, far into the night, but few were visible in the morning. Passed the Cape May lightship at 3 h. 55 m. A.M.; saw the rockets of the Enchantress, and the blue signals of the Negus; saw the Widgeon; passed the schooner A, at 5 h. 50 m. A. M.; hauled in by the wind and stood in at 5 h. 15 m. the wind N.E.; pushed on with short tacks all the morning with wind about N. N. E.

Saw a little yacht about six o'clock, Saturday morning, supposed to be the Eva. Saw the Negus and Widgeon off northeast, about seven o'clock; also the Dreadnaught off shore, hull down. Off Absecom the Fish bore west seven miles. The Negus and Widgeon were then in sight. Then passed the Dreadnaught and Alarm, and the schooner A was astern out of sight. The Dreadnaught about half-past two carried away something about her jib and furled it. Both yachts then put one reef in their mainsails. The other pilot boats reached off shore at dark, and the Fish lost sight of them.

In the morning saw the Elwell under the lee, and she soon crossed our bow. The Widgeon was off north. Stood in to Highlands and anchored in a calm, with the Elwell a mile off. At two o'clock yesterday afternoon a light breeze sprung up from the southeast ; hauled southwest, drew up on Elwell and passed her. Passed the Lightship at twenty minutes to eight. The Elwell passed at twenty minutes to nine, the Olio at seventeen minutes to nine. The E. Blunt was then off shore. Came up the bay and river with a light breeze.

THE DREADNAUGHT'S EXPERIENCE.

At 4 h. 32 m. the Enchantress rounded the Southwest Spit and trimmed aft on her course on the port tack, followed by the Alarm at 4 h. 38 m. and by the Dreadnaught an instant later. The pilot boats and working vessels, still on the starboard tack came up in the following order: The Mary E. Fish leading, the Widgeon next, then the Reindeer, the Negus, and the James W. Elwell following closely, with the ruck astern. The breeze was now freshening, and on each yacht and boat a vast cloud of canvas was piled aloft, every stitch of which was drawing finely ; driving the vessels through the water at a lively rate of speed. At 4 h. 43 m. the Eva and half a minute later, the Van Name tacked and squared away. Meantime the Olio catching the breeze to best advantage, had shot ahead of the Enchantress, leaving the Alarm third in position, the Dreadnaught fourth, and the Eva and Van Name nearly abreast astern. The Dreadnaught now set her staysail, and with this additional canvas gained rapidly upon the Alarm, who found it necessary to substitute her balloon jib for her forestaysail jib. The Dreadnaught, however, gained perceptibly upon her, and when, just as the sun was sinking, the Alarm passed the Highlands of Navesink at 5 h. 20 m, the Dreadnaught was abreast of her, and both vessels going through the water like racers, making a very pretty spurt of it with a fresh full sail breeze blowing and everything drawing on both boats. The sky was perfectly clear, and the fleet at this time presented a beautiful appearance and one well calculated to excite the admiration of the most ordinary observer.

The Dreadnaught had gained constantly upon the Alarm and was just passing her when the latter parted the tack of her balloon jib. This was quickly got inboard and reset without checking her headway; but the Dreadnaught caught a freshening breeze just then, and went bowling down the Seabright beach at a tearing pace, with her late antagonist well on her lee quarter. As the darkness began to gather, the position of the vessels had changed but little, though the rate of speed had brought those who were well in the race far down the Long Branch beach, which was still plainly visible, with its long line of bathing houses, behind which towered the spires of the town, while from the open sea to the westward a steady, long "white-capped" swell came rolling in continually. At the rate at which the Dreadnaught was now running, and with the pile of canvas which she had set, there appeared to be but little doubt, that she would soon overhaul the Clio and Enchantress, who alone of all the fleet led her in the race, when a suddening freshening of the breeze split the Dreadnaught's staysail with a bang, parting everything so that the sail flapped 'out to leeward and went astern, held only by the sheet and the guy ropes. The yacht was at once thrown into the wind and headway checked before the truant sail struck the water, and thus the canvas was saved and hauled aboard by the sheet while the vessel lay to.

It was then deemed advisable to send down the balloon topsail, as that sail was doing no good; but, owing to a further mishap, this became entangled with the toping lift of the mainsail, and had to be got in with great care and at considerable loss of time. At this time it was also found that the bonnet of the jib was badly split, so that when the Dreadnaught again got on her course she had lost nearly forty minutes of most valuable time, during which it was quite impossible to say what portion of the fleet had passed her or what advantage had been gained by those already ahead. Finally, however, she got under way again, and thanks to the constantly increasing wind was by nine o'clock picking up the yachts ahead very rapidly when Barnegat Light bore due west. The Dreadnaught gained rapidly on the leading yachts for a time, but soon carried away the bonnet of her jib before rounding the Lighthouse off Cape May, and afterwards breaking the rod leading from her stern, just at the weld, in such a manner as to loosen the jib stay and set the masts back from their position over eight inches. This mishap occurred when she was homeward bound after having rounded the Cape May Lightship well up with the leaders of the race, and necessitated her running to southward for fully an hour, thus putting her fairly out of the race at a time when, in spite of rough weather and a constant series of mishaps, her chance of finally winning was by no means bad. After this the light winds and a heavy swell, together with her crippled condition, retarded her progress so much that at one o'clock yesterday she was becalmed somewhat south of Highland Lights, and reaching the Lightship at 8 h. 40 m.

The New York Herald, New York, October 13, 1873.

THE OCEAN RACES.

Return of the Fleet to Sandy Hook—The James W. Elwell's Experience— Working Schooner William H. Van Name Wins the $250 Prize of Her Class and the Smack Wallace Blackford Walks Over the Course.

The Ocean Races are ended and general satisfaction reigns at the result. The yacht clubs of America have often been accused of a fondness for smooth water sailing; but a contest from Owl's Head, Long Island, to the Five Fathom Bank Lightship is one over a course that is at times as bad as can be traversed by a sailing vessel. At this season of the year strong winds, or, at least, fresh breezes may always be expected, and it requires a vessel well built, ably manned and properly governed to win a race such as that which has just terminated. The yachts, pilot boats, working schooners and schooner smacks which competed for the prices offered had their work cut out from the start; and, though the breezes were strong and baffling at times, light at others, and frequently variable, it was conclusively proven that the skill of the competent mariner is more than a match for the subtleness of old Neptune. Among the arrivals last Saturday evening were the working schooner William H. Van Name and schooner smack Wallace Blackford, which completes the list of winners, the former beating the Reindeer, her only competitor, and the latter walking over the course. There are now but the yachts Alarm and Eva and working schooner Reindeer to hear from. Annexed will be found additional reports of the races:

THE RACE AS SEEN FROM THE JAMES W. ELWELL.

On Board Pilot Boat James W. Elwell, No. 7,
October 11, 1873.

At just three minutes after three last Thursday, by the clock on board the pilot boat Elwell, the signal and the lowering of the Yacht Club flag on board the steam yacht Herald was given by the Judges for the competing vessels in the ocean race to get ready. An anxious ten minutes succeeded. The thirteen competitors were ready for the start; mainsail and foresails were set, and jibs and topsails were ready to be run up as soon as the final signal was given. Promptly it came, anchors were weighed and the vessels were off.

Rather an amusing incident occurred just previous to and at the moment of getting under way. The schooner smack Wallace Blackford, the only one in the race, lay near the Elwell. There was a good but noisy crew on board of her. Though she was the only boat of her class in the contest she was evidently determined to make it hot for some of the more pretentious looking vessels of the fleet, if possible. As soon as the order to be away was given the work on the deck of that smack was lively. She had not only her anchor under bow first, but she went round as if she was on a pivot. "How's that for getting under way?" sang out her skipper, with a proud consciousness of having accomplished something smart.

Down through the Narrows the racers flew, with every stretch of canvas they could carry. The sight from the deck of the Elwell was a beautiful one. Numbers of steamboats and tugs, heavily freighted with sight-seers, waved adieu to the competing vessels. Yachts of every rig, from cat to schooner, saluted them as they flew by. The wind was fresh from the northeast, but baffling. The Enchantress was among the first yachts around the Southwest Spit, followed by the Alarm, the Dreadnaught and the working schooner Van Name. At 4 h. 32 m. the pilot boat Fish rounded; then came the Widgeon, schooner Reindeer, pilot boat Negus, fishing smack Blackford, then the Elwell and the Blunt. The difference between the time of the passing of the Fish, which was the first pilot boat around, and the Blunt, the last, was about seven minutes. After leaving the buoy we had the wind abeam. It was still fresh, with a heavy sea running. All hands had now gone amidships, and not a head was seen above the rails. The Elwell, owing to the wind veering a little, was not able to weather the point of the Hook, and had to make another tack. The Blunt, taking advantage of this manœuvre, continued on her course and obtained the lead of the Elwell. The point of the Hook was passed at ten minutes after five o'clock. With every sail that would draw, the whole fleet were now fairly off for the Cape May Lightship. About a quarter past five the steam yacht Herald passed by, going in, and with good wishes for a pleasant voyage we waved adieu to the New Yorkers. The race now began in earnest, with the Elwell engaged in a stern chase. The wind was behind us, and with foresail and mainsail boomed out we were going through the water at a lively rate. Shortly after the pretty little village of Seabright loomed up, and the beach at Long Branch showed prettily in the distance. At sundown we were still astern of the fleet, but hoping for better things. The Widgeon, with all her yacht sails on, was taking every advantage of the wind, and was slipping through the water like a race-horse. So long as the wind continued light it was the Widgeon's "pie," but if it came to blow, and it did during the night, we knew she, and the others of her class, would be compelled to come down to pilot boat sails proper, and then the pilot yacht Widgeon, good boat as she is, might not have so fair a record. About a quarter to six o'clock the Elwell overhauled the Blunt, and allowed her the honor of following in her wake. The fishing schooner Blackford was next brought abeam, and shortly after allowed to drop astern. There was some satisfaction in knowing we were picking up with the group and getting into good company. At ten minutes after eight o'clock the moon rose in all its splendor. We were now ten miles north of Barnegat, with the wind increasing, but puffy. At half-past eight o'clock we sighted Barnegat light. Fifteen minutes later the man at the lookout sighted three of the racers to leeward. Shortly after another of the boats hove in sight. We now felt we were overhauling the fleet and gaining our lost ground, and all on board felt in better spirits. The wind, too, was freshening, and, although nearly all on board were paying their respects to Neptune in the cockpit of the Elwell, Captain Warner made no objection, and jolly Jack Reardon, who stood at the wheel, sang out to one of the party, " Go in, old man, we mayn't be shipmates in a long time again." At half-past ten o'clock we had Barnegat Light abeam, bearing west. Four of the leaders were still in sight. At half-past twelve o'clock Absecom Light, bearing northwest, was in sight. The wind was increasing every moment, but not blowing nearly as strong as the larger boats wished for. At forty-seven minutes past two o'clock on Friday morning the Lightship, on Five Fathom Bank, appeared in sight. All was anxiety on board the Elwell. Every one on board was on the lookout for the lights, which were to tell the story of the racers' whereabouts.

At seven minutes to three, two rockets went into the air, indicating that one of the fleet was close by the ship. In twenty minutes two more were seen. A sharp lookout was kept for the color of the lights, but the roughness of the sea prevented the lookout from being able to see them. At a quarter past three two more rockets were seen from the deck of the Elwell, and at half-past the stars of another pair lighted up the heavens. We were now nearing the Lightship. At four o'clock the Elwell sent her rockets up to announce her coming. Up to this time the fireworks of four of the vessels had been seen. About 4 h. 3 m. the Widgeon, as nearly as could be made out, turned the Lightship. The wind had increased in strength since midnight, and the order to shorten sail was given. The mainsail was accordingly single reefed, the gafftopsail was stowed, staysail and flying jib taken in.

At 4 h. 15 m. we wore around the beacon, having made the run down in thirteen and a half hours. Going by we hailed those on board:

" How many have gone round ? "

" Six."

" Has the Widgeon yet rounded ? "

" Yes, sir."

Before we had time to ask any more questions we were out of hearing. It was consoling to know we were not the last boat at this stage of the race, as we had been in leaving the Hook. After passing, the course was altered, and, heading the Elwell north by west half north, we commenced to beat home against a strong head wind and heavy sea.

It was now blowing a stiff nor'easter, and under a single reefed mainsail we were ploughing through the waters at a terrible rate. At 4 h. 30 m. another of the racers passed the Lightship. In another quarter of a mile two more rockets showed the whereabouts of one more of the craft. A little before five, a yacht, which we took to be the Clio, by the lights she showed, paid her respects to the beacon, and commenced the burst on the wind homewards. At six o'clock Friday morning the reefs were shaken out of the mainsail, although the wind was still blowing fresh and our decks were wet nearly all the time. The good boat did nobly. It was the kind of a blow that suited her. At times we had the rails under, and nearly all on board were seasick. The sea since we left the Lightship had been running very high, sweeping the decks from stem to stern every few minutes. Now and then a glimpse of five of the racers could be had as the Elwell rose on the crests of the sea, but what boats they were it was impossible to tell. At 10 h. 30 m. we lost sight of land and stood off shore. The wind continued stiff and came down in chunks. We were driving through the water at a terrible rate against a heavy head sea under flying jib, jib, jib staysail, foresail and mainsail. The

Blunt, in sight all the morning, was hull down before noon.

At 12 h. bearings were taken, lat. 39 12, Absecom bearing west northwest about twenty-five miles. Since daybreak we had made about twenty miles on our direct course. We were now well out to sea, the wind continuing to blow with great violence and the sea was rolling heavily. Before nightfall seven of the vessels were in sight, the greatest number we had seen since we lost sight of them on Thursday evening.

At 6 h. 20 m. Barnegat was sighted on our weather quarter. The Elwell was now pointing about northwest by north. Egg Harbor light was well under the lee and Absecom could only be seen at intervals as we rose on the swell of the sea. Darkness was fast settling over the face of the water. The racers to the windward of us were no longer to be seen. A yacht, looking like the Clio, passed astern of us a couple of miles on the port tack. Our reckoning at this time showed that since leaving the Lightship at Five Fathom we had beaten about fifty-five miles. The Widgeon, the Fish and the Negus were to windward hull down; one of the smaller yachts was about three miles astern and another just beginning to show on the horizon. This was the position of the boats as seen from the Elwell as darkness came on.

· Nothing of interest occurred during the night, only the parting of the flying-jib sheets, which was soon righted. The wind was light through the night, giving indications of dying out before noon. At daybreak, we found we had overhauled the Fish and left her about three miles astern. The Widgeon was also in sight to the windward. She did not have so much water between us as she had at nightfall. The Negus was nowhere to be seen, and it was thought possible that the new boat, untried as she was, had showed some of the older boats a trick in speed worth knowing. Every sail we could carry was set, but there was no "draw" in them.

At 9 h, 30 m. in the morning, we sighted the Lightship with the breeze fast giving out. The Fish was at this time to leeward of us about three miles, and in shore; the Widgeon about five miles to windward, slowly nearing the Lightship with a light breeze. The beacon was only seven miles distant. By ·10 h. the sails were flapping, and we came to anchor. The blow had spent itself and we were becalmed. The Fish, to leeward of us, after trying to crawl up, also anchored. None of the others were at this time in sight. For four hours, we lay at anchor praying for a blow, and not getting it. The yacht Dreadnaught began to show up about noon, with the light breeze that was stirring. The Fish weighed anchor about 3 h. 30 m. and set every inch of canvas she could pnt on, to catch the capful of wind. On board the Elwell there was also a stir, and at 4 h. the anchor was brought under her bow. The Fish was now creeping slowly upon the Elwell in the light wind, and at 7 h. 45 m. showed her light at the Lightship. At 8 h. 30 m. the Elwell also showed her light and hailed the beacon:—

" How many have passed ? "

" One yacht and three pilot boats."

" What yacht ? "

" The Enchantress."

" Good enough, Cap.   What time ? "

" The Enchantress at 6 h. 12 m. this morning; the Negus at 8 h. 30 m. and the Widgeon at 12 h. 30 m."

Just after passing, the Dreadnaught showed her signal lights. There was scarcely five minutes difference between the yacht and the pilot boat. The race was so far run. Two yachts and four pilot boats had announced their arrival. The Elwell headed for Staten Island, all on board satisfied with the fifty-three hours which had elapsed since the start, and all hoping that the next ocean race in which the Elwell would be engaged, would be run with a fiercer blow, in a heavier sea, and under close-reefed canvas out and back.

REPORT OF WORKING SCHOONER W. H. VAN NAME.

The working schooner W. H. Van Name, which won the prize of $250 for vessels of her class in the ocean races, passed Sandy Hook Lightship at 10 h. 50 m. Saturday night. A brief report of the part she took in the contest is as follows:—The Van Name was the fourth vessel around the Southwest Spit. Off Long Branch passed the Dreadnaught and Alarm, and off Absecom went by the Clio. Carried all lighter sails to Barnegat. At 2 h. 30 m. Friday morning made the Five Fathom Bank Lightship and sent up rockets according to instructions from the Regatta Committee. At 2 h. 44 m. rounded the Lightship the second boat, the first passing being the yacht Enchantress. Was under reefed mainsail, full foresail, and bonnet out of jib at the time. Trimmed in all the sheets, hauled on the wind and stood in shore, the schooner making good weather and not taking any water on deck. The sea was rough, and there was plenty of wind. Continued beating to the northward until daybreak, when we sighted to leeward the Widgeon, Mary E. Fish, Thomas S. Negus and yacht Alarm. The pilot boats stood off shore, and we hugged the beach, experiencing baffling winds. Passed yacht Dreadnaught on Saturday morning at three o'clock, on port tack. Beat along in company with yacht Alarm for some three hours, the Van Name being to windward, when the Alarm up helm, started sheets, and ran back before the wind. Off Squam Beach got becalmed and remained there until eight o'clock in the evening, when a light breeze sprung up from the southwest, which enabled the schooner to pass Sandy Hook Lightship at 10 h. 40 m. The Van Name in this race demonstrated that she is a fast boat and has excellent seagoing qualities. She did not take a barrel of water on deck during the run down and back, and came in with whole canvas. She was sailed by Captain Samuel Greenwood, late of the yacht Sappho.

PILOT BOAT THOMAS S. NEGUS, NO. 1.

In the great Ocean Race the fortunate pilot boat Thomas S. Negus, No. 1, the winner of the $1,000 prize, was commanded by Pilot William Lewis, her captain, assisted by Messrs. Sylvester, Lennon, Cooper, Robert and William Hall, Mr. T. S. Negus, one of the New Jersey Pilot Commissioners, and after whom the boat was named, together with Messrs. T. D. Harrison, E. C. Neilson, William F. Taylor and Freeman A. Smith, the latter appointed a Judge by the Regatta Committee, were on board. These gentlemen speak in the warmest terms of the seagoing qualities of the Negus, and state that she was at all times during the eventful race able to carry all her canvas and topmasts, and at no time shipping any water, while other boats seem to have quite as much sea and wind as they could stagger under.

Captain Lewis and his company are entitled to credit for the confidence which they had in their boat and the pluck displayed in entering her for the ocean contest, as she was only launched on the 6th of September last. Her first trial was on the 2d inst., the day of the autumn regatta of the New York Yacht Club, when she proved herself to be fast in light winds, and with her recent victory, stamps her to be a grand success.

The Sun, New York, October 13, 1873.

THE GREAT OCEAN RACE.

A Test of the Seagoing Qualities of Our Yachts—A Lively Dash Over the Waves—Beautiful Moonlight Scenes—A Fine Run to Cape May Lightship—Dead Beat Back to Windward—The Last Boat Back.

The great Ocean Race which commenced on Thursday afternoon, and was concluded yesterday by the arrival of the last of the contestants, brilliantly terminated the yachting season of '73. The weather was magnificent throughout, the racers ploughing their way through "white caps" glittering in the sun's rays by day, and through moonlit seas by night. The fleet had a splendid run down to Cape May Lightship with a free wind and a dead beat to windward returning. For two days it blew fresh, with high seas, and in fact from start to finish no element was wanting to make the race a satisfactory test of the seagoing qualities of the various craft engaged in the contest.

The run down to the point of Sandy Hook was without any

special incident. Off the Hook the accompanying steamers left the fleet and turned their prows homeward. Off the Highlands the wind freshened, coming from the eastward about two points abaft the beam. At this time the Clio and Enchantress were leading the fleet, closely followed by the Alarm and Dreadnaught. A short distance astern were the Eva, A. Van Name, Mary E. Fish, and Widgeon. The Thos. S. Negus, Reindeer, Elwell, Edmund Blunt, and smack Wallace Blackford brought up the rear. At 5:15 the Widgeon, yacht rigged throughout, set jib-topsail, and commenced to overhaul the Mary Fish. Off the Highland lights the Negus and Reindeer also began to make play to the front. About 5:30 the fleet encountered considerable sea, into which bowsprits were pitched in a lively manner. All had every inch of muslin piled on which they could carry; but about dark staysails, jibtopsails and flying jibs began to come in. A rolling sea at supper time made the crockery jingle and sent the landsmen aboard the various craft on deck, too sick to nibble a biscuit, and the seas shipped sent them below again, drenched in spray, to seek consolation if possible in the arms of Morpheus. At 6:30 the wind was east by south, and the Enchantress was leading the fleet, having passed the Clio, which, however, struggled manfully for precedence with the big yachts Alarm and Dreadnaught. Off the weather bow of the Mary Fish were the Eva, Widgeon, and Van Name, and a short distance astern were the Negus and Reindeer. After dark the vessels of the fleet began to string out, the Enchantress being five or six miles ahead of the one bringing up the rear. About 9 the Mary Fish parted head rope of staysail and took it in. At 9:15 Barnegat light bearing west by half south, saw the Negus to leeward and the Reindeer to windward, both a little astern. The Eva and Widgeon were on weather bow. Wind from the eastward, two points abaft the beam.

As the moon rose high in the heavens the scene was grandly beautiful. The Mary Fish dashed through the waves, gaily sending showers of spray aloft, which flashed in the moonlight like diamonds, and left a glittering wake of foam far behind her.

Ever and anon she plunged into a sea which swept her decks and washed in torrents out of the lee scuppers. Vast hills of water threatened to overwhelm the little craft, but as they overhung her she would ever mount the waves and dash through the sea like a duck. At 10:30 P. M. Little Egg Harbor light bore west by north. Wind east northeast and puffy, with light fleecy clouds obscuring the moon. At 12:20 A. M., Friday, Absecom light bore west. Wind northeast. About this time the Mary Fish shipped a tremendous sea and the jibboom was rigged in. Things began to look squally, and Capt. Brown called Pilots Watson, Hussey, Germond, and Maxwell on deck for a consultation. No harm was done except wetting the watch forward, and "freshening the nip" made everything serene.

At 1:30 rockets were seen, an indication that a yacht was nearing the Lightship. At this time winged our foresail. Wind northeast. At 2:30 sighted the Lightship from aloft. Took reef in foresail and bonnet out of jib. Rockets began to go up in all directions to the astonishment of an old sailor aboard a coaster, who hailed the Mary Fish, and wanted to know what the—— was up. Blue lights and red lights burning showed that some of the fleet were rounding the Lightship, and rockets off to the southward showed that two or three vessels had gone too far in that direction. At 3 sent up two rockets. Viewed through a night glass the scene at the Lightship was a brilliant one. As the craft successively passed blue and red lights lit up the sea, and flashed on the Lightship enveloped in a shower of spray and foam. The Mary Fish dashed through the waves and came up rapidly. At 3:45 got ready to jibe, dangerous manœuvre in a heavy sea. Single reefed mainsail and lowered the peak. At 3:53 jibed and came on a wind on the starboard tack, passing the Lightship at 3:55. Hailing the Lightship found only five vessels had passed, a small yacht being the last one. The wind was stiff from the northeast, a heavy sea running, and the barometer 30° 38', and rising. At 4:10 shook out reefs, and about the same time saw a pilot boat, supposed to be the Elwell, passing Lightship. The morning broke damp and chilly, and the spray flying over the deck of the Mary Fish brought out sou'westers, peajackets and India rubber boots. At 6 A. M. off Hereford passed to windward of the working schooner Van Name. Three yachts were seen astern, but it was too foggy to make them out. The wind about this time came out due north, and the long dead beat to windward up the Jersey coast had fairly commenced. On the wind, with plenty of it, is the Mary Fish's best point of sailing. As she came in sight of three or four of the white winged racers ahead a grim smile broke over the face of Capt. Dick Brown, and the recollection of fifty yachting triumphs, from the time he won the Queen's cup in the America to the present day, illumined his countenance. Says he to the Sun reporter : " Sonny, we are the smallest boat in the fleet, but the harder it blows down the coast, and the heavier the sea, the better for us."

As the sun rose, made out the yachts Alarm and Clio or Eva astern, and the Elwell and Blunt. At 7:15 made out the Widgeon, Negus and Dreadnaught ahead. A minute later the lookout aloft sighted the Enchantress on the weather bow, going like a race horse, with topmasts housed. She soon went out of sight and was not seen afterwards. At 7:30 the Mary Fish was gaining fast on the Widgeon, Negus and Dreadnaught. Standing off shore at this time on the port tack, the Mary Fish met the Alarm and Elwell standing in on the starboard tack. The two latter tacked in her wake, but were soon far astern. Near the Alarm and Elwell was the working schooner Van Name. No other boats were in sight. Great Egg Harbor bore northwest at 8 A. M., at which time the Molly Fish had the fifth place in the race, with a chance of something better if the wind held. By the time breakfast was over the sun came out bright and warm. Everybody came on deck and things were made snug for a twenty-four hour dead beat to windward. The veteran darkey cook poked his head up out of the fore-castle, and as he tossed a lot of potatoe peelings to leeward exclaimed, "Golly, Capt. Brown, give it to her. Dis is de breeze de Molly wants." At 9:20 the Dreadnaught took in her jib, having evidently torn it badly. Soon after she took a reef in her mainsail, and gradually dropped to leeward. At ten A. M. the wind was north·northeast and the barometer 30:42 and rising. Absecom light bore north by east about eight miles off. The Alarm, Van Name and Elwell were six miles off on the lee quarter of the Mary Fish and nearly out of sight. The Negus and Widgeon were ahead on the lee bow and the Dreadnaught placed at a disadvantage by the accident to her jib, was gradually dropping astern.

As the sun rose high in the heavens a more glorious subject for painter's brush or poet's pen than the scene presented could not be imagined. The vast hills of water which were following the Molly Fish the night previous were now ahead, and she dashed into and over them with an ease and buoyancy perfectly delightful. The sickening rolling seas of the night before had vanished, and in their stead was the inspiriting motion of a vessel by the wind. As far as the eye could reach "white caps" crowned the billows. Around the Mary Fish the gallant yachts were ploughing along with lee rails buried in foam, throwing the spray in showers over the decks and far to leeward. At one moment the bowsprits would point toward the zenith, and at another would plunge into the waves as if never to emerge therefrom. Over all was a clear, blue sky and an October sun. About 11:30 the Mary Fish, which had been rapidly gaining on the Negus and Widgeon, was unfortunately headed by the wind a couple of points, and the shift of wind of course gave the two latter a corresponding advantage. At this time the Negus was under whole sails, and the Widgeon had set her flying jib. The shift of wind placed them some distance to windward of the Fish. At 11:50 the Mary Fish tacked off Atlantic City. At 1 P. M. the Elwell was ahead of the Dreadnaught on her lee bow. All day long the Molly Fish made tacks up the coast in and off shore, Capt. Brown and Pilot Watson spelling each other at the helm. At 3 sighted the Negus and Widgeon ahead some distance to windward, tacking in shore. The Elwell could be seen astern tacking off shore. The Dreadnaught, Van Name, Blunt and Alarm were out of sight astern. At 3:30,.

while passing Little Egg Harbor, saw Commodore Belling's pretty yacht Meta at anchor. In the mouth of the harbor the Mary Fish went about on port tack, and stood off shore on the same tack for two hours and a half, when she went about and stood in shore on starboard tack. The wind was northeast, and sea going down all the time. The Negus was carrying staysail and jibtopsail with ease, and the Widgeon also had all her muslin spread. At 5:40 the Mary Fish set her main gafftopsail. The Negus and Widgeon tacked off shore about the same time as the Fish, but when she tacked in shore continued standing to the eastward, and thereby gained a decided advantage over her. Had the Mary Fish continued standing off shore till midnight she would have held the easterly wind, and doubtless have been at Sandy Hook by daylight, and won the $1,000 purse. In so close a race with so powerful opponents as the Negus and Widgeon it was bad policy to " break tacks," and by doing so she lost all chance of winning the race. The indications were, however, that the wind would come out from the westward, which it did for a while, but not long enough to do any good.

Barnegat was passed at 10.45, at which time the wind shifted to the northwest, and the Mary Fish rigged out her flying jibboom and set balloon flying jib and main staysail. It soon veered back again to the northeast, and the momentary advantage was lost. At 1 A. M. wind hauled to the westward again for a few minutes, and the flying jib was again set, but taken in again, as the wind veered around once more to the northeast. From this time out had light and baffling breezes. At 6:30 A.M. Saturday, Toms river bore due west; wind nor' nor'west, and variable.

The Widgeon and Elwell were seen ahead. None of the other vessels of the fleet were in sight. At 11 A. M. continued in the doldrums, and the sails flapped idly against the masts. The Widgeon and Elwell were also lying becalmed a short distance to the westward, the Widgeon being nearest the Sandy Hook Lightship. An unknown yacht, and pilot boat Edmund Blunt were seen coming up the coast. At 11:30 the Mary Fish

aud Elwell anchored just north of the taverns at Long Branch.
At 1:45 P. M. the wind came out light from the southeast, and
the Mary Fish and Elwell hauled up their mud hooks and made
sail for the Lightship, which the Widgeon had passed a few
minutes previous. The Clio and Blunt were seen astern about 2
P. M., bringing up a light breeze from the southward. After
drifting about for several hours the Mary E. Fish finally passed
the Lightship, and was told by Capt. Cosgrove that she was the
fourth vessel to arrive. The Enchantress passed the Lightship
at 6:12 A. M., Thomas S. Negus at 8:49:30, Widgeon at 12:33:30
P. M., Mary E. Fish at 7:40 P. M., James W. Elwell at 8:35 P. M.,
and the Dreadnaught, Clio, Edmund Blunt, and smack Wallace
Blackford, a few minutes apart in the order named. The working schooner William H. Van Name arrived at 10:40. The
Alarm up helm and started sheets and ran down the coast again
about noon on Saturday, and the Eva and Reindeer were
reported off Sandy Hook yesterday. The Enchantress thus
wins the $1,000 cup for schooner yachts, the Thomas S. Negus
takes the $1,000 purse, the William H. Van Name pockets one
$250 purse, and the Blackford, the only vessel in her class, of
course, "mug-hunted" the other $250.

The New York Times, October 13, 1873.

THE OCEAN RACE.

From Our Special Correspondent.

PILOT-BOAT JAMES W. ELWELL,

Sunday, October 12, 1873.

In my dispatch sent from off Long Branch, on Thursday afternoon, I sent you a description of the start made by the yachts,
pilot-boats, and others engaged in the Ocean Race for the prize,
offered by Commodore Bennett, of the New York Yacht Club
the course being from an anchorage off Owl's Head, to and
around the Cape May Lightship and return to Sandy Hook
Lightship. I also described the positions of the different ves-

sels as they were overtaken by the darkness, which was as follows: The Enchantress leading, with Clio somewhat astern,
which in turn was followed by the Dreadnaught, Alarm, Van
Name, Eva, Mary E. Fish, Widgeon, T. S. Negus, E. Blunt, James
W. Elwell, Reindeer, in the order named, with the little smack
Wallace Blackford bringing up the rear. At this time the sea
was running very heavy, and the breeze freshening from the
north-east, betokening anything but a pleasant night's sail; but
as everything on board was strong and taut, no apprehensions
were entertained that anything would part. Shortly after 7
o'clock the wind again hauled a little more to the eastward and
increased to nearly half a gale, and about an hour later we were
bowling along in fine style, and beginning to think that our
chances of final success were improving, as the Elwell is a boat
that sails well in a heavy, choppy sea and strong breeze, such as
we had at this time. We were carrying all the canvas we
could set, consisting of foresail, mainsail, maintopsail, jib, flying
jib, and jib-topsail, together with a small maintopmast staysail.
In the moonlight we could see that we were overhauling the
Blunt, and shortly afterward passed her, when we could distinguish nothing further. At 10 o'clock we were abreast of and
passed Barnegat light. The sea at this point was particularly
lumpy, causing our boat to pitch and roll considerably; but we
took in no water beyond a little spray occasionally over the bows
The maintopmast staysail had just before this been taken in, and
we were making good headway, notwithstanding the sea running.
We passed little Egg Harbor, which bore nearly due west at
11:32, having run from Barnegat, a distance of about nineteen
miles, in one hour and thirty-two minutes. Nothing of interest
occurred from this point until we arrived within about two miles
of the Lightship at Cape May, when the mainsail was lowered
and a single reef put in on account of the increased wind and sea.

At this time we noticed some schooner firing rockets as a
signal to those at the Lightship that she was rounding that
point, and by the aid of powerful glasses recognized it as Pilot
boat No. 10 (the Widgeon). We rounded at 4:15 A. M., and

stood on the starboard tack on the beat back. As we rounded the Lightship we inquired what boats had passed, and were informed that three yachts and three pilot-boats had already gone by, which we understood to be the Enchantress, Dreadnaught Alarm, Thomas S. Negus, and Widgeon. The Blunt rounded the turning point shortly after us, as we could see by her signals, as also the Eva. The sea, as we stood toward home, was worse than it had been yet, and we shipped two or three rather heavy doses of salt water, but, fortunately, without damage, and after standing first on one tack and then on the other for about two hours, the weather moderated somewhat and we shook the reef out of the mainsail. At daybreak every one was on deck, and eyes and glasses were turned in every direction to see if any of the racing fleet was in sight. It was at once discovered that the Blunt was about five miles astern of us, and the Mary E. Fish about the same distance ahead, although considerable to leeward, but none of the others were in sight. All became excitement to overhaul and pass the Fish, and every care was taken not to lose a single foot or slightest advantage. After sailing for some little time in this position, we appeared to be gaining on our leader, and shortly after caught and passed her, when we saw the Widgeon ahead of us and to windward, and soon after saw the Alarm to leeward and astern and seemingly laboring considerably. All hands were somewhat concerned about the little schooner Clio, and an anxious lookout was kept, but nothing could be seen of her. We had also seen nothing of the Van Name, Reindeer or Blackford, or of the leading yachts. From this point we lost sight of the Widgeon and Alarm, although we could still see the Mary E. Fish a little way astern of us and doing her utmost to regain the position we had wrested from her.

So we sailed along until the darkness again fell and hid everything from view. All hands then went below and talked over the exciting events of the tussle we had had with the Fish. During the night we continued to make good way, and hopes were freely indulged in that we might reach the termination of our voyage by early morning. In the morning, as the light began to dawn, we no-

ticed the Fish still a long way astern and some distance to windward; but could not see anything else in sight.   The sea at this
time was calming down and the wind continuing to drop lighter and
lighter so that grave doubts arose as to whether we should not become becalmed before many hours were over.   This was soon reduced to a certainty, for after standing in and off shore and making
but little headway, we found ourselves off Long Branch although
some distance at sea almost perfectly in the doldrums, the wind being scarcely sufficient to cause a wave in the canvas. We then drifted
about in this way for sometime, when the anchor was let go about
eleven o'clock, and we patiently waited for the breeze to come up.

The Fish was about one-half mile behind, but considerably
nearer in shore.   She was also obliged to adopt the same course
as the Elwell, and wait for a breeze.   Shortly after letting her
anchor drop we noticed the Widgeon on our windward bow
crawling up to the Lightship, but with her sails flapping lazily
against the mast in the almost dead calm that prevailed.   She,
however, every now and then got a slight puff, although it was
hardly enough to give her steerage-way.   At half-past one
o'clock the Fish caught a slight slant of wind off shore, and immediately weighed anchor and headed for the Lightship, passing
the Elwell, which was again getting under way.   Both boats
then drifted about until nearly seven o'clock, when a slight
breeze sprang up, enabling them to continue their course.   The
Fish passed the Sandy Hook Lightship ahead of us at 7:40, and
our boat at 8:35.   On inquiring of the judges at that station, we
were informed that the Enchantress had rounded at 6:12 A. M.
the Thomas S. Negus at 8:49:3, the Widgeon at 12:30, and the
Fish at 7:40.   Previous to our passing the Lightship, and at
about dark, while we were drifting hopelessly about the sea, we
noticed a black yacht a long way off to windward, which was
taken for the Clio, but it was afterward discovered to be the
Dreadnaught, as she rounded the Lightship at 8:38.   This we
were enabled to make out as she showed her signals in passing
the Judges' station.   The wind again dropped quite away, and it
became apparent that we could not hope to reach shore that

night.   We, however, headed for home, and after scarcely doing more than drift, we arrived off Quarantine at 2 A. M., when we came to a final anchorage.   Here also we found the Enchantress, who remains there to be in readiness for her match with the Dreadnaught on Friday next.   Mr. Loubat, her owner, stated to your correspondent that should the Dreadnaught not start, he will sail over the course the same as the one just sailed and claim the cup.

Of the boats which started on the race just made the following are now in, viz.:   The yachts Enchantress, Dreadnaught, Clio and Eva ; the pilot boats Thomas S. Negus, Mary E. Fish, and J. W. Elwell; the schooner Van Name.   There remains yet to be heard of, the Alarm, Blunt, Reindeer and Wallace Blackford.

The Enchantress wins the $1,000 cup ; the Thomas S. Negus the $1,000 in money ; the Van Name, the $250 purse.   The winner of the third prize of $250 is not yet decided.

The New York Daily Tribune, October 13, 1873.

THE OCEAN YACHT RACE.

A QUICK RUN TO CAPE MAY—THE ENCHANTRESS THE WINNER.

The Ocean Races for the Bennett Challenge Cup from Owl's Head to Cape May and return, began on Thursday afternoon, and the competing yachts, pilot-boats, and working schooners have been drifting at irregular intervals since 6 A. M. Saturday. The race which opened so brilliantly closed rather tamely.   The course was from Owl's Head to and around the Lightship on Five-Fathom Bank off Cape May, and thence to the Sandy Hook Lightship where the Judges were stationed.   The length of this course was about 245 miles.   The prize of a $1,000 cup was to be awarded to the first yacht home, regardless of time allowance. A second prize of $1,000, and two of $250 each, were also offered to pilot boats, working schooners, and fishing smacks, under the condition that the first boat home of each of these classes should receive one of the prizes.

Of the yachts the Enchantress and Dreadnaught were the favorites. The Eva and Clio were also well watched, though it was hardly expected that they could compete successfully with the Enchantress and the Dreadnaught. With the coming of Friday morning the intervening distances had been widely increased. The run to the Lightship had been accomplished with marvelous speed, the breeze having continued and freshened throughout the night. Slight disasters had occurred. The Enchantress had encountered a tremendous sea and had split her jib. The balloon jib of the Alarm and the staysail of the Dreadnaught were out of order. Similar misfortunes had occasioned slight delay to other yachts, and nearly all had been obliged to reef their mainsails. The Enchantress was the first of the yachts to round the Lightship. Of the pilot boats, the Negus had taken the first place, with the Widgeon second, the Fish third, the Elwell fourth, and the Blunt last. The race home was a " beat dead to windward," and progress was necessarily slow. The Enchantress maintained the lead she had obtained. The Negus increased the gap behind her. The Elwell overhauled and passed the Fish, and bade fair to obtain soon a similar position with relation to the Widgeon. The fishing smacks and working schooners were not to be seen, but as there was no interest in their race, it mattered little. The Enchantress made good progress, and was the first vessel to reach the Sandy Hook lightship at 6:12 A. M. on Saturday. The remaining yachts were a long distance astern, and at about 8 A. M. the wind died out completely and left nearly all the racers becalmed within a few miles of the goal. This nearly killed the interest in a race which would otherwise have been an unprecedented success.

The Negus had, however, obtained a position so favorable that she was not seriously crippled by the calm and drifted across the line at 8:49:30 Saturday morning. These vessels, of course, were the winners of the races in which the interest centered, but the remaining vessels of both classes were hopelessly becalmed. It was 12:33:30 when the Widgeon crossed the line. The Fish did not arrive till 7:40 P. M., and the Elwell's time was 8:35. Then came the yacht Dreadnaught at 8:38, and the remainder of the fleet drifted about several hours longer before accomplishing the few miles intervening between themselves and the Lightship.

Of the working schooners the Van Name arrived yesterday forenoon thus winning the $250 prize awarded to the winning schooner.

[*The World, New York, October* 13, 1873]

THE RETURN OF THE YACHTS.

A REVIEW OF THE OCEAN RACE AND A LIST OF THE WINNING BOATS.

For many days previous to last Thursday the interest of all aquatic sport lovers had centered in the great Ocean Race for the Bennett Cup and money prizes, to be sailed over the course from Owl's head to and around the Lightship off Cape May and back to the Lightship off Sandy Hook. Much speculation has been indulged in as to the probable result and most men familiar with the qualities and condition of the various yachts and other vessels had fixed upon Mr. J. F. Loubat's yacht, the Enchantress, as likely to win the race and the cup. Under other circumstances perhaps the splendid reputation for seaworthiness won in many hard contested battles with rough weather and heavy seas by Mr. A. B. Stockwell's Dreadnaught would have made her a great favorite. But it seemed to be well known that the Dreadnaught was very "foul" from her summer's cruising, and in sad need of clean copper, new canvas, and other repairs. The Enchantress, on the other hand, was just off the dock, with bottom pumice-stoned till it shone like a mirror. She had a full crew, and above all her owner was bound to win the race or bring her back without a stick in her or a stitch on her. Mr. A. C. Kingsland's Alarm, though in many respects a fine sailer, was not expected to win, and the Clio and Eva were looked upon as quite too small to be reliable should the weather prove heavy, as might reasonably be expected at this season of the year. Some thought that one of the twelve pilot boats, working schooners, or smacks entered might come off victor by some happy chance, but after all the Enchantress was by long odds the favorite, and justified the prediction of her admirers by a successful trip and the fair winning of a fair ocean race over a course 122 miles and return in thirty-nine hours. The Enchantress' trip was not marked by the occurence of any serious accidents beyond the splitting of her jib by the force of the wind and the carrying away of her bobstay by a heavy sea. These do not appear to have caused any considerable delay, so that her cruise may be considered a fair criterion of the seaworthiness and ability of the yacht. The Dreadnaught, on the contrary, having shipped a chance crew at starting, met with a constant series of disasters, and was prevented from making a good showing in the race. The loss of her staysail and the unfortunate snarl into which her club-topsail got when being sent down preparatory to rounding the Cape May Lightship caused a dead loss of thirty-five minutes, and the subsequent parting of her jibstay rendered it necessary to run before the wind for nearly an hour in a direction exactly opposite to her course, by which she lost nearly four hours on her true course, and was therefore becalmed when the wind died away after some of her antagonists had reached the goal. In addition to this she carried away her jib owing to an imperfect splice in her leach-rope, and the mainsail showed signs of weakening at the reef cringle. Had the Dreadnaught been less unfortunate the Enchantress might perhaps have been more closely pressed and possibly her laurels would have been won in a much severer contest. Little is known of the course pursued by the Alarm after rounding the Cape May Lightship, and it was believed on board the Dreadnaught that owing to the carrying away of some portion of her rigging she was obliged to run before the wind to the Delaware breakwater for shelter. The leading boats rounded the Five Fathom Lightship in the following manner: Enchantress, Dreadnaught, Alarm, Widgeon.

The Enchantress made the Sandy Hook light-ship at 6 h. 12 m, Saturday morning, winning the yacht cup; the Thomas S. Negus. No. 1. at 6 h. 49 m. 30 s., winning the first money prize; the Mary E. Fish, No. 4, at 7 h. 40 m.; the Dreadnaught at 8 h. 40 m. Saturday afternoon.   Off the Lightship after dark Saturday evening the scene was an unusual one.   There was a dead calm, and the sea, which had been so heavy during the entire trip, had quieted down to a long and steady swell.   The moon in the eastern sky sent a long wake of light across the water, and on all sides the distance was filled with the signal lights and shadowy forms of vessels of every sort, some at anchor and others lying to, idly yielding to the long sweep of the swell and describing with their tall masts huge arcs among the stars.   Now and then a steamer or a tug with a seaward-bound craft in tow would cross the wake of the moon and steam away for the harbor or disappear in the offing.   Presently "eight bells" sounded from the Lightship, and a few moments after a red rocket shot from some vessel far in shore into the sky, exploding in a shower of colored lights.

Another followed from the same quarter, and then another and another from boats more or less distant, while on the Elwell and the Dreadnaught, then just drifting past the Lightship, blue and red signal fires were burned, casting their weird, strange light upon rigging, spars, and sails, and leaving as they died out a momentary sense of utter darkness.   Soon after this a light breeze sprung up, offering an opportunity to those who desired to make an anchorage inside the Hook.

The Commercial Advertiser, New York, October 13, 1873.

THE STORY OF THE RACERS.

WHAT IT DEMONSTRATES—LIGHT VESSELS IN A ROUGH SEA.

Now that the winning boats of the great Ocean Regatta are known and are safely in port, it is pleasant to hear the story of the sailing-masters and the passengers.   Taking the reports as they come to us, the yacht Enchantress, which wins the first prize, should be proud of herself. She made the run from New York to Cape May in excellent time, and in a heavy sea. The problem of light vessels, such as the yachts of the New York Club generally are, crossing the Atlantic, was solved by the race between the Fleetwing, Vesta, and the Henrietta, in which the Henrietta was the winner, and since that time the white sails of the yachts have been spread in all the pleasant places of the world, from the British coast to Spain, and up in the Mediterranean, where Mr. Lorillard left his yacht, a wreck, and gave to us, through the medium of the foreign correspondents, a story of romance in which life ashore, under a tent, guarded by Arabs, needed only the presence of the requisite number of *houris* to make it a chapter from the "Arabian Nights." Yacht-owners' comfort divides itself into two distinct features—the comfort of lazy indifference, and the comfort of a cruise. The fact that vessels of the class of larger boats of the New York Yacht Club can go almost anywhere with safety, has placed a new complexion upon yachts and yachting in America. It is an expensive luxury, but there is something indefinably "nice" and commendably jolly in having a yacht, and being able to go where one pleases— providing always that there be a wind. Here comes in the point where the demonstrated safety of the vessels at sea adds to the first division of the yacht-owners' comfort, and where the lazy indifference of the occasion is made doubly grateful by the safety.

The records of the racers in the race to Cape May and back are interesting in more ways than one. They tell just what the other boats did—the boats which are not yet home, and the work done by the Enchantress is worthy of remembrance. Notwithstanding a heavy sea, the yacht made the run from Owl's Head, in New York Harbor, to Five Fathom Lightship, off Cape May, a distance of 121$\frac{1}{4}$ miles, in ten hours and forty-five minutes, and beat back again in twenty-eight hours and fifteen minutes, making the entire run of 247 miles in thirty-nine hours. This is not a quick run home, but it shows that vessels built for pleasure, well manned and properly equipped, may be used to an advantage

in a sea, and, with ordinary " luck at sea," may be depended upon for long and even tempestuous voyages.

The race to Cape May and back is also important, since boats
of several classes were thrown into competition and contrast.
The pilot boats of New York Harbor have measured their distances and ability with the yachts, and are a representative
class, with which sea work is not a specialty, but a general occurrence.

The pilot boat Thomas S. Negus is the winner of the prize
for her class, and the run made by this vessel shows that the
pilot boats are to be trusted also, since the new boat has done
so well, and the working schooner, Wm. H. Van Name, is
winner of the third prize.

The contest demonstrates the fact that the " pleasure-boat
navy " of America is worthy of representation at home and worthy of imitation abroad.   The old idea that size and weight were
necessary at sea is exploded by the record of the performances
of these light-craft, and the improvements made in such architecture as yacht-building are each year adding new wonders to
the performances of the vessels of the various yacht club fleets.
The ocean regattas are a benefit—far more so than the ordinary
races over the Yacht Club course from Staten Island to the
Lightship and back, as it makes a necessity that the vessels should
be in thorough sea-going trim, and should be handled with care
to procure speed and yet keep the yacht in good condition for
the work required of her—and the repetition of such regattas
will doubtless bring forward more boats that have yet to win a
sea record, and inaugurate a new system of ocean navigation in
pleasure craft as beautiful as they are seaworthy.

The New York Herald, October 15, 1873.

In the recent Ocean Regatta the Clio, Messrs. Asten & Bradhurst, was the winner of a $250 cup from the Eva, Mr. E. Burd
Grubb. It is only fair to state that the owners of the Clio are
willing to sail any yacht of her size and tonnage to wind-

ward and return, feeling assured that she will give a good account of herself.

The schooner Alarm, Rear Commodore Kingsland, passed Sandy Hook Lightship at nine o'clock Sunday night, having made the run from Five Fathom Bank Lightship in twelve hours. The reason that Commodore Kingsland ordered his yacht to abandon the ocean race on Friday morning, when she held a capital position, is that one of the men on board was seriously ill requiring immediate medical aid, so they bore away for Cape May, where a physician was found. There is no doubt that the Alarm would have done well in the contest could she have continued.

The schooner Eva, one of the yachts which started in the Ocean Regatta and did not return, has been heard from at Burlington, on the Delaware, the residence of her owner. She arrived there on Sunday morning in a disabled condition. Among the accidents that happened her were the disabling of her steering apparatus, and the breaking of her fore-chain plate, which carried away the bolt out of the topping lift and sprung the flying jib-boom. At this time the sailing master of the Eva concluded that it would be safer to abandon the race, and so changed the course of the yacht.

The New York Herald, October 18, 1873.

THE OCEAN RACES.

Official Report of the Committee of the New York Yacht Club Announcing the Winners of the Great Ocean Race Prizes.

NEW YORK, Oct. 16, 1873.

The Regatta Committee of the New York Yacht Club submit the following report of the ocean regatta sailed on the 9th inst. for prizes presented by James Gordon Bennett, Esq., Commodore of the Club:—

THE PRIZES.

The prizes offered were as follows, viz:

First—Prize of the value of $1.000, to be sailed for by schooner yachts belonging to any organized yacht club, from an anchorage off Owl's Head, New York Harbor, to and around the Lightship on Five Fathom Bank, off Cape May, N. J., and return to Sandy Hook Lightship.

Second—Three purses; one of the value of $1.000, and two of the value of $250 each, to be sailed for over the same course, upon the same day, and open to the following classes of vessels, hailing from any port in the United States:—

1. Pilot boats.

2. Working schooners of not less than 25, nor over 300 tons, old measurement.

3. Schooner smacks.

In this race the first vessel arriving at the winning post to take a purse of $1.000; the first vessel arriving of each of the other two classes to take a purse of $250.

ENTRIES.

The entries were as follows, viz:

YACHTS.

Name.	Owner.	Tonnage.
Enchantress	J. F. Loubat	276.16
Alarm	A. C. Kingsland	225.77
Clio	{ T. B. Asten } T. C. P. Bradhurst	59.18
Eva	E. Burd Grubb	77.50
Atalanta	William Astor	145.41
Dreadnaught	A. B. Stockwell	240.00

PILOT BOATS.

Name.	Owner.	Tonnage.
Widgeon No. 10	New York Pilots	105.09
Hope, No. 1	New York Pilots	132.04
Edmund Blunt, No. 21	New York Pilots	—
C. H. Marshall, No. 3	New York Pilots	85.00
James W. Elwell, No. 7	New Jersey Pilots	165.00
Thomas S. Negus, No. 1	New Jersey Pilots	—
Mary E. Fish, No. 4	New Jersey Pilots	—

WORKING SCHOONERS.
Designating letter.

W. H. Van Name	A	W. H. Van Name	180.00
Reindeer	B	Captain Howard	140.06
Sharpshooter	C	F. M. Crossman	120.00
Racer	D	Eugene Howard	—

SCHOONER SMACKS.

Wallace Blackford..........E.....H. C. Rogers & Co. 80.00

CONTESTANTS.

On the day appointed for the regatta the following vessels were at the anchorage prepared for the start :—

YACHTS.

Name.	*Owner.*	*Tonnage.*
Enchantress	J. F. Loubat	276.16
Alarm	A. C. Kingsland	225.77
Clio	{ T. B. Asten	59.18
	{ T. C. Bradhurst	—
Eva	E. Burd Grubb	77.50
Dreadnaught	A. B. Stockwell	240.00

PILOT BOATS.

Widgeon, No. 10	New York Pilots	105.00
James W. Elwell, No. 7	New Jersey Pilots	165.00
Thomas S. Negus, No. 1	New Jersey Pilots	—
Mary E. Fish, No. 4	New Jersey Pilots	—
Edmund Blunt, No. 2	New York Pilots	—

WORKING SCHOONERS.
Designating Letter.

W. H. Van Name	A	W. H. Van Name	180.00
Reindeer	B	Captain Howard	140 00

SCHOONER SMACKS.

Wallace Blackford..........H. C. Rogers & Co...... 80.00

The preparatory signal was given at 3:02 P. M. The vessels were started at 3:12 P. M.

The person who was sent to Cape May to take the time of rounding the Five Fathom Bank Lightship was unable to board that vessel, because of the strong northeast wind and high sea prevailing, and no official time at that point can be given.

HOME TO THE LIGHTSHIP.

The time of arrival at Sandy Hook Lightship was as follows

YACHTS.

	H.	M.
Enchantress, October 11..............	6	12 A.M.
Dreadnaught, October 11......................	8	30 P.M.
Clio, October 12................................	1	22 A.M.
Alarm Not taken		
Eva—Not taken		

PILOT BOATS.

	H.	M.	S.
Thomas S. Negus, October 11..............	8	49	30 A.M.
Widgeon, October 11......................	12	33	30 P.M.
Mary E. Fish, October 11.................	7	40	00 P.M.
James W. Elwell October 11,..............	8	25	00 P.M.
Edmund Blunt, October 11.................	9	44	00 P.M.

WORKING SCHOONERS.

W. H. Van Name, October 11..............	10	52	00 P.M.
Reindeer—Not taken			

SMACK.

Wallace Blackford October 11..............	11	44	00 P.M.

THE WINNERS.

The prizes are awarded as follows :—
The Yacht Prize to Enchantress.
The $1,000 Purse to Pilot boat Thomas S. Negus.
One $250 Purse to schooner William H. Van Name.
One $250 Purse to smack Wallace Blackford.
All of which is respectfully submitted.

FLETCHER R. WESTRAY ⎤
  WILLIAM KREBS,   ⎟ Regatta
E. E. CHASE,   ⎬ Commttee.
CHARLES A. MINTON, ⎦

The New York Herald, October 23, 1873.

OCEAN RACING.

From Owl's Head to Five Fathom Bank Lightship and Return—The Schooner Smack Wallace Blackford willing to Sail any Vessel of her class for $2,000,

To the Editor of the Herald:—

Through the liberality of the Commodore of the New York Yacht Club our schooner smack was lately permitted to test her sailing qualities in the Ocean Race with some of the swiftest sailing craft of New York Bay; but, very much to our disappointment, the Wallace Blackford had no competitor of her class, thereby depriving us of the privilege of demonstrating that she is the fastest sailing fishing smack afloat.

Permit us to say, through the columns of the Herald, that the smack Wallace Blackford is open to sail over the same course against any fishing smack (with a well) for a purse of $2000, at any time before December 30, 1873.   Respectfully yours,

EUGENE G. BLACKFORD.
H. C. ROGERS & Co.

CHAPTER V.

THE CAPE MAY CHALLENGE CUP RACE.

The New York Herald, September 23, 1873.

The Owner of the Enchantress Looking for the Cape May Challenge Cup
—The Dreadnaught Called Out—Mr. Loubat Willing to Sail any
Yacht of an Organized Club across the Atlantic.

UNION CLUB, NEW YORK, Sept. 22, 1873.

Captain STOCKWELL, Yacht Dreadnaught, New York Yacht
Club :—

DEAR SIR :—I hereby challenge your Yacht Dreadnaught to
sail my yacht Enchantress, on Tuesday, the 14th day of October
next, at twelve M., for the Cape May Challenge Cup, presented
by Commodore J. G. Bennett to the New York Yacht Club,
Course, from Sandy Hook Lightship to Five Fathom Lightship
(Cape May) and return.

Should you desire any extension of time please name any
day to suit your own convenience up to the 1st of November
next, although, according to the tenure by which you hold said
challenge cup, you are obliged to race any challenger during the
racing season—that is, from the third Thursday in June to the
third Thursday in October in each year, on a fifteen days' notice,
or forfeit the cup to the challenger.

I shall, therefore, hold you to such race, and if you do not accept
this challenge I shall go over the course on Tuesday, the 14th of

October next, starting from Sandy Hook Lightship at 12 M. and claim said challenge cup, as I recognize no right in a holder of a challenge cup to refuse a challenge on any plea whatsoever.

As to the ocean race from Sandy Hook Lightship to Cowes (Isle of Wight), of which you spoke yesterday, I can but repeat that I am not willing to stake such a large sum as $25,000 on a race, but that, should it be agreeable to you or any member of any organized yacht club in the United States to challenge my yacht, Enchantress, for a race across the Atlantic—entrance $5,000 or less, play or pay—to be sailed from Sandy Hook Lightship at 12 M., on any day which may suit your or their convenience from the 8th to the 16th of November next, I will be most happy to accept any such challenge or challenges.

I should require notice thereof, however, before the 1st of October next.

I send copy of this letter to Mr. Charles A. Minton, Secretary of the New York Yacht Club, to be placed by him on file, and remain,   Yours truly,

J. F. LOUBAT.

The New York Herald, September 25, 1873.

The Cape May Challenge Cup—Letter of the Secretary of the New York Yacht Club to the owner of the Enchantress—Mr. Loubat's Reply—Resolved to Sail for the Cup and claim it, unless beaten.

CLUB ROOMS, Sept. 23, 1873.

J. F. LOUBAT, ESQ.:—

DEAR SIR—I have your favor of yesterday and note contents. I saw Mr. Stockwell to-day, and, as far as I can understand it, there appears to be some misunderstanding between you and himself as regards the Cape May Challenge Cup. He considers himself still under challenge from the Magic, and until that is settled, either by the withdrawal of one of the parties, or sailing of the match, that he is not open to be challenged by any other vessel. Your impression on the contrary, as expressed on Sunday, I understood to be, that the match was off. It appears to be a question as to how long a yacht under challenge can hold a cup when neither of the parties intends to sail for it. I have my own views upon the subject but would prefer laying the matter before the Regatta Committee before expressing them.

As soon as a definite opinion is arrived at I will advise you.

Yours, very truly,

C. A. MINTON, Secretary.

MR. LOUBAT'S REPLY.

CHAS. A. MINTON, Secretary N. Y. Y. C.:

UNION CLUB, NEW YORK, Sept. 24, 1873.

DEAR SIR:—In answer to your favor of yesterday's date I beg to remark that, without assuming that "neither of the parties intend to sail," I must insist that the only proper answer to my challenge is notice of intended sailing this season under a challenge which precludes the possibility of accepting mine. There is not, nor can be, a misunderstanding. I intend to sail over the Cape May Challenge Cup course on Tuesday, the 14th of October next, starting from the Sandy Hook Lightship at twelve M., and to claim the challenge cup, unless I am beaten.

Yours, very truly,

J. F. LOUBAT.

I send a copy of this letter to Captain Stockwell.

The Field, London, October 11, 1873.

ANOTHER YACHT RACE.

We learn from the *Spirit of the Times* that there is a chance of a race being made across the Atlantic by the Dreadnaught, Capt. Stockwell, and the Enchantress, Capt. Loubat. We learn from the same paper that the Dreadnaught, holder of the Bennet Challenge Cup, is under challenge from the Enchantress to sail a match from Sandy Hook to Cape May

Lightship and back on the 14th of October. There however appears to be some difficulty about the challenge, as the owner of the Dreadnaught declares that he is under challenge from the Magic, and cannot accept two challenges. The New York Yacht Club is probably used to this sort of thing, and will prove quite equal to the occasion. As the matter at present stands, Capt. Loubat insists on the legitimacy of his challenge, unless the Dreadnaught and Magic intend sailing this season; at any rate the Enchantress will be at Sandy Hook Lightship at twelve noon on the 14th inst., and will sail over the course and claim the challenge cup, unless the Dreadnaught is there to beat her.

The New York Herald, October 14, 1873.

The challenge of Mr. J. F. Loubat, owner of the Enchantress, to Mr. A. B. Stockwell, owner of the Dreadnaught, to sail from Sandy Hook Lightship to and around Five-Fathom Bank lightship and return, for the Cape May Challenge Cup (now held by the Dreadnaught), was accepted by the latter gentleman and this day fixed for the race. Yachtsmen in general agreed that the event would be very interesting, and since the great ocean races they have expressed the opinion that it could not be otherwise than particularly exciting. In the late run to the Cape May Lightship and back the Dreadnaught was quite unfortunate in splitting sails and receiving other damage, which will prevent her from appearing at the starting point, thus leaving the Enchantress to " walk over" the course. It is certain that the owner of the Dreadnaught desires to sail the race, but as his yacht is not in fit condition to attempt it he must accept the alternative.

The Sun, New York, October 13, 1873.

THE DISPUTES OF THE YACHTSMEN.

The Clio, though the smallest of the fleet, sailed over

the course, without a mishap, carrying sail through wind and sea in a manner which proved her seaworthy qualities. During the race other and larger yachts came to grief, and her immediate competitor, the saucy Eva, was left by the fleet Clio far astern.

The race for the $500 Cape May Challenge cup was to have been sailed to-day between the Enchantress and the Dreadnaught, the latter of which won the cup last year. Owing to her disabled condition she will not be ready to sail to-day, and as the owner of the Enchantress will not give her any further time it will be a "mug hunt" for the Enchantress, which will appear at the starting point and claim and receive the cup.

The World, New York, October 14, 1873.

MUG HUNTING.

THE ENCHANTRESS REFUSES TO ACCEDE TO THE DREADNAUGHT'S

REQUEST FOR DELAY.

The Bennett Cape May Challenge Cup has for the past year been held by Mr. Stockwell, owner of the Dreadnaught, which last fall won it from the Palmer in a well-contested race over the prescribed course from Sandy Hook to Cape May light-ship and return in twenty-six hours. According to the rule by which this challenge cup is held its holder is bound to have his yacht in readiness to sail a race over the prescribed course whenever called upon to do so from the opening of the yachting season up to the 16th of the present month, or relinquish the cup. Hardly had the Dreadnaught returned from her recent encounter with the Enchantress in so crippled a condition as to render her quite unseaworthy when her owner finds himself challenged by Mr. Loubat, the owner of the Enchantress, to sail a race for this cup over the same course, starting to-day at 12 M. The limit of time during which a holder of this cup may be challenged is looked upon as simply a protection for the holder, preventing the necessity of keeping his yacht in the water and in sailing trim the year round. Understanding this, Mr. Stockwell sent word to Mr. Loubat representing the impossibility of putting the Dreadnaught in fit sailing condition, or even repairing her injuries so as to make her safely seaworthy at so short notice, and offering, if a delay of a few days could be afforded, to waive his right of refusing to sail after the 16th instant. To this message the following reply was yesterday received:

A. B. STOCKWELL Esq.

My Dear Sir: I regret that I cannot accede to your request for delay. The challenge cup, as you will probably recollect, must be sailed for by Thursday next. I shall, therefore, sail from Sandy Hook Lightship Tuesday the 14 inst. at 12 M., and shall claim the challenge cup, as also our private cup, unless defeated.

Yours, respectfully,
J. F. LOUBAT,
Yacht Enchantress, N. Y. Y. C.

New York, October 12, 1873.

The private cup alluded to in the above note is a $1,000 cup which these gentlemen have individually wagered upon the result of this race, and goes with the challenge cup mentioned above. It is said that several gentlemen, members of the New York Yacht Club, yesterday visited the Dreadnaught to satisfy themselves of the truth of her reported condition, and then called upon Mr. Loubat for the purpose of dissuading him from a course which they consider unfair "mug hunting" and but little designed to promote sport on the water or harmony and good feeling in the Club. Mr. Stockwell desires that it may be announced that he will be ready, if notified at once, to race the Enchantress for these two cups over any course known to the New York Yacht Club at any time after Friday next, though he should certainly decline to yield the private challenge cup if the race is insisted upon before that time, on the ground that the bet was a verbal one and not made "play or pay."

The Evening Mail, New York, October 14, 1873.

A VERY SMALL BUSINESS.

Mr. Joseph F. Loubat, the owner of the yacht Enchantress, appears to be disposed to play what in lower circles is called an "open and shut game," in order to get away from the owner of the Dreadnaught the challenge cup so fairly won by that fine yacht last Fall. By a strict construction of the rules of the yacht club, the winner of the challenge cup is bound to be ready to sail a race whenever called upon to do so between the opening of the subsequent yachting season and the 16th of October. As is well known, the Dreadnaught has just come into port from a recent race, in so crippled a condition as to be unfit for sailing; and the owner of the Enchantress takes advantage of the circumstance to send in his demand for a race, together with the claim that both the challenge cup and a $1,000 cup privately wagered shall belong to the winner. In view of this fact that the Dreadnaught is really disabled and notwithstanding the protests and wishes of the members of the Club, Mr. Loubat insists upon compliance with his challenge and churlishly notifies the owner of the Dreadnaught of his intention to sail over the racing course to-day and thereafter assert his claim to the two cups. This, too, in spite of the announcement that the challenged party will waive his right to refuse sailing after the date fixed by the rules, and will be ready to sail at any time after Friday next. Of course, there can be but one opinion touching Mr. Loubat's conduct in this matter, for, independently of the mug-hunting disposition it evinces, there is certainly about it such a repudiation of the commonest principles of courtesy and fair play as ought to make the winner in such a mean game forever feel as if he had paid a very high price for his surreptitious gains. We dislike to characterize, in type, an action so utterly antagonistic to the high-toned code which is generally supposed to govern yachtsmen.

The Sun, New York, October 15, 1873.

Mr. J. F. Loubat, of the yacht Enchantress, seems to us to be acting rather ungenerously in requiring Mr. Stockwell, of the Dreadnaught, to sail a race without giving him a fair time to refit his yacht and make her seaworthy after the damages she received in the recent contest for the Cape May cup.

The New York Times, New York, October 15, 1873.

COCKLE-SHELLS.

A controversy is said to be pending between the owners of two of our leading yachts, which may appropriately be made the occasion of recurring to certain views on the subject of yachting, which we expressed the other day. Last year, the Cape May Challenge Cup was won by the Dreadnaught, from the Palmer, in a match race from Sandy Hook to Cape May and back within the allotted time of twenty-six hours. By the terms on which the cup is given, it must be held by the winner, at all times during the yachting season, open to challenge for a trial over the same course, or else it must be relinquished. The late ocean race which the Enchantress won, beating the Dreadnaught and others, was not, it must be understood, for this but for another special prize. Now, the owner of the Enchantress, as is clearly his right, challenges the Dreadnaught to a race for the Challenge Cup before Thursday, the 16th inst. at which date the season ends. The owner of the Dreadnaught pleads for delay on the ground that his yacht has been so strained by the late race as to be unseaworthy, and offers, if time be given, to waive his right of refusing to sail after the 16th.

To many this proposition will appear perfectly fair, and Mr. Loubat, the owner of the Enchantress, will be charged with all sorts of unworthy motives for insisting upon his technical rights. We do not coincide with this view. Stanchness, not less than speed, is an element, if it be not the chief element of merit in an ocean race ; and the fact that, after such a race, the Enchantress is in better trim to encounter another than the Dreadnaught, shows of itself that she is better entitled to the award of superiority. The cup is given on condition that its holder shall be always ready, during a prescribed term, to vindicate his right to hold it; and for a yachtsman to attempt to evade such an express obligation, on the ground that his boat is unseaworthy, is simply to admit the whole question put at issue by the offer of such a prize, and to confess that he has forfeited his claim to retain it.

We refer to the matter because disputes of this kind are constantly arising, and because such an excuse, if seriously put forth and entertained, is a stain upon the name of American yachting. The truth is, our amateur mariners have so educated themselves to believe that swiftness and beauty of outline were alone essential to a model yacht, that everything like solidity appears to have been sacrificed to these graces. If yachts are meant for playthings, to amuse a summer fancy, this is well enough. But let our yacht clubs have this clearly understood, and resign all claim to be anything but smooth-water sailors. When Mr. Ashbury came over here after the American cup, and went away without it, everybody was well pleased. But if, at the end of that week of races, a sailor had been asked to choose between the Livonia—stanch and sound as when she entered—and any one of the three or four yachts that almost went to pieces in the effort to beat her, is it likely that he would have long hesitated ?

We look with regret on controversies like this between the Enchantress and Dreadnaught, because their very nature implies a degeneration in the spirit of our yachtsmen and the build of our yachts alike. For this reason, and as one means to check this demoralization, we hope to see Mr. Loubat press his claim, and, if possible, set a precedent which may not be disregarded. A yacht that is knocked up by a single race ought to be content with such trophies as may be gathered on light winds and smooth water, and leave worthier triumphs to worthier and stouter competitors.

The World, New York, October 15, 1873.

THE PAST YACHTING SEASON.

The season of the New York Yacht Club for 1873 has not, we regret to say, reflected any credit whatever on that organization. It has been proved, indeed, although it was sufficiently evident before, that the Club possesses a number of vessels capable of making high speed in smooth water and with a light breeze. But upon the annual cruise of the club it was proved also either that the majority of the yachts were not fit, or that the majority of the yachtsmen were not inclined to face the summer breezes of the Sound, although while the large schooners and sloops of the Yacht Club were lying wind-bound, open boats were racing across the same Sound. The recent outside races have been still more discreditable than the summer cruise. The race of the Meta and the Vision proved nothing except that those sloops, which are certainly large enough to be good sea-boats, are not sea-boats at all. The sloop Vindex, which would have no possible chance with either of them in the inside summer races to which the majority of yachtsmen addict themselves, put them both utterly to shame in weather which they ought to have been equally well prepared to encounter. The recent race to Cape May and back, in which no severer weather was encountered than any coasting schooner pursues her voyages in without difficulty, crippled or drove into harbor nearly all the contestants in it. The result of these races has been to show that our yachts, superior as they probably are to the English yachts for speed in light weather, are utterly inferior to them for sea-going qualities. For the English yachts habitually sail races with no greater disaster than the occasional loss of a light spar or a light sail in such weather as drove the Meta into port, rendered the Vision utterly helpless, and seriously injured the Eva and the Dreadnaught. It is evident that in some cases by reason of model, in other cases by reason of rig, most of our yachts are very ill-suited to improve marine architecture, which is one chief reason of being of yacht clubs, or of developing a class of amateur sailors, which is the other. This is a valuable lesson, if our yachtsmen will consent to learn it and act upon it. But it seems that some of them are much in need of learning a lesson in courtesy and fair dealing. These qualities the New York Yacht Club has always prided itself upon promoting, the assertions of the defeated Mr. Ashbury to the contrary notwithstanding. And these qualities are conspicuously absent from the recent behavior of the owner of the Enchantress in insisting that the Dreadnaught shall sail against his yacht in a crippled condition or surrender without a contest the prize which was fairly and well won by the Dreadnaught a year ago. In either case the prize could have no possible value as a trophy. If yachting is to be regarded merely as a means towards the acquisition of a collection of silverware, the owner of the Enchantress may be called a yachtsman. But if yachting is a " manly sport," his course in relation to the challenge cup held by the Dreadnaught does not suggest to us that he is qualified to succeed in it.

The New York Times, New York, October 17, 1873.

THE CAPE MAY CHALLENGE CUP.

Between 9 and 10 o'clock Tuesday morning the yacht Enchantress left her anchorage off Staten Island and proceeded to Sandy Hook. At noon she started alone over the course prescribed for the Bennett Cape May Challenge Cup, from the Hook to Cape May Lightship and return. The present holder of the cup, the Dreadnaught, is now refitting damage received in the ocean race of the 9th inst., and was unable to join in the contest. The sloop yacht Vixen, with a member of the Racing Committee on board anchored off the Lightship shortly before 12 o'clock, and at 12:16 gave the signal for the Enchantress to start. She had her small-main topsail and jib-topsail set, there being at the time a good west by north breeze. The distance between the point of the Hook and the Ocean House at Long Branch—fourteen miles—was made in one hour and fifteen minutes. Commodore Stockton's house, twenty-two miles from the Hook, was passed at 4:18 P. M. About this time the breeze decreased, whereupon the large balloon topsail was set. At 6 P. M. Little Egg Harbor was passed bearing west-south-west five miles off, and at 6:20 Absecom Light was made and passed at 7:35. The wind fell, and the yacht slowly drifted toward the Lightship, which was sighted at 11 P. M. At 11:15 the large maintopmast staysail and balloon jib were got ready to set as the Lightship was turned, which was accomplished at 1:30 A. M. on Wednesday morning. Mr. Loubat hailed the light-ship and asked the people on board to take the yacht's time. The balloon sails were then set, but at 3:25 A. M. the wind hauled to the nor'ard, and the balloon jib had to be taken in. At 5:25 A. M. her head was east by north. At 5:30 A. M. the jib topsail and maintopmast staysail were hauled down and the yacht went about, heading on this tack north by east; went about again at 6:10 A. M. the wind shifting and light, and now headed north-north-east. At 6:40 the balloon maintopsail was shifted for a working topsail Absecom bearing north-west by west, six miles away. At 7:30 the small maintopmast staysail was set. At 8 a new Philadelphia schooner-yacht, bound south, was passed. At 8:55 the maintopmast staysail was hauled down and the yacht went about, setting the staysail again on the other tack. At 9:55, after tacking off shore, the yacht was put about on the starboard tack and stood inshore again, a brisk cool breeze blowing. At 11:40, closing the land, the maintopmast staysail was hauled down and the yacht went about on the port tack. The balloon jib topsail was set, Little Egg Harbor bearing west. with a light breeze. At 11:50 the balloon maintopsail was set and the yacht went about at 1 P. M., Heading north-north-east. The small maintopmaststaysail was now set. At 1:35 Barnegat Point was made, a point and a half on the weather bow, eight miles off, ship heading north by west. Barnegat was passed at 3:25 P. M., and the balloon jib was set, wind freshening from the eastward. At 7 P. M., the wind hauling to the southward and eastward, the sheets were slackened off, the wind being very

light.   At 7.50 P. M., the Highland Lights were sighted.   At
8:25 the maintopmast staysail was hauled down, and the balloon
jib at 8:40, the small jib being set instead, and the wind dead
aft.   At 9 P. M. the foresail was boomed out, and Sandy Hook
Light was sighted a little on the starboard bow, the wind very
light. At 11 P. M. the mainboom was jibed. At 11:33 the Lightship was spoken and asked to take the yacht's time.   The ship
then hauled to the wind on the port tack, and stood in for the
Hook with a nice breeze. Sandy Hook was passed at 12:20, and
the yacht sailed up the bay for Staten Island where she arrived
at 5:50 A. M., yesterday, and anchored off shore, as the wind
failed.   At 9 A. M., the yacht hove up again, went close in, and
let go the anchor at 9:15 A. M.   All well on board, and the cup
won, as also a private cup wagered with the owner of the
Dreadnaught.

The World, *New York, October* 20, 1873.

CONCERNING MUGS AND YACHTING.

If Mr. Loubat, the owner of the Enchantress, had challenged
Mr. Stockwell, the owner of the Dreadnaught, upon the heels of
a race in which the Dreadnaught was badly damaged and the
Enchantress not at all damaged, to run another race which
the Dreadnaught by racing-rules would be obliged to run or lose
a cup, yet could not possibly be refitted and made ready for, the
common-sense opinion would be that Mr. Loubat was more
anxious to acquire a collection of silverware than to prove the
quality of his yacht and uphold a manly sport.

That opinion The World expressed, basing the same upon its
reporter's statement, which was as follows :

"Hardly had the Dreadnaught returned from her recent encounter with the Enchantress in so crippled a condition as to
render her quite unseaworthy when her owner finds himself
challenged by Mr. Loubat, the owner of the Enchantress, to sail
a race for this cup over the same course, starting to-day at
12 M."

Our reporter was grossly misled, we cannot pretend to say by whom, but if by any yachtsman, then that person is not a fit associate for the gentlemen of the New York Yacht Club.

Mr. Stockwell did not return with the Dreadnaught disabled from the ocean regatta of the 9th, to "find himself challenged" by Mr. Loubat, the owner of the winning Enchantress. On the contrary he had been challenged on the 22d of September to a race on the 14th day of October, for the Cape May challenge cup. That cup was last year won by the Dreadnaught from the Palmer, and is held by the Dreadnaught on condition of racing any challenger during the racing season on a fifteen day's notice, or forfeit the cup.

But Mr. Loubat's challenge gave twenty-one day's notice. The Dreadnaught need not have entered the ocean regatta on the 9th in which she is alleged to have been disabled. The Enchantress underwent the same rough weather with the same risk to her condition for the challenge-cup race on the 14th. The Dreadnaught was beaten 14 hours in the ocean regatta from New York Harbor to Cape May and back to Sandy Hook Lightship, but had still three nights and two full days to repair her alleged damages, to say nothing of providing beforehand for haste.

It is obvious, therefore, that Mr. Loubat was perfectly right to refuse delay, right to sail the course, and right to claim the challenge cup as well as the private cup staked upon the same race; it is also obvious that an undue preference for silverware over good yachting cannot justly be imputed to *him*.

Mr. Stockwell's position in the matter was thus represented —we hope misrepresented—to our reporter:

"Mr. Stockwell desires that it may be announced that he will be ready if notified at once, to race the Enchantress for these two cups over any course known to the New York Yacht Club at any time after Friday next, though he should certainly decline to yield the private challenge cup if the race is insisted upon before that time, on the ground that the bet was a verbal one and not made 'play or pay.'"

What distinction between a verbal and a written agreement a gentleman becomes able to perceive by being a member of the New York Yacht Club we cannot pretend to guess, nor why the private cup does not follow the challenge cup; but perhaps a yacht-owner may have a nicer code than land-lubbers would imagine.

The Sun, New York, October 21, 1873.

Any person who labors under the impression that Mr. J. F. Loubat has taken an unfair advantage of Mr. A. B. Stockwell in compelling him to sail his yacht Dreadnaught against Mr. Loubat's Enchantress when the Dreadnaught could not be got into condition, has been the victim of a mistake. The challenge was given and accepted for a certain day long before the race took place. Meanwhile, Mr. Stockwell put the Dreadnaught into another race, taking the chances of her being disabled, but without obtaining from Mr. Loubat any conditional release from the meeting between them. Accordingly when the day for that match arrived Mr. Loubat sailed it, and of course won the cup which was at stake. This was all perfectly fair, and involved nothing ungenerous or improper on his part.

Th New York Times, New York, October 21, 1873.

Mr. J. F. Loubat, owner of the yacht Enchantress, has been very shamefully abused by some of the papers for challenging the Dreadnaught to race for the Commodore's challenge cup. We ventured to protest against these attacks last week, without fully knowing all the facts of the case. Now that we do know them, we are more strongly of opinion than before that Mr. Loubat has been very badly used. The challenge was not issued after the Dreadnaught was injured—supposing she ever was injured, which is doubtful—but dates back as far as September 22. The Cup is held under certain very clear conditions, and Mr. Loubat could not foresee that the owner of the Dreadnaught would endeavor to evade those conditions on the plea that his yacht was not in sea-going condition. If the attacks on Mr. Loubat have been prompted by Mr. Stockwell, we can only say that Mr. Stockwell has been guilty of conduct which reflects no credit on the Yacht Club. Indeed, the Yacht Club itself does not appear to have treated Mr. Loubat very generously, for the Secretary must have known that the challenge was not issued under the circumstances described in the papers which assailed him, and the true facts might easily have been placed before the public. Mr. Stockwell seems to have striven hard to keep the cup, when he knew that he could not keep it by fair means— that seems to be the long and short of the story. Mr. Loubat's conduct has been perfectly fair and straightforward from first to last; and, as will be seen from the report of the Regatta Committee in our news columns, the cup has been awarded, and very properly, to the plucky owner of the Enchantress.

The World, New York, October 21, 1873.

The Regatta Committee of the New York Yacht Club publish a decision such as we expected, awarding the Cape May challenge cup from the Dreadnaught to the Enchantress.

Mr. Stockwell, in a letter which we also print, withdraws from the untenable position taken in his former statement to our reporter, and very properly leaving also the private cup for assignation to the same committee, goes into winter quarters wondering if any Enchantress can be truly enchanting, all whose cups have not been won in actual strife and electro plated with the fine gold of courtesy.

THE CHALLENGE CUP.

Report of the Regatta Committee on the Challenge of the Dreadnaught by the Enchantress—the Enchantress awarded the cup.

To Charles A. Minton, Esq., Secretary New York Yacht Club:

The Regatta Committee submit the following report in reference to the challenge of the yacht Dreadnaught by the yacht Enchantress for the Cape May challenge cup won by the former on the 10th October, 1872.

On the 22d September, 1873, Mr. Loubat, of the Enchanress, sent to the Secretary of the club a copy of a note of that date, which he had addressed to Mr. Stockwell, of the yacht Dreadnaught, in which he challenged the latter for a race between their respective yachts for the Cape May challenge cup held by the Dreadnaught. In the note he named Tuesday, the 14th October, as the day upon which the race should be sailed, but expressed his willingness to sail it on any other day to suit Mr. Stockwell, up to 1st November.

On the 7th October Mr. Stockwell informed a member of the Regatta Committee that he had received the challenge, and would sail the race on the day named.

The Regatta Committee appointed Mr. C. A. Minton a sub-committee to start the yachts, with power to associate other members of the Club with himself to assist in the performance of the duties, and to act as judges on board the competing vessels and take the time of each.

On the 14th October Mr. Minton proceeded to Sandy Hook and found the Enchantress there prepared to start for the race. He appointed Mr. Frederic Tams, a member of the Club, onboard the Enchantress, to act as judge on board that vessel, and report the time of her rounding the Five Fathom Bank Lightship, off Cape May, and of her arrival at the home stake-boat. The Dreadnaught did not make her appearance. At thirteen minutes past twelve the Enchantress sailed from the starting point. By report of Mr. Tams—a copy is submitted herewith—she rounded the Five Fathom Bank Lightship at thirty-five minutes past one of the 15th, and at thirty-five minutes past eleven P. M. of the 15th she passed Sandy Hook Lightship.

The rules which govern races for the cup, as presented by the donor, are as follows, viz.:

First—The cup is to be held by the winner for thirty days after the race without liability to challenge.

Second—Upon the expiration of that period the winner must accept any challenge, and be prepared to sail a race over the same course within fifteen days from the receipt of such challenge, or forfeit the cup to the challenger; but should any yacht succeed in holding the cup in two consecutive races during one season it will not again be liable to challenge until the commencement of the yachting season of the following year. The cup will become the bona-fide property of any yacht holding it successfully through three consecutive contests.

Third—The yachting season in American waters in reference to this cup is understood to be from the third Thursday in June until the third Thursday in October in each year.

The Regatta Committee are of the opinion that the Enchantress is entitled to the cup, and so award it.

The letter, above referred to, of Mr. Loubat, conveying the challenge, is submitted herewith.

FLETCHER WESTRAY,
WILLLIAM KREBS,
E. E. CHASE,

NEW YORK, Oct. 20, 1873.　　　　　　　　Regatta Committee.

53 EXCHANGE PLACE, NEW YORK, October 16, 1873.

To the Regatta Committee of the New York Yacht Club.

DEAR SIRS: As Judge appointed on the Enchantress in her match with the Dreadnaught for the Cape May challenge cup, I beg to report that after having been started by Mr. Charles A. Minton at thirteen minutes past twelve P. M. on the fourteenth day of October, 1873, she sailed around the Lightship off Cape May, which she rounded at thirty-five minutes past one A. M. of the 15th October, keeping it to starboard, and returned to the Lightship off Sandy Hook, which she passed to starboard, at thirty-five minutes past eleven P. M. of the 15th October, having complied with the regulations governing the contests for said cup. I remain, yours respectfully,

(Signed)　　　　　　　　　　　　　J. FREDERIC TAMS.

Union Club, New York, September 22, 1873.
Captain Stockwell, Yacht Dreadnaught, New York Yacht Club.

Dear Sir: I hereby challenge your yacht Dreadnaught to to sail my yacht Enchantress on Tuesday, the 14th of October next, at twelve m., for the Cape May challenge cup, presented by Commodore J. G. Bennett to the New York Yacht Club, Course from Sandy Hook Lightship to Five Fathom Lightship. (Cape May) and return.

. Should you desire an extension of time please name any day to suit your own convenience up to the 1st of November next, although according to the tenure by which you hold said challenge cup, you are obliged to race any challenger during the racing season, that is, from the third Thursday in June to the third Thursday in October in each year, on a fifteen day's notice, or forfeit the cup to the challenger.

I shall, therefore, hold you to such race, and if you do not accept this challenge I shall go over the course on Tuesday, the 14th of October next, starting from Sandy Hook Lightship at twelve m., and claim said challenge cup, as I recognize no right in a holder of a challenge cup to refuse a challenge on any plea whatsoever.

As to the ocean race from Sandy Hook Lightship to Cowes (Isle of Wight), of which you spoke yesterday, I can but repeat that I am not willing to stake such a large sum as $25,000 on a race, but that, should it be agreeable to you or any member of any organized yacht club in the United States to challenge my yacht Enchantress for a race across the Atlantic—entrance $5,000 or less, play or pay—to be sailed from Sandy Hook Lightship at twelve m., on any day which may suit your or their convenience from the 8th till the 16th of November next, I will be most happy to accept any such challenge or challenges.

I should require notice thereof, however, before the 1st day of October next.

I send copy of this letter to Mr. Charles A. Minton, Secretary of. New York Yacht Club, to be placed by him on file, and and remain yours truly.   J. F. Loubat.

LETTER FROM MR. STOCKWELL.

To the Editor of the World.

Sir: Observing a statement in your columns this morning, purporting to come from me, I now enclose a copy of a letter addressed by me to the Regatta Committee of the New York Yacht Club; and I beg further to say that, my boat being laid up for the winter months, I have no intention of issuing or accepting any challenge whatever.

Yours, very respectfully,

A. B. Stockwell.

To the Regatta Committee of the New York Yacht Club.

Gentlemen: In calling your attention to a letter I have already addressed to you on the subject of the challenge cup claimed by the owner of the yacht Enchantress, I now hand you herewith my check for $1,000, being the amount of my private bet with that gentleman, and I rely on your courtesy to decide the question, if any, of the private bet, as well as of the challenge cup.

I desire here to reiterate that the only doubt in my mind is whether a challenge cup, which seems to me held by a peculiar tenure and subject to be won only by a bona-fide race between the yachts, can be acquired by a walk-over without contest. Should you decide that it can I shall most cheerfully acquiesce in your decision, which will then establish a technical claim on the part of the owner of the yacht Enchantress, but will not remove my feeling that common courtesy between yachtsmen should have induced him to accord me time to refit my vessel, and thus enhance his possession of the cup, which now can have no real value in his hands, as it represents no victory.

Yours, very respectfully,

Alden B. Stockwell.

The Evening Mail, New York, October 21, 1873.

MR. LOUBAT'S CHALLENGE.

The decision of the New York Yacht Club in regard to the challenge of the Dreadnaught by the Enchantress, which we publish elsewhere, relieves Mr. Loubat, the owner of the latter, from unjust imputations that were more or less extensively made upon his conduct as a yachtsman. The *World*, which criticised Mr. Loubat pretty severely, as we did, has gracefully retracted its charges against that gentleman, as we do. There are very few newspapers that can be conceded to be infallible or omniscient, and we have no ambition to be counted among the fortunately limited number of journals which never correct, or seek to atone for, their own mistakes.

The fact that Mr. Loubat's challenge was sent upon the 22d of September materially changes the situation, as it was stated to us by gentlemen who ought to be well informed. He. is naturally sensitive to the criticisms made from this mistaken report of the facts—as any honorable gentleman would be—and we are glad to rectify, so far as we can, the false impression produced by what we said without a full knowledge of the case. Mr. Loubat has acted honorably, and the better public opinion, for which he should most care, will do him full justice.

The New York Herald, New York, October 24, 1873.

NEW YORK YACHT CLUB.

Important Meeting—the Question Regarding the Cape May Challenge Cup Amicably Settled—New Signals adopted.

The New York Yacht Club held a regular meeting last evening, at its rooms in Twenty-seventh street, Vice Commodore William P. Douglas in the chair.

The following gentlemen were proposed and accepted as members:—John A. Barnham, Jr., George W. M. Sturgis and A. Lumley.

The report on the classification of yachts was then laid over.

Mr. Talboys moved that the reports of the Committee on summer races at Newport and elsewhere, be accepted without reading and ordered on file, and that the thanks of the club be tendered to the committee.   Passed.

Some changes were then proposed in the by-laws providing for the election of a permanent yearly Regatta Committee, instead of the temporary Regatta Committee only empowered to act during the June regatta.   Mr. Minton explained what was to be gained by the change, and the amendment to the by-laws was passed.

THE CAPE MAY CHALLENGE CUP.

The following letter was read :—

UNION CLUB, NEW YORK, Oct. 22, 1873.

WILLIAM P. DOUGLAS, Esq., *Vice-Commodore and Acting Commodore of the New York Yacht Club :—*

SIR—I cannot but express to you my regret that the New York Yacht Club should hitherto have shown such indifference to the unworthy attacks made upon me—one of its captains.

I now most respectfully beg to say that if it should take no steps to ascertain how my letter of the 12th inst. to Captain Stockwell should have found its way into the columns of the New York World of the 14th inst., and given rise to various unfounded charges in that and other papers, which have since been so handsomely retracted by their editors, it will then be a grave question with me what should be my future conduct in the matter.

The Regatta Committee, as you are aware, have but justly awarded me the Cape May challenge cup, but pending the club's action, I place it in your hands as I will not inscribe on it the name of the Enchantress without the fullest endorsement of the New York Yacht Club, to which I have the honor to belong,   I remain, etc.,

J. F. LOUBAT,
Captain of the Yacht Enchantress, N. Y. Y. C.

THE DECISION OF THE REGATTA COMMITTEE SUSTAINED.

A lengthy discussion then followed as to what course should be taken regarding this letter. Almost all the members spoke upon the question, and three resolutions were offered, two of them being somewhat too personal to be carried. The discussion was at one moment quite excited. At length the following resolution was proposed by Mr. G. G. Haven :—

Resolved, That the action of the Regatta Committee is fully endorsed and approved by the club, but that in the absence of any specific charge against any member of the club they do not feel empowered to investigate the authorship of any newspaper article, while they consider Mr. Loubat fully justified in accepting and retaining the cup as honorably and fairly won.

The resolution was unanimously carried.

The action of the Regatta Committee was to award the cup to Mr. Loubat as spoken of in his letter. It was also stated that the private bet of $1,000 had been sent by Mr. Stockwell to the Regatta Committee to hand to Mr. Loubat.

On vote the Club adopted Caston's night signals, Messrs. Stuyvesant, Bend and Colgate being appointed a committee to revise the code of signals.

A WINTER RENDEZVOUS IN GEORGIA.

A proposition was received from a Mr. Arkwright, of Savannah, Ga., giving the club a tract of land at a watering place near that city for the purpose of making it a winter rendezvous. The proposition was accepted and the thanks of the club tendered to Mr. Arkwright.

AN UNACCEPTED RESIGNATION.

The following letter was read from the Vice Commodore:—
C. A. Minton, Esq.:—

Dear Sir:—I beg, through you, to tender my resignation of the office of Vice-Commodore of the N. Y. Y. C. While naturally reluctant to resign so honorable a position, I feel it my duty to do so, inasmuch as I am persuaded that the flag officers of the club should always be active members. For two years

back the Sappho has not been in these waters, and it is very un-
certain if I shall put her in commission next summer. While
placing my resignation in your hands I desire to thank the yacht
owners for the honor which they conferred on me in electing
me as their Vice Commodore, and to assure them that, although
relieved from office, my interest in the welfare of the club shall
never flag. W. P. DOUGLAS.

Oct. 23, 1873.

It was moved that Mr. Douglas be requested to reconsider his
action and to withdraw his letter. Mr. Douglas did so, after
some hesitation, and shortly after tendered to the club the
die for the new medal, which was struck some time since in com-
memoration of the victory of the America in winning the Queen's
Cup. The gift was accepted with thanks.

The meeting then adjourned.

The New York Times, New York, October 24, 1873.

THE NEW YORK YACHT CLUB.

A regular meeting of the New York Yacht Club was
held last night at the club-house, Madison Avenue and Twenty-
seventh street, Vice-Commodore William P. Douglass in the
chair. After the ordinary routine business had been transacted
and a number of new members had been admitted, the following
letter from Mr. Loubat was read: (*See page* 129.)

The reading of the letter was followed by an excited
discussion, in which various theories respecting the publication
of Mr. Loubat's letter were rehearsed. While some of the
members were in favor of investigating the matter and appoint-
ing a committee for that purpose, the majority felt that Mr.
Loubat should rest satisfied with the retractions which, according to his letter, had been made in the newspapers. One
member indignantly repudiated the suggestion that the members
of the club should act like a body of detectives and try to find
out who supplied certain information to the newspapers—a

course entirely beneath the dignity of gentlemen and true yachts-men.

Mr. Talboys said that he had conversed with Mr. Stockwell on the subject, and that gentleman denied that he had ever sup-plied any information to any newspaper, and declared that he had been in no way concerned in the publication of the letter in question.

Mr. Krebs presented the following :

Whereas, Mr. Stockwell having disclaimed any agency in procuring the publication in the *World* of the letter to which Mr. Loubat refers, or in the publication of any of the newspaper articles of which Mr. Loubat complains,

Resolved, The opinion of the meeting is that there is no rea-son why Mr. Loubat should hesitate to accept the cup, and inscribe upon it the name of his yacht.

Mr. Talboys said that he hoped the resolution would not pass. It was not right that a document which was to be placed among the archives of the New York Yacht Club should con-tain the name of Mr. Stockwell in connection with the charges alluded to. Mr. Stockwell was not present to speak for himself, and he thought it was an injustice to him to pass such a resolu-tion.

The resolution was lost.

Mr. Bend proposed the following :

Resolved, That the Secretary notify Mr. Loubat that the club approves the action of the Regatta Committee in awarding to the Enchantress the Cape May challenge cup, but that the club does not consider it within its province to notice the publi-cation of the letter of Mr. Stockwell.

A vote was called for, and the resolution declared lost. After some further animated discussion the following resolution, proposed by G. G. Haven, was unanimously adopted :

Resolved, That the action of the Regatta Committee is fully endorsed and approved by the club, but in the absence of any specific charge against any member of the club, they do not feel empowered to investigate the authorship of any newspaper article, while they consider Mr. Loubat fully justified in accepting and retaining the cup as honorably and fairly won

This ended the discussion of the Loubat-Stockwell dispute, and the meeting proceeded to transact other business.

A plot of ground in Savannah, offered to the club gratuitously as a winter rendezvous by Mr. Arkwright, was accepted, and a committee appointed to draw up resolutions expressing to Mr. Arkwright the thanks of the club.

It was resolved that Coston's night signals be adopted as the signals of the club, and that a committee, consisting of Messrs. Stuyvesant, Bend and Colgate be appointed to revise the present book of signals. A Mr. Wolfe, of Southampton, England, was, at his own request, appointed flag-maker to the club.

A letter from Vice-Commodore Douglass, tendering his resignation, on the ground that his yacht, the Sappho, had not been in these waters for two years, and that he considered all officers of the club should be active members, was read. At the earnest request of the members, Mr. Douglas consented to withdraw his resignation. A magnificent gold die and medal of the club was presented by Vice-Commodore Douglas, and thankfully accepted. The meeting then adjourned.

The World, New York, October 24, 1873.

NEW YORK YACHT CLUB MATTERS.

A Letter from Mr. Loubat—The Difficulty Arranged—A Resignation Made and Withdrawn.

A regular meeting of the New York Yacht Club was held last night at its rooms corner Madison Avenue and Twenty-seventh Street. Vice-Commodore William P. Douglas presided, and considerable routine business of a private nature was transacted. Charles A. Minton, the Secretary of the Club, read the following communication from J. F. Loubat, who had recently been awarded the challenge cup by the Regatta Committee and whose action in the matter of the challenge to the Dreadnaught in her then disabled condition was the subject of comment in yachting circles. (*See page* 129.)

The reading of this communication gave rise to considerable discussion, which brought out the statement that as soon as the Committee had decided the race in favor of the Enchantress Captain Stockwell forwarded to the Committee the cup with the private prize of $1,000 previously arranged. Mr. Talboys said that Captain Stockwell had disclaimed to him all knowledge of how the letter had reached the newspaper in question, and the following compromise resolution was offered by G. G. Haven-and it was unanimously adopted:

Resolved, That the action of the Regatta Committee is fully indorsed and approved by the Club, but that in the absence of any specific charge against any member of the Club they do not feel empowered to investigate the authorship of any newspaper article, while they consider Mr. Loubat fully justified in accepting and retaining the cup as honorably and fairly won.

A motion was then made that the Club acknowledge the communication of Mr. Arkwright, of Savannah, Ga., who offered to give all the property in Savannah harbor that was required for a winter rendezvous. A vote of thanks was accorded him, and Messrs. Wright, Bend and Johnson were appointed a committee to consider the expediency of accepting the offer. Mr. Bend moved that a committee be appointed to revise the code of signals of the Club and report at the next meeting. It was adopted, and Messrs. Bend, Stuyvesant and Colgate were appointed such committee.

The Secratary then read the following letter of resignation from Vice-Commodore Douglas, of the yacht Sappho: (*See pages* 130, 131.)

Rear Commodore Kingsland rose, and sincerely hoped that the resignation would be withdrawn. After passing a few fitting words on the action of Commodore Douglas, he moved that the Club request Mr. Douglas to withdraw it. The motion was adopted with cheers, and Commodore Douglas then gracefully withdrew his resignation, thanking the members for their flattering action.   The Club then adjourned.

CHAPTER VI.

MR. LOUBAT'S GIFT TO THE PILOTS.

The New York Herald, New York, October 26, 1873.

YACHTING.

Generous Donations by Mr. J. F. Loubat, of the Enchantress, to the Pilot's
Benevolent Funds of this Port.

Mr. J. F. Loubat, of the yacht Enchantress, in view of Mr.
Stockwell sending him his check for $1,000, as a winner of a
private bet between the Enchantress and Dreadnaught, in the
Cape May challenge cup contest, has made a charitable disposition of the amount, and more, he has added his own check for a
like sum, the whole to be credited to two of the pilots' benevolent associations of this port. The following report from official
source tells the story:—

Mr. A. B. Stockwell, of the yacht Dreadnaught, a few days
ago sent to the Regatta Committee of the New York Yacht Club
his check for $1,000, with authority to hand the same to Mr. J.
F. Loubat, of the yacht Enchantress, in payment of the private
bet between the two gentlemen upon the result of the recent
challenge for the Cape May challenge cup. The committee
sent the check to Mr. Loubat and received from him the following communication:—

UNION CLUB, NEW YORK, Oct. 25, 1873.

FLETCHER WESTRAY, ESQ., *Chairman N. Y. Y. C. Regatta Committee:*—

SIR.—I beg to acknowledge the receipt of your official communication of the 23d inst., with check of Mr. A. B. Stockwell for $1,000, our bet upon the race you decided won by the Enchantress. Enclosed please find that check endorsed by me to the order of the Regatta Committee of the N. Y. Y. C., as well as my own for the same amount. I beg the Regatta Committee to hand one to the Treasurer of the Sandy Hook Pilots' Charity Fund (care of J. W. Avery, No. 309 Water Street), and the other to the Treasurer of the New York and New Jersey Pilots' Benevolent Society, corner of South and Fulton Streets.

I remain, sir, very respectfully,

Your obedient servant,

J. F. LOUBAT,

Captain Yacht Enchantress N. Y. Y. C.

The New York Herald, New York, October 29, 1873.

THE PILOTS' BENEVOLENT FUND.

Acknowledging the Receipt of Mr. J. F. Loubat's Generous Donations—Letters of Thanks.

The annexed letters, acknowledging the receipt of the generous donations recently made by Mr. J. F. Loubat, of the yacht Enchantress, to the benevolent funds of the pilot organizations of this city, tell their own story :—

NEW YORK, Oct. 27, 1873.

CAPTAIN J. F. LOUBAT, *Yacht Enchantress, N. Y. Y. C.*

DEAR SIR—We have this day received from the N. Y. Y. C. Regatta Committee your check for the sum of $1,000, as a donation to the New York and Sandy Hook Pilots' Charitable Fund, and beg leave to submit the following extract from the minutes of the Board of Trustees of said organization :—

At a meeting of the trustees of the New York and Sandy

Hook Pilots' Charitable Fund, held this day, at their rooms, No. 309 Water street, it was unanimously resolved that the thanks of this association be tendered to Captain J. F. Loubat, of the yacht Enchantress, N. Y. Y. C., for his generous donation to our fund.

And we, as officers of said fund, beg leave to convey to you our heartfelt acknowledgment for your liberal gift, coming, as it does, when we greatly need it, and can assure you that it will be a source of much gratification to the numerous pensioners on our fund.

With our best wishes for your future welfare, we remain, yours, very respectfully,

H. Harbinson, *President.*

Walter Brewer, *Secretary.*

New York, Oct. 28, 1873.

To the Editor of the Herald :—

The members of the New York and New Jersey Pilots' Benevolent Association gratefully acknowledge the receipt of $1,000, generously donated by Captain Loubat, of the yacht Enchantress, N. Y. Y. C., the first intimation of which we received through the columns of the *Herald.*

Henry Devere, *Secretary.*

New York, Nov. 11, 1873.

Captain J. F. Loubat, *Yacht Enchantress, N. Y. Y. C.*

Dear Sir—Continued absence from the city and a misunderstanding on the part of my associates, will, I trust, be accepted by you as sufficient apology for not acknowledging earlier your generous donation of one thousand dollars to the New York and New Jersey Pilots' Benevolent Association.

I am instructed by the trustees to convey to you the sincere thanks of the Association for your liberal gift at this opportune time, having recently lost one of our members, and a large portion of your present goes to his orphan child for it's maintenance

Trusting that your sea voyage will be pleasant and that you will safely return with renewed vigor, and that the Enchantress will sustain her well-earned reputation.

I remain, yours very respectfully,

(Signed) Henry Devere, *Secretary.*

CHAPTER VII.

THE ENCHANTRESS GOES TO COWES.

New York, October 29, 1873.

Captain J. F. Loubat, Yacht Enchantress, N. Y. Y. C.

Dear Sir:

I am requested by the pilots of the port to say that they will, with great pleasure, furnish your vessel on her voyage to sea with a pilot, *free of charge.*

Please send me word when she will be ready for sea.

Very respectfully yours,
John W. Avery,
309 Water Street, N. Y.

The New York Times, New York, November 27, 1873.

STATEN ISLAND.

Mr. Loubat's yacht Enchantress has been at anchor off Stapleton for the last three weeks. She is undergoing a thorough overhauling in rigging and spars, and will have a new suit of sails, preparatory to making her European trip. She is expected to sail early in the present month.

The New York Herald, New York, November 9, 1873.

YACHTING.

THE ENCHANTRESS TO CROSS THE ATLANTIC.

The schooner yacht Enchantress, New York Yacht Club,

will leave her anchorage off Stapleton, Staten Island, this morning, about eleven oclock, for a trip across the Atlantic. She will proceed to Cowes, where Mr. Loubat will join her as soon as his business in New York will give him an opportunity. A tugboat with the owner and a few friends, will accompany the yacht outside the Sandy Hook Lightship, when adieus will be spoken and wishes for a safe and pleasant voyage heartily extended to all on board. She is in excellent trim for such a trip, and no doubt will arrive out in good season. Captain Fairchild is in command.

The Spirit of the Times, New York, December 27, 1873.

The schooner yacht Enchantress arrived at Cowes on Dec. 1 from New York. She left here on the 9th ult., and thus made the passage in twenty-two days. The Enchantress experienced variable weather, westerly winds however prevailing. The dingy is reported to have been stove in the davits, a contingency the reverse of unlikely to happen to a boat carried thus at sea. The Enchantress will ship an English crew, and fit out at once for the Mediterranean.

The Field, London, February 23, 1874.

AMERICAN YACHTS.

Mr. Fish, the yacht designer, of New York, arrived at Cowes in the steamship Hermann this week, having been requested by Mr. Loubat, the owner of the American yacht Enchantress, now lying in the Medina, to come to England, and carry out whatever improvements he thought necessary in order to bring her out as a racer this season. Mr. Fish is well known for the success with which he altered the Sappho, and made her one of the fastest yachts ever sailed. We understand that immediate steps will be taken to put the Enchantress in racing trim. Mr. Fish brought over with him in the Hermann a new suit of cotton-racing sails for her.

Bell's Life in London, London, May 2, 1874.

Whether the American schooner Enchantress, now being lengthened at Cowes, will join in the open matches, will only be decided after a trial. She is being drawn out some 10ft. aft, and is to have a lead keel and bustlings over garboards, after the English fashion. Should these alterations be successfully carried out, we anticipate another revolution in the yachting world, as there is little doubt that she is capable of being made faster than the Sappho, and consequently able to tackle any English schooner. Her builder, Mr. R. Fish, is superintending alterations and Mr. J. White is carrying out the work. The yacht is in the Medina Docks, at Cowes, and is well worthy a visit.

Bell's Life in London, London, May 30, 1874.

THE SCHOONER YACHT ENCHANTRESS.

The following letter appears in the *Field* :—

Sir.—Perhaps one of the most interesting experiments we have ever witnessed in yacht construction is now being made in Mr. John White's graving dock, by Mr. Fish, an American yacht designer. Mr. Fish is, I understand, a self-made man, and he appears to be wonderfully alive to picking up and utilising ideas, from whatever source they may come, providing they are good for anything. For many years he informs me he has been thinking out and experimentalising on the proper form of a midship section for a clipper yacht. Of course it is well-known that on this section depends the whole of the ultimate form of a vessel, and whether she will carry sail, and as Marrett says, "rolling, direct resistance, lateral resistance, and stability are affected by the form of the midship section;" but prior to this question the form or shape which would offer least resistance and most stability in passing through the water had to be considered. This, after a series of experiments, Mr. Fish decided to be that of a cone, pointed each end, similar to the cigar ships which the Messrs. Winan have made us southerners familiar with. The first experiment with the cone was a decided success, so much so that he at once adopted that principle, and fully carried it out with a deep hollow bottom (in fact, reversing the cone below water instead of putting on a deep keel) in building the Enchantress, the principle making the vessel much stronger and enabling her to carry her weights much lower than would have been the case with a deep keel only. To carry it down in the V shape was to compel the carrying a large quantity of ballast to overcome the resistance of her sails, and to keep down the tendency which her bilge would have to float whenever the vessel heeled over.

All this Mr. Fish took into consideration, and the result is the Enchantress, which he built in New York, 1871, for Mr. George Lorillard for a cruising and sea-going yacht, which she has thoroughly proved herself to be, having crossed the Atlantic five times at all seasons of the year and cruised in the Mediterranean for two seasons, carrying all the while her immense spars; and now that she is in dock I do not notice the least sign of weakness or wrinkling of her copper in any part, which proves her to be well put together, also showing that her form is peculiarly easy in a sea way in rough weather. To give any person an idea of her construction without lines is a difficult matter; but, to commence with, she is unlike any yacht which our builders have ever sent out, her midship section being a true ogee. From there she begins to taper off to each end, so that her entrance and her leaving the water appear to be perfection, and, with very little ballast, her sail-carrying power will be enormous, as directly she begins to heel over, her bilge, instead of pushing up from below, and so heeling her still more, will be pushed down by the weight of water in the hollow, and will consequently render her more stable. The alterations now being made in her at Mr. John White's establishment are, first, that of lengthening by the stern thirteen feet, as Mr. Fish thought she was far too abruptly finished there to carry out his idea in perfection, which, by the alteration now being made in her, appears

to be exactly what was required.   Since she has been in the dock
a number of scientific gentlemen have visited her, and the criticisms appear to be generally very favorable.   Her principal
dimensions we may quote as under :

	Feet.		Feet.
Length between perpendicu-lars.	128	Ditto masthead	11
Ditto over all	144	Length maintopmast	52
Ditto on load water-line	120	Ditto of foremast	85
Beam extreme	24	Ditto deck to hounds	64
Ditto on load line	24	Ditto masthead	10
Depth of hold	11	Ditto foretopmast	48
Displacement, English meas. 350 tons.		Ditto main gaff	50
SPARS.		Ditto main boom	82
		Ditto fore gaff	26
Length of mainmast	91	Ditto main topsail yard	44
Ditto deck to hounds	69	Ditto topsail yard	35

At the present moment she is in a very forward state, considering the short time she has been in hand, and the amount
of work required to be done in lengthening a yacht of this
description, as she had to be opened so far back to avoid anything like a too sudden alteration in her contour.   Below, her
accommodations for the crew are materially improved ; the fittings for the men, which were put up in America, have been
knocked away, and, without entrenching any more on the accommodations aft, quite double the room has been made for the
crew, which is a great desideratum.   Aft the fittings will not be
touched, except to be redecorated.   We believe that Mr. Loubat,
who now owns her, intends sailing as many matches as he can
with her this season ; and there is no reason to doubt but that
she will prove herself to be very fast.   The uniform success
which has always attended the efforts of Mr. Fish in building or
altering yachts give confidence that the Enchantress will be another success.

We should very much like to see our American friends do
something now in the cutter line.   Cutters are essentially English yachts ; schooners we have had very fast, very weatherly,
and possessed of all the qualities of good yachts, but the Americans always beat us in schooners, without any of our schooners

can go in and beat the Enchantress, which is a question unsolved at the present time; but cutters have never yet been built by any nation to equal our forty, sixty, and one hundred tonners, and here is another field open for our American brethren, who, we prophesy, will not be long before they commission Mr. Fish to try his skill in that way. The Enchantress will be commanded by Captain Poland, who was with Sir Edward Sullivan some years, and last year in the Shamrock. VECTIS.

The Field, London, July 4, 1874.

The Enchantress, Mr. Loubat, is now between the piers at the entrance to Mr. John White's graving dock, and will be ready for sea next week. We have now four American schooners at Cowes—the Enchantress, the Sappho (now lying in the harbor, Mr. Douglas, her owner, not seeming to wish to fit out this season), the Faustine (now in the roadstead), and the Viking (having a refit at the present moment, all of which, excepting the Sappho) may be expected to take part in any races they can enter for.

CHAPTER VIII.

AN INTERNATIONAL YACHT RACE,

SOCIETE DES REGATES DU HAVRE.

SATURDAY, 25TH JULY, AT 7 A. M., PRECISELY.

MATCH FOR YACHTS OF ALL NATIONS OF 10 TONS AND UPWARDS FROM HAVRE ROADS TO SEA AND BACK.

Length of Course about fifty miles, time allowance Fiftcen seconds per ton.

1st Prize—A work of art (Grand Prize of the City of Havre), value F 2,500.

2nd Prize—A work of art value F 1,000 and a Marine Glass.

3rd Prize (to the first French yacht)—A work of art and a telescope, value F 1,000.

N. B. The yawls and schooners shall be allowed to enter as follows, viz: Yawls at $\frac{3}{4}$ and schooners at $\frac{3}{5}$ their tonnage measured according to the rule of the Societe des Regates du Havre.

EXTRACT OF INSTRUCTIONS AND REGULATIONS.

First. The races will be run according to the sailing regulations of the Societe des Regates du Havre, the decision of the Committee shall in all cases be final.

The Sailing Committee reserve to themselves the right of altering any of the arrangements or regulations that they may deem needful ; copies of regulations and instructions may be obtained at the time of entry, by application to the Hon. Secretary of the society.

Second. Time shall be allowed for difference of tonnage, according to the scale of the Society.

Third. Three boats to start or no race, the third prize will not be given unless three French yachts sail the course.

Fourth. Yachts to anchor in a line as directed by the sailing Committee.

Fifth. To weigh anchor and start by the following signals, which must be strictly complied with—viz: A gun will be fired as a signal to prepare ; after an interval of one minute a second gun will be fired as the signal to weigh anchor and start.

Sixth. Vessels may set their mainsails, but neither foresails, headsails nor topsails until after the signal to start.

Seventh. No restriction as to canvas.

Eighth. Yachts may anchor during the races, but before starting again, must weigh their anchors.

Ninth. The vessels must leave all mark boats including the winning markboat on the starboard side.

These boats will have a red flag flying at the masthead by day, and by night there will be three red lamps hung in a triangle.

If dark, the yachts are to fire rockets, and must past close to the markboat to report their names.

Tenth. Yachts sailing in matches shall carry their racing colors at the main-masthead.

Eleventh. The Owner, Captain or Master of every yacht entered or some duly authorized person, shall attend at the Hotel-de-Ville on the day preceding the race (exclusive of Sunday) at 9 P. M. for the purpose of receiving instructions and a chart, relative to the course to be sailed.

Twelfth. Entrance fee, not returnable, F 1 per ton. Minimum F 25. Maximum F 75.

NOTICE.

Application for entrance may be previously made by letter to the Hon. Secretary, L. Mandrot, Esq., 31, quai d' Orleans, Havre.

Entries to close for Monday's race 20th July, on Saturday 18th July at noon.

Post entries at double fees not returnable up to 9 P. M. on the day preceding the race.

Entries to close, for Saturday's race 25th July, on Thursday 23d July at 9 P. M.

Post entries at double fees, not returnable, up to 9 P. M. on the preceding race.

The Regatta ball will take place at Frascatis on 18th of July at 10 P. M.

The other annual regattas sailing and rowing matches, will be held on the 19th and 20th July at 1 P. M.

The prizes will be distributed in the grand salon at Frascatis on Monday 20th of July at 9 P. M.

By order of the Committee.

HAVRE March 15th 1874.

<table>
<tr><td>L. MANDROT,
Hon. Secretary.</td><td>Ed. WINSLOW,
President.</td></tr>
</table>

1874—VILLE DU HAVRE.—36eme Anneé

SOCIETE DES REGATES DU HAVRE.

SAMEDI 25 JUILLET 1874, A SEPT HEURES DU MATIN.

COURSE POUR BATEAUX DE PLAISANCE DE TOUTES NATIONS.

De la rade du Havre au large et retour. Au Chronometre avec compensation de temps de 15 secondes par tonneau. Parcours : environ 50 miles marins.

1er Prix. Un Objet D'art, Grand Prix de la Ville du Havre, Valeur F 2,500. 2me. Prix. Offert par la Societe des Regates du Havre. Valeur F 1,000

Et une Jumelle offerte par le Ministre de la Marine.

Prix au premier Bateau de Plaisance Francais, Offert par la Societe des Regates du Havre, Valeur F 1,000.

Et une Longue--vue offerte par le Ministre de la Marine.

A moins de trois Concurrents Francais, ce Prix ne sera pas delivre.

INSCRIPTIONS :

1 Octonia......Lion blanc sur fond bleu......goëlette Anglaise,
Wm. Turner, 14 Tons.

2 Corinne...Rouge et damier bleu et blanc horizontal, au centre
goëlette anglaise, N. Wood, 122 Tons.

3 Faustine........Rouge avec raies blanches diagonales.......
goëlette américaine, G. Peabody Russell, 74 Tons.

4 Hirondelle.........Hirondelle verte sur fond jaune..........
côtre dandy anglais, W. C. Quilter, 60 Tons.

5 Comte-de-Chambord...Blanc avec carré bleu...côtre Francais,
Cardon, 22 Tons.

6 Scapin.....Bleu et blanc horizontal.....côtre Francais, Baqué,
24¼ Tons.

7 Mésange.....Damier bleu et blanc.....côtre Francais, Le Roy
d'Etiolles, 36½ Tons.

8 Panthère...Damier jaune et bleu...côtre Francais, Crandalle,
10½ Tons.

9 Florinda......Damier Rouge et noir......côtre dandy Anglais,
Wm. Jessop, 102½ Tons.

10 Egeria...Orange et bleu...goëlette anglaise, John Mulholland

11 Enchantress.Bleu, blanc, bleu horizontal.goëlette Américaine,
J. F. Loubat, 200 Tons.

12 Gertrude.....Jaune clair et bleu en diagonale.....côtre dandy
Anglais, J. G. Watt, 48½ Tons.

13 Verveine....Rouge avec une boule blanche....côtre Francais,
Legru, 17 Tons.

14 Gertrude..Rouge avec une boule blanche.côtre dandy Anglais,
Langtry, 60½ Tons.

Le Secrétaire du Comité d'Administration,

L. MANDROT,

Le Président du Comité d'Administration,

E. WINSLOW,

Le Président d'honneur,

E. BIGOT DE LA ROBILLARDIRE,
Maire du Havre, Chevalier de la Légion-d'Honneur.

Bell's Life, London, August 1, 1874.

SOCIETE DES REGATES DU HAVRE.

It was unfortunate for Havre that after having been the means of bringing together several of the most notable English racing yachts, and the American schooners Enchantress and Faustine, the weather should have been of a character such as to make sailing results wholly unreliable as a guage of racing abilities. In other respects, however, the last day of the Societe des Regates du Havre was as pleasant as its predecessors, and went far towards toning down many of the annoyances and impositions to which yachtsmen are subjected in French ports. We heard more than one owner affirm it would be their last visit until some of the existing regulations and penalties, as far as respected yachts were repealed, and really some customary forms are unnecessarily vexatious and frivolous. There was great excitement consequent upon the meeting of the Enchantress and Cetonia, when, on Thursday, these vessels were known to have arrived in the Roads, and then the Gwendolin and the Florinda's presence contributed additional interest, the Corinne being little thought of as the "coming ship;" seeing that in every match she previously competed in she had shown lamentably inferior in speed to the Cetonia. We bore in mind, however, a display of reaching ability in the first half of the race from Dover to Boulogne, and conjured up a day in store when she might get suitable weather. Few, however, were prepared to see Ratsey's last so much improved, but unshipping tanks and a little additional lead has worked wonders. We were told that she would display in a breeze greatly increased stability, and for this *on dit* without reserve there would have been obviously accountable reasons. The day was a somewhat remarkable one, the wind for the first half being taken fresher by the Enchantres and the Corinne—the weather line, while in running back, the lee line —had more wind than the Enchantress; the latter, consequently, never having had a chance of showing her true form, added to which, her throat halliard iron on the main gaff gave out, and delayed her quite 10 minutes, but she afterwards reached fast enough in the same streak of wind as the Corinne to give an insight of the possession of marvellous speed on that particular point of sailing. Like other long vessels of the American model, she made a sorry show with the wind dead on the mast, this being simply to be accounted for through the vast amount of friction on her large submerged body; whilst with reference to her weatherly qualities, it may be taken as demonstrated that on this point she will never be able to compensate by speed in head-reaching for a palpable deficiency in weatherliness. The Oetonia and the Florinda did not show by any means to advantage. Every one knows Mr. Turner's schooner, by reason of being somewhat under-canvassed, to be no great flyer in light winds, but zephyrs are the Florinda's *forte*, yet she sailed in anything but brilliant form. The Faustine, a most objectionable vessel to the eye in point of shape, figured wretchedly badly, and the Flying Cloud, in her best day, would have made a humiliating exhibition of the angular-looking American. The two Gertrudes did as well as the wind favored them, and the Hirondelle went apparently as fast as allowed to. The conditions, &c., are appended, viz. :—

Match, open to yachts of all nations of 10 tons and upwards; course from markboat off Havre Harbor piers to a markboat moored in a W. N. W. direction, and returning to a markboat moored about one mile N. N. W. of Cape Le Heve, distance about 45 miles; time race, 15 sec. per ton; tonnage computed according to the society's rule, viz :—The length taken from stem to stern post, and breadth and depth at extremes, all in metres; the length is multiplied by the depth and the product by quarter breadth, the whole being divided by four to find tonnage. Three prizes, viz :—First (Grand Prize of the City of Havre) a work of art valued at F 2,500 second F 1,000 third (to the first French yacht of any rig) F 1,000 in addition to the above the owner of the first vessel was presented with a pair of marine glasses, and the owner of the second vessel with a telescope. The entries, American and English, were :

		TONS,	
YACHT.	RIG.	FRENCH.	OWNER.
Cetonia	schooner	148	Mr. W. Turner.
Corinne	schooner	122	Mr. N. Wood.
Gwendolin	schooner	—	Major Ewing.
Egeria	schooner	—	Mr. J. Mulholland.
Enchantress	schooner	200	Mr. J. F. Loubat.
Faustine	schooner	74	Mr. J. P. Russell.
Gertrude	yawl	60½	Mr. E. Langtry.
Gertrude	yawl	48½	Mr. J. F. Watt.
Hirondelle	yawl	60	Mr. W. C. Quilter.
Florinda	yawl	102½	Mr. W. Jessop.

Yawls sailing at three-fourths, and schooners at three-fifths their tonnage. The Gwendolin, although in harbor, did not start, and the Egeria, not having arrived from Ireland, was another absentee.

Seven o'clock A. M. would be thought the height of lunacy by the metropolitan clubs for starting a match over a course of about 40 miles, but the Havrais are an early rising people, and kept exemplary punctuality in starting the match of July 25. The yachts were out of dock at 5, and jilting about in readiness at 6:45. There was to be, according to French custom, a drift of 15 minutes after starting gun, wherewith to cross the line, and then into the book of reckoning went time, Dr. or Cr. according as the race was commenced by each, and to be added or deducted as the case might be at the finish of the match. With a light balloon topsail breeze from the N. N. W. we thus logged them:—

START.

	H. M. S.		H. M. S.
Gertrude (48½)	7 7 45	Corinne	7 11 15
Enchantress	7 9 46	Florinda	7 13 30
Hirondelle	7 10 0	Faustine	7 14 30
Cetonia	7 10 5	Gertrude (60½)	7 20 0

With a W. by N. ½ N. course, on a N. N. W. breeze, the wind was on the starboard beam, and the Enchantress must have had her head up to about N. W. soon after start, for the purpose of having weather guage of the rest should the breeze narrow.

On the other hand Gertrude (Watt) headed as far to leeward of her course, or about W., while the Cetonia would have followed the Enchantress in luffing out into a fresher breeze to windward, had the Hirondelle not been just in her wind at the opportune time. The latter, who looked as if her sails had been given a douche bath, perhaps showed a little judgment in leaving the heavy weights and wiping away in chase of her class—the lesser Gertrude—who was now spinning along, with the mouth of the Seine well open, and, keeping the shore aboard, leading vessel. The Corinne picked the breezy track in the Enchantress's trail, and was quickly upon the Cetonia's starboard beam, with the Florinda in a position that about split the distance between the two English schooners, the Faustine and the Gertrude (60½) making a waiting race of it, Mr. Langtry's craft losing a minute or two over and above the allowed quarter of an hour. Balloon-topsails and staysails, jib topsails and big jibs were carried on all but the Cetonia and the Florinda, who had working topsails, the two American vessels spread of sail beggaring description compared with the rest. At 7:30 the Enchantress and the Corinne led weather line, with a palpable advantage in amount of breeze over the Cetonia and the Florinda, while away on the lee beam of the Cetonia, a mile distant, was the Gertrude, reaching fast, with the Hirondelle far in her wake, but both with less of the motive power in their sails than the vessels further north. Two miles astern were the Faustine and the Gertrude (Langtry), bringing up a clipping burst to what the rest had. This was obvious from the style in which the Gertrude was heeling up, but the wee Yankee, with her delta topsails, had a good deal of the sentry-box upright carriage. The wind was free enough, and there should not have been a difference in so short a space of water, but the Enchantress certainly had more than either the Cetonia or the Florinda, while the Corinne planted herself at 7:35 right on the Cetonia's weather beam. Settling at 7:40 to a nice steady balloon topsail breeze, a weak spot in the iron work of the Enchantress's gaff brought the sail with a run down at the throat, and it was ten minutes—and smart work too—before the mainsail was again set up and balloon topsail resheeted. In this opening the Cetonia walked up on the Enchantress, and drew level with her port quarter, although three-quarters of a mile to the southward, the Corinne closing in to about half a mile of the American's wake, and being third vessel, the Florinda in the Cetonia's trail fourth, the Gertrude (Watt) fifth, Hirondelle sixth, Faustine seventh, and the other Gertrude whipping up with the little Scapin, going in very good form indeed, leading French yachts.

At 8 o'clock a little roll from seaward made us look for more wind, but it kept light and unsteady, until 9 o'clock, when the Corinne had reached past with the breeze on her beam very wide to windward of the Cetonia, now being second vessel to the Enchantress, a mile distant, the Cetonia was about 200 yards east of the Corinne, and the Florinda some three cables' lengths astern of the Cetonia, the others in same position, but the Hirondelle was being nearly played out by both the Faustine and Gertrude (Langtry), and then a quarter of an hour later certainly last vessel. Two miles from the markboat (that was discernible through the haze only a short time previously) the wind shortened, and the Enchantress screwed up to be certain of fetching her W. limit on starboard tack, and a little later on all came close-hauled. Nearing the mark the wind again freed slightly, but the weather-most boats, the Enchantress and Corinne, had a good bit the best of it, the northing giving the additional advantage of a free slant when round. The Enchantress made the most of her position, and showing great speed, even in so light a breeze, had an undeniably creditable lead, when she tacked to round the W. mark steamer 20 miles from Havre; the time of each staying being:—

	H.	M.	S.			H.	M.	S.
Enchantress	10	2	30	Gertrude 60½		10	44	0
Corinne	10	10	0	Faustine		10	48	0
Cetonia	10	15	45	Mesange		10	50	0
Florinda	10	20	40	Hirondelle		10	52	0
Gertrude 48½	10	41	0					

The wind was just abaft the port beam when they steadied for their course to the Le Heve mark, the Enchantress ran with two balloon topsails, balloon maintopmast-staysail and balloon-forestaysail, beside all lower canvas, the Corinne being similarly treated, but for some time appeared to have her foretopsail sheet adrift. The weather, which had been overcast with but occasional bursts of sun improved about 11 o'clock, but when the summer haze rolled away and the sun came out strong, the breeze lost heart, and now on the English craft spinnakers were set jib fashion, the American, with not so much wind as the Corinne and Cetonia, coming back very fast, until at 11:30 the stranger had lost position to the Corinne, and the Cetonia had also gone past her. Mr. Turner's vessel and the Corinne drew within hail, and the Florinda on being treated to her favorite jib, picked up her heels in vulgar haste and left the American flax pile as though brought up. With a rally of wind astern, the tail of the fleet rose their hulls on the leaders until the big Gertrude could be seen feathering at the stem, and the lesser American doing better with the ruck than on sailing west. The breeze towards noon drew round on to the quarter, and then spinnaker booms were dropped, and sails set square. The Corinne's fore-spinnaker, as jib, drawing well, and picking up a breeze at 12:30 that made the sheet tauten out, she with additional help of main spinnaker went fast away from the Cetonia, while the Florinda got into a vein that drew her up in under the Cetonia's beam, and lasted of sufficient strength to ramp her through the schooner's lee. An unaccountable burst at 1:30 put the Corinne double the distance, or about a mile and a half ahead of the Cetonia in a short space of time. Of course it was a little wind favor, but it obviously settled the destination of the prize, as the Florinda, although going again in her best form looked little like saving time on Mr. Wood's craft, and both were going far faster than either the Cetonia or the Enchantress. The latter towards the close ran up slightly on the Cetonia, but we saw enough of her to judge that down the wind there are a number of faster craft on this side ; but, perhaps, other than the untried Gosport frigates there is no tried vessel, the Sappho included, capable of reaching with Mr. Loubat's Enchantress. She was very well taken care of in the race, but, as we have said before, we attach but very little importance to the result of this match. The finish made the Corinne an easy winner, and the Florinda more particularly so of second prize, the little French cutter, Scapin, having revenge on the Mesange by winning her prize with a lot in hand. The times of arrival were :—

	H. M. S.		H. M. S.
*Corine	2 1 45	Gertrude (Langtry),	.2 49 0
†Florinda	2 12 30	Faustine	2 49 30
Cetonia	2 14 0	Hirondelle	.2 50 20
Enchantress	2 19 30	‡Scapin	2 50 30
Gertrude (Watt)	..2 46 0		

*Winner of £100, first prize, and marine glasses.
†Winner of £40, second prize, and telescope.
‡Winner of £40, for first French yacht.

The Field, London August 1, 1874.

SOCIÉTE DES REGATES DU HAVRE.

Saturday, July 25.

The good yachtsmen of Havre brought their regatta to a close on this 25th day of July; but the vessels that sailed for their prizes are to compete in another match across Channel on Monday. So far as we know, everyone is satisfied with the arrangements the Regatta Society has made, and the liberality displayed has been simply charming. However, the society has determined to go still farther, and next year promises three prizes of F 2000 each for " each rig," and a prix d'honneur of F 3000 for first yacht by classification. Such startling liberality will no doubt induce a large number of English yachts to flock to Havre.

The race to-day was mainly remarkable for the *debut* of the American yacht Enchantress, and if she were something like a Cetonia among Flying Clouds, her *entree* would be regarded with some interest. Allowing for her great size, she will no doubt be always a formidable competitor ; but it would be absurd to suppose that there is anything wonderful about her. She will always beat small vessels in breezes, just as the Sappho would ; but we should expect to see her pretty well tied up with such a weight of wind as a vessel like the Guinivere would have to haul down a reef in. The Cetonia got an exemplary beating from Corinne, but the beating was a little too much to be true. However, the Corinne ran and reached right well, and she may cause some anxiety on board Egeria and Pantomime ere the season is out. In dismissing the doings of the Havre Regatta Society this year, we can only re-echo a feeling we have heard expressed on board most of the yachts present, that the arrangements for the matches were in many instances superior to those of English clubs, and that the liberality as to prizes was such as not only to call forth satisfaction, but astonishment, considering the flying visits the yachts make to the place.

The starting hour was appointed for 7 A. M., and it was early on tide (5:30) when the fleet came out from the floating docks into the roads.

The weather on the previous night had been overcast and wore an unsettled look, but, after a thunderstorm, cleared away and somewhat brightened up. With the first of the morning a thick haze rolled in from the N. W., bringing a light, chilly air from that quarter, and it looked all over like a day for flying kites. Enchantress showed her hand by setting her two balloon topsails, huge flying jib, and staysail; and her competitor Faustine copied this sail plan to the letter. Corinne set 'main balloon-topsail, the rest of the fleet big working sails. The French vessels, however, could not let such an eligible opportunity pass without airing their balloon canvas, and (it little recked whether on or off the wind) boom water sails were rigged with a view of accelerating speed. Once we thought the north wind had heart in it for a pipe up, but there was little more than enough to keep their sails asleep when the line was crossed after second gun fire (7 h. 5 m.). We timed them to commence the race thus ·

	H. M. S.		H. M. S.
Gertrude (Watt)	7 7 45	Corinne	7 11 15
Enchantress	7 9 4	Florinda	7 13 30
Hirundelle	7 10 0	Faustine	7 14 30
Cetonia	7 10 05	Gertrude (Langtry)	7 18 0

On heading her course Enchantress trimmed her sheet for a breeze about two points abaft the beam, Gertrude being broad on her lee (port) bow, and evidently intending to keep the shore closer aboard. When Cetonia luffed for the mark boat she found Hirondelle too close to clear her bowsprit of the yawl's mizen, and had to bear away under her lee beam; here the schooner hung for a time, and was prevented thereby getting fair in the wake of Enchantress, and in a breeze to windward, which the Hirondelle's captain could not appreciate the advantage of. On the other hand, Corinne luffed out into it and soon came up on the beam of Cetonia; while the weather-beaten dandy, Hirondelle went in to share a streak of calm to leeward with Mr. Watt's Gertrude, at once losing any chance she might have had in the race. Florinda came on almost in the wake of Cetonia, slightly drawing up on Mr. Turner's schooner, while Faustine was being fast left astern by all the vessels which had crossed the imaginary line before her, and was coming back fast to Mr. Langtry's Gertrude—who, by the way, lost some three minutes over and above the fifteen allowed at the start. Briefly, there was more wind by far with the weather line—where were the Enchantress and Corinne—than with those further to the southward, viz., Cetonia, Florinda, and Gertrude; and seeing this Poland, of the Enchantress, wisely luffed out into it, eventually getting a nice sailing breeze, and, with every available inch of fore and aft sail set, was grandly drawing away from Cetonia, who was, at 7.30, second vessel. Jibtopsails were set by all at, 7.35, although the wind, from two points free, was now fair on the beam, and northing as they sailed west. At 7.36 the Enchantress found wind enough to wring and break the iron work of the main gaff that the lower main halyard block was connected to, and of course the mainsail settled down at the throat; the topsail sheet, however, held on, and the vessel was kept going her course, with but the slightest diminution of speed. Ten minutes elapsed ere the luff of the mainsail was again taunt, and then Cetonia had ranged herself up on the American's port beam, Corinne being far in her wake some three quarters of a mile distant. Florinda was a quarter of a mile astern of Cetonia, with Gertrude (Mr. Watt) two miles distant on the lee beam. Faustine and Gertrude (Mr. Langtry) were sailing along in close company two miles astern of Florinda. The weather was yet dull and overcast, with a slight motion of sea, when the N. E. tide came away, and then, after a little burst of sunshine, the air came very chilly. At nine o'clock the wind had drawn forward the beam, and, through keeping a course close to windward of the mark, Enchantress and Corinne got a fine lift, as well as having about double the power of wind Cetonia and Florinda had; whilst Gertrude (Mr. Langtry) and Faustine were bringing up a breeze that put them up close to Gertrude (Mr. Watt) and passed Hirondelle by some two miles. How much better the Enchantress went when she took wind just forward the beam then she did running, was obvious enough, and now that it freshened a little neither Cetonia nor Corinne could by long chalks compass her speed; the Corinne was in the same streak of wind, but neither Cetonia nor Florinda had the same weight. Ere the markboat was reached they came to a close haul, and with it a softening of the wind ; maintopmast-staysails were run down on the schooners and jib topsails also, for rounding; and, as will be seen by the appended times, the tailing from first to last was so considerable that it would be futile work to attempt to show how partial and spotty the breeze must have been on the twenty miles, reach down to the western mark, viz.:

	H. M. S.		H. M. S.
Enchantress	10 2 30	Gertrude (Langtry)	10 44 0
Corinne	10 10 0	Faustine	10 48 0
Cetonia	10 15 0	Mesange (1st French	
Florinda	10 20 40	yacht)	10 50 0
Gertrude (Watt)	10 41 0	Hirondelle	10 52 0

Enchantress ran up fore balloon topsail and balloon maintop-mast staysail, after having taken nearly a minute and a half in staying round the mark. There was no tide to consider, and thus, with a free wind, the direct course was steered for the winning mark off Cape Le Heve, bearing E. by N., distant twenty-four miles. Up to 10:30 the leading vssssls ran with a light and failing breeze just abaft the port beam, but which kept gradually drawing more aft. At eleven o'clock the sun came out intensely hot, and so dried up the wind as to become nearly a case of doldrums. Enchantress might have got into a calmer streak than either Corinne or Cetonia, the last named pair taking a wide berth on her port (lee) side, and leaving her in turn, fast as the American was going through the water. Noon brought a little more air, with a light summer haze, and at 12.30 there was a beautiful true balloon topsail breeze. Corinne now, with a clear lead, of half a mile from Cetonia, set her spinnaker on bowsprit, and then Florinda, who had now also run past Enchantress, followed the fashion. At one o'clock Cetonia had nearly drawn up on Corinne's beam, when the latter spurted off in a little extra lift of wind, and at the same time Florinda came blowing at the bow with a double measure from the bellows. Enchantress had the wind lighter, there was no doubt, but, even when in the same strart, could not run as fast as either of the English schooners. Corinne, with a thorough racing fit-out, was materially helped by having two spinnakers when the wind came far enough aft to set the main one and carry the other on the bowsprit; but as to area of sail, of course the Enchantress should on any point have had the heels of the smaller vessels, even in light winds. Florinda carried a breeze from a mile astern of Cetonia right through her lee and out ahead, and wanted but a little distance to have taken time from the Corinne. Gertrude (2), Faustine, Hirondelle, and Scapin (first French yacht) brought a breeze up that closed them in with the leading vessels, but not near enough to in any way affect the result. Two miles from home Corinne took in main spinnaker, and finished with one fore jib.

" Corinne.

THE INTERNATIONAL CHANNEL MATCH.—THE " C(

"Enchantress."

AND "ENCHANTRESS" STRUCK BY A SQUALL.

CHAPTER IX.

INTERNATIONAL CHANNEL MATCH.

YACHT CLUB DE FRANCE AND ROYAL ALBERT YACHT CLUB.

From Havre to Southsea July 27, 1874.

OPEN TO YACHTS OF ALL NATIONALITIES.

By the Yacht Club De France and the Royal Albert Yacht Club.

First Prize.—(Given by the Yacht Club de France) the Gladiators, two silver statues, unpublished models, offered by M. J. L. Gerome, Painter, member of the "Institut de France," value £320 besides the value of art, the value of metal only is £120.

Second Prize.—(Given by the Yacht Club de France) a silver cup (Grande Patere Minerve, du Tresor de Hildesheim), value £80.

Third Prize.—A silver cup, value £25, given by the Royal Albert Yacht Club.

Special Prizes.—A purse of £12, offered by the Yacht Club de France, to the yacht arriving first, whatever the rig, but floating the French flag.

A purse of £8, offered by the Yacht Club de France, to the yacht arriving second, whatever the rig, but floating the French flag.

To start from Havre roads, on the 27th of July, at four o'clock, at high water.

The time of starting of each vessel will be taken by chronometer, at the moment of passing through an imaginary line drawn from the shore to the starting buoy floating special flag, by the Committee of the Yacht Club de France.

In like manner, the time of each yacht will be taken on its passing the winning mark off Southsea, by the Committee of the Royal Albert Yacht Club.

If the first vessel in is a cutter and if she saves her time on her rig, she will take the first prize.

The second prize can only be won, on the same conditions, by a schooner or a yawl.

The third prize will be taken by the first yacht of a different rig to the former ones and on the same conditions.

The allowance of time for tonnage (which is only to be applied with regard to yachts of the same rig) as well as the tonnage measurement, will be according to the Rules of the Royal Albert Yacht Club.

In all other respects with the exception of time allowance and tonnage measurement, the Rules of the Yacht Club de France will be adhered to.

In case of dispute, the Committee of the Royal Albert Yacht Club and the Committee of the Conseil Maritime du Yacht Club de France will decide.

There will be no entrance fee for any yachts carrying the flag of the Yacht Club de France.

For all others it will be £4.

But, on payment of this sum, the vessel so doing acquires the right of carrying the flag of the Yacht Club de France and of enjoying the privileges attached to it during the present year, and during the following years by payment of 16s. per year.

Each yacht on entering must state the distinguishing colors of her racing flag and at the same time pay the entrance fee.

In the event of the vessels arriving in the night, the Markboat, at Southsea, will show three vertical lights and throw up a rocket on the arrival of each vessel.

Yachts are to pass near enough to the markboat to give their names and tonnage.

COMMITTEE OF THE MATCH.

President, M. G. Benoit-Champy, Vice-President of the Yacht Club de France.

Members, The members of the "Conseil Maritime" of the Yacht Club de France; MM. de Rouge (Marquis), the Capt. J. H. Anderson; the Members of the Committee of the Royal Albert Yacht Club; MM. Champeaux, Larue, Mandrot and Marcel, Members of the Committee of the Societe des Regates du Havre.

YACHTS TO ENTER UP TO THE 15TH JULY.

At Paris, at the Secretaryship of the Yacht Club de France rue Louis le Grand.

At Southsea, at the Secretaryship of the Royal Albert Yacht Club Club House.

At Havre at the Secretaryship of the Societe des Regates du Havre, 31, quai d'Orleans.

VICE-ADMIRAL BARON CL. DE LA RONCIERE-LE NOURY,
President of the Yacht-Club de France.

COUNT E. BATTHYANY, R. N. R.
Rear-Commodore of the Royal-Albert-Yacht-Club.

The Commercial Advertiser, New York, July 29, 1874.

THE INTERNATIONAL YACHT RACE.

It quickens all hearts on this side of the Atlantic to read that in the International Yacht Race on Monday, in the English channel, the American yacht Enchantress came in first, leading the fleet by eleven minutes and forty seconds. Unfortunately she lost the fruits of her prowess through time allowance, but it is gratifying to know that the stars and stripes were the first to greet the eyes of our English neighbors at Southsea. The race had been arranged by the Yacht Club of France, and the point of departure was Havre. Ten yachts started, but the cable only tells us that the American came in first, followed by the Corinne, the latter taking the prize by time allowance. The Enchantress is schooner built, is owned by M. J. F. Loubat, and belongs to the New York Yacht Club. The brilliant feat of the American champion will give a new impetus to international contests in deep water.

The New York Times, New York, July 31, 1874.

Mr. Loubat's fine yacht the Enchantress, appears to be sustaining abroad the reputation for speed and stanchness which she won in our waters. In the recent international race from Havre to Southsea, under the management of the French Yacht Club, the Enchantress, although becalmed all night, came in ahead of the fleet by nearly twelve minutes. The cup, indeed, she failed to secure, that being awarded to her nearest competitor on time allowance; but her performance shows that American yachts have little to fear from any foreign rivals. Some months ago Mr. Loubat suffered a great deal of ill-considered and wild criticism from certain newspapers because he insisted, as he had a clear right to do, upon claiming a challenge cup for which his only contestant had refused to sail. It gives us the more pleasure, therefore, to record his present success.

Bell's Life in London, London, August 1, 1874.

CHANNEL RACE FROM HAVRE TO SOUTHSEA.

After Saturday's match the whole fleet of competitors, excepting the Enchantress, came into harbor, and thus ensured a quiet day preparatory to the Channel Race on Monday. On Saturday night the wind freshened, and on Sunday morning blew strong on the rise of the flood, a nasty roll coming into the bay, and the long counter of the Enchantress popping very unpleasantly. She consequently joined the harbor division, and came out with the rest about 9 o'clock on (Monday) the morning of the race.

The start had with the first issue of the program been set for 4 P.M.—high water—so it was stated, but low water would have been nearer the mark, seeing that the morning tide of Monday was at 8.50. In consequence of this, and the glaring unsuitability of the appointed time, an effort was made to induce the committee to alter the starting hour, the idea being readily enough taken up by the executive of the French Yacht Club, and debated on. Many matters, however, having been prearranged, it was elicited that it would be impolitic to interfere with existing arrangements, other than that of postponing the start until the day following at 8 o'clock. To this proposition many present were willing to accede; but in the end it was determined to stand by the original program, and out of this expressed ultimatum some little unpleasantness arose, which, however, has doubtless by this time been smoothed over, and will have no more lasting impression upon French yachtsmen than upon those from this side the channel. Sunday's breeze had blown itself out, and St. Adresse Bay was as smooth as a dyke by noon on Monday, at which hour the whole of the competitors—except Mr. Langtry's Gertrude—nine in number, showed up, and the time dragged wearily enough without the slightest prospect of a breeze. With a delay of an hour came a little chill, but this, the lightest of topsail breezes, was nearly spun out by sundown. In the first watch came a clock calm, and the air—from a close haul at starting, when a little draught did come—breezed up dead aft, then with a temporary burst came a fight between an easterly and westerly breeze, the catspaws prevailing in the end from the latter quarter; in one of these vagrant airs Corinne got a start, such as is often seen in the Channel, which sent her away roaring from the Gwendolin, and giving her quite an eight mile lead, sufficient, in fact, to put a heavy mortgage in her favor on the most valuable prize of the year, and this before nearly half of the course had been sailed. Subsequently, however, she well held her place, and is, no doubt, a greatly improved vessel since the early part of the season. A palpable error in judgment at the finish might, however, have nullified her first advantage, and lost the Corinne the race, the outrageous carrying on at such a juncture being out of all countenance. The Enchantress when a breeze came, illustrated the utter futility of anything in the race attempting to reach with her, and we should think that in a fresh breeze, with the wind on the beam, she could open out a two mile lead in every hour from the best one pitted against her on Monday last. Run, however, she will not, and in sailing to windward, the task of rendering a satisfactory result might be safely left with the Cetonia.

Of the rest we feel convinced that had the Gwendolin started on the previous form her winning chance was far before the Corinne's, and in the result of this race one cannot but trace the same provoking run of ill-luck Major Ewing's schooner has encountered so persistently of late. The Cetonia we knew to be out of trim and required docking. This there seems to be no doubt was the cause of her not appearing in her previous fine form. The Florinda was within an ace of getting served by the Hirondelle, as the Corinne did the Gwendolin, Mr. Quilter's yawl sailing a very good race with Mr. Jessop's notability, and only being out of it when simply overpowered by weight of breeze. The Florinda, reckoning the second prize in this race, has thus accomplished nine consecutive wins, a very remarkable yachting coincidence. Of the Faustine nothing need be said, but the Mesange deserves a passing compliment. The first part of the race, as we have said, was paltry in the extreme, but the end, as will be seen in our detailed report, made some little amends for the unsatisfactory outset. The following were conditions and entries, the Gertrude alone not starting :—

The race was under the auspices of the Yacht Club de France and the Royal Albert Yacht Club of England, open to yachts of all nations. Course, from Havre to Southsea; The entries were:

YACHTS.	RIG.	TONS.	OWNERS.
Cetonia	Schooner	202	Mr. W. Turner.
Comte de Chambord (F)	Cutter	26	Mr. M. E. Cardon.
Corinne	Schooner	165	Mr. N. Wood.
Enchantress (American)	Schooner	320	Mr. J. F. Loubat.
Faustine...... ...."	Schooner	120	Mr. J. P. Russell.
Florinda	Yawl	136	Mr. W. Jessop.
Gertrude	Yawl	80	Mr. E. Langtry.
Gwendolin	Schooner	192	Major Ewing.
Mesange....(French)	Cutter	40	Mr. M. Le Roy d'Etiolles.
Scapin........."	Cutter	31	Mr. M. Leon Baque.

From a flat calm at 4 o'clock there came a few stray veins, and at an hour after the appointed starting hour a neutral tint on the sea away in the northern board gave notice of a breeze that, in a few minutes, ruffled the whole of the bay, and set several at shifting. Very quickly the Corinne's balloon topsails disappeared for working ones, and then the Enchantress and the Gwendolin came to two jib-headers, the Cetonia's two working sails appearing after all about the correct thing; but one and all seemed to be of a mind that wind was meant from the clouds and dark sea-line. A further provoking delay made some rather impatient to be sent off, but it was 5.12.10 before the gun was fired, and then this was the order and time of their being logged crossing the line:

	H.	M.	S.			H.	M.	S.
Hirondelle	5	17	0	Chambord		5	20	50
Florinda	5	18	0	Gwendolin		5	21	0
Cetonia	5	19	0	Enchantress		5	22	50
Mesange	5	20	0	Faustine		5	27	0
Scapin	5	20	30	Corinne		2	30	10

The Hirondelle, Florinda, Cetonia, Mesange, Enchantress, and Corinne, shot round the markboat in stays, and headed off about N. W., with a light breeze from N. by E. The Corinne lost some three minutes at start, and the Gwendolin and the Faustine, who were far under Cape La Heve, made a poor beginning indeed. For the first half hour the breeze continued northerly, and jib-topsails were run up to bend a hand on the close haul. At 6 o'clock the breeze had so freed that a course N. by W. for the Nab was being made good. At this time the Cetonia had drawn out from under lee of the Florinda, and become leading vessel, the Corinne and the Gwendolin coming up fast away fine on the weather quarter of the Florinda, the Hirondelle being close upon the latter's weather quarter, while far away astern of all was the Faustine. All the time of the close haul the Enchantress had been dropping to leeward of the Cetonia; and, although in the first instance she had tacked at the markboat, well clear of the Cetonia's wind, she was now fairly under her lee-quarter, and, forereaching not a whit faster and not looking within a point of the Cowes schooner course. The Corrine brought up a luffing breeze, which put her up with the Hirondelle; and, at 6:30, with a failing wind—free enough for maintopmast-staysails, and spinnakers on bowsprit—jib-headed topsails came down and ballooners went up on the Enchantress, Corinne, and Gwendolin, and then balloon staysails were bent to the stays and hoisted.

At 7 o'clock the Cetonia was the leading vessel, with the Florinda second, and the Enchantress third. The Gwendolin and Corinne, however, away to the eastward, were bringing more wind up with them, and at 7:45 Major Ewing's vessel went fairly past the Florinda to windward, and by 8 was up on the Cetonia's starboard beam, carrying a breeze. The Corinne also went past the Florinda and Cetonia, the Enchantress hanging under the lee quarter of the Cetonia, and not altering her position a jot. The water was as smooth as a lake at 8:15, and at 8:30 the wind had nearly died out in the eastward. A light breeze was yet playing, but the Cetonia and the Enchantress, to the westward, were in the doldrums, and had both the Gwendolin and the Corinne now ahead of them. The Corinne drew up close to the Gwendolin, and after a luff the Cowes schooner took the lead, both carrying a little breeze, but the Corinne having apparently the best. Heavy thunderclouds were hanging in the N. W. when the sun went down, but other than a passing blow out of one of these steely-looking banks, the sky had not the least appearance of wind. By 9 o'clock the evening had deepened so quickly as to render the Corinne and the Gwendolin almost indistinct from the Enchantress and the Florinda, but from the Octonia the Corinne could be made out drawing away from the Gwendolin, and astern the Faustine and the Hirondelle had a little breeze, by which they closed the land in fast from the Enchantress, Florinda, and Octonia, who had the wind on the masthead. At 9 Cape Antifer Light bore S. E. by E., and La Hevc Lights S. By 9:30 a little air came up right aft, and spinnakers were set, the Octonia and the Florinda running along almost beam and beam, with the Enchantress a quarter of a mile astern of Mr. Turner's schooner. Gwendolin also set her spinnaker, and stealing up on the Corinne unperceived, went past her to windward ere the latter thought of squaring off her boom and setting sail for a run. By 10 o'clock there had been several gybes ; but after this the wind came from the S. W., and the Corinne once more drew up on the Gwendolin's beam, the Octonia and the Florinda's position being now equally good with those of the Corinne and Gwendolin, and in fact both they and the Enchantress were nearer than any of the rest to the Nab ; a freeing of the wind to the southward would, of course, however, give the lee vessels the best chance through drawing to and getting everything to draw, while the weather line would be more off the wind.

At 11.30 the Corinne, about 200 yards from the Gwendolin took a westerly draught, which freshened as she went on, and with a lee tide she made herself a breeze which lasted her out until she was fairly out of sight of everything else, the rest meanwhile lying with scarcely steerage way. Save a light eye where the sun went down, the night was cloudy, and it was 4 o'clock when the Corinne was made out with a good six miles lead of the Octonia, the Gwendolin being third in position, then the Enchantress, Florinda, Hirondelle and Faustine. At 4.30 a clinking breeze came up from the westward, and the Enchantress soon drew out from the Octonia, the Gwendolin fairly reaching away from the last named, but the Florinda being left fast by schooners. As before stated, the two lee vessels, the Corinne and Gwendolin, had an advantage in being in a position to get their sails drawing better than the Cetonia; but the Enchantress, although similarly situated, drew fast on the pair, and quickly reached past the Gwendolin, going at a tremendous pace after the Corinne, and illustrating that the vaunted 16 knots was not moonshine. It was only a question of distance for the Enchantress to have won; she passed the Corinne about the Nab, the latter now, with the same strength of wind that had come up at 4.30, being smothered with sail, and with a little sea on the tide the gear was getting hardly used. The Corinne had two ballooners and spinnaker for jib when, at 7 o'clock, the wind shortened, and made the big headsail lift; one shake and all full again, and down came both topmasts, the maintopsail yard and main-gaff also going, and leaving Mr. Wood's smart little craft a pitiable object. She was kept going her course while the wreck was cleared away, the flying Enchantress of course picking up precious minutes; but from the Nab it was too short to hope to save her time from the Corinne, even in her crippled state. Gwendolin stuck to her ballooners to the finish, but was wary in running down headsail and maintopmast staysail. Major Ewing's vessel came in in such style that we thought it a pity the Corinne's fluke had left the Gwendolin out of it, especially as we hear she will not sail again this year. The Enchantress finished first, her performance at reaching—during the time there had come a fair sailing breeze—being a splendid one; but the Corinne was well within time, and took the big £320 prize, the Florinda second (£40), and the Mesange the prize for French yachts. The official times of arrival were:—

	H. M. S.		H. M. S.
Enchantress	7 21 40	Hirondelle	8 48 35
Corinne	7 33 20	Faustine	9 1 20
Gwendolin	7 53 15	Mesange	9 23 10
Cetonia	7 54 56	Scapin	9 36 30
Florinda	8 12 45	Chambord	9 49 50

The Field, London, August 1, 1874.

THE YACHT CLUB OF FRANCE.

Monday, July 27.

We have been over and over again asked why the members of the Yacht Club de France gave £400 in prizes to bring about a match between English and American yachts. Knowing the fondness our Gallic friends have for the sea and all its influences, we replied—a little too simple was that reply perhaps—it was their love of watching a good contest upon water. A satisfactory confirmation was given to this answer at Havre on Sunday, by the announcement that many members of the club had arrived from Paris, and had chartered a steamer to accompany the match across Channel. This was evidence that a keen interest was taken in the coming contest, and the Englishmen present were charmed; indeed, so warm was the enthusiasm evoked at Frascati's, that they would have embraced their admirers had it been a custom the phlegmatic Britishers were tutored in. As it was, Mr. Midshipman Easy took Alphonse by the hand, and assured him that all the yacht owners present felt proud of the admiration they had excited in the minds of Frenchmen, and that they would only be too glad to teach them the art of yachting, as they had taught them everything else before. The mutual adulation being over, and its debilitating effects removed by all round doses of B. and S., the expert Britisher began to think it was time to question some of the arrangements of the contest. There is no doubt our countrymen—and we might say countrywomen—do like to see a yacht match sailed; and it is very certain, if the match be sailed in the dark, they cannot so see it. Accordingly, as the Yacht Club de France had arranged that the start should be an afternoon one—four o'clock—the Englishmen present ventured to ask that they might be allowed to start at 9 A. M., especially as they would have to be outside in the bay at that hour. But the Frenchmen who delight in yacht sailing are made of stubborn stuff, and would not yield an inch, even

though they themselves were barred viewing the contest. Arrangements should not be changed, they argued, out of mere caprice;
and moreover they had agreed to banquet themselves at one
o'clock, three hours before the start, and then rise to view the
fight with emotions that the gods might envy.

The morrow came, and a wet, dirty-looking morrow it was,
very little wind, a leaden sky, and a drizzling rain. At eight
o'clock all the yachts that were to meet in the contest were
towed outside and anchored in the bay, to wait a dreary eight
hours for four o'clock. Two o'clock came, and we began to look
anxiously for the steamer freighted with the members of the
Yacht Club; but they came not yet, and the Dollond which we
turned upon the glittering corridors of Frascati told us the
carousal was still unfinished. But banquets, like other good
things, must come to an end, and presently—at three o'clock--
the steamer, flying the tri-color of the Yacht Club de France
and the blue ensign of the Royal Albert Yacht Club, came out
of the harbor. At 3.30 she was alongside the nearest yacht,
and gave final instructions that the match would be started at 4
P. M. across an imaginary line. The steamer then made off to
the other yachts, and, as they were very much scattered about,
it took her just one hour and a half to go to them all and then
get into position W. N. W. of Cape La Heve to form the line of
the start. And so five o'clock came before the gun was
fired, and, with only three hours of daylight before us, we began
to think that the good things partaken of at Frascati's would
lose our French friends a sight of the match. We were thinking how best we could condole with them on this disappointment,
when lo! directly the start had taken place away steamed the
Club vessel straight for the Culvers, leaving the yachts to themselves and Davy Jones. "There," says Dipsey Sounding in our
ear, "Talk of Mossoo taking an interest in a yacht match! they
know as much about it as a Kaffer does of the Sanscrit for peak
purchase; I tell ye it's all done for political reasons." Well, it
was rather a nose-ender to see that steamer steam away, but in
ten minutes we had sunk our wonderment, the steamer, Dipsey

Sounding's political reasons, and all the rest of it; and thought only of the contest and that very wicked-looking young lady La Belle Americaine.

There had been a nice sou'-westerly breeze during the early morning; but after noon the breeze died away, and up to three o'clock there was scarcely a ripple upon the water. Then there came a smart breeze from the northward, straight across from the Nab, and the vessels that had sent up balloon topsails hauled them down. These were Gwendolin and Enchantress, and they now sent up jib-headers, and Corinne sent up big workers. But before the gun was given for the start the breeze died out to light airs, and everybody wished that the dark clouds and the chill from them had not frightened ballooners off the vessels. The match did not, for the first part, prove a very exciting affair, and told us very little concerning the merits of the vessels. However, we could see that the Enchantress is a slouch close-hauled off a light wind, and that the Gwendolin is better than Cetonia under similar conditions ; but then we knew that before. The Corinne moved very fast in the light wind, and from the first half-hour looked the most dangerous vessel in the race. It was a pity she got so far away from the others during the night, whilst they were becalmed, as we could not fairly judge of her performance in the fine reaching breeze which blew after three o'clock on Tuesday morning; but there is no doubt she kept up the reputation she made on the Thames for fast reaching. The Cetonia, we take it, was not doing quite her best, whilst Gwendolin never sailed better, and had she been lucky enough to have shared in the breeze that took Corinne away from her at mid-night, she would have won. The Florinda no doubt would have given the schooner some trouble had the northerly wind held ; but of course, when it came to reaching, she had no chance against such big schooners. The Hirondelle sailed very well, and it was no disgrace for her to be beaten 36 minutes by such a vessel as Florinda over an eighty miles course. The Faustine is a funny kind of racing craft, but she might find a worthy antag-onist in the Harlequin, and we should be inclined to back the

latter.   We know this is rather hard on the Faustine, but it is
only right she should be pitted against a vessel she has some
chance of beating.   The three French yachts were sailed remarkably well, and everybody was pleased to see a French gentleman win one of the three prizes.

Match, from Havre to Southsea, for three prizes.   The first
vessel in to determine the rig of the winner of the first prize.
Time allowance, twice the Royal Albert Yacht Club scale.   The
start to be made underway, and the time each vessel crossed the
line to be taken and accounted for at the finish ; no time beyond
fifteen minutes to be allowed for at the start :

ENGLISH YACHTS.

YACHT.	RIG.	TONS.	OWNER.
Cetonia	Schooner	202	Mr. W. Turner.
Gwendolin	Schooner	192	Major Ewing.
Corinne	Schooner	165	Mr. N. Wood.
Florinda	Yawl	136	Mr. W. Jessop.
Hirondelle	Yawl	68	Mr. W. C. Quilter.

AMERICAN YACHTS.

Enchantress	Schooner	320	Mr. J. F. Loubat
Faustine	Schooner	120	Mr. P. Russell.

FRENCH YACHTS.

Mesange	Cutter	40	M. Le Dr. leRoy d'Etiolles
Scapin	Cutter	31	M. Leon Baque.
Comte de Chambord		26	M. E. Cardon.

At 5 o'clock the club steamer took up a position three miles
W. N. W. of the Lighthouse on Cape La Heve, forming the line
for the start.   All the yachts were to the southward of the line,
the Gwendolin, Faustine, Scapin, and Count de Chambord inside
the bank, close under the Cape, and the others on the leeward
end of the line.   Course: from the line of Cape La Heve to a
markboat off the Horse Shoal, near Southsea ; about eighty
miles N. by W.

At 5.15 the gun was fired for the start, and Hirondelle was
the first across at 5.20, standing on starboard tack N. W. by N.
½ N.; wind light from N. N. E.   Florinda was the next over

under Hirondelle's lee quarter at 5.22.30, and in the wake of her came Cetonia at 5.24.0. The Mesange struck into the latter's trail, and crossed the line at 5.25; and the Enchantress went across close after her at 5.26. Then came the Gwendolin inshore and high on their weather at 5.27, followed by the two other Frenchmen and the Faustine. The Corinne was still to the southward, and, standing in on port tack, crossed the line about midway at 5.33, so far as we could judge, having thus lost three minutes at the start.

The wind, as we have said, was light, and flying about a great deal, directly after the start altering to N., much to the disadvantage of those who had started inshore. Jib topsails went up all round, and there was enough heart in the wind to send Florinda through Hirondelle's lee half an hour after the start. Gwendolin and Corinne, too, were doing well in the light breeze, and were gradually creeping up on Enchantress and Cetonia—wide on their port beam. At six o'clock the Enchantress hauled down her fore jib-header, and sent up a wooden-headed one, Gwendolin at the same time shifting hers for a ballooner, both sticking to main jib-headers. The wind now commenced to eastern in earnest, but remained dreadfully light; their heads by 6.15 were up to N. $\frac{1}{2}$ W., and this brought Gwendolin and Corinne from the weather quarter to weather beam of Cetonia and weather bow of Enchantress. These four schooners seemed pretty evenly matched in the light wind, and if there was any difference in their speed Corinne was the fastest, gradually eating up to Gwendolin. The wind seemed inclined to free them still more, but Cetonia shifted her balloon fore staysail for a working one, whilst Corinne and Gwendolin thought it an occasion for exactly the reverse, and shifted workers for ballooners. As the breeze easterned there came a little more weight in it, but still it was only of balloon topsail strength, and the passage over promised to be a protracted one. At 6.50 all could head N. by E. two points above their course, and Enchantress sent up maintopmast staysail, and Gwendolin shifted No. 2 for big reaching jib. Corinne, too, now had a leading wind, went in for a change, and, stowing her jib and jib topsail on the bowsprit, hauled up spinnaker, instead for head sail; but we fancied Gwendolin reached away from her after she made the change. With sheets started, the schooners were marching up to the two yawls, and both dandies hauled up a bit to show the former a leeward passage. At 7.10, with a beam wind all easterly, Gwendolin hauling up maintopmast staysail, burst through Hirondelle's lee, and went on in the wake of Florinda, who was still a quarter of a mile ahead. Corinne, sending up a balloon maintopsail, followed Gwendolin through Hirondelle's lee, and both had reached past the Enchantress. The latter now sent up main balloon topsail, and Gwendolin main working topsail, the sky at present having anything but a pleasant look about it. At 7.30 Gwendolin went past on Florinda's weather, and became the leading vessel, having fairly sailed past everything in the fleet.

But there was a rival for honors close astern of the Gwendolin in the person of Corinne, and that young lady, with a weight of wind in her sails, was luffed out across the stern of Gwendolin with the idea of passing on her weather. It is much the quicker way, as everybody knows, to pass a vessel to windward, and Corinne had already been long enough under Gwendolin's lee quarter to know she could find no passage to leeward. At first it looked as if she could not get past to windward either, but presently a fresher breeze took hold of her, and up she marched to Gwendolin. The latter, out of politeness or flurry, conceded her a weather passage, and so at eight o'clock Corinne became a leading vessel. Then Gwendolin, sorry for her good nature, hauled up across Corinne's stern, in order to repass her if she could, and surely Corinne was bound to yield the passage. But Corinne's sailing master has evidently not learnt his manners in a high bred French school, and instead of taking off his cap and bowing a weather passage to Gwendolin, commenced luffing at her savagely. Gwendolin, stung by such ingratitude, commenced luffing too, and presently the pair were by the wind, heading N. E., the spinnaker of the Corinne's bowsprit falling into folds. Still Gwendolin could not get past, although she got well nigh abeam, and the wind falling light, she gave up the attempt, and as Gwendolin eased her helm Corinne did the same, so both bore up to their course N. by W., and were still the leading vessels at 8.30. The wind continued to die away, and as the red glare left by the setting sun disappeared the evening became very dark ; but the full moon would soon be due, and then the sailing would become prettier. As the wind lightened it got round southerly, and at 9.15 Gwendolin's crew, going to work very quietly, got out main spinnaker to starboard, Corinne at the time being under her port beam, Florinda and Hirondelle astern, and Cetonia and Enchantress away under her lee quarter. Slowly, but surely, Gwendolin went past on Corinne's weather, and at 9.30 was again leading vessel. Corinne now ran off main boom and set spinnaker, but only just in time to prevent Gwendolin getting clear away.

The wind now got to the westward of south and brought the vessels by the lee, and to keep on their course Gwendolin and Corinne gybed to port tack at 9.45. The wind came westerly very fast, and at ten o'clock it was abeam due west, whilst at nine they had it abeam easterly. The westerly wind brought a smart shower of rain, but by half-past ten the sky had cleared, and the bright full moon showed up all the vessels. Gwendolin, with Corinne on her port (weather) beam, was still leading, and Cetonia and Enchantress were broad on their weather quarter ; whilst Florinda and Hirondelle were dragging along in the wake of Corinne. At eleven o'clock all were in a roaring calm, with noontide heat. Then a little air came from S. S.W., which brought about a squaring of booms, and Gwendolin set fore spinnaker, reserving her main for a probable gybe in the course of a few minutes.

They lay with very little motion up to 11.30, when Corinne was seen to take a light breeze abeam westerly, and stole ahead of Gwendolin. The latter was not a cable's length from her, but was left becalmed, her sails flapping in folds as she yielded to the swell. In twenty minutes the Corinne was lost to the rest of the fleet, having sailed clean away with the westerly breeze, and we suppose a greater fluke was never scored. Gwendolin now, for want of something better to do, set about shifting her main balloon topsail, and when that job was completed hauled up maintopmast staysail. But it was all to no purpose, and one after the other she saw Octonia and Enchantress steal past broad on her weather, and Florinda ranged up abeam. They were now about thirty miles from Cape La Heve, and where Corinne was gone no one knew on board the other craft.

From midnight up to 2 A. M. Gwendolin lay well-nigh becalmed, with Florinda in the same plight, when at that hour a light air came out from S.W.; by 2.30 it had increased in strength and backed to S.S.W., so spinnakers were got out— Gwendolin setting hers on foremast, and water-sail under main boom. Up to four o'clock the wind continued to increase and hauled more westerly, and at last, coming out W.S. W., due abeam, brought in spinnakers. It was now sunrise, and Corinne, that had been lost so many hours, was made out leading five miles ahead of Enchantress, on the latter's weather bow, and to windward of her course; two miles under the lee-quarter of the Enchantress was the Octonia, and half a mile under the lee-quarter of Octonia were Gwendolin and Florinda abeam. Scattered about three miles astern of Florinda were Hirondelle, Mesange, Faustine, Comte de Chambord, and Scapin, all having closed up during the darkness by bringing up the westerly breeze.

They now had a fine scupper breeze on the port beam, and the big Yankee was tearing along with a tremendous burst of speed, hauling Corinne back to her, and leaving Octonia and Gwendolin fast. The latter two were carrying a pretty white feather in their teeth, and both, we think, were gaining on Corinne. But Gwendolin was showing the finer speed, and, dropping Florinda, marched through Octonia's lee in a way we did not expect. It was now really fine sailing, and the cool morning breeze refreshed one after the sultry calm of the middle watch. Soon the white Culver Cliffs of the Isle of Wight loomed up in the bright sunshine, and Enchantress, going as fast perhaps as Guinevere could in such a breeze, was rapidly getting hold of Corinne. At 6 o'clock, at the eastern end of Sandown Bay, the Yankee was within a half a mile of the Cowes boat; but the latter was making a bold fight of it, and her fine speed was bound to carry her home the victress. But Corinne, after her good fortune of the night, was now about to get her turn of ill luck, and we must admit it was rather a severe one when it came. At 6.45 Enchantress went past on her weather, and gave her such a shake up that when she filled again down came her fore and main topmasts, spinnaker on bowsprit breaking the fore one and main ballooner and main topmast staysail the other. Worse than this, the balloon topsail yard fell across the main gaff, and smashed that; so Corinne was indeed in trouble. However, with all the wreck hanging about her—it was impossible to clear it whilst under way—spinnaker was cut adrift altogether—she kept her course for the channel between the Norman and Horse Shoal, the Yankee clipper going clean away. Gwendolin immediately stowed jib-topsail and hauled down main topmast stay. sail, determined to risk no spar breaking now her chance of winning was over. Cetonia, however, continued to drag hers along, but it was doing her little good, as Gwendolin continued to gain a trifle on her the whole way in to the winning Markboat. But little else need be said concerning the match; Enchantress continued to extend her lead when once past Corinne, and the latter, in her crippled state, was yet able to keep the prize for herself. The yachts passed the winning mark, and were timed by the Secretary of the Royal Albert Yacht Club, as under:

	H. M. S.		H. M. S.
Enchantress	7 21 40	Hirondelle	8 48 35
Corinne	7 33 20	Faustine	9 1 26
Gwendolin	7 53 15	Mesange	9 23 10
Cetonia	7 53 56	Scapin	9 36 30
Florinda	8 12 45	Count de Chambord	9 49 50

The Corinne won the silver images, the Florinda the silver salver, and the Mesange the Royal Albert Cup. The Mesange also won a prize, value £12, for the first French yacht in; and and Scapin an £8 prize for second French yacht.

Hunt's Yachting Magazine, London, September, 1874.

THE YACHT CLUB DE FRANCE.

It certainly appears a curious liberality on the part of our friends across the Channel to offer two prizes, amounting to £400 for a race from France to England. If it was not that they bribe the yachts of "perfidious Albion" largely, to visit their coasts, and entertain them hospitably when they get them there, we might be inclined to suspect that the liberal prizes were given in order to get quit of them; but as this is not the case, we must conclude that they are only "speeding the parting guest." Another curious part of the proceeding is that the starting time should be fixed for so late an hour as 4 P. M., which makes sailing all night a necessity. But, whilst we wonder at their arrangements, we admire their generosity.

The yachts were carefully towed out of the harbor at 8 A. M., and had to drop their anchors and wait patiently until the starting hour, which, as the sailing committee and their friends were anxious to secure a substantial feast before venturing on the treacherous ocean, was delayed until 5 h. 15 m. P. M. Like most ocean matches this one had the usual amount of fluking, and was a very excited affair, excepting just at the finish, when owing to the wholesale smashing on board the Corinne, some degree of excitement took place. The Gwendolin was very unlucky, and the Corinne got hers and her own luck, whilst the Cetonia seemed quite out of form, and did not sail in the style we know she is capable of. The Hirondelle surprised us by the manner in which she went, and had she not carried away her spinnaker boom at a critical period of the race, might have even saved her time on Florinda. Of the Americans the Faustine cut up very badly, and she certainly can have very little claim to being considered a racing vessel; and the Enchantress, although reaching very fast, could do nothing beating to windward in a light breeze. During the night the Corinne got away from every-thing else whilst they were becalmed, sailing very fast indeed, and with go.d luck just before the finish, won from the En-chantress with something in hand, notwithstanding that she lost both topmasts and main-gaff at one fell swoop.

The conditions and entries were:—Match from Havre to Southsea for three prizes. The first vessel in to determine the rig of the winner of the first prize. Time allowance, twice the Royal Albert Yacht Club scale. The start to be made underway, and the time each vessel crossed the line to be taken and accounted for at the finish; no time beyond fifteen minutes to be allowed for at the start :—

Numbered as in Hunt's Universal Yacht List, for 1874.

NO.	NAME OF YACHTS.	RIG.	TONS.	OWNERS.
264	Cetonia (English)	Schooner	202	W. Turner, Esq.
841	Gwendolin "	Schooner	192	Major Ewing
340	Corinne "	Schooner	165	N. Wood, Esq.
683	Florinda "	Yawl	136	W. Jessop, Esq.
924	Hirondelle "	Yawl	68	W. C. Quilter, Esq.
	Enchantress (Amer'n)	Schooner	320	J. F. Loubat, Esq.
	Faustine "	Schooner	120	J. P. Russell, Esq.
	Mesange (French)	Cutter	40	M. Le Dr. le Roy d'Etiolles
	Scapin "	Cutter	31	M. Leon Baque
	Comte de Chambord	Cutter	26	M. E. Cardon

The Hirondelle was the first across the line at 5 h. 18 m., with Florinda next, whilst the Corinne was last, losing some two or three minutes at the start. The wind was very light and shifty, but coming in little gusts from the north and north-east, and balloon sails were set to make the most of it whilst it lasted.

Soon the wind got a little stronger, and with more east in it the yachts had it pretty free, and the Gwendolin picked them all up, and at half-past seven was leading vessel. But the Corinne luffing up, unopposed by the Gwendolin, went out on her weather, and passed her; then the Gwendolin tried to do the same, but without the same success, as the Corinne luffed up very hard, and both were standing away from their course. But the Gwendolin at last got her spinnaker out again, and, bearing away, got past the Corinne and once more was leading vessel. After this the wind came so far round that a jibe was necessary, and about eleven p. m. all lay becalmed.

The first to feel the wind again was the Corinne, which just before midnight got a breeze all to herself, and actually ran clean out of sight of every vessel in the race. Until two A.M. the others were lying as still as if at moorings, when a nice breeze sprung up from southwest, which, backing more southerly, came stronger, and with a beam wind the yachts were bowling along at fair speed. At daybreak the Corinne was leading by about five miles, but with just the wind to suit her, the Enchantress was picking her up like a race horse following a dray horse; but the former was so far ahead that she was certain to get in within her time, let the American sail ever so fast. A little before seven o'clock the Enchantress over-hauled her,* and passing on her weather took the wind from her, and as the wind once more filled the unfortunate Corinne's sails, down came both topmasts, the topsail-yard falling with such force on the main-gaff as to break it in two. Of course it was no use stopping to pick up the pieces, so the wreck was cut adrift, and the Corinne held her course, winning the first prize notwithstanding her accident. The time of arrival off Southsea was:

	H. M. S.		H. M. S.
Enchantress	7 21 40	Hirondelle	8 48 35
Corinne	7 33 20	Faustine	9 1 26
Gwendolin	7 53 15	Mesange	9 23 10
Cetonia	7 53 56	Scapin	9 36 30
Florinda	8 12 45	C. de Chambord	9 49 50

The Corinne took the first prize, value £320; the Florinda the second, value £80; the Mesange the Albert cup, also £12 prize for first French yacht; and the Scapin the £8 prize for second French yacht. The Gwendolin stowed flying jib and main staysail on seeing the Corinne's accident, and appeared to sail all the faster for the change. The Enchantress went past the winning flag-boat at a great speed, and with all her canvas set was a sight not easily forgotten.

CHAPTER X.

THE PRINCE OF WALES'S CHALLENGE CUP RACE.

ROYAL YACHT SQUADRON OFFICIAL PROGRAMS.

TIME ALLOWANCE FOR YACHTS SAILING FOR THE PRINCE OF WALES CHALLENGE CUP.

THURSDAY, AUGUST 6, 1874.

	M.	S.		M.	S.
Enchantress, 320, allows Shark..	23	48	Shark, 201, allows Egeria..9		48
" " Egeria..	33	36			

1874.

ROYAL YACHT SQUADRON REGATTA, ON THURSDAY, AUG. 6.

CHALLENGE CUP, THE GIFT OF H. R. H., THE PRINCE OF WALES.

For all American and British schooners and yawls of 100 tons and upwards. Yawls to have half their tonnage added. All yachts to be measured by a person appointed by the Sailing Committee of R. Y. S., according to Thames measurement. Time allowance, 12 seconds per ton. No restriction as to hands, canvas, or boats; in other respects the R. Y. S. Sailing Regulations to be adhered to.

COURSE :

From Cowes round the Light Vessel on the Shambles, and back round the Nab, leaving both Light Vessels on the port hand (passing to the Southward of the Isle of Wight), winning between Cowes Castle and a Flagboat moored in the Roads, keeping outside all the buoys and marks on the shoals extending from the Island Shore (Peel and Princess included), except the Middle and Sturbridge.

TO START UNDERWEIGH:

Three to start or no race.			To start at	A. M.
Shark,	-	201.	Duke of Rutland.	
Egeria,	-	152.	J. Mulholland, Esq.	
Enchantress,	-	320.	J. F. Loubat.	

Mark Boat Off Castle—Union Jack.

MARK BOAT OFF CASTLE,—TWO LIGHTS HORIZONTAL BY NIGHT.

PREPARATIVE.

The owner of any vessel winning a prize, will be required before the prize is delivered, to sign a declaration that the Sailing Regulations have been strictly conformed to.

RICHARD GRANT, *Secretary.*

Bell's Life in London, London, August 8, 1874.

Cowes, Friday, August 17, (*by telegraph.*)

The Challenge Cup, presented by H. R. H. the Prince of Wales, for all American and English schooners and yawls of 100 tons and upwards; yawls to have half their tonnage added; course from Cowes round the Shambles Lightship and back round the Nab to Cowes; time race; Thames measurement; allowance 12 sec. per ton; no restriction as to hands, canvas, or boats; the cup to be won three times by the same vessel.

The holders were—Egeria 1870, Aline 1871, Gwendolin 1872, Egeria 1873. The entries this year were:—

YACHT.	RIG.	TONS.	OWNER.
Egeria (holder)	Schooner	152	J. Mulholland, Esq.
Shark (challenger)	Schooner	201	Duke of Rutland.
Enchantress (do American)	Schooner	320	J. F. Loubat.

The race was started at 6 A.M. on Friday morning. There was a strong breeze from the westward, with a west going tide, and each went across the line at gun fire under whole lower canvas, the Egeria and Shark with housed topmasts, the Enchantress having maintopmast on end. It was a dead beat down to the Needles, and from the first, the Enchantress justified the remarks which have been passed on her, that her weatherly qualities are far inferior to the English vessels. There was but lttle sea, of course, in the Solent, but she did not care, even with a breeze fresh enough for housed topmasts and second jibs, to turn about, and under the north shore was hanging from five to ten minutes in the wind. The Egeria and the Shark both under the circumstances weathered her, and it looked as though she would have a rough Channel passage, as when full and before gathering way fairly wallowing down until waist deep, in fact, buried up to the skylights. The Egeria and Shark were meanwhile spinning to windward in a manner that made the American's lee berth a more extended one every minute.

* * *

The Field, London, August 8, 1874.

The match round the Shambles was started this morning at six o'clock. The starters were Egeria, Shark and Enchantress. It was a dirty-looking morning, a S.W. wind blowing, with rain. The Enchantress started with housed topmasts, and, as the yachts would most likely fetch right out to the Shambles, she will probably come in a long way ahead. The match will not be concluded before evening; but the Egeria weathered the Enchantress on the second board. The latter then carried away her jibboom, and hove to for the purpose of reefing her mainsail. After getting under way again she was catching Egeria; off Newtown she carried away her forestay, and returned to Cowes. Shark also gave up, so Egeria sailed over the course alone.

The Daily News, London, August 10, 1874.

ROYAL YACHT SQUADRON REGATTA.

Cowes, Saturday Evening.

In consequence of the series of mishaps to the Enchantress, American schooner, from whom so much had been expected, the race for the Prince of Wales's Challenge Cup was virtually decided on Saturday morning, but still there was just the bare possibility that the Egeria might not be able to complete the course. The Enchantress fell early into difficulties, for off Yarmouth she lost her jibboom; off Sconce Point her jib tack went; and off the east buoy of the Shingles away went her forestay. With these accumulated casualties there was nothing left for her but to return to her anchorage at Cowes. After getting through the Needles Passage, the Egeria met the Channel tide, and took in sail, and on the return from the Shambles Light made easy sail, and arrived at Cowes at 11.50 P.M. Thus the Egeria became the absolute winner of the Prince of Wales's Challenge Cup, having won it three times, though not in consecutive years, as was originally the conditions of the race. These terms were looked upon as very hard ones, for if they had been adhered to the Cup would doubtless have remained as a challenge for all time, and this being represented to the Prince of Wales, the original conditions were modified, and instead of it being required that the same yacht should win it three years in succession, it was altered to allow any yacht to take it who had won it on three seperate occasions. This good fortune has fallen to the lot of the Egeria; but during the whole time that the prize has been instituted there was always a difficulty in getting yacht-owners to start for it, as there was only a very problematical prospect of getting anything for their pains, and in consequence of the course taken few persons ever had an opportunity of witnessing it, inasmuch on every former occasion the greater part of the race was done in the darkness of the night. The following is the order of winners of this prize:—In 1870, by the Egeria; 1871, by the Aline; 1872, by the Gwendolin; and in 1873 and 1874, by the Egeria.

The Shark after having gone far enough bore up for home, the Duke of Rutland having merely entered for the purpose of making up the conditional three starters. Ere Yarmouth was reached the Enchantress was upwards of a mile to leeward of the Egeria, and hereabout some of her innumerable stays of head-gear gave out, and the jibboom was carried away. She was pitching badly enough even here, but what sort of a figure she would have cut at St. Albans must be left to conjecture. The question was, however, quickly set at rest, through the vessel bearing up, and running back for Cowes, where she arrived about 9 o'clock, her standing jib-stay having apparently given out, as the foremast looked to have come aft. The Egeria, consequently hauled down reefs, and sailed over the course by herself, her owner thus becoming possessor of the Prince of Wales's Cup.

The Field, London, August 15, 1874.

ROYAL YACHT SQUADRON.

We stated last week that the American yacht Enchantress, after a series of mishaps, was obliged to return to Cowes. At the time Enchantress bore up off Hurst, having carried away her forestay, Egeria was a good mile and a half out on her weather, and holding a much better wind than the American yacht. The Egeria had lost some time through the clew of her jib bursting out, and having thereby to shift jibs.

The Egeria passed out through the Needles at 8 A. M., and, with the wind strong at W. S. W., had well nigh a dead beat of something like thirty miles before her. There was a big sea on, but Egeria, snugged down to double-reefed mainsail (foresail stowed), reefed staysail, and small jib, jogging along easily, was making excellent weather of it. She weathered the Shambles Lightship at 3.55 P. M., having worked down by long leg on port tack and short one on starboard off shore. For the run up Channel to the Nab, foresail was set, but no other change made, and she made the Lightship at the eastern end of the island at 10 P. M. Cowes was reached at 11.50, and Egeria at midnight let go her anchor in the Roads. The Egeria won the Prince of Wales's Challenge Cup in 1870, beating the Guinevere, &c.; she again won it last year, beating the Morna. Having again won it this year, she has complied with the conditions of the donor, and won it three times. Mr. Mulholland thus becomes the winner of the cup.

The prize was originally offered as an inducement to get the American yachts to compete against those of England, but up to the time the Enchantress entered no American had competed for it. Everyone seems rejoiced that the cup is finally disposed of, and we assume that challenge cups are not popular-

---

Hunt's Yachting Magazine, London, September, 1874.

August 7th:—The race for the Prince of Wales's Challenge Cup was to have have been sailed round the Shambles to-day but the request of the Egeria it was postponed for a day in order to allow her to prepare for the fight.

August 8th.—The race round the Shambles for the Prince of Wales's Challenge Cup was started at six o'clock in the morning, the only entries being:—

Numbered as in Hunt's Universal Yacht List for 1874.

No.	Names of Yachts.	Rig.	Tons.	Owner.	Builders
542	Enchantress......	Schooner	320	J. F. Loubat, Esq.	
492	Egeria..........	Schooner	152	J. Mulholland, Esq., M.P.	Wanhill
2105	Shark..........	Schooner	201	Duke of Rutland.	Wanhill

The Egeria got away first, and the Enchantress, slow in stays, lost some time; but when she got really set going she began to pick up the Egeria, when her jibboom carried away. After getting the wreck in she began to overhaul the Egeria; but before getting to Hurst Castle her forestay parted, and, after nearly losing her mast, she had to run back to Cowes. The Shark gave up soon afterwards, and so the Egeria sailed over the course, and claimed the cup, which, as she had won it twice before, is now her property.

CHATPER XI.

MR. LOUBAT'S FIRST EUROPEAN CHALLENGE.

The Times, London, August 14, 1874.

Should it be agreeable to any member of an organized
European yacht club, owning a yacht of at least 300 tons R. T.
Y. C. measurement, to sail a match for a hundred guinea cup
with the Enchantress over the Prince of Wales's Challenge cup
course, according to the rules, regulations, and time allowance
established for the said course, Mr. J. F. Loubat will be happy
to sail any such match in July next, the race to be sailed on the
day appointed without regard to wind or weather. This offer is
to remain open until the 15th day of September.

Bell's Life in London, London, August 15, 1874.

INTERNATIONAL YACHT CHALLENGE.

To the Editor of Bell's Life in London.

Sir : Should it be agreeable to any member of an organized
European Yacht Club, owning a yacht of at least 300 tons, R. T.
Y. C. measurement, to sail a match, for a one hundred guinea

cup, with the Enchantress, over the Prince of Wales's Challenge
Cup course, according to the rules, regulations, and time allowance
established for said course, I shall be most happy to sail any
such match in July next. The race to take place on the day
appointed without regard to wind or weather. This offer re—
mains open until the 15th day of September,

Yours, &c.   J. F. LOUBAT.

Cowes, August 12, 1874.

The Field, London August 15, 1874.

THE AMERICAN YACHT ENCHANTRESS,

Although it is contrary to our custom to insert challenges,
we give the inclosed, as it relates to a matter of international interest:

SIR:—Should it be agreeable to any member of an organized
European yacht club, owning a yacht of at least 300 tons, R. T.
Y.C. measurement, to sail a match for a one hundred guinea cup
with the Enchantrsss, over the Prince of Wales's Challenge Cup
Course, according to the rules, regulations, and time allowance
established for said course, I shall be most happy to sail such a
match in July next.

The race to take place on the day appointed, without regard
to wind or weather.

This offer remains open until the 15th day of September.

Cowes, August 12, 1874.   J. F. LOUBAT,

Yacht Enchantress, N.Y.Y.C.

The Evening Express, New York, August 15, 1874.

PLUCKY MR. LOUBAT.

There was some good sailing with the fleet-winged vessels
abroad, across the Channel, and the Enchantress made good time

displayed excellent sea-going qualities, and her enterprising owner did not lose heart in the contests nor faith in his boat because
the sail makers were employed in repairing her canvas and the
spar-makers on her spars after the race. The true spirit of an
American yachtsman is dominant in Mr. Loubat's composition ;
he represents the New York Yacht Club, and the spirit which
sent the Henrietta, Vesta, and Fleetwing over to England in an
ocean race, and the Sappho and Dauntless, afterward, into foreign waters in racing trim, is well supported by Mr. Loubat's
challenge to all other clubs. The Enchantress is to sail against any
yacht club in Europe for a one hundred guinea cup, the race to
take place next July. There is time enough for the entries, and
the course chosen is the Prince of Wales's cup course, so that the
stranger who throws his gauntlet into the face of the foreign
yachtsmen gives them the privilege of sailing the race over their
own favorite track. We may justly admire Mr. Loubat's pluck,
and may trust that the competing vessels may be worthy of the
Enchantress—that it may be a fair race and a good one, and that,
if defeated, Mr. Loubat may console himself with the fact that
his courage brought him a good contestant, and he suffers no disgrace by a defeat fairly accomplished.

THE " EN(

From the Illustrated Sporting and Dramatic News, London, Saturday, Aug

CHAPTER XII.

THE ENCHANTRESS IN ENGLAND.

THE FLY-AWAY.

Have you seen the fish with a great long tail ?
The fish that tried to make the " Enchantress " sail ;
She went across to France, on purpose for to win,
Where she got severely beaten by the little yacht " Corinne."

CHORUS :

Have you seen the fish with a great long tail,
A little wiggle waggle, a winkle or a whale ?

She tried again, this day, the challenge cup to catch,
But found, to his surprise, that the " Egeria " was his match,
So home he had to run, with his great long tail,
Followed by the " Shark " a winkle, or a whale.

Have you seen the fish, &c.

Now back to Yankee Land this fish will have to go,
Where he can calculate, and guess, and bounce, and blow
And tell his fellow-countrymen what folly he has seen,
In coming o'er to England, on purpose for to win.

Have you seen the fish, &c.

THE YANKEE BOAT.

O, if you listen, I will sing a little ditty
  Of that Yankee boat that came across the sea,
Which caused a great to do throughout the country,
  Excitement, and great anxiety.

Chorus.—So attention pay,
      To what I say,
        And of this Yankee boat you soon shall hear,
        For you see she came across the ocean,
        From that noted place that is called America.

Now they sent her to old England for improvement,
  Which of course she has been and boldly done her part;
For she's shown them all a wrinkle in the channel,
  Like a little fish away from them did dart.—*Chorus.*

Now that noted little yacht that's called Cetonia,
  Which was thought to be the order of the day;
But this Yankee boat she caused them for to wonder,
  When from her she boldly marched away.—*Chorus.*

Now this long tail fish that came across the ocean,
  It takes a swifter fish than the shark for him to catch;
And, if he hadn't lost his little nosegay.
  Egeria would not seen the way he went.—*Chorus.*

Now the owner has just sent out a challenge,
  But there's something I can scarcely understand,
For those noblemen that thought she was a duffer—
  But still they haven't the nerve to try their hand—
                              [*Chorus.*
Now the rumor was this Yankee boat had foundered,
  And gone to the bottom of the sea;
But I am happy to inform you she is still reigning,
  And they will find her a torment still to be.—*Chorus.*

Now, with all the advice that I have given.
  Of this Yankee boat I hope you understand;
And I guess she'll give our racers all a licking
  Before she goes home to Yankee land.—*Chorus.*

The Field, London, October 10, 1874.

A SEASON YACHT RACING.

*   *   *   *   *   *   *

But the achievements of the English yachts were completely eclipsed by the performances of the American yacht Enchantress, and she certainly did earn a distinction no English yacht could make claim to, although not in the way expected. She appears to have been a moderately good vessel, as originally built; but some improvements, wrought upon her by her designer, turned her into a regular laughing-stock. That she is very fast with the wind well on the quarter, there is no denying, and in the Havre-Southsea match passed the Corinne (35ft. shorter on the load line) in pretty much the same way that the Guinevere or Livonia could. But it was not on this point of sailing that her performances were eccentric, nor in going before the wind, but in beating to windward. She took nearly as long to stay as a coal brig, and then was not certain of doing it, and when her sheets were hauled aft, in a breeze at sea she tumbled about so that it was next to impossible to sail her. Lead ballast—to the tune of seventy tons we believe—has made her capable of standing up much better in a breeze, and it is just as likely she would come out and repeat the Sappho-Cambria performance if any small vessel were matched against her over an open course. The American papers repudiated the notion that she is an "American yacht;" but one inhabitant of the United States, more generous than his compatriots, came forward and claimed her—defects and all. Englishmen ought certainly to be grateful for this; for it is quite bad enough to have to bear with all our own failures, without having to stand sponsors to those we have had nothing to do with.

The Evening Post, New York, November 24, 1874.

AMERICAN YACHTS IN FOREIGN WATERS.

THE EXPLOITS OF THE ENCHANTRESS.

Yankee clippers and American sewing machines have become

pretty well-known all the world over.   The dearest wish of the
manufacturers of the latter article, that no family should be without a sewing machine, is gradually accomplishing itself.   In the
mean time we have given our English cousins "some new wrinkles"
in the matter of yacht-building.   Witness the Sappho and other
American boats built for purposes of speed.   There is now-a-days
scarcely a yacht race of any importance in European waters but
Brother Jonathan is sure to put his keel into it.   Even "Mossoo"
as represented by the Yacht Club of France, cannot get up a
quiet little International Channel Race with the sons of perfidious
Albion but the inevitable Yankee must needs assist.   At the
match from Havre to Southampton, a distance of about eighty-
three miles, held under the auspices of the Yacht Club of France
on the 27th of July last, for prizes amounting to £400, there
were five entries of English yachts, of which we give only the
schooners, and two entries of American yachts :—

ENGLISH YACHTS.

	RIG.	TONS.	OWNERS.
Cetonia,	Schooner	202	Mr. W. Turner.
Gwendolin	"	192	Major Ewing.
Corinne	"	165	Mr. N. Wood.

AMERICAN YACHTS.

	TONS.	OWNERS.
Enchantress	320	J. F. Loubat.
Faustine	120	Mr. P. Russell.

It will be seen that the contest was substantially between
English and American yachts, for the Frenchmen had entered
three small cutters of twenty-six, thirty-five and forty tons respectively.   "Mossoo" in fact organized a little yachting entertainment for the benefit of his foreign friends.   Individually
"Mossoo" much prefers *Les Grandes Eaux de Versailles*.   At 5
o'clock P. M., the club steamer took up a position three miles W.
N.W. of the lighthouse, on Cape La Heve, forming the line
for the start.   The Enchantress went across the line at 5:26, and
the Gwendolin at 5:27, followed by the Faustine, the Corinne
being the last at 5:33.   At 11 o'clock the yachts all found them-

selves becalmed thirty miles from Cape La Heve. The Gwendolin with the Corinne on her port (weather) beam, was leading, and the Cetonia and the Enchantress were broad on their weather quarter. They lay thus becalmed till 11:30, when the Corinne was seen to take a light breeze abeam westerly, and stole away from the Gwendolin. The latter was not a cable's length from her, but got no wind, her sails flapping in folds as she lay almost motionless on the water. In twenty minutes the Corinne was lost to the rest of the fleet, as she sailed off with the westerly breeze. A greater "fluke" was never scored. At sunrise the Corinne was leading five miles ahead of the Enchantress, on the latter's weather bow and to windward of her course. They now had a fine breeze, and the Enchantress went flying along, rapidly overhauling the Corinne and leaving all the others behind. At 6:45 the Enchantress went past the Corinne on her weather, and gave her such a shake up that when her sails filled again down came her fore and main topmasts. She kept on her course for the channel between the Noman and Horse Shoal, the Yankee clipper going clear away. The yachts passed the "winning mark" as follows:—

	H. M. S.		H. M. S.
Enchantress	7 21 40	Gwendolin	7 53 15
Corinne	7 33 20	Faustine	9 1 23

The Corinne, of one hundred and sixty-five tons, was entitled to time from the larger yacht, and won the first prize, namely, two silver statues of gladiators, from models by J. L. Gerome (*Institut de France*) estimated at £320 in value.

The performance of the Enchantress was on this occasion very remarkable, and shows what she can do in a stiff breeze. From sunrise till twenty-one minutes past 7, a not very long period, on the morning of the 27th of July, she gained more than five miles on the Corinne, and came in ahead—thus more than making up all the time she had lost in the calm. The owner of the Enchantress was so well pleased with her performances that we find the following challenge in the columns of the leading English sporting paper, the *Field*, in its number of August 15, last:

" THE AMERICAN YACHT ENCHANTRESS.

" Although it is contrary to our custom to insert challenges, we give the enclosed, as it relates to a matter of international interest :

" SIR :—Should it be agreeable to any member of an organized yacht club, owning a yacht of at least 300 tons R. T. Y. C. measurement, to sail a match for a one-hundred guinea cup with the Enchantress over the Prince of Wales's Challenge Cup course, according to the rules and regulations and time allowance established for said course, I shall be most happy to sail such a match in July next. The race to take place on the day appointed, without regard to wind or weather.

" This offer remains open until the 15th day of September.

"COWES, August 12, 1874.

" J. F. LOUBAT,
"Yacht Enchautress, N. Y. Y. C."

This challenge was not taken up.

Mr. Loubat bought the yacht Enchantress from Mr. George Lorillard, who had her built in this country after a model of Robert Fish. At the close of the yachting season of 1873, in American waters, Mr. Loubat went abroad, his yacht having preceded him ; and during the last winter he engaged the services of Mr. Fish to superintend and direct the alterations he proposed making on her. She was lengthened and otherwise improved at an expense of more than twenty thousand dollars. These alterations were made in England.

When the Enchantress appeared in English waters as a *debutante* this last season, she was the subject of a good deal of comment in yachting circles, and was criticised in a not unkindly spirit by the leading English sporting papers, including the *Field*, which was impartial till some considerable time after the challenge of the Enchantress. But, in an article in the *Field* of October 11, 1874, entitled "A Season's Yacht Racing", the writer goes considerably out of his way to criticise the Enchantress in a spirit which, if not directly dictated by an unfriendly feeling, is certainly in the very worst of taste, more especially (to use his own words, and his own reason for printing the challenge), as it relates to a matter of international interest." While the challenge of the Enchantress remained unanswered it would, perhaps, have been more graceful—certainly more delicate—had those criticisms been left unwritten. The article winds up in the following words :

" The American papers repudiated the notion that she is ' an American yacht .' But one inhabitant of the United States, more generous than his compatriots, came forward and claimed her, defects and all. Englishmen ought certainly to be grateful for this, for it is quite bad enough to have to bear with all our own failures, without having to stand sponsors to those we have had nothing to do with."

We very much doubt if these playful sneers in any manner represent the true sentiments of English yachtsmen, and we are quite certain that the *Field* is not commissioned to speak for "American papers."

The Field, London, October 17, 1874.

The Enchantress, Mr. J. F. Loubat, arrived here on Monday from the eastward. Although there can be no doubt that she did not this season turn out such a success as was expected, yet Mr. Fish, her constructor, is still sanguine of beating the crack yachts of England, and openly states that before returning to America Mr. Loubat's yacht will beat the whole of our English yachts.

The Hampshire Advertiser, Southampton, October 17, 1874.

Mr. Loubat's schooner Enchantress is being stripped, and will go on the mud in a few days to lay up for the winter. Mr. Fish, her designer, is very sanguine that, without any alterations, he will be able next season to beat all the English yachts, and with-

out prejudice to the talents of our English builders, we should
not be surprised if his prognostication was to turn out correct.
We perfectly recollect the Cambria and Sappho matches, and
how we who were believers in the Cambria were surprised to see
the Sappho beat her in the way she did, not but that the Sappho
was as big again as the Cambria, but then we all thought that
in beating to windward she would be beaten so much by the
Cambria that in the run home the Sappho would be unable to
catch her. Recollecting this and also the fact that Mr. Fish,
who made the Sappho what she is, has the Enchantress in hand
and that on her his reputation in a great measure rests, we shall
be very chary of giving an opinion against her.

The Field, London, October 31, 1874.

THE ENCHANTRESS.

Sir:—In *The Field* of the 17th inst. it is stated under head of
"Yachting Intelligence" that Mr. Fish still maintains that the
Enchantress will beat all English yachts.

Those who remember the career of the little Flying Cloud,
how she carried all before her, beating all the small schooners
will scarcely doubt that Mr. Fish is right, and that the Enchantress
will do the same among the large schooners, for she is almost
an exact model (enlarged) of the Flying Cloud. I do not suppose that Mr. Fish has ever seen the Flying Cloud dry, or it
might be said that the Enchantress is a copy of that celebrated
little clipper.

In strong breezes (for these long, sharp vessels can do nothing
in light winds) I do not doubt that the Enchantress will astonish
the Englishmen.

Liverpool, Oct. 22.   Mersey.

CHAPTER XIII.

THE ENCHANTRESS IN RUSSIA AND IN SWEDEN.

The Times, London, July, 1875.

KING OSCAR AT ST. PETERSBURG.

(FROM AN OCCASIONAL CORRESPONDENT.)

St. Petersburg, July 18.

The visit of the King of Sweden is almost ended, as His Majesty is to leave Peterhof for Stockholm late to-morrow night. I may remind your readers that, what at first sight, considering the intricacy of the Cronstadt Channel, might seem an imprudence, is not so in reality, as there is no real night at this season in these latitudes. The smallest print can be read with ease in the open air at midnight. The close of His Majesty's visit was celebrated by a review of some 35,000 troops on Friday, and yesterday there was a grand naval inspection, when almost every available thing that could float belonging to the Russian Government was brought into requisition. It was a gloriously fine day, with just enough breeze to prevent the hot sun being disagreeable. The fleet was anchored in three parallel lines in Cronstadt Roads, and consisted of the following vessels:—Ironclads:— Peter the Great, 4 guns, 12in. (when she gets them); Sebastopol, 18 guns, 8in., broadside, frigate; Petropaulovsk, 18 guns, 8in., broadside frigate; Kreml, 16 guns, 8in., floating battery; Pervenetz, 14 guns, 8in., floating battery; Admiral Lazareff, 6 guns, 9in., in three turrets; Admiral Spiridoff, 4 guns, 9in., 8 in two turrets; Smertch, 4 guns, 9in., in two turrets; Tcharodeika. 4 guns, 9in., in two turrets; Rousalka, 4 guns, 9in., in two turrets; Lava, Latnik, and five other monitors, having a freeboard of about 9in., and carrying one 8in. gun in a single turret. Next come the Voievoda and seven other wooden corvettes, variously armed; the Rurik and six other paddle vessels, including the Emperor's large yacht, the Derjava, which was not used, as she was said to be too long to handle with safety in so crowded a roadstead; and the Erch, screw gunboat, and ten others, carrying one gun each, of various calibres.

Besides the above, at the request of the authorities, the American ships Franklin and Alaska, the Swedish vessels Vanadis and Blenda, the Norwegian frigate St. Olaff, in which His Swedish Majesty came over, and the English Royal Yacht Osborne had positions in about the centre of the lines. The total number of vessels was thus a little over 50, without counting a long line of tiny yachts belonging to the Petersburg Yacht Club. Vice-admiral Gregory Boutakov, so well and favorably known in England as Naval Attache to the Russian Embassy, and author of the able treatise on Naval Tactics, was really in command of the fleet, although the flag of the Grand Duke Constantine as Grand Admiral was flying on the Rurik, Rear-Admirals Erdmann, Geikung and Pilkin, with Captains Selivanov and Drecher, flew their flags and broad pendants, and commanded the various divisions. Vice-Admiral Surdin and Rear-Admiral Warden flew their flags on board the Vanadis and Franklin respectively, and Commander F. Durant was in command of the Osborne, which brought the Duke and Duchess of Edinburgh hither from England.

At about noon, the Emperor, the King of Sweden, the Duke of Edinburgh, the Grand Duke Constantine, and other members of the Imperial family, with their numerous suites, arrived at Cronstadt from the Summer Palace at Peterhof in the yacht

Alexandra.   After steaming up and down the lines and paying visits on board the St. Olaff, the Franklin, and the Petropaulovsk, which last was Admiral Boutakov's flagship, the Imperial and Royal party returned to Peterhof about 2:30.

It is needless to say that during the inspection yards were manned, that cheers were given and salutes fired in great profusion.   The orthodox number of cheers on each occasion was six from each ship, and the salutes consisted of 31 guns.   The din was deafening, and, after their manner, the Americans certainly contributed more than their fair share.   The forts also joined in, and some time after each general salute was finished, as far as the ships were concerned, far-off booms were heard and white wreaths of smoke seen rising from forts apparently miles away inland.   These same wreaths, too, made their appearance in all sorts of odd and unlooked-for spots.   Along the coast line, where no one would have expected to find batteries, the puffs betrayed the existence of many " snakes-in-the-grass."   With regard to the character and efficiency of the ironclads, if Russian accounts are to be trusted, there is not one that would be formidable for five minutes to the Hercules, to say nothing of the Thunderer or Devastation.   The Peter the Great will take nearly a year before she can go to sea.   She has, as yet, no turrets whatever, but so desirable was it considered to make a good show that, actually, false turrets of wooden scantling were constructed and painted to look like what it is hoped the real ones will be some day when their plates are ready and fixed in place. She was begun before the Devastation, so I think the little " scare " that once existed in English Naval circles about her may be considered to be without basis.   There were two other things to strike an English observer yesterday—one, that the seamanship which declined the task of manœuvring the Derjava must be vastly inferior to that which animates the Victoria and Albert on similar occasions ; the other, that the Alexandra, the yacht which could be manœuvred, emitted volumes of black smoke that would have disgraced a Newcastle collier.

The Osborne is expected to reach Portsmoth about the middle of August, when she will be refitted and decorated for her cruise to India with the Prince of Wales.

Brentano's Aquatic Monthly, New York, April, 1879.

THE SCHOONER-YACHT ENCHANTRESS.

The following reminiscence of the long cruise of the Enchantress, Mr. J. F. Loubat, owner, in European waters, we deem of sufficient interest for publication, the more especially as it has not previously appeared in print: During the long cruisings of the Enchantress she visited the principal ports and capitals of the Old World. Wherever she anchored she was received with "all the honors," her generous owner receiving and dispensing unstinted hospitalities and courtesies. She was sailed by Captain Robert Fish, whose handling of the Sappho, to whom England's best lowered their colors, is a matter of yachting history. That the Enchantress made a most favorable impression, and caused her private signal and the signal of the New York Yacht Club to be respected by the yachtingfraternity of distant lands, is as true as the fact that Mr. Loubat issued the broadest and boldest challenge ever published to the yachtsmen of Great Britain, in offering to sail them on their own time allowance and rules, thus virtually "handicapping" his yacht's American model materially; and yet she was permitted to go into winter quarters without an acceptance. The good yacht Enchantress now sails under a foreign flag, having been sold in England.

The following official communication from Gen. Andrews, Minister of the United States in Sweden, explains fully the cordial reception accorded the Enchantress at Stockholm.

LEGATION OF THE UNITED STATES,
STOCKHOLM, SWEDEN, JULY 29, 1875.

Hon. HAMILTON FISH, Secretary of State, Washington, D. C.:

SIR:—As indicating the disposition of King Oscar II., to reciprocate attentions, I would state that Mr. J. F. Loubat, of New York (but now residing in Paris) having arrived here with his remarkably elegant yacht Enchantress, and made an informal visit to the King, in company with the Swedish Admiral Lagercrantz, he was invited with myself to visit His Majesty on Sunday last, at the palace of Drottningholm, and stay to dinner.

We went out in the Swedish Government yacht, accompanied by a small Government steamer, with Admiral Lagercrantz, and by invitation, breakfasted with the King at 1 P.M. Soon after, his Majesty accompanied us in an excursion on the same yacht on Lake Melar, for three hours or more. Returning to Drottningholm, rooms were assigned to Mr. Loubat and myself in the palace, and we had the honor of dining with His Majesty at 5½ o'clock. The Crown Prince Gustaf, four officers of the Household and the Admiral, were of the party on the occasion and at dinner. His Majesty took leave of us at about 8 P. M. He was, of course, very civil and kind during the day.

On Monday, His Majesty and the Crown Prince, accompanied by the Minister of the Marine, Admiral Lagercrantz and four officials of the Court, accepted Mr. Loubat's invitation to visit the Enchantress. At about 1 P. M. a fine lunch was served. Including Gen. Crawford and Mr. Phœnix (Mr. Loubat's traveling companions) and myself, there were twelve seated at the table in the spacious dining saloon of the yacht. His Majesty remained on board upwards of two hours, and the occasion was remarkably pleasant.

Several private dinners have been given to the owner of the yacht. He has been made an honorary member of the Royal Swedish Yacht Club, and has accepted the King's invitation to be present at the annual review of that club on Sunday next.

It seems to be understood that the Enchantress is the first American yacht that has visited Stockholm.

I have the honor to be, etc., etc.,

C. C. ANDREWS.

The New York Times, New York, August 9, 1875.

OUR EUROPEAN SQUADRON.

NORTHERN CRUISE OF ADMIRAL JOHN L. WORDEN.

Cordial reception of the American Officers in Germany, Sweden Norway, and Russia—Magnificent Military and Naval Reviews at St. Petersburg and Cronstadt.

From an Occasional Correspondent.

CRONSTADT, Russia, Tuesday, July 20, 1875.

In the early part of last May a portion of the American squadron now on duty in European waters was ordered to rendezvous at Villefranche, near Nice, to make preparations for a Summer's cruise along the northern coast of Europe. The vessels selected for this duty were the Franklin, bearing the flag of our old Monitor hero, Rear-Admiral John L. Worden; the corvette Alaska, Capt. Carter, and the sloop-of-war Juniata, Commander S. D. Greene, Worden's First Lieutenant in the memorable action at Hampton Roads.

Leaving the harbor of Villefranche May 17, this squadron arrived at Gibraltar on the 23d of the same month, and while there took part in the festivities on the celebration of the Queen's birthday. The officers of the squadron were present, by invitation on the afternoon of that holiday, at the annual review of the garrison upon the famous Neutral Ground, the Admiral accompanying the Governor, Sir E. Williams, the heroic defender of Kars, of Crimean fame, as reviewing officer. By a somewhat curious coincidence, it happened that several of the regiments taking part in this display were representatives of the same bodies whose regimental numbers figure so prominently in our present centennial newspapers. The most noticeable among these was the Twenty–third or Royal Welsh Fusiliers, whose traditional goat appeared on the ground with his regiment. The present incumbent of that time-honored position is a magnificent white cashmere animal, presented to the Fusiliers on their return from the Ashantee campaign by the citizens of Portsmouth. "Billy" had evidently been well drilled, for he marched past the reviewing stand with the precision of a veteran, leading his six or seven hundred masters with becoming gravity. After the review, and during the few days of their stay in port, many civilities were exchanged between the navy men and the officers of the garrison. The Governor led off with a ball, which was followed by dinners on board the flagship and at the various regimental mess rooms. The visit, however, was necessarily a short one, and, on the 28th of May, the squadron again put to sea and the northern cruise proper began.

On the 8th of June the squadron arrived off the mouth of the Elbe, at Cuxhaven, where the German gunboat Loreley was found waiting to receive and convey the Americans to their anchorage further up the river. To many of the new comers the scene on the lower Elbe presented quite a novel spectacle; the long lines of dikes shutting out the water from the green stretches of meadow-land on either side; the fact of reversing the natural order of things so far as to look down to see the surrounding country on a level with the vessel's keel; the first view, in short, of a land where

"People do not live, but go aboard,"

formed a subject of lively discussion. The prevailing sentiment in regard to this curious country is best summed up in the words of one of the spectators, who hazarded the opinion that "Those fellows may think their landscape very fine, but if they ever have water scape, Lord help 'em!" The larger vessel being left at Gluckstadt, about thirty miles from Hamburg, the rest of the squadron proceeded to the city, the Admiral's flag being transferred temporarily to the Alaska.

Nothing could have been more cordial or more flattering than the marked attention with which the American visitors, were officially received in Berlin. The Ministers of War and the Navy entertained the Admiral and his suite at dinner, and Mr. Davis having expressed a wish to present the visitors to his Highness, the Crown Prince, in the absence of the Emperor at Ems, an immediate reply was received inviting the Admiral and staff to dine at Potsdam on the following day with the Prince and his wife, the Princess Royal of England.

The American guests were received at the so-called "New Palace," in Potsdam, built at the close of the Seven Years' War by Frederick the Great. The monarch's object in erecting this splendid building was to show his enemies that he still had plenty of the sinews of war, though it was only by the greatest efforts that he succeeded in obtaining the necessary funds to complete the costly pile. The reception of the Americans on this occasion was one of the pleasantest features of the visit to Germany. The Crown Prince and Princess were most cordial in their welcome conversing freely with their naval guests and conducting their entertainment with gratifying absence of formality. Both expressed a good deal of curiosity in regard to the exhibition at Philadelphia next year, mingled with hopes for its success, to to which the Prince added his regrets at not being able to attend the great World's Fair. Seventy guests were present at the dinner, including Minister Davis and Mrs. Davis, the Admiral and staff,and Lord Odo and Lady Russell, Gen. Dannenberg, Col. Lestocq, and other heroes of the late war represented the military element. At the close of the banquet, and when the Americans were about to retire, they were shown instead through all the historical grounds of Potsdam and Sans Souci at the Prince's invitation, the fountains at the latter resort being played for their benefit, and all the sights of the place opened for their inspection before the party returned to Berlin.

Leaving Berlin on the following day, the Admiral returned to the squadron and started at once for Kiel, where the German iron-clad fleet was awaiting his arrival. This port was reached June 24th by the Franklin and Alaska, the Juniata remaining at Hamburg to undergo some repairs. From a military point of view, it is difficult to overestimate the value of Kiel in its present use as the great naval arsenal of Germany. One can hardly wonder that for the sake of such a prize the Prussians crossed the Eyder that had been for centuries the boundary line dividing them from Denmark. It is perhaps a matter of equal surprise that, in its defenseless state during the early part of the late war, the French did not seize it. One of the German works recently published on the great struggle calls attention to this fact, and adds the laconic comment, ' If they had been Yankees' some would have gone in," a neat tribute to the glories of New Orleans and Mobile Bay. Now that the entrance to the place is so well protected—by the great earthworks at Friedrichsort and elsewhere, and with torpedoes substituted for the beer casks that blocked the channel to the imaginative Bouet Willaumez—an attack would be rendered very difficult. As the Americans came to anchor in this beautiful harbor, a flood of invitations of all kinds was poured on board the Flagship. In spite of the shortness of the visit, the variety of the entertainments offered and the hearty welcome from all sides rendered the few days of the stay thoroughly enjoyable. The iron-clad squadron, four magnificent vessels—Konig Wilhelm, Kaiser, Kronprinz and Hansa under the command of Admiral Henck, had been detained in port several days to participate in the reception of the visitors. Admiral Werner, the commandant of the arsenal, whose career on the coast of Spain attracted so much attention a few years ago, was especially cordial in his welcome. A banquet at his residence, followed by another on the Flagship Wilhelm, were among the first entertainments. During our stay the first Schleswig-Holstein musical festival took place at Kiel, and the Americans were invited to attend as guests of honor. With the renowned Joachim as leader and Clara Schumann as one of the performers the festival proved a great success. It was during a banquet given at the close of these three days of musical feast that the Admiral took occasion to express the thanks of the squadron for the unexpected warmth and cordiality of the welcome extended to the Americans. In conclusion the speaker dwelt upon the valuable qualities of our German citizens at home, and spoke of the pleasure he felt in visiting in person the former home of some of our best Americans. These expressions were received by the assemblage of over 500 guests with enthu-

siastic applause, the allusion to the distant kinsmen evidently re-
calling personal associations to many present.

Leaving Kiel on the 1st of July, the American squadron
fired the usual national salute on the 5th, amid the beautiful
cluster of islands that shut out the Venice of the North from the
open sea. The passage from the Baltic to the city reminds one
irresistibly of the beautiful Thousand Isles with which so many
of your readers are familiar. The ships anchored on the evening
of the 5th at Waxholm, twelve miles below the capital, the channel being too intricate to permit of their proceeding further inland. Their arrival was the signal for the immediate appearance
of the Swedish " mosquito" fleet of light-draft gun-boats, sent
down from Stockholm to receive the visitors. On the same
evening, the Royal yacht Amazon brought down from the capital the American Minister, Gen. Andrews, with the message
that the King had postponed his proposed trip to Russia to greet
the Americans in person.

On arriving at Stockholm the party were driven at once to the
Royal Palace. King Oscar, a tall, fine-looking man, somewhat past
the middle age, appeared in the audience hall as soon as he had
been notified of the arrival of his guests. His Majesty wore the
Swedish naval uniform, not only as a compliment to the visitors
but probably to remind them that in the by-gone times he had
been "one of them," as his early life was spent in the Swedish
Navy. Of this his cordial manner left no reason to doubt, his
greeting being that of a brother officer in a similar service. His
Majesty expressed much regret at having to leave Stockholm,
"but," said he, "I have given orders that you shall be received as
my own guests," and to judge from the result, they obey the
royal mandates tolerably well in Sweden. In reply to a question
from one of the officers, his Majesty said : "I look forward to
my trip across the Baltic with great interest, as I am still fond
of the sea. I like it so much better than this duty." At the
close of the interview his Majesty replied to the Admiral's fare-
well by saying that it should be only an *au revoir*, as they would
meet again in Russia. The King left on the same evening for

Cronstadt, but his instructions as to the entertainment of his guests were most pleasantly observed.

Detained at the Waxholm anchorage by unfavorable weather, the Franklin and Alaska did not reach Cronstadt until the early morning of July 12. The vessels were met on their arrival off the harbor by an officer from the flagship Rurik, with an invitation from the Lord High Admiral to take part in a naval review, for which preparations were being made near the harbor forts. The invitation having been accepted, the American ships were given a position of honor as leading vessels of the central column of "heavies." Even at this early date (the review not taking place until the 17th) the assemblage of war-vessels presented a most imposing appearance. West of Fort Nicholas, a formidable battery defending the southern side of Cronstadt, were arranged four columns of vessels. The southern line was formed of the smaller craft, yachts and dispatch boats. The tall, symmetrical spars and jaunty appearance of the leading vessel in this column were a guarantee of her nationality, and more than one keen eye had picked her out as a Yankee craft before she hoisted her colors and displayed the well known burgee of Loubat's yacht, the graceful Enchantress. North of the small-fry a column of seven single-turreted monitors formed a second line, headed by their Flagship, the gun-boat Volga. Still further to the northward came seven wooden corvettes and frigates, including, as a rear guard, the St. Olaff and Vanadis, which, with the gun-boat Blenda, formed the Swedish contingent. The above mentioned gun-boat was the last vessel in the fourth line of nine similar craft that formed the northern boundary of the van division. On one side of this fleet were the fortresses of Peter and Alexander, the southern line running from Fort Paul westward to battery No. 3. In the rear of this division lay the yacht Rurik, bearing the flag of the Grand Duke Constantine, the Lord High Admiral of Russia, under whose management the whole fleet had been placed. Immediately to the rear of his vessel and stretching far away to the westward were grouped the heavier ships, in three columns, double and three turreted monitors to the southward;

iron-clad gun-boats (led by the Duke of Edinburgh's yacht Osborne) on the north flank, and in the centre led by the Franklin and Alaska, the pick of the Russian iron-clad Navy, Peter the Great, an immense turreted ram, a project of Admiral Popoff's, and then the Peter and Paul, Sebastopol, Kreml, and Pervenentz, heavy iron-clad frigates, in the order named, the line ending with the Bogatyr and another corvette, the name of the former probably a familiar one to those who witnessed the reception of the Grand Duke Alexis.

The Grand Duke Constantine repaired on board the Flagship in person to welcome the Admiral to Russia, and to tender his thanks for the proposed participation of the Americans in the coming ceremony. When the Admiral expressed his acknowledgment of the honor accorded to his ships in placing them in the leading line, his Highness replied, pointing to the long rows of monitors: "You are here, Admiral, among the children of your gallant deed; it is only right that you should take the first place," a graceful compliment, which was duly appreciated by the naval men present. At a dinner, given the same evening aboard the Rurik, the Grand Duke spoke most feelingly of the intimate relations between the two countries, and proposed the health of "The President," which was received with all the honors.

During the few days preceding the naval review the Americans busied themselves in a sort of steeplechase through the different sights of St. Petersburg, the time of their stay being unfortunately too limited to admit of extended visits anywhere. The magnificence of St. Isaac's; the gloomy grandeur of the Kazan Cathedral; the beautiful Hermitage, with its gaudy frescoes and treasures of art; the famous Winter Palace; the fortress of St. Petersburg, church and castle in one, with the tombs of the Czars; the little hut, so carefully preserved and piously revered, where Peter the Great once held his court; the thousand and one monuments of departed monarchs or of glorious triumphs—all passed before them, like the shifting scenes of a kaleidoscope. It was too much like the model railroad dinner—one mouthful, obtained by dint of much labor and bodily toil, and then—all aboard? The excursionists from the ships did their best under these discouraging circumstance, their uniforms being an " open sesame " to all places of amusement or interest, and their search for novelties much lightened by the kindly services of the Russian officers, who piloted them about in gallant style.

Meanwhile the official entertainments formed a part of the daily occupation of the Admiral and his suite. The Czar was at Peterhoff, the Russian Versailles, a beautiful palace and park opposite Cronstadt, on the southern side of the bay, with his guests, King Oscar II., of Sweden, and the Duke and Duchess of Edinburgh. On the 13th a grand review of the Imperial Guard and other troops took place at Krasnoe Selo, fifteen miles from Peterhoff. The review was one of the most brilliant military pageants I have ever seen, over 50,000 men of the different arms being upon the field. The King of Sweden was the reviewing officer, attended by the Czar and a brilliant suite. A novelty to the American visitors was the presence in line of a large body of Circassians and Cossacks in their curious national costumes. The manœuvering was simply perfect; battalion after battalion of foot marched past, double company front, with uniform step, and with aligments such as columns of fours might envy; following them came the cavalry—walk, trot, gallop, walk—as the different signals rang out from the bugle, the changes being so instantaneous as to seem almost marvelous.

Once, a squadron of Circassians rode by, a signal was made to "wheel and charge," and this difficult movement was so perfect that even in the staff there was an unofficer-like "buzz" of approval, while the King of Sweden openly expressed his admiration, and as the squadron rode back the Czar himself said a few words of compliment. Instantly the air rang again with a mighty shout from the delighted troopers, as different from the regulation "cheer" as one can well imagine. It is not often that soldiers get such a compliment from the Emperor on the reviewing grounds, but that none ever deserved it more would be the testimony of all who witnessed the feat.

At noon precisely on the 17th, the Emperor's yacht Derjawa, followed by two other small vessels as escort, appeared at the head of the in-shore line of vessels off Cronstadt. The presence of the Czar was at once acknowledged by all the vessels manning yards, (or turrets, as the case might be,) but no further demonstration was made until the yacht had passed down the centre of the van division and anchored abreast of the Rurik. As she came to, the Emperor's standard was hauled down, and the blue and yellow of Sweden took its place at the Derjawa's mainmasthead. Then from every fort and every vessel of the great fleet the national salute came thundering forth, mingled with the cheers of the seamen and the martial strains of the Swedish and Russian national anthems. Nothing I have ever seen afloat could equal this imposing display; the review at Portsmouth in 1867, in honor of the Sultan, and considered a magnificent spectacle, was far inferior to this. Fancy a fleet whose line of anchorage covered a space of nearly two miles and a half, treble columns, with fifty vessels of war in the line, many of them among the most formidable ships afloat, add to this the shouts of the men, the roar of the artillery, the clash of the music, and you have a scene not to be forgotten. After a short visit to the Swedish Flagship, the imperial barge came alongside of the Franklin, and the Czar, King Oscar, the Duke and Duchess of Edinburgh, the Grand Duke Constantine, the Czarewitch, and his pretty wife, the Princess Dagmar, with a large retinue, came on board the American vessel, were the imperial standard was hoisted at the main. The Grand Duke Constantine presented the officers to the Czar, the King of Sweden greeting them as previous Stockholm acquaintances, with a cheery, "How are you all now, gentlemen?" which provoked an audible smile from some of the "unterrified." The imperial party inspected the ship throughout, praising her appearance very highly, and seeming especially surprised by the prevailing neatness. In truth, that seems the most noticeable feature of our Yankee men of

war as compared with those of other nationalities, most of which
are anything but successful in that respect.

At the Krasnoe-Selo review, where the Americans were
seated in the Empress' pavilion, directly opposite the reviewing
officers, I had seen the Czar again for the first time since that
memorable Summer day in Paris in 1867, when Berezowsky
attempted his life. When on board the Franklin I had an
opportunity of viewing him still more closely. Time has
wrought its inevitable changes, but the dignified bearing, the
firm set of the lips, and the clear eye of the great ruler of all
the Russias are as of old. His character lies written on his
face, a proud, determined, but kind-hearted and liberal-minded
man. His brother Constantine has the appearance common to
many aristocratic Englishmen, that the British cut of his
whiskers seems to increase still further. But in spite of his
grave, reserved appearance, his Highness can crack a joke and
enjoy one with the best of them, and many are the stories told
by his officers in corroboration thereof. Among the suite I
noticed a tall, distinguished looking officer, with iron-gray hair,
a quiet, rather sad-looking face, and a decided stamp of superiority about his whole appearance. Though he appeared in the
uniform of a general officer of engineers I could not place him
at first, but on inquiry I found how much he deserved attention
as the commander of Sebastopol, the famous Todleben. I was
no longer surprised at his being one of the very few present
who wore the Cross of St. George, of the first class, a decoration
that the Czar himself does not wear, as being one reserved, in his
opinion, " for those to whom the country is indebted for deliverance
from imminent danger or for heroic efforts to that end."

On leaving the Franklin, as the imperial standard was hauled
down it was saluted as before by the American Flagship and all
the vessels and forts. The Emperor then repaired on board his
yacht, signalled to the fleet his commendation and thanks, and
on his way back to Peterhof passed close to the Franklin, bowing repeatedly in answer to the salutes from that ship and the
Alaska. On the same evening the Grand Duke Constantine

conveyed officially to Admiral Worden the thanks of the Czar for his reception on board, coupled with an invitation to attend an evening fete at Peterhof on the following day.

This closing scene in the gala week was fully equal to any of the other magnificent displays that had previously taken place. For miles the grounds in the vicinity of the Czar's Summer palace were illuminated *a giorno* with colored lanterns; the palace and the islands on the lake, the "*piece des suisses*" of the park were one mass of lights of every kind. Even the walks winding about in every direction were traced in glowing devices of every hue. On one of the largest islands all the invited guests were assembled to witness a ballet by the imperial troupe, after which an elegant collation was served, the fete concluding with a brilliant display of fireworks.

The King of Sweden left on the evening of the 19th for Stockholm his squadron being accompanied by all the vessels of the van division. All the ships in the harbor were brilliantly illuminated in his honor. As the Vanadis passed the American Flagship, during a pause in the cheering, the King sang out, "goodnight, Admiral, and bon voyage," a compliment instantly acknowledged by three times three from the Yankee men-of-war.

On the following morning the American vessels got under way and left the harbor, escorted by the Peter the Great to the offing, the Russian vessels of the rear division, at anchor, saluting the Admiral's flag with thirteen guns. With a short visit to Copenhagen, where the Juniata is expected to join, the northern cruise of our squadron will terminate, the vessels touching as Flushing and Plymouth on their return to Gibraltar and the Mediterranean.

While there will be quite a general satisfaction among the members of the squadron when the fatted calf of welcome has been killed for good, and the quiet of ordinary routine is restored, there are few who do not appreciate the advantages to the country of a trip of this kind. It is impossible to give an adequate idea of the interest taken by the mass of foreigners in anything American—in that far-off country which in spite of its original ideas of government seems to enjoy such great prosperity. It was touching to find among the thousands of visitors who flocked to see the strangers, many who came hundreds of miles to have one glimpse of the Stars and Stripes, for the sake of personal associations, or with the thought of some friend or relative who had left the Fatherland for a new home beyond the seas. The universal cordiality of the welcome extended to our ships by German, Swede, and Russian alike is most gratifying to all who feel that even in this slight way some knowledge may be gained by them of the great country of which they so often hear. While it is a subject of general regret that these visits could not have been made in more modern types of naval architecture, one finds not a little consolation for this drawback in the high terms of praise accorded to the personnel of the squadron. No notice of their movements has appeared in any journal unaccompanied by the highest terms of praise of the officers and men, and in every port especial mention has been made of the splendid bearing of the officers and the discipline and efficiency of their subordinates.

The American Register, Paris, September 25, 1875.

THE YACHT ENCHANTRESS.

Mr. J. F. Loubat, the proprietor of the yacht Enchantress, has returned to Paris, after a two months' cruise in his beautiful vessel. He visited Sweden, Norway and Russia, and everywhere during his trip was the recipient of marked favor and courtesy. The King of Sweden visited the American yacht; he remained several hours on board and lunched with Mr. Loubat. In Russian waters Mr. Loubat met with the same extreme kindness and attention. Admiral Popoff, of the Russian Navy, visited the Enchantress; as did also the

Grand Duke Constantine, who received in return the visit of Mr. Loubat and the American gentlemen who were his guests. The Enchantress is now at Cowes, where she will be laid up during the winter.

The Commonwealth, Boston, November 6, 1876.

FROM ENGLAND.

Special to the Commonwealth.

COWES (ENGLAND), Oct. 15, 1875.

THE NEW YORK YACHT ENCHANTRESS IN RUSSIAN AND SCANDI-NAVIAN WATERS.

Having vainly sought to have his challenge to all English yachts accepted, and finding that the French Yacht Club were to give no international channel race, Mr. Loubat, owner of the yacht Enchantress, of the New York Yacht Club, decided upon making a cruise to Sweden, Norway and Russia, and started on the 18th of June from Cherbourg, accompanied by his friends General Crawford and Lloyd Phœnix as his guests. They reached Copenhagen on the 24th of June, remained there two days, and on the 2d of July arrived at Cronstadt. The yacht had no sooner anchored than an officer came on board, sent by Captain Koupreyanoff, of the Russian iron-clad man of war Pervenetz, which was acting as guard-ship, to offer his compliments and services. On the morning of the 4th of July the Enchantress was duly " dressed," having the Russian flag at the fore. Again was a Russian officer sent on board with thanks for the compliment, and with renewed expressions of good-will. Admiral Popoff, who twice commanded the Russian fleet in the Pacific, and is well-known in San Francisco, which city he several times visited, came on board the yacht, and after remaining some time informed Mr. Loubat that the Grand Duke Constantine would call on the 6th. On that day the Grand Duke came on board, and after a very pleasant visit took Mr. Loubat to dine

with him. During the course of the conversation the Grand
Duke referred in the kindest terms to the mission upon which
the Hon. G. V. Fox went to Russia some years since, and at
which time Mr. Loubat was one of his secretaries. The Grand
Duke also evinced much interest in Captain Robert Fish, the
well-known modeller, and now sailing-master of the Enchantress.
He consulted him as regards the modelling of some new war
vessels to be constructed for the Russian Navy, and was exceedingly courteous to the American gentlemen during the whole of
their interview. Admiral Popoff took Mr. Loubat with him to
visit the new Russian ship Peter the Great, an immense turretted
iron-clad ram, considered the most powerful vessel afloat—and
which was constructed after the plans and under the supervision
of the Admiral—and in every way displayed the utmost friend-
liness to the owner of the Enchantress and his party.

On the 12th of July the members of the St. Petersburg
Yacht River Club came to Cronstadt in their yachts, and were
entertained on board of the Enchantress. The next day the
American party dined at the club-house, which was most ele-
gantly decorated and festooned with the American and Russian flags. There were very complimentary toasts proposed in
honor of the United States, and most amicable speeches were
pronounced by the Russian gentlemen and responded to by the
Americans. The next day the Enchantress, by order of
Grand Duke Constantine, was towed into the outer roads and
placed at the head of the line of yachts which were to take positions in a grand naval review at which were to be present
fifty-three men-of-war, the American vessels Franklin (Admiral
Worden's Flagship,) and the Alaska among the number. The
King of Sweden was there in his frigate, the Vanadis. There
were also the Swedish Gunboat Blenda, and the Norwegian
frigate Saint Olaf, and the Queen of England's yacht Osborne,
which had brought over the Duke and Duchess of Edinburgh.
The review was one of the most imposing of its kind, in fact,
it was so very brilliant as to excite the jealousy of the reporter
for the London *Times*, who in his letter published in that journal

went out of his way to reflect in a sarcastic manner upon the seamanship of the Russians, the Emperor not coming out in his yacht, the Derjava, but taking a smaller vessel. This course was unfavorably contrasted with that pursued in English waters by those who command the royal yacht Albert and Victoria. The good taste of the strictures in question will be the better appreciated when it is added that the Czar's yacht was not made use of simply because there was not a sufficient depth of water for her to reach Peterhof, the Imperial summer residence.

On the 19th the Enchantress weighed anchor, sailing away along the line of war vessels. On passing Admiral Boutakoff's ship—the second in command, Grand Duke Constantine being commander-in-chief—the Enchantress dipped her colors, where-upon the band on the Russian ship played " Hail Columbia," the Admiral and officers remaining uncovered until the air was finished. These were unusual honors to render to a yacht, but the Enchantress was the first American vessel of the kind which had visited Cronstadt, save Vanderbilt's North Star, many years since, and the Russians made the most of the opportunity for giving proof of their friendship and good-will to our people.

On the 22d of July the Enchantress reached Stockholm, and on the Saturday following Mr. Loubat was presented to the King at Drottningholm Palace by Admiral Lagercrantz, and by invitation of His Majesty the proprietor of the Enchantress and the American minister, Gen. C. C. Andrews, spent the following day with him. They sailed to the palace on the King's yacht, lunched and dined with His Majesty, who, the next day, came on board the Enchantress, where he was entertained at lunch, and remained several hours. The King expressed his regret at not being able to visit the centennial exposition, but will send his second son—an officer in the Swedish navy. With His Majesty on board the Enchantress were the Crown Prince, Baron Von Otter, Minister of the Navy; Admiral Lagercrantz; Baron Flake, Master of the Royal Household; Major Ribbing, tutor of the Crown Prince; also the Chamberlain on duty. The American minister was present. On this occasion the King, for the first time, tasted Catawba wine.   He drank with American wine, said he, to the prosperity of the United States and perpetual friendship between the two countries.   We may add that His Majesty found the wine so much to his liking that he ordered a supply to be purchased for the palace.

It should have been mentioned above that the Enchantress passed near Elsinore, in the Sound, the Russian war vessel Swetlana, commanded by the Grand Duke Alexis, who is to make a two-years' cruise in the Mediterranean, will then be appointed Admiral, and in command of a fleet will again visit the United States.

As the Enchantress was to continue her cruise, the King of Sweden himself wrote out the itinerary of a tour through Norway for the American party, and said he should advise one of his chamberlains for Norway to take charge of them upon their arrival at Christiania.   Before leaving, however, Mr. Loubat and his friends were invited by King Oscar to remain and be present at the regatta of the Royal Swedish Yacht Club, of which the King is president, and of which His Majesty caused Mr. Loubat to be made an honorary member.

On Sunday, August 1st, the American party spent the day upon the King's steam yacht, where they were joined after the regatta by His Majesty, who had been sailing his yacht with the other vessels of the kind belonging to the club.   The American visitors noticed with pleasure the affable manner, in fact, the true sailor-like bluffness, with which the King went among the people.   From the highest to the lowest all sailed their own yachts; and it was a pleasant thing to witness the King distributing prizes and shaking hands with the winners.   After the Minister of the Navy had addressed the yachtsmen and caused the report of the races to be read, a pause took place to allow time for objections, if any were to be made, and then the names of the fortunate parties were read out aloud amid the applause of the people assembled; and, as said above, the King personally complimented them.

Returning to Stockholm, the yachts were all towed by

steamers ablaze with Venetian lights and firing rockets. The villas along the coast were illuminated, and also sent up rockets, and thus for a distance of over eight miles the Americans witnessed one of the most beautiful sights one could behold.

Leaving Stockholm, the Enchantress visited Gottenborg, Christiania and Bergen, in which places the vessel first displayed the New York Yacht Club Flag. Wherever they went, Mr. Loubat and his friends met with the same kindness. It was evident the people were delighted to greet Americans with more than usual courtesy. Many of them have relatives and friends in the United States who are prospering in their new home, and, it was, doubtless, pleasant to them to have the opportunity of greeting cheerfully and cordially citizens of the great Republic. The Enchantress was visited by all classes, and the party on board of her will long remember this most interesting cruise. Doubtless the popularity of our representative at Stockholm, Gen. C. C. Andrews, added to the favor shown to the party upon the yacht, as the General was so much with them ; but, above all, was the sincere desire of the people to evince goodwill towards Americans. The official reports made by General Andrews upon the institutions of Sweden and Norway have attracted much attention in European political circles, and have rendered him very popular, as we said above, in these countries, and the party on the Enchantress found the Minister most willing to be of service. The Enchantress is at present being laid up for the winter at Cowes, from which place lately sailed the celebrated American yacht Sappho, now the property of Prince Sciarra of Rome. NAUTILUS.

CHAPTER XIV.

MR. LOUBAT'S CUP TO THE ROYAL ALBERT YACHT CLUB.

The Evening Post, New York, July 7, 1875,

AN AMERICAN YACHTSMAN'S GIFT TO THE ROYAL ALBERT YACHT CLUB.

Messrs. Tiffany & Co., of Union Square, have just finished a silver cup ordered by an American gentleman, now residing abroad, for presentation to the Royal Albert Yacht Club. The cup, including pedestal, is forty inches in height and nineteen inches in width, and in originality of design and workmanship is one of the finest pieces of silver plate ever executed in this country.

The pedestal is of ebony, and ornamented with a large silver plate in the form of a square-sail bent to a yardarm. It is inscribed as follows: "Presented to the Royal Albert Yacht Club by J. F. Loubat, Esq." The cup is supported on a circular base, ornamented with dolphins' heads in high relief, and bound with a massive hawser. The lower part of the body of the cup is burnished, but above the rim or belt, upon a concave surface, it bears an elaborate design of sailor-boys with joined hands, forming a ring upon the greensward and dancing. Various nautical objects, such as capstans, tillers, anchors and cables, are grouped in with the figures. This design forms a most elegant piece of repousse.

From either side of the body two gracefully curving arms or handles spring, and are ornamented with laurel blossoms at the top and laurel wreaths hang pendant at the curves. The neck of the cup is ornamented in relief with tridents and female heads crowned with cereal productions peculiar to America. To relieve the somewhat formal shape of the neck sprays of palm are introduced, springing from the body at the point of union with the handles and forming a curve to the crown of the neck. The introduction of these palm branches serve to carry off the lines of the arms, and adds greatly to the general effect of the design.

The crown of the neck is ornamented with a winged figure of Victory, kneeling and with outstretched arms holding the laurel wreaths of victory. This figure is exquisitely modelled, and is, as well as the cup which it surmounts, a triumph of the silversmiths' art. The neck of the vase shows the rich satin finish, but the figures and ornamentations in relief are tinted with gold, which greatly enhances the richness of the general effect.

The cup is to be shipped to Europe on Saturday, but in the meantime it will remain on exhibition at the store of Messrs. Tiffany & Co., in Union Square. It is eminently worthy of the notice of connoisseurs. Its destination will give the art-workers in silver in England a good idea of the progress of the art in this country, and that it will be accepted as a creditable production of artistic skill we have no doubt.

* * *

Hunt's Yachting Magazine, London, September, 1875.

ROYAL ALBERT YACHT CLUB REGATTA.

Third day.—The liberal prizes offered on Thursday, the final day of the regatta, attracted nearly all the most famous of our racing vessels, and of the nineteen names figuring on the card, only one or two were not yachts which have won world-wide reputations. Only two were absent at the start, namely, the Odetta and Hypatia, and had there been a sailing breeze the match would have been something to remember. Unfortunately, as is so often the case when unusually handsome prizes are given, the weather was unfavorable, and so the great match for Mr. Loubat's cup was unsuccessful in providing sport. With such a paltry and baffling wind none of the yachts engaged had any fair chance of showing their sailing powers, and the disposal of the prizes was more the result of luck than anything else. The following were the conditions of the match:—First prize (presented by J. F. Loubat, Esq.), value £200; second, value £70, and third, value £50, for yachts of 40 tons and upwards, belonging to any royal yacht club, or to any recognized yacht club of a foreign country. The rig of the first vessel in to determine the rig of the winner, the second prize to be awarded to the vessel of different rig saving her time, and the third prize to the vessel of other rig saving her time. Course, from starting vessel round the Nab Light, thence round a Flagboat moored off Yarmouth. Once round. The starters were:—

Numbered as in Hunt's Universal Yacht List for 1875.

NO.	NAMES OF YACHTS.	RIG.	TONS.	OWNERS.	BUILDERS.
1237	Iona	Cutter.	66	J. Ashbury, Esq., M.P.	Ratsey.
402	Cuckoo	Cutter.	93	Harry Hall, Esq.	Fife.
1365	Kriemhilda	Cutter.	105	The Count Batthyany,	Ratsey.
1839	Neva	Cutter.	62	R. K. Holms-Kerr, Esq.	Fife.
1927	Oimara	Cutter.	159	J. Wylie, Esq.	Steel.
725	Fiona	Cutter.	78	E. Boutcher, Esq.	Fife.
2873	Vol-au-Vent	Cutter.	102	Col. Markham.	Ratsey.
1934	Olga	Schoon'r	220	J. A. Hankey, Esq.	Henderson.
541	Egeria	Schoon'r	155	J. Mulholland, Esq.	Wanhill.
947	Gwendolin	Schoon'r	192	Major Ewing.	Nicholson.
384	Corinne	Schoon'r	162	N. Wood, Esq.	Ratsey.
780	Flying Cloud	Schoon'r	75	F. Cox, Esq.	Inman.
1408	Latona	Yawl.	163	A. B. Rowley, Esq.	J. White.
861	Gertrude	Yawl.	68	Sir A. Fairbairn, Bart.	Wanhill.
762	Florinda	Yawl.	163	W. Jessop, Esq.	Nicholson.
1047	Heron	Yawl.	45	F. Blackwood, Esq.	Ratsey.

The Odetta and Hypatia entered, but did not start.

The morning was hazy and without a breath of wind, but about 9 h. 30 m. a light south-west breeze sprung up, but the yachts in shore did not get it, and the start had to be delayed until about 10 h. 45 m., when a light S. S. W. wind gave the yachts steerage way, and they were sent on their journey. With balloon topsails and spinnakers on bowsprits, the yachts drifted across the line in the most leisurely manner, the Flying Cloud being first away. They continued working down towards the Nab until about twelve o'clock, when the wind entirely ceased and kedges were let go by many, and thus they lay for about an hour when an air came from the south, which gradually westered until it was about south-west, and they got round the Nab Light ship thus:—Vol-au-Vent 3 h. 17 m. 15 s., Gertrude 3 h. 17 m. 15 s., Fiona 3 h. 19 m. 35 s., Neva 3 h. 26 m. 25 s., Arrow 3 h. 28 m., 25 s. Latona 3 h. 28 m. 30 s., Cuckoo 3 h. 29 m. 15 s., Iona 3 h. 30 m. 5 s., Corinne 3 h. 31 m. 0 s., Egeria 3 h. 31 m. 5 s. Florinda 3 h. 32 m. 30 s., Kriemhilda 3 h. 34 m. 10 s., Gwendolin 3 h. 34 m. 15 s., Olga 3 h. 35 m. 10 s., Heron 3 h. 41 m. 0 s. Flying Cloud 3 h. 43 m. 0 s.

The wind now freshened a little and with spinnakers on bowsprits they were making better progress. Vol-au-Vent left the others a little, and Kriemhilda getting past Iona closed up to Cuckoo. Off Egypt the wind westered more and rain began to fall, and the Vol-au-Vent was far ahead of the others and got round the mark-boat off Yarmouth about 9 h. 30 m. Nearly all the yachts lay becalmed until about 9 h. P.M., when a nice W. S. W. breeze came, and soon afterwards they all got round the mark-boat and began the homeward journey to Southsea. The wind was shifting about very much but the Vol-au-Vent got to the end of the course before meeting the tide, whilst the others being caught by it, and getting so little wind that kedges were let go, and some were hours afterwards in finishing. The times taken were:—

	H. M. S.		H. M. S.		H. M. S.
Vol-au-Vent.	12 41 50	Gwendolin	3 2 20	Gertrude..	3 12 50
Corinne........	2 45 40	Fiona	3 4 30	Florinda ..	3 18 25
Egeria........	2 49 52	Neva	3 11 20	Kriemhil'a	4 2 20

The Vol-au-Vent thus takes the £200, Corinne the £70, and the Gertrude the £50. The race was one of the most tedious ever sailed and was a tiresome wind up to an otherwise excellent regatta.

———

To J. F. Loubat, Esq.,

      Owner of the yacht Enchantress,

           New York Yacht Club.

Sir :—In the name of the Royal Albert Yacht Club, we the undersigned desire to express to you our thanks for the munificent gift recently presented by you to our club.

America has ever been foremost in promoting yacht building and yacht racing, and it is most gratifying to us to welcome to our shores an American gentleman in many ways distinguished both in his own country and in Europe, and whose love of a noble sport must powerfully contribute to strengthen this natural bond of union between the two nations.

We have accepted this handsome trophy as a token of the good-will and fellowship which have long existed and will long endure between the yachtsmen of America and England.

That our club should be selected by you to receive this beautiful specimen of American art, and above all this noble token of personal generosity demands more than our silent acceptance.

We trust, therefore, that you will accept our sincere thanks for the gift itself, and our expression of admiration and sympathy with the motives which have prompted you to present to our club such a valuable and lasting memento of the kindly feeling and generous sentiments entertained by yourself.

Alfred,*

Commodore.

Wm. Corring Gordon,   Batthyany,
     Vice Commodore.   *Rear Commodore .*

*H. R. H. the duke of Edinburgh.

CHAPTER XV.

THE YACHT RACING ASSOCIATION.

SAILING RULES, 1876.

MANAGEMENT OF THE RACES.

1. All Racers, and all Yachts sailing therein, shall be unaer
the direction of the Flag Officers or Sailing Committee of the
Club under whose auspices the Races are being sailed. All matters shall be subject to their approval and control; and all doubts,
questions, and disputes, which may arise shall be subject to their
decision. Their decisions shall be based upon these rules so far
as they will apply, but as no rules can be devised capable of
meeting every incident and accident of sailing, the Sailing Committee should keep in view the ordinary customs of the sea, and
discourage all attempts to win a Race by other means
than fair sailing and superior speed and skill. The decisions of the Sailing Committee shall be final, unless they
think fit, on the application of the parties interested, or
otherwise, to refer the questions at issue for the decision
of the Council of the Yacht Racing Association. No
member of the Sailing Committee or Council shall take part in
the decision upon any disputed question in which he is directly
interested. The Sailing Committee, or any officer appointed to

take charge for the day, shall award the prizes, subject to rule 30. If any yacht be disqualified, the next in order shall be awarded the prize.

POSTPONEMENT OF RACES.

2. The Sailing Committee, or officer in charge for the day, shall have power to postpone any race, should unfavorable weather render such a course desirable.

MEASUREMENT FOR TONNAGE.

3. The tonnage of every yacht entered to sail in a race shall be ascertained in the manner following: The length shall be taken in a straight line at the deck, from the fore part of the stem to the after-part of the stern-post; from which deducting the breadth, the remainder shall be esteemed the length to find the tonnage; the breadth shall be taken from outside to outside of the planking, in the broadest part of the yacht, and no allowance shall be made for wales, doubling planks, or mouldings of any kind; then multiplying the length by the breadth, and the product by half the breadth, and dividing the result by 94, the quotient shall be deemed the true tonnage; provided always that if any part of the stem or stern-post, or other part of the vessel at or below the load water-line project beyond the length taken as above mentioned, such projection or projections shall, for the purposes of finding the tonnage, be added to the length taken as stated. In the case of a yacht whose stern-post has an elbow, the length shall be taken to a point where the stern-post, if its rake were continued, would cut the deck-line; and in measuring schooners or other yachts with overhanging stems, the length shall be taken to a point half the distance between the fore part of the stem at the deck line and a perpendicular to the true load water, line at its fore-end. The fraction $\frac{47}{94}$ and over to be counted as a ton and any fraction under   to be disregarded. If, from any peculiar ity in the construction of a yacht, or other cause, the measurer shall be of opinion that this rule will not measure the yacht fairly, he shall report the circumstances to the Council or Sailing Committee, who, after making such inquiries as they may con-

sider necessary, shall award a certificate of tonnage accordingly. The certificate of tonnage of The Yacht Racing Association shall be deemed a yacht's true racing tonnage, so long as she remains unaltered.

TIME ALLOWANCE.

4. Time shall be allowed on arrival for difference in tonnage, according to the annexed scale, increased or decreased in proportion to the length of different courses. If it is necessary during a race to shorten the course, the time allowance shall be reduced in proportion.

ENTRIES.

5. Entries shall be made with the Secretary at least forty-eight hours previous to the time appointed for starting each race. In case of a Sunday intervening, twenty-four hours to be added,

Form of entry to be signed by the owner, or his representative, previous to the race.

Please to enter the ———— yacht for the ———— race at ———— on the ————. Her distinguishing flag is ————, and her tonnage, in accordance with rule 3, is ———— tons. I undertake sailing under this entry she shall not have on board any bags of shot; that all her ballast shall be properly stowed under the platform or in lockers, and shall not be shifted or trimmed in any way whatever; and that I will obey and be bound by the Sailing Rules of The Yacht Racing Association.

Signed this   day of

Should any yacht duly entered for a race not start, or having started should she give up, or be disabled during the race, such yacht shall, in the event of the race being resailed, be entitled to start; but no new entries shall be received under any circumstances whatever for a postponed race.

OWNERSHIP.

6. Each yacht entered for a race, together with her gear, must be the *bona fide* property of the person or persons in whose name or names she is entered, who must be a member or members of a recognised yacht club.

ONLY ONE YACHT OF SAME OWNER.

7. No owner shall be allowed to enter more than one yacht in a race, except in cases in which a prize is given for each rig, when one yacht of each rig may be entered.

ONE YACHT ENTITLED TO SAIL OVER.

8. When a prize has been offered for competition, any yacht, duly entered, may claim to sail over the course and shall be entitled to the prize; subject, however, to Rule 2.

SLIDING KEELS.

9. No yachts which are fitted with machinery to shift keels, or otherwise to alter their form, shall be permitted to enter.

MEMBER ON BOARD.

10. Every yacht sailing in a race shall have on board a member of a recognised yacht club, who, before the prize is awarded, shall, if required, sign a declaration, that the yacht under his charge has strictly conformed to all the sailing regulations.

DISTINGUISHING FLAGS.

11. Each yacht must carry, at her main topmast head, a rectangular distinguishing flag, of a suitable size, which must not be hauled down unless she gives up the race. If the topmast be lowered on deck or carried away, the flag must be rehoisted in a conspicious place, as soon as possible.

INSTRUCTIONS.

12. Every yacht entered for a race shall, at the time of entry, or as soon after as possible, be supplied with written or printed instructions as to the conditions of the race, the course to be sailed, marks, &c., and nothing shall be considered as a mark in the course unless specially named as such in these instructions.

SAILS.

13. There shall be no restrictions as to sails, or the manner of setting and working them; but steam power must not be used for hoisting sails.

CREW AND FRIENDS.

14. There shall be no limit as to the number of paid hands, and no restrictions as to the number of friends, or to their working. No paid hand to join or leave a yacht after the signal to start. [This rule is not intended to apply to Corinthian matches.]

FITTINGS AND BALLAST.

15. All yachts to be fitted below deck with the ordinary fittings of a yacht, including two transverse bulkheads of wood, and their platforms to be kept down, and bulkheads standing. No water shall be started from or taken into the tanks after the signal to start has been made. No more than the usual anchors and chains to be carried during a race, which must not be used as shifting ballast, or for altering the trim of the yacht. No bags of shot shall be on board, and all ballast shall be properly stowed under the platform or in lockers, and shall not be shifted or trimmed in any way whatever during a race. No ballast to be shipped or unshipped after 4 A.M. on the day of the race. A race resailed shall, so far as regards this rule, be considered a new race.

BOATS AND LIFE BUOYS.

16. Yachts exceeding thirty and under seventy tons, shall carry a boat on deck not less than ten feet in length and three feet six inches beam, and yachts of seventy tons and over, one of not less than twelve feet in length, and three feet six inches beam, with oars lashed in them ready for immediate use. Each yacht to carry at least one life buoy on deck.

STARTING.

17. The yachts to start from moorings, anchors, or under way, as directed by the Sailing Committee. Half an hour before the time of starting one of the following flags of the Commercial Code shall be hoisted as a preparative flag for the yachts of each successive race; in case of a start from anchors or moorings to take up their stations for the start with headsails down, or all

sails down, as the Sailing Committee may direct; or in case the start be a flying one, to approach the starting line, viz:—

B of Commercial Code for the yachts of the 1st Race

C ....2nd "

D ....3rd "

F ....4th "

and so on.

Five minutes before the start the preparative Flag to be lowered and a Blue Peter hoisted, and a gun fired. At the expiration of five minutes exactly the Blue Peter to be hauled down and a second gun fired as a signal to start. If the start is to be made from anchors or moorings, lots shall be drawn for stations, and springs shall be allowed on the same bridle or anchor chain or warp as the bowfasts, but are not to be carried to a buoy, pier, other vessel, or fixed object. If any yacht lets go or parts her bridle before the signal to start, or if she drags any moorings or anchor to which he is made fast for the purpose of starting, she shall be liable to be disqualified, unless such parting or dragging be explained to the satisfaction of the Committee, or unless she has returned, after the signal to start, within the line of starting buoys, so as not to obtain any advantage by the accident. In case of a flying start, no yacht to cross the line previously pointed out until after the signal to start; or should she have done so, she must return and recross the line. Should the gun miss fire, the lowering of the Blue Peter to be the signal to start.

MEETING END ON.

18. If two yachts are meeting end on, or nearly end on, so as to involve risk of collision, the helms of both shall be put to port, so that each may pass on the port side of the other.

TWO YACHTS CROSSING.

19. When two yachts are crossing so as to involve risk of collision, then if they have the wind on different sides, the yacht with the wind on the port side shall keep out of the way of the

yacht with the wind on the starboard side, except in the case in
which the yacht with the wind on the port side is close hauled
and the other yacht free, in which case the latter yacht shall
keep out of the way; but if they have the wind on the same
side, or if one of them has the wind aft, then the yacht which is
to windward shall keep out of the way of the yacht which is to
leeward.

OVERTAKING, ROUNDING, MARKS, ETC.

20. A yacht overtaking another yacht shall keep out of the
way of the last mentioned yacht, but when rounding any buoy
or vessel used to mark out the course, should two yachts not be
clear of each other at the time the leading yacht is close to, and
actually rounding the mark, the outside yacht must give the
other room to pass clear of it, whether it be the lee or weather
yacht which is in danger of fouling the mark. No yacht to be
considered clear unless so much a-head as to give a free choice
to the other on which side she will pass. An overtaking yacht
shall not, however, be justified in attempting to establish an overlap, and thus force a passage between the leading yacht and the
mark after the latter yacht has altered her helm for the purpose of rounding.

OBSTRUCTIONS TO SEA ROOM.

21. When passing pier, shoal, rock, vessel, or other obstruction to sea room, should yachts not be clear of each other, the
outside yacht or yachts must give room to the yacht in danger of
fouling such obstruction, whether she be the weather or the leeward yacht; provided always that an overlap has been established before an obstruction is actually reached.

LUFFING AND BEARING AWAY.

22. A yacht may luff as she pleases to prevent another passing to windward, but must never bear away to hinder her passing to leeward—the lee side to be considered that on which the
leading yacht of the two carries her main boom. The overtaking vessels, if to leeward, must not luff until she has drawn
clear ahead of the yacht she has overtaken.

CLOSE HAULED APPROACHING SHORE.

23. If two yachts are standing towards a shore or shoal, or towards any buoy, boat or vessel, and the yacht to leeward is likely to run aground, or foul of such buoy, boat or vessel, and is not able to tack without coming into collision with the yacht to windward, the latter shall at once tack, on being hailed to do so by the owner of the leeward yacht, or the person acting as his representative, who shall be bound to see that his own vessel tacks at the same time.

RUNNING AGROUND ETC.

24. Any yacht running on shore, or foul of a buoy, vessel, or other obstruction, may use her own anchors, boats, warps, &c., to get off, but may not receive any assistance except from the crew of the vessel fouled. Any anchor, boat, or warp used must be taken on board again before she continues the race.

FOULING YACHTS, MARKS, ETC.

25. Each yacht must go fairly round the course; and must not touch any buoy, boat, or vessel used to mark it out, but shall not be disqualified if wrongfully compelled to do so by another yacht. If a yacht, in consequence of her neglect of any of these rules, shall foul another yacht, or compel other yachts to foul, she shall forfeit all claim to the prize, and shall pay all damages.

SWEEPS.

26. No towing, sweeping, poling, or pushing, or any mode of propulsion except sails, shall be allowed.

ANCHORING.

27. Yachts may anchor during a race, but must weigh their anchor again, and not slip. No yacht shall during a race make fast to any buoy, stage, or pier, or send an anchor out in a boat, except for the purpose of rule 24.

SOUNDING.

28. No other means of sounding than the lead and line allowed.

MAN OVERBOARD.

29. In case of a man falling overboard from a competing yacht, all other yachts in a position to do so shall use their utmost endeavors to render assistance; and if it should appear that any yacht was prevented thereby winning the race, the committee shall have power to order it to be re-sailed.

PROTESTS.

30. Should the owner of any yacht, or the person acting as his representative, consider that he has a fair ground of complaint against another for foul sailing, or any violation of these rules, he must, if it arise during the race, immediately signify the same by showing an ensign conspicuously in the main rigging. The protest shall be made in writing, and under such regulations (if any) as the Sailing Committee may determine, within twelve hours of the termination of the race, and shall be heard and decided by the Sailing Committee after such inquiries as they may consider necessary.

REMOVAL OF FLAG BOAT.

31. Should any flag vessel or boat be removed from its proper position, either by accident or design, the race shall be sailed over again, or not, at the option of the Sailing Committee.

PENALTY FOR DISOBEYING RULES.

32. Any yacht wilfully disobeying or infringing any of these rules, which shall apply to all yachts whether sailing in the same or different races, shall be disqualified from receiving any prize she would otherwise have won, and her owner shall be liable for all damages arising therefrom.

Should a flagrant breach of these rules be proved against any yacht, her sailing master may be disqualified by the Council for one season from sailing in any race held under the rules of the Yacht Racing Association.

CRUISING TRIM.

33. When yachts are ordered to sail in cruising trim, the following rules are to be strictly observed:—

1. No doors, tables, cabin skylights, or other cabin or deck fittings (davits excepted) are to be removed from their places before or during the race.

2. No sails or other gear are to be put into the main cabin.

3. Anchors and chains suitable to the size of the yacht are to be carried, one at the cathead, which anchor is not to be unshackled from the chain before or during the race.

4. Yachts exceeding thirty and under seventy tons, shall carry a boat on deck not less than ten feet in length and three feet six inches beam—yachts of seventy tons and over, their usual cutter and dingy.

5. No extra hands, except a pilot, beyond the regular crew of the yacht, are to be allowed.

APPENDIX.

The Yacht Racing Association further recommend for the consideration of Sailing Committees :—

ALLOWANCE TO SCHOONERS AND YAWLS.

1st. That as mixed races are no satisfactory test of the relative speed of yachts, whenever possible, the different rigs should be kept separate; but when mixed races are unavoidable, the following rule shall be observed:

The tonnage of schooners and yawls to be reckoned for time allowance as follows: viz., schooners at three-fifths, and yawls at four-fifths of their actual tonnage. In calculating the deduction for difference of rig, the tonnage by certificate to the exact fraction to be used. In computing the time allowances from the result, $\frac{47}{94}$ and over to be considered a ton. Schooners and yawls to be allowed to enter in classes at the reduced tonnage.

FLYING STARTS.

2nd. That flying starts should be adopted when practicable, but no time should be allowed for delay in starting.

NO LIMIT TO RACE.

3rd. That any limit to the time for concluding a race should be avoided as far as possible.

CLASSIFICATION.

4th. That the classification of yachts should, when practicable, be as follows :

Not exceeding	. . . .	10 tons.
Above 10 tons and not exceeding	. .	20 "
" 20 " " "	. .	40 "
" 40 " " "	. .	80 "
" 80 "		

COURSES.

5th. That as distance is an important element in the calculation of time allowance, the marks and Flagboats should be placed so as to mark as accurately as possible the length of the course, for which time is allowed.

ROUNDING MARKS.

6th. That in heavy weather it should be arranged, if practicable, for yachts to stay instead of gybe round marks.

CHAPTER XVI.

THE RULE OF THE ROAD AT SEA.

The Field, London, April 8, 1876.

THE ALBERTA AND THE MISTLETOE.

The papers relating to the collision between the Alberta and the yacht Mistletoe were issued a few days ago. Amongst the inclosures is the following from Rear-Admiral Robert Hall, C. B., Secretary of the Admiralty, to the Commander-in-chief at Portsmouth, communicating the decision arrived at by the Lords of the Admiralty as to the responsibility of the officers of the Alberta in regard to the disaster:

"ADMIRALTY, Dec. 28, 1875.

"SIR:—With reference to the report of the Court of Inquiry, which was held in pursuance of the Lords Commissioners of the Admiralty's order of the 30th August last, into the circumstances of the collision between Her Majesty's ship Alberta and the yacht Mistletoe, I am commanded to acquaint you that my lords have not taken any action in the matter pending the result of the Coroner's inquests upon the bodies of the persons who were unfortunately drowned on the occasion. I am now to in-

form you that my lords desire that you will acquaint Captain H
S. H., the Prince of Leinengen and Staff Captain Welch that,
having given careful consideration to the report of the officers
who formed the court, and concurring generally in the finding at
which they arrived, my lords have come to the conclusion that as
the attention of Prince Leinengen is frequently and unavoidably
taken up by the attendance on the Queen during the time Her
Majesty is on board the Alberta in crossing the Solent, the conduct of the navigation is properly left to the staff captain, and
that the latter officer must be held responsible for it. My lords
further consider, in accordance with the finding of the court,
that the course steered by the Alberta should have been such,
that she could not have been brought into collision with the Mistletoe through any alteration of course made by that vessel ; and
my lords cannot therefore acquit Staff Captain Welch from
blame in not having exhibited sufficient care and attention so as
to have avoided all risk of accident, and he is to be reprimanded
accordingly. My Lords are satisfied that after the collision
every effort was made with the utmost rapidity for the preserva-
tion of life. I am to add that, in dealing with this matter, my
lords have taken into consideration that Staff Captain Welch has
now for a great many years been in charge of the Alberta on
the occasion of her Majesty crossing the Solent; and that, up to
the time of the unfortunate occurrence above referred to, no
accident of any kind has taken place, and that his proceedings
have given entire satisfaction.—I am, &c.,

ROBERT HALL

"Admiral George Elliot, &c., Portsmouth."

The Field, London, September, 1876.

BALMORAL, August 30, 1875.

DEAR LORD EXETER :—It has appeared in the course of the
inquiry, at Gosport, that it is a common practice for private
yachts to approach the Royal yacht, when her Majesty is on

board, from motives of loyalty or curiosity. It is evident that such a proceeding must at all times be attended with considerable risk, and in summer, when the Solent is crowded with vessels, such manœuvres are extremely dangerous. The Queen has therefore commanded me to request that you will kindly assist Her Majesty in making it known to all owners of yachts how earnestly the Queen hopes that this practice, which may lead to lamentable results, should be discontinued.

Believe me, dear Lord Exeter, yours faithfully,

HENRY J. PONSONBY,

The Commodore of the Royal Victoria Yacht Club, Ryde.

The Field, London, May 27, 1876.

AXIOMS FOR YACHTSMEN.

We cull the following from the *New York Nautical Gazette*: " Don't—Don't stand up in a boat; don't sit on the rail of a boat; don't let your garments trail overboard; don't step into a boat except in her middle; don't rise in a boat before you are alongside; don't pull under the bows of a ship—it looks green, and the consequences might be fatal; don't forget to ' in fenders ' every time you shove off; don't forget that a loaded boat keeps her headway longer than a light one; don't make fast with a hitch that will jam; don't lower away with the plug out; keep the plug on hand by a small lanyard to it, so that it cannot be ' led astray ' and have to be hunted up when needed. Do.—Do hoist your flags chock up—nothing betokens the landsman more than slovenly colours; do haul taut all your geer; do see that no ' Irish pennants ' are flying adrift aloft; do have a long scope out in a gale; do see that your crew keeps in its place and does not boss the quarter deck; do keep your men tidy and looking sailor-like; do limit the ' cocktails ' aft, and pay more attention to working ship; do keep to leeward of competing yachts when you are not in the match yourself; do learn to be your own skipper and navigator—it is not so difficult and impossible a thing to acquire; do read the *Nautical Gazette* if you wish to be considered any kind of a yachtsman."

NEW THAMES YACHT CLUB.

THE RULE OF THE ROAD AT SEA.

NAIL THIS UP IN THE FORECASTLE—READ, MARK, LEARN AND INWARDLY DIGEST IT.

" When both side lights you see ahead
    Port your helm, and show yours Red.
    Green to Green—or Red to Red—
    Keep your course and go ahead.

" If on your starboard Red appear,
    It is your duty to keep clear,
    To act as judgment says is proper,
    To port, or starboard, back, or stop her,

" But when upon your port is seen
    A steamer's starboard light of Green,
    There's not so much for you to do,
    If Green do port, keeps clear of you.

" Both in safety and in doubt
    Always keep a good look-out,
    In danger, with no room to turn,
    Ease her! stop her! go astern!"
    With the COMMODORE'S *compliments.*

        Northwood Park, Cowes.

CHAPTER XVII.

MR. LOUBAT'S SECOND EUROPEAN CHALLENGE.

The American Register, Paris, April 15, 1876.

THE ENCHANTRESS.

The following letter, which has been addressed to the editor of *Bell's Life*, cannot fail to interest many of our readers:

Paris, April 12, 1876.

To the Editor of *Bell's Life*, London.

Sir.—My attention has been called to the following lines, which appeared in your paper of Saturday, May 29, 1875:

The American Enchantress is bound on a Norway cruise, and has turned up racing business—a very profitable move, more than likely.

I beg leave to repeat the offer that I made through your columns (August 15, 1874) that, if it should be agreeable to any member of an organized European yacht club owning a schooner yacht of at least 300 tons, Royal Thames Yacht Club measurement, to sail a match for a one hundred guinea cup, with the Enchantress, over H. R. H. the Prince of Wales's Challenge Cup

course, according to the rules and regulations and time allowance
established for said course, I shall be most happy to sail such a
match on any day after the 15th of August next.

The race to take place on the appointed day, without regard
to wind or weather, and to be play or pay.

This offer remains open until the 15th of May next.

I am Sir, your obedient servant,

J. F. LOUBAT.

Bell's Life in London, London, April 15, 1876.

INTERNATIONAL YACHT CHALLENGE.

We have authority to announce that Mr. J. F. Loubat, owner
of the American schooner yacht Enchantress, New York Yacht
Club, is willing to repeat the offer made in " Bell's Life," in August, 1874, respecting an international sailing match over a fair
open water course.   Mr. Loubat's challenge is as follows :

" If it should be agreeable to any member of an organized
European yacht club, owning a schooner yacht of at least 300
tons, Royal Thames Yacht Club measurement, to sail a match
for a one hundred guinea cup with the Enchantress, over H. R.
H., the Prince of Wales's Challenge Cup Course, according to the
rules and regulations and time allowance established for the said
course he (Mr. Loubat) will be most happy to sail such a match
on any day after the 15th of August next.   The race to take
place on the appointed day without regard to wind or weather,
and to be play or pay. · This offer remains open until the 15th
of May next.

Mr. Loubat's offer is couched in fair, sportsmanlike terms,
but unfortunately, through restricting the weight to 300 tons,
there would be but the Boadicea, Elmina, and Guinevere eligible
to compete with the Enchantress.   The Guinevere's past performance would, of course, cause her to be regarded as the
English representative vessel, but now that she has dropped to
the cruising class racing in her case is out of the question, and

neither the Boadicea nor the Elmina is equipped for racing. There is Mr. Adrian Hope's new schooner Fortuna, up to the size, but we have nothing to justify us in supposing that she is intended for other than a cruiser, and we are, therefore, afraid that, as in the case of Mr. Loubat's challenge of August, 1874, the present will be also allowed to pass by unnoticed by English yachtsmen.

The Field, London, April 15, 1876.

THE AMERICAN YACHT ENCHANTRESS.

SIR:—My attention has been called to some remarks which appeared in print some time since relating to the Enchantress having "turned up racing."

I beg leave to repeat the offer that I made through your columns August 15, 1874, that, if it should be agreeable to any member of an organised European yacht club owning a schooner yacht of at least 300 tons, R. T. Y. C. measurement, to sail a match for a one hundred guinea cup with the Enchantress over H. R. H. the Prince of Wales's Challenge Cup course, according to the rules and regulations and time allowance established for said course, I shall be most happy to sail such a match on any day after the 15th of August next, the race to take place on the appointed day without regard to wind or weather, and to be play or pay.   This offer remains open until the 15th of May next.

PARIS, April 12, 1876.   J. F. LOUBAT.

Land and Water, London, April 15, 1876.

CHALLENGE FROM YACHT ENCHANTRESS.

I beg leave to repeat the offer that I made on August 15, 1874, that if it should be agreeable to any member of an organized European yacht club owning a schooner yacht of at least 300 tons, R. T. Y. C. measurement, to sail a match for a one hundred guinea cup with the Enchantress over H. R. H. the Prince of Wales's Challenge Cup course, according to the rules and regulations and time allowance established for said course, I shall be most happy to sail such a match on any day after the 15th of August next; the race to take place on the appointed day, without regard to wind or weather, and to be play or pay. This offer remains open until the 15th of May next.

J. F. LOUBAT.

' Hunt's Yachting Magazine, London, May, 1876.

CHALLENGE FROM THE YACHT ENCHANTRESS.

I beg leave to repeat the offer that I made on August 15, 1874, that if it should be agreeable to any member of an organized European yacht club owning a schooner yacht of at least 300 tons, R. T. Y. C. measurement, to sail a match for a one hundred guinea cup with the Enchantress over H. R. H. the Prince of Wale's Challenge Cup course, according to the rules and regulations and time allowance established for said course, I shall be most happy to sail such a match on any day after the 15th of August next; the race to take place on the appointed day, without regard to wind or weather, and to be play or pay. This offer remains open until the 15th of May next.

J. F. LOUBAT.

The New York Herald, New York, April 16, 1876.

SPECIAL DESPATCH TO THE HERALD BY CABLE.

Herald Bureau, No. 61 Avenue de l'Opera,
Paris, April 15, 1876.

. A YACHTING CHALLENGE.

Mr. J. F. Loubat publishes a challenge to any European schooner yacht of 300 tons to sail a match for a hundred guinea cup against the Enchantress, of the New York Yacht Club.

Galignani's Messenger, Paris, April 18, 1876.

We are requested to reproduce the following communication addressed to the editor of *Bell's Life in London* :—

" PARIS, April 12, 1876.

My attention has been called to the following lines, which appeared in your paper of Saturday, May 28, 1875 :—

"*The American Enchantress is bound on a Norway cruise and has turned up racing business—a very profitable move, more than likely.*

I beg leave to repeat the offer that I made through your columns (August 15, 1874), that, if it should be agreeable to any member of an organized European yacht club owning a schooner yacht of at least 300 tons Royal Thames Yacht Club measurement to sail a match for a one hundred guinea cup, with the Enchantress, over H.R.H., the Prince of Wales's Challenge Cup course, according to the rules and regulations and time allowance established for said course. I shall be most happy to sail such a match on any day after the 15th of August next. The race to take place on the appointed day, without regard to wind or weather, and to be play or pay. This offer remains open until the 15th of May next. Accept, etc.,

J. F. LOUBAT.

The American Register, Paris, June 27, 1876.

THE YACHT ENCHANTRESS.

The *Sport* calls particular attention to the challenge of Mr. Loubat, which it published on the 19th of April, and which also appeared in our columns, and says that its readers will be surprised to find that no English yacht has yet decided to race with the Enchantress. It will be remembered that she came out to Europe to sail for the Prince of Wales's Challenge Cup open to English and American yachts. The race was to take place on the 6th of August, 1874, but on the 5th, Mr. Loubat was officially informed by the Royal Yacht Squadron, that Mr. Mulholland's yacht, the Egeria, having sprung her gaff, the only yacht ready to sail against the Enchantress was that of the Duke of Rutland, the Shark; and as, according to the terms of the Prince of Wales's gift, three starters were required, there could be no race, unless Mr. Loubat would defer it until Friday. To this request he readily acceded. On the day selected the Enchantress broke down, and notwithstanding his subsequent challenges, in 1874 and 1876, Mr. Loubat has not yet been able to have a race.

CHAPTER XVIII.

THE LOUBAT CAPE MAY CUP RACE.

The New York Herald, New York, March 26, 1875.

NEW YORK YACHT CLUB.

The second general meeting of the New York Yacht Club was held last evening at the club rooms, Madison avenue and Twenty seventh street Commodore Kingsland in the chair.

MR. LOUBAT PRESENTS A CUP.

The Secretary presented and read the following letter from Mr. J. F. Loubat, owner of the schooner Enchantress :—

PARIS, February 20, 1875.

To the Commodore, Officers and Members of the
New York Yacht Club :—

GENTLEMEN:—Should it be agreeable to the New York Yacht Club, I should be most happy to present the club with a $1,000 cup, to be sailed for on the second Thursday of October, 1876, by schooner yachts of 100 tons and upward, belonging to any organized yacht club in the world.

All yachts to be measured by a person appointed by the New York Yacht Club, according to the club measurement; time allowance to be the same as that for His Royal Highness the Prince of Wales's Challenge Cup yacht race, *i.e.*, twelve seconds per ton; the New York Yacht Club regulations to be adhered to ; no entrance fee. Course, from off Owl's Head, New York harbor, to and around the Sandy Hook Lightship, leaving the same on the starboard hand, thence to and around the Lightship on Five Fathom Bank off Cape May, N. J., and return to the Sandy Hook Lightship, leaving both on the port hand.

The owner of any vessel winning the prize will be required, before the prize is delivered, to sign a declaration that the sailing regulations have been strictly conformed to.

I remain, gentlemen, your very obedient servant,

J. F. Loubat.

This cup was accepted, with the thanks of the Club, and referred to the Regatta Committee, with power to arrange terms and necessary details with Mr. Loubat.

The election of new members being in order, forty-one gentlemen were added to the roll of the club. Adjourned.

The New York Times, New York, August 23, 1876.

A NEW CHALLENGE CUP.

The silver cup ordered by Mr. J. F. Loubat, owner of the yacht Enchantress, of Tiffany & Co., for presentation as a token of regard to the New York Yacht Club has just been completed and is now on exhibition at Tiffany's salesrooms, in Union square. The cup, with the base, is forty-two inches in height, and is entirely different from any yet made by the firm. It is ornamented in the Renaissance style, with a broad base, tapering gradually to a fluted, basket-like top, ornamented with laurel wreaths. Two heads are wrought at the terminus of the neck, between them being gold anchors, the cordage of which entwines the body of the cup. The handles represents the prows of barges, imitative of the early Eastern craft. From each side of these prows heavy gold chain cables are run into holes at the bottom of the bowl. The standard of the cup is decorated with a group of anchors, its broadest portion being ornamented with the heads of nymphs rising from leaves of water lilies. The resting base of the cup is made of rich ebony, ornamented on one side with a broad shield trimmed with palm leaves, and intended for future inscription. The side of the cup itself is engraved with the name of the donor, and the Club to which the gift is presented. The cup will be sailed for during the second week in October, in a regatta open to yachts of 100 tons and upward, of any club in the world.

The New York Herald, New York, October 15, 1876.

YACHTING.

The Race to Cape May Lightship and Return for the Loubat Cup.—The Schooner Atalanta Wins—Light and Variable Winds Throughout the Race.

The yachting season came to a conclusion yesterday with the finish of the race for the Loubat Cup. It is a matter of regret that the Atalanta and Idler were the only two competitors for what is, without doubt, one of the handsomest pieces of plate ever offered as a prize in a yacht race, but the lateness in the season prevented many yacht owners from entering their boats, as they had already laid them up for the winter. The result of the race astonished most yachtsmen, as they had made up their mind that the Atalanta was no match for the Idler, the heroine of so many aquatic triumphs. Probably, with the exception of Mr. William Astor, the owner, and some few of his friends who were aware of the excellent sailing qualities of their yacht, the Atalanta had no friends that cherished a hope of her coming out ahead. She certainly won the Kane regatta last year, but that was hardly considered a fair test of her merits, and then her antagonist on this occasion owned a reputation for speed in all weather second to none in the country. The race to Cape May and back, though not exactly a thorough trial of the qualities of the two yachts, certainly gives the Atalanta the right to a position in the front rank of our flyers, and take her in a race of twenty miles to windward and return it would be hard to find any boat of her size that would not be badly pushed to beat her. Of course the Atalanta was favored by the wind going down to the Five Fathom Lightship, but coming back both yachts had about the same breeze, and then she appeared to make the fastest time. Mr. Samuel S. Colgate, the owner of the Idler, is naturally very much disappointed at the result of the race, as he felt pretty confident of winning, but next season he will probably be able to have another trial over a course where the speed of the two yachts will be thoroughly tried.

Early this season Mr. Loubat sent a communication to the New York Yacht Club offering a $1,000 cup to be sailed for over the Cape May course under certain stipulations mentioned in the following circular:—

NEW YORK YACHT CLUB, Oct. 2, 1875.

The race for the Loubat Ocean Cup, for schooners, will be sailed on Thursday, October 12, 1876, and is open to schooner yachts of all nations of 100 tons and over; time allowance to be the same as that for His Royal Highness the Prince of Wales' Challenge Cup yacht race—*i. e.*, twelve seconds per ton. New York Yacht Club regulations to beadhered to—No entrance fee.

The course will be from off Owl's Head, New York harbor, over the regular regatta course of the New York Yacht Club, to and around the Sandy Hook Lightship, leaving the same on the starboard hand; thence to and around the Lightship on Five Fathom Bank, off Cape May, and return to Sandy Hook Lightship, leaving both on the port hand.

The start will be made at three o'clock P. M., and the time of the competing yachts will be taken as they pass between the judges' boat and the Long Island shore. The signals for starting will be given from the judges' boat, as follows:—For a preparatory signal, one gun, and the club signal will be lowered; ten minutes later, for the yachts to cross the line, the same signals will be repeated. No yacht's time will be taken after the expiration of fifteen minutes from the second signals, unless instructions to the contrary are given on the day of the race.

The owner of any vessel winning the prize will be required before it is delivered, to sign a declaration that the sailing regulations have been strictly conformed to.

Entries must be made to the Secretary of the club at the club house, Madison avenue and Twenty-seventh street, on or before Wednesday, October 11.

G. L. Haight,

Chairman Regatta Committee, N. Y. Y. C.

C. A. Minton,

Secretary N. Y. Y. C.

The fact that the race was to be sailed with time allowance is said to have deterred some of the large keel schooners from competing, but considering that it was a race of about 228 miles, twelve seconds per ton did not make much difference.

THE RACE.

On Thursday afternoon a number of gentlemen who were going to participate in the race for the Loubat Cup left the city by the two o'clock boat for Stapleton, Staten Island. On arriving there the two competing yachts, the Idler and the Atalanta, were tacking about, waiting for the starting signal. Mr. S. M. Mills, accompanied by Mr. G. L. Haight, the chairman of the Regatta Committee, went on board his schooner yacht Vesta, which he had kindly placed at the disposal of the judges, and getting under weigh stood across toward the Long Island shore and let go her anchor off Owl's Head. It was a beautiful afternoon, and although a trifle more wind would have been an improvement there was a light southerly breeze that gave promise of strengthening.   In order to lose no time Mr. G. L. Haight gave orders to fire the peparatory signal, and at 3 h. 15 m. P. M. a gun was fired that gave the racing yachts ten minutes to get ready.   They were both under main and foresail, main club topsail, jib, flying jib and jib-topsail.   The second gun was fired at 3 h. 25 m., and then the yachts came up toward the imaginary line between the Vesta and Owl's Head.   The Atalanta was the first to cross and make a reach across to the Staten Island shore on the port tack. The Idler followed two minutes later on the starboard tack, hugging the Long Island shore.   The following is the time of the yachts as they crossed :—

			—TIME.—		
YACHT.	NAME.	TONNAGE.	H.	M.	S.
Atalanta.....Mr. William Astor.......		145.56	3	32	30
Idler.........Mr. Samuel J. Colgate....		191.26	3	34	30

The steam yacht Ideal was out to see the start, and followed behind the racers.   As soon as the yachts had crossed the line Mr. Mills weighed anchor, and the Vesta accompanied them a a short distance outside the Narrows.   The wind was rather variable, as on the Staten Island side it appeared to have a little westing, while off Long Island it was nearly southwest.

The Atalanta made a short leg on the starboard, and then stayed and headed again for Staten Island, fetching to the leeward of Fort Wadsworth.   She then stretched across toward Fort Lafayette, but the tide was running flood, and she only crossed the Idler's bow about 300 yards ahead.   She tacked under the lee of Fort Hamilton and made a stretch back, and only just succeeded in weathering the Idler.   On the next leg she again opened the gap, and going in stays headed well up toward Gravesend, from whence she reached out in the bay.   Returning on the starboard tack the Atalanta crossed the Idler's bows, the latter giving way; and when they came together again the Atalanta tacked under the lee of the Idler, as the latter had the right of way, and the pair ran alongside of one another up to Murray's Dock, when they went about, the Atalanta off the Idler's weather beam.   After a short contest the Idler gradually eat up to windward and came out off the Atalanta's weather bow. The Idler was well handled and out manœuvred the Atalanta, which would probably have done better to pass under her stern than to tack under her lee. The breeze was still steady, but appeared to be hauling more to the westward. Both yachts now headed toward the Quarantine ship, and the Idler was doing good work, forereaching and going to windward of the Atalanta. Off Quarantine Island the Idler broke tacks and stood to the eastward, the Atalanta holding on the port tack. She finally stayed off the Hospital ship, and making a stretch to the eastward crossed the Idler's wake about a quarter of a mile astern. The sun was just setting and its golden rays were illuminating the autumnal tinted foliage of the woods on Staten Island. The Atalanta tacked and followed after the Idler, both yachts making a long leg on the port tack. On the next stretch they weathered the Southwest Spit buoy, passing as follows :— Idler, 6 h. 00 m.; Atalanta, 6 h. 05 m.

They both then gave a little sheet, and the Atalanta set a stay sail. They ran very quickly past the point of the Hook, and with sheets lifted made fast time on their road to the Lightship. The night was rather chilly, and the breeze appeared to be freshening every minute. They ran down to the Lightship with their booms to port, and the Idler turned first about five minutes ahead of the Atalanta. The yachts then parted company, and the Idler stayed and stood in shore on the port tack, and the Atalanta trimmed in her sheets and headed off southeast. The breeze began to edge round to the westward, and in about three-quarters of an hour the Atalanta was laying her course and skipping along at a fast gait. At midnight Barnegat was southwest from the Atalanta, and at 1 h. 30 m: A. M. it bore west by north. The breeze then begun to let up, and at 3 h. 15 m. the Atalanta sent up club foretopsail and balloon-staysail. The Atalanta must have passed the Idler about 3 h. A. M., as the latter was then well in shore, near Little Egg Harbor, with hardly any wind. At 4 h. 05 m. A. M. Little Egg Harbor bore west northwest, and presently the gloom of night began to pass away and daylight coming up disclosed the Idler some seven miles astern of the Atalanta. The breeze was then about west northwest, but very light, and the Atalanta was making about two or three knots an hour, running a couple of points free. At first the Idler appeared to be closing up the gap as her hull became more apparent, but after an hour or so she went back, hull down. At 6 h. 05 m. A. M. Absecom Light bore west northwest, and shortly afterward the breeze freshened a little, and the Atalanta was making about four knots. The morning was bright and pleasant, with a pretty hot sun, making it more like an August than an October day. At 8 h. 30 m. the breeze began to die, and the Atalanta sent up a balloon staysail and set a balloon jib. The Idler was still some six or seven miles astern, evidently not much better off in the way of wind. The sea was as smooth as a millpond, and there was just sufficient breeze to give steerage way. At 9 h. 43 m. the lookout on the Atalanta sighted the Five Fathom Lightship.

For the next two hours there was a light fanning breeze from the westward and about 11 h. A.M. it hauled round to the northward. The Atalanta winged out, but it did not do her much good as the wind died away entirely, For the next half hour there were little catspaws of air coming from all directions and finally a light breeze settled down from south southwest. The Atalanta then trimmed down on the wind and after tacking around for about an hour and a half rounded the Five Fathom Lightship at 1 h. 37 m. P.M. She then headed for home, starting at first under all her light canvas, with her booms to starboard. The breeze gradually strengthened and she slipped along at about a four knot gait. The wind coming more aft the fore-boom was shifted out and she went along wing and wing. In the meantime the Idler was tacking around and trying to weather the Lightship, a feat she finally accomplished at 3 h. 23 m., just 1 h. 46 m. behind the Atalanta, equivalent to about seven miles. The Atalanta trotted along on her course, improving her gait as the breeze freshened, and the Idler sank lower and lower on the horizon, until at last—5 h. 05 m. P. M.—she disappeared all together. Absecom Light then bore west, about ten miles distant. After passing Absecom Light the Atalanta sent over her foreboom and hauled up a couple of points, skipping along at about an eleven knot gait, on the port tack. The breeze was now pretty fresh and dead on the beam, so that the main sheet stood a little trimming down. At 10 h. 25 m. P.M. Barnegat Light was northwest, and at 11 h. 05 m. it was bearing west about a point and a half abaft of the beam. Toward morning the breeze lightened up a little, and the Atalanta finally rounded the Sandy Hook Lightship at 4 h. 01 m. 30 s yesterday morning, the winner of the Loubat Cup. She was well handled during the race, and Captain S. W. Freestone and his mate, Charles Johnson, deserve credit for the way they worked her light canvas. Captain Peter Roff and Captain Dan, of the Wanderer, were also on board lending a helping hand. The Idler rounded the Lightship at 6 h. 54 m. and followed the Atalanta, which had started immediately after rounding for Staten Island.

The following is the time of the race:

	Start.	Finish.	Actual time.	Corrected time.
	H.M.S.	H.M.S..	H. M. S.	H. M. S.
Atalanta	3 32 30	4 01 30	36 29 00	36 19 52.
Idler	3 34 30	6 54 00	39 19 00	39 19 00.

The Atalanta therefore won the cup by 2 h. 50 m. actual time; and 2 h., 59 m., 8 s. corrected time. She was built by David Caril, of City Island, on about ten feet of the keel of the old Calypso that was destroyed by fire. She left last night for Rhinebeck on the Hudson, where the owner Mr. Astor has his country residence. Mr. Astor intends to start shortly for a cruise in Southern waters.

CHAPTER XIX.

MISCELLANEOUS.

The Field, London, October 6, 1877.

THE ENCHANTRESS SOLD.

Mr. J. F. Loubat has disposed of this yacht to Major Williams.

The Illustrated Sporting Dramatic Times, New York, June 12, 1878.

YACHTING OF THE UNITED STATES.

The lover and amateur of this time-honored pastime of yachting cannot help, if he be at all observant, feeling joyous and encouraged at its rapid progress in American waters. Indeed one has to watch the press to possess a correct idea of its rapid advancement. In every section of the country—not only in the harbors, bays and rivers of the older States, but on the little lakes, bayous and inlets of the most distant part of our country's broad domain, the white wings of the yacht and pleasure-boat and their picturesque beauty to the panorama. We have been led to this brief reflection by indulging in a retrospective glance at the number of yachts which have been built, and the many yachting organizations which have been formed around us during the past twenty years. As an ardent amateur of the pastime, it affords us heartfelt pleasure to record this fact; and we sincerely hope the prevailing spirit will never culminate until the American yachting marine outnumbers—as it now outsails—the world.

It is not •many years since those who evinced an interest in aquatic matters could almost enumerate the pleasure-craft throughout the country. Then, the yachts belonging to the gentlemen of New York, Boston, Philadelphia, Baltimore, Mobile, New Orleans, etc., were familiarly known to all amateurs of yachting. Now, the case is far different; the increase and influence, especially of the clubs located in the vicinity of the metropolis have given an extraordinary impetus to yachting recreation in every locality. Clubs composed of vessels of large and small dimensions, are found in every seaport of our land. Inland places and the harbors of our great lakes, as well as the river towns and villages, attest and give practical evidence of our assertion.

The New York Yacht Club, the pioneer club of the country, has performed yeoman service in developing the pastime; and its signals and vessels have conferred an unfading lustre upon our yachting annals. As we are now in the regatta season, it may not be inappropriate to briefly recall some of the principal events which adorn and honor the yachting record of the United States. First of all, in regard to its importance and to the name it won for us, from the entire yachting world, must be mentioned the America's visit to Great Britain. Of her beauty of model (a monument to this hour of the lamented George Steer's genius and talent as a naval architect;) of her hollow victories over England's crack yachts, in fleets and singly, not one being able to give her a decent race, we will not dilate, as it long since passed into familiar and glorious American yachting history. The gallant little schooner is now the property of General B. F. Butler, and has proven herself as hard to beat in modern times, notwithstanding all modern improvements, as she was in the days of Auld Lang Syne. Long may she fly the legend she so nobly won when she distanced the British fleet. " The Yankee's ahead, the rest nowhere!"

The sloop yacht Silvie's visit to England in 1853, although not resulting in any great amount of sailing honors is worthy of mention as Mr. Louis A. Depau, her owner, after starting in a regatta which he did with reluctance, as the wind was very light, and the whole sail turned out a drifting, instead of a sailing match. She came in second, the Julia, a craft about half her size coming in first. The Silvie was a centre-board sloop, of one hundred and six tons, eighty feet long, twenty-four feet beam. The second prize, a cup, was won by the Silvie, but Mr. Depau wishing to gain some honors for his sloop and the New York Yacht Club, before returning across the Atlantic, naturally desired another and more satisfactory test. In the regatta above alluded to, all the yachts approaching the tonnage, and double the tonnage of the Silvie, were nowhere, among them being Mr. Weld's champion schooner Alarm. Mr. Depau in the hope of getting on another trial, made the following proposition to English yachtsmen :

First.—"That the cup awarded to the yacht Silvie should be sailed for by all yachts in the Royal Yacht Squadron, or of any other yacht squadron in England, the Silvie to remain at anchor, or if the committee desired, she would enter for the race with the understanding that the distance must be performed by the winning vessel in a certain number of hours, according to the distance to be sailed over, in order thus to determine that the race was sailed with a good breeze."

Second.—"The Silvie would sail any yacht in the Royal Yacht Squadron a round race, one-half distance to windward, for any reasonable amount of money, according to above rule concerning time.

Third.—"The Silvie would sail any yacht for the honor of the American flag."

As may be imagined, the Silvie did not get any other chance from a people, who, as George Wilkes says, are accustomed to "*hive* their victories," and soon after she voyaged to Russia and "up the straits ;" from thence returning to New York. She crossed the Atlantic in sixteen and one-half days, returning in thirty-five making the homeward voyage under shortened sail in consequence of carrying away her bowsprit and main boom. The Silvie, now rigged as a schooner, hails from Boston, and flys the signal of the Eastern Yacht Clubs. She was built by George Steers.

"Another event, second only in importance, and perhaps not second but superior in its beneficial effects upon this country's yachting status was the renowned mid-winter ocean race across the Atlantic of the schooner yachts Henrietta, owned by Commodore James G. Bennett, Fleetwing, owned by Messrs. George and Frank Osgood, and the Vesta owned by Messrs. Pierre and George Lorillard. The America's hollow victories placed us ahead of the world in speed and model; while the ocean race silenced forever the sneers and criticisms of those who were accustomed to deride us as "sunshiny or feather-bed yachtsmen, whose craft seldom ventured off soundings or outside the Light ships." The manhood and daring of our yachtsmen, and the staunchness and sea-going qualities of our yachts, have never been lampooned since by any yachting writer of intelligence. The course was from Sandy Hook lightship to the Needles Light on the western end of the Isle of Wight, in the English Channel, for a purse of ninety thousand dollars, thirty thousand dollars for each yacht.

The Henrietta is a keel yacht of 205 tons, the Fleetwing, a keel of 212 tons, and the Vesta, a centre-board of 201 tons. The Henrietta won the race, although the Vesta and Fleetwing had defeated her in match races of twenty miles to windward and return, off Sandy Hook. A race of three thousand miles is evidently as much a test of skillful navigation as it is of speed. Mr. Bennett crossed on the Henrietta, and Mr. George Lorillard on the Vesta; it was one of the closest and fastest races ever known between sailing vessels, and all three yachts after separating, the first night, outside of Sandy Hook, and never sighting each other in the interim, arrived at the Needles within a period of a little over two hours. This race will be forever memorable

in American yachting annals, and no subsequent yacht sailing of
either a hazardous or peaceful character, can ever cast it in the
shade or dim its lustre.   Of a truth, it forms a picture upon our
yachting escutcheon to which both our old and young yachtsmen
will always revert with true joy and satisfaction.

Happily for our limited amount of yachting literature, this
notable event has been portrayed in a highly talented manner,
which insure for it, as it richly deserves, something more than
an ephemeral existence.   Colonel Stuart M. Taylor, who shared
the perils of the voyage on board the Vesta, has written " The
Log of the Vesta," which was published in five numbers of the
Aquatic Monthly, and we venture the assertion that no superior
or more beautiful composition on a yachting subject has ever
been printed on either side of the Atlantic.   Colonel Taylor, a
true Knickerbocker gentleman, for many years an energetic
member of the New York Yacht Club, is now Recorder of the
City and County of San Francisco, and we most respectfully
salute him, feeling fully sensible that the " good cause " of yachting in our land possesses no warmer defender, no more talented
advocate, and no sincerer disciple.

Of the two voyages of the schooner yacht Sappho, to England from New York we shall speak at another time in the
first of which she was defeated by entering in a regatta, as the
Silvie did, and could not get any other chance from our cousins
before the yachting season was over.   But on her second visit,
sailed by Captain Bob Fish, she literally "came the America
over them," duplicating that celebrated schooner's performances
and triumphs, and distancing all competitors in Brittannia's own
waters, showed the greatest yachting on the globe—how squadrons were defeated and fields were won.

The cruise of Mr. Loubat's Enchantress, an elegant specimen
of this country's yachting marine, lasting some two or three
years and visiting all navigable foreign waters, would be highly
entertaining.   Distinguished people everywhere were entertained
handsomely by her hospitable owner, and she carried creditably
the New York Yacht Club's time-honored signal all over the

world. Neither must it be forgotton that, with Bob Fish at the helm, she set her racing colors and challenged any yacht in England, upon their own time allowance, for which handicap an American model could not get a customer, and was obliged to go into Winter quarters. "PEVERLLY."

Sunday Times and Noah's Weekly Messenger, New York, July 14, 1878.

A YACHTSMAN ON SHORE—COLUMBIA'S HISTORICAL MEDALS*.

Mr. J. F. Loubat, so favorably known as a leading yachtsman of the United States, from his ownership and long cruisings in his schooner-yacht Enchantress, one of the largest and most elegant yachts ever launched, has just published the above work, which for patient research, ability and good taste evinced in its composition will render it always invaluable to the student of bibliographic reminiscences of our land. The work was commenced in 1862; the author has therefore devoted sixteen years to its accomplishment, and made the generous outlay of twenty-five thousand dollars to place the magnificent volumes before the literary world. It is truly gratifying to know that this work has been accomplished in such a thorough and talented manner; and that the historical facts, as depicted, leave scarcely anything for the future student to do, but to familiarize himself with the data and record so plainly set before him.

In these volumes are remembered and honored our naval heroes, Paul Jones, Preble, Decatur, Bainbridge, Hull, Burrows, Porter, Macdonough, etc.; and on land, Mad Anthony Wayne, Brown, Ripley, Miller, Scott, Gaines, McComb, Andrew Jackson, Zachary Taylor, and many others whose names and deeds enrich our country's patriotic annals.

---

*The Medalic History of the United States of America, 1776-1876. By J. F. Loubat, Member of the New-York Historical Society, &c. With 170 etchings by Jules Jacquemart. Two volumes. Text and plates. New York. Published by the Author. 1878.

Yachtsmen will not miss a thorough inspection and perusal of page 447, vol. I, which contains an etching of the first-class life-saving medals given to Col. J. Schuyler Crosby, now consul to Florence, and Carl Fosberg, for saving the life of Miss Edith May, and endeavoring to rescue the late Miss Adele Hunter and Commodore William T. Garner and his wife, at the sinking of the yacht Mohawk, in New York Harbor, July 20, 1876; awarded June 8, 1877. Many of our readers may remember that the late Mr. Louis B. Montant and Mr. G. G. Howland, also exhibited on board the Mohawk, heroic conduct, and a perfect disregard of self during this sad fatality. Many thought they would be remembered also, and perhaps they would have been, if the attention of the government had been directed toward a public recognition of their bravery during this time of peril.

The perseverance which Mr. Loubat has exhibited in the preparation of this history, stamps him not only as an accomplished but as a most indomitable historian; and his tact and judicious system as a collector is evinced in almost every paragraph of this truly great work; and that his years of labor and research have been pursued *con amore*, is apparent on every page. Our first national token was struck in honor of George Washington, as a reward of the government for his capture of Boston in March, 1776. From this medal to the one awarded to John Horn, of Detroit, for life-saving, by the act of June 20, 1874, our national medals number just eighty-six. Our struggle for independence is commemorated by seventeen; the war of 1812 by twenty-seven; the Mexican war by four, and medals to ex-President Grant and the late Commodore Vanderbilt for services during the late civil war render the enumeration complete. A large number of the first medals were specimens of the skill of the most accomplished French engravers, such as A. Dupre, Duvivier, and Gatteaux.

Later medals attest the admitted skill and talent of Andrieu Gayrard, Paquet, Rembrandt Peale, Barber, and other engravers of the highest reputation. One of the most talented reviewers connected with our metropolitan press thus speaks of this portion of Mr. Loubat's labors : " The engravings and designs are of all degrees of merit, from the rude and monstrous carving of the 'Red-Jacket Medal' to the finest examples of numismatic art. Mr. Loubat arranges the medals in chronological order, and not only tells the story of each one, but gives a biographical sketch of the person honored by it, an account of the designer and engraver, and a complete transcript of the official documents, reports of battles, etc., which the medal was struck to commemorate. Some of these documents he tells us are now printed for the first time, and we need hardly say that they give his work a high historical value. These descriptive and documentary pages, together with a copious introduction in which he tells of his long, patient, and ingenious search after missing medals, and gives a narrative of the agency of Franklin, Jefferson, Humphreys, and others in procuring the preparation of American medals in Paris, make up the first of Mr. Loubat's stately volumes.

" The second volume contains 170 etchings, 85 plates, by that renowned master of his art, M. Jules Jacquemart, of Paris, whose etchings of the best pictures in our metropolitan museum of art render his name familiar to New Yorkers. The printer of the plates, A. Salmon, of Paris, is deserving of mention for his perfect style of working off the etchings. The hand-made paper, of superb linen fabric, was manufactured expressly for Mr. Loubat, at Rives. The letter-press is the work of Francis Hart & Co., of New York, and its execution reflects great credit upon the head of this house, Mr. Theodore L. De Vinne. In this work the most experienced judge is left nothing to criticise in its elegant type, superior press work, and perfect arrangement.

" The following letter from the President of the New York Historical Society pays an intelligent and deserved tribute to the work :

New York, 76 University Place, May 29, 1878.

Mr. J. F. Loubat, LL. D., etc. •

Dear Sir:—I hasten to acknowledge the receipt of the copy of your splendid work on the Medallic History of the United States, which you have sent to me for our Historical Society; and I do

LIBRARY
OF THE
UNIVERSITY
OF CALIFORNIA

THE NEW YORK PILOT

From the Painting presented to Mr. J. F. Loubat, by the owners.

J.F. LOUBAT
16

CHAPTER XX.

THE NEW YORK PILOT BOAT JOSEPH F. LOUBAT NO. 16.

New York, Dec. 14th, 1880.

The new pilot boat "Joseph F. Loubat," No. 16, will be launched at Tottenville, Staten Island, on Saturday, December 18th, 1880.

Boat to connect with Rail Road, will leave Staten Island Ferry, foot of Whitehall St., New York, at 8 o'clock, A. M.

Very Respectfully,

E. COMFORT,
W. J. BARRY,
J. McCARTHY,
M. J. MARIGA.

The New York Herald, New York, December 19, 1880.

LAUNCH OF A PILOT BOAT.

THE JOSEPH F. LOUBAT ADDED TO THE SANDY HOOK FLEET.

At Ellis' shipyards in Tottenville, S. I., a number of persons gathered yesterday morning to assist in the ceremonies of launching and christening pilot boat No. 16, of the Sandy Hook pilot's fleet. The boat is a schooner, like all her sisters of the fleet, and was built by Jacob S. Ellis, at an expense of $13,000, for pilots Electus Comfort, W. J. Barry, James McCarthy and Maurice J. Mariga. Her length, over all, is 88 feet, breadth of beam 21 feet 2 inches, depth of hold is 9 feet, and her burden, by carpenter's measurement, 140 tons.

The party, consisting of the four owners, all their friends of the force of pilots who were ashore, ladies, the Eckford Social Club, of Brooklyn, and Mr. and Mrs. Bradish Johnson, jr., and a party of their friends were on hand early in the morning, and as the vessel was started on her ways Mrs. Johnson smashed the traditional bottle of champagne (extra dry) on the bows and christened the gliding boat the "Joseph F. Loubat." The name was chosen, it should be said, out of compliment to Mr. Loubat, the yachtsman, whose contributions to the benevolent societies of the pilots has earned him their friendship, and Mrs. Johnson was chosen as the vessel's sponsor because of her relationship to Mr. Loubat, she being his cousin.

The launch was accomplished at a quarter of ten A. M., and was a reasonably successfully one, the vessel sliding gracefully down to a point below high water mark. She did not float, but stopped above the water, and it was found impracticable to coax or drive her further down. The next high tide, however, floated her off, as a sailor remarked, "high and dry" and she swam like a cork in the water.

The Joseph F. Loubat is one of the handsomest of all the fleet in appearance, and is furnished and fitted out in the most thorough and comfortable style known to the pilots. So far as can be judged by her model and general appearance, and by the favorable start in life which she received yesterday, she will, as pilot boat No. 16, prove a credit to the gallant fleet that is already known the world over.

The New York Times, New York, December 19, 1880.

A NEW PILOT-BOAT LAUNCHED.

A large number of persons gathered yesterday in Jacob S. Ellis's ship yard, at Tottenville, Staten Island, to witness the launch of the new Sandy Hook pilot boat, Joseph F. Loubat. A special train on the Staten Island Railway conveyed a large number of pilots and their families to Tottenville. When the blocks were knocked from uuder the vessel, she glided down the ways, but before her bow slipped off her stern became stuck in the mud.

Mr. Ellis announced that pontoons would be placed each side of the vessel, and that she would be floated at high tide. The Loubat is larger than any pilot boat now in the service. Her dimensions are as follows: 74 feet keel; 88 feet over all; 21 feet beam; 9 feet hold; draught of water, 11 feet. Her cabins and state rooms are finished with hard wood, and she is fitted up with all the latest improvements. She is owned by Staten Island and New York pilots, and will take the place of Pilot boat No. 16. Capt. Comfort, of Brooklyn, will command her. The total cost of the vessel is about $11,000.

The World, New York, December 19, 1880.

A NEW PILOT-BOAT LAUNCH.

The new Sandy Hook pilot boat, Joseph F. Loubat, was launched yesterday at Captain Jacob S. Ellis's yard at Tottenville, S. I. When the blocks were knocked from under the vessel she slid easily down the ways till the bow floated, but then the stern stuck in the mud, and pontoons will be needed to free her. She is the largest of the pilot boat fleet and will take the place of No. 16. Her dimensions are: Length along the keel, 74 feet; length over all, 88 feet; beam, 21 feet, and draft, 11 feet, and she cost $11,000. Captain Comfort, of Brooklyn, is to be in command.

CHAPTER XXI.

THE DEATH OF CAPTAIN ROBERT FISH.

The Sun, New York, January 18, 1883.

A FAMOUS YACHT BUILDER.

DEATH OF CAPTAIN ROBERT FISH WHO FASHIONED THE SAPPHO AND THE ENCHANTRESS.

Captain Robert Fish, the yacht builder, died at his home in Pamrapo, N. J., early yesterday morning, 70 years old, of disease incident to age. His father, David Fish, kept a boat-house at the foot of Roosevelt street, in this city. Robert finally opened a shop in Front street, and in 1840 he removed to 404 Water Street. In 1850, he established his yard at Pamrapo. Among his earliest achievements were the Annie, a cabin yacht, built for Anson Livingston, and the cabin yacht Julia for Dr. Patten.

What he considered his greatest triumph was the remodelling of the Sappho, a schooner of 300 tons, the work of another builder. She was sent to England, and in the international races at Cowes, was defeated.

She was brought back and sold to W. P. Douglass. Captain Fish puts hips on her, widening her in such a way above the bilge strake that she had much greater stability and was able to stand up under a much greater press of canvass in a stiff breeze. He gave the masts a greater rake, and shifted them so as to make her steer more easily.   Her ballast also was shifted, leaving her a little by the stern, In 1870 she returned to Cowes and won three successive races, defeating the famous English yacht Cambria. Captain Fish was in command during the races.

Among other models made by Captain Fish were those of the Eva, the Enchantress, and the Meteor. The Eva was built for George Lorillard, and was never defeated. The Enchantress was built by Pine of Greenpoint for George Lorillard. One of her famous races was that of October 9, 1873, from Owl's Head Point around the Lightship off Cape May and return. It was a scrub race, yachts, working schooners, and pilot boats participating, but the Enchantress carried off the cup, valued at $1,000. J. F. Loubat was the owner of the Enchantress at this time. Mr. Loubat afterward made an extended tour of European waters in the Enchantress, with Captain Fish in charge. While on this trip he noticed a number of yachts of familiar model in an English fleet. Asking a member of the club, a stranger, where they came from, he was told that they were made after the model of a Yankee yacht called the Truant, built by one Fish in New York. The Truant was built for Moses H. Grinnell.

The Enchantress challenged all England, but there were no takers. The Meteor tried to get a race at Cowes, but she failed. In 1873 she sailed for the Mediterranean, and from the English Channel to Lisbon she was logged at seventeen knots* an

---

The World, New York, March 24, 1887.

A WORLD READER, E. F. F., writes to know something about the speed of transatlantic sailing ships and yachts. A ship captain could not tell the truth about his own ship if he tried. It is not that he is untruthful. He may be a second GEORGE WASHINGTON, but the moment the speed of his own vessel is called into question he forgets the day he started and always omits the day he arrives in telling the time of passage. There is no "official time" of sailing vessel's crossing the Atlantic Ocean, except in the races of the Cambria and Dauntless to New York and the Henrietta, Vesta and Fleetwing to the other side. Even for the Sappho's time we have to depend upon the unsupported testimony of her sailing-master. There was no starter, no starting gun, no judges and no one to receive her. It is the same with the Red Jacket's time. Either made the passage in about thirteen days. The report, or rumor, that the Dreadnought made the run from Sandy Hook to Queenstown Bar in 9 days, 17 hours, 3 minutes, has no more foundation than LOCKE's story concerning the inhabitants of the moon.

hour. By an error made by the navigator the Meteor ran aground near Cape Bonn, on the coast of Africa, and was a total wreck. Mr. Fish was among the Arabs some time, but eventually reached home.

The Challenge, built from Mr. Fish's model, had a record of seventeen and one-half knots an hour. Louis Lorillard's yacht, Wanderer, was built at Greenpoint from a model by Mr. Fish. She was 104 feet on the water line, 23 feet beam, and 8 feet depth of hold.

Among the famous open boats built or modeled by Mr. Fish, were the Fulton and the Bob Fish. The Fulton won in the famous races of New Jersey against New York. The Bob Fish was built for Bergen Point owners, but afterward she became the property of Colonel Varian of this city. She won a number of races.

The funeral will take place from the Methodist church, Pamrapo, at 3 o'clock to-morrow.

-- ——

The Sun, New York, January 20, 1883.

AT CAPTAIN ROBERT FISH'S FUNERAL.

The snow was falling yesterday when Captain Robert Fish, the yacht builder, was buried in New York Bay Cemetery, Pamrapo, N. J. "We were sailing," said the Rev. R. M. Alysworth, who conducted the services in the Pamrapo Methodist church, "over the troubled ocean from which Captain Fish has landed. His life, filled with activity, was a romance. Travelling in many lands, in different classes of society, he made friends wherever he went."

On the coffin lay a wreath and an anchor of white flowers, one of which was the gift of J. F. Loubat, formerly the owner of the schooner Enchantress, which Captain Fish modelled for Mr. Lorillard. Captain Fish sailed with Mr. Loubat for three years. The pall-bearers were Captain Joe. Ellsworth, owner of the sloops Admiral and Captain and other yachts; William Elsworth, E. C. Allaire, Jr., Daniel and Jasper Cadmus, of Pamrapo, and Peter Stewart, sailmaker of New York. Among those present were Messrs. J. F. Loubat, Samuel H. Pine, shipbuilder of Brooklyn; W. J. Jones, of Jones & Dobb, ship painters; New York; Jas. Stewart, sailmaker, New York; Philip Ellsworth, who modelled the yacht Montauk; A. Carey Smith, yacht designer; Elia Morton, W. Bishop, ship plumber, New York, and W. B. Nichols, of East Seventy-fourth street, New York, for whom Captain Fish built the Julia, the Cumming, and other yachts, and for whom, at the time of his death, he was about to build a yacht, of which he has left the model.

The World, New York, January 20, 1883.

FUNERAL OF CAPTAIN FISH.

The funeral of Captain Robert Fish took place yesterday afternoon from the West View Avenue Methodist Episcopal Church at Pamrapo, N. J., the Rev. Robert M. Aylsworth, the pastor, officiating. The chief mourners were Mrs. Robert Fish, the widow; Mr. John Fish, the son, and the Misses Hattie and Evelyn Fish, the daughters. Among those present were Mr. J. F. Loubat, former owner of the Enchantress, modelled by Captain Fish; Captain Wm. Burril, of Hoboken; Mr. Francis, of Bloomingdale, inventor of the Francis lifesaving car and the earliest employer of Captain Fish; Mr. Samuel Pyne, Captain Frank Hopkins, Mr. A. Cary Smith, Captain Philip Elesworth and Mr. Elia Morton. After the close of the services the casket was opened and all present in the church defiled past it and took a last look at the remains, which were immediately after conveyed to the New York Bay Cemetery at Greenville, where, after the reading of the burial service by Mr. Aylsworth, the interment took place.

THE END